PASSION'S FIRE

As Merrie sat, transfixed on the bank, Lord Rutherford calmly lifted her skirt and slipped the stocking over her foot with a skill that bespoke practice.

Merrie, after a moment's frozen horror, lashed out. Her flat palm cracked against his cheek.

Rutherford's face, seared with the scarlet mark of her hand, was quite expressionless. "You would do well to remember, Merrie Trelawney, that that is the one and only time you will do such a thing without my permission." He bent and, before she had time to realize his intention, scooped her up into his arms.

Enraged, Merrie slapped him again. There was an instant of dreadful silence during which she fancied she could still hear the resounding crack of her palm against his face. Then he spoke very softly. "You will not, I trust, deny my right to retaliate."

A long-fingered hand encircled the slender colum of her neck, the thumb feeling the wildly beating pulse at the base of her throat.

"What exactly *are* you, Merrie Trelawney?"

Before she could reply she found herself unable to do so—as his mouth came down hard on hers . . .

SMUGGLER'S LADY

BOOK YOUR PLACE ON OUR WEBSITE AND MAKE THE READING CONNECTION!

We've created a customized website just for our very special readers, where you can get the inside scoop on everything that's going on with Zebra, Pinnacle and Kensington books.

When you come online, you'll have the exciting opportunity to:

- View covers of upcoming books
- Read sample chapters
- Learn about our future publishing schedule (listed by publication month *and author*)
- Find out when your favorite authors will be visiting a city near you
- Search for and order backlist books from our online catalog
- Check out author bios and background information
- Send e-mail to your favorite authors
- Meet the Kensington staff online
- Join us in weekly chats with authors, readers and other guests
- Get writing guidelines
- AND MUCH MORE!

**Visit our website at
http://www.kensingtonbooks.com**

JANE FEATHER

Smuggler's Lady

ZEBRA BOOKS
Kensington Publishing Corp.
http://www.kensingtonbooks.com

ZEBRA BOOKS are published by

Kensington Publishing Corp.
850 Third Avenue
New York, NY 10022

All Kensington titles, imprints, and distributed lines are available at
special quantity discounts for bulk purchases for sales promotion,
premiums, fund-raising, educational, or institutional use.

Special book excerpts or customized printings can also be created
to fit specific needs. For details, write or phone the office of the
Kensington Special Sales Manager: Attn. Special Sales Depart-
ment. Kensington Publishing Corp., 850 Third Avenue, New
York, NY 10022. Phone: 1-800-221-2647.

Zebra and the Z logo Reg. U.S. Pat. & TM Off.

ISBN 0-8217-7986-9

First Printing: December 1986
20 19 18 17 16 15 14 13 12 11

Printed in the United States of America

Chapter One

"The sky will clear before long." The short, stocky Frenchman peered anxiously up into the black canopy where an ominous gray tinge threatened.

"Aye, but 'tis only a quarter moon." The slight figure of his companion shrugged. "We cannot always bend the elements to our will, *mon ami.*"

"More's the pity." Jacques frowned at the busy, silent scene in the small cove, where a fishing boat rocked without lights in the shallows, figures moved with orderly speed, each so certain of his task that they carried crates and bundles ashore with a familiarity that required neither words nor light. "We shall be away before the clouds break," he said. "It is you will face the danger, Meredith."

" 'Tis not an unfamiliar one, Jacques." Another shrug and the figure adjusted the knitted cap that fitted tightly around a small, well-shaped head. "The coastguard are a pesky lot these days, though. For some reason, they appear to have taken uncommon offense at our activities." A low musical laugh accompanied the statement and the Frenchman smiled his understanding.

"A fact that adds to your pleasure, I'll be bound."

"You were always a sharp one, Jacques."

"Never a fool, that's for sure, and never one to court danger without cause." He began to move across the sand, his companion keeping pace beside him. "Our task is completed, it seems," the Frenchman resumed, taking in the neat piles on the sand, the sudden stillness of one group of men, the movement of others back to the boat. "We'll make good our escape until our rendezvous next month."

"I think it would be as well to change the position of the signal," Meredith said thoughtfully. "If all's well, we'll show the beacon at Devil's Point, four nights into the new moon. It is agreed?"

"Agreed. God keep you until then."

"And you, Jacques."

Meredith did not linger, after the firm handclasp, to watch the Frenchman and his crew into the boat. The task facing the group of Cornishmen on the beach was onerous and fraught with danger as they loaded onto patient ponies the casks of brandy, bales of silk and lace, well-wrapped bundles of tobacco that were so eagerly awaited by the customers in the villages and hamlets of the county. The deliveries could not be made immediately, and for this night the contraband must be transported to the safety of the cool, dry cave beneath the cliff some two miles to the west of this secluded cove.

As the procession moved across the beach toward the narrow path snaking up to the cliff road, Meredith looked back to the dark Atlantic Ocean. The French boat was nearing the line of surf crashing against the hidden reef at the entrance to the cove. There was one small break in the reef, invisible to all but the skillful and initiated. Jacques was both, and the watcher on the beach could not tarry to see him safely through.

As they reached the cliff head, the clouds parted and for a breathless instant the moon shone clear, shedding its silver illumination on the dark-clad, silent group.

"We're like butterflies on the end of a pin," a rough voice grumbled.

"If anyone's out to pin us tonight, Bart, we'll have a surprise for them," Meredith replied with a sardonic laugh that somehow conveyed both confidence and reassurance.

The clouds closed over the treacherous light once more, and the procession moved on, the ponies' hooves, muffled in sackcloth, making little sound on the stony road.

Saracen lost his footing for the hundredth time in the hundredth pothole and Damian, Lord Rutherford, gave vent to his ill temper in a powerful oath, deciding for the hundredth time that Cornwall was only fit for Cornishmen. He had been riding for hours along murky, ill-paved roads, through an unfriendly countryside, until evening became blackest night and the journey's end appeared no closer. He was alone—a condition he tended to prefer these days, anyway—Walter's horse having gone lame some two hours back, and his lordship, after one look at the only accommodation available in the nearest hamlet, having decided, with a well-bred shudder, that the open road was infinitely preferable. Now, he was regretting the impulse. Better a flea-bitten mattress and dirty sheets than this wasteland.

The directions had seemed straightforward, if he'd understood them, given as they'd been in that abominable accent that bore little relation to human speech as Lord Rutherford knew it: Keep to the coast road some ten miles, bear left at the gibbet at Hacket's Cross, and the village of Landreth would somehow appear. So far, he had come upon nothing remotely resembling a gibbet, with or without a swinging corpse, and the dark Cornish night enclosed both man and horse, the crash of the breaking surf to his right the only sound.

Until the sudden clash of steel upon steel drove irritation to the four winds, sending the soldier's blood racing and drawing a long whinny from the horse, as seasoned a campaigner as his master.

"Easy, Saracen." The soft command was hardly necessary as the Mameluke training reasserted itself, and the black quivered in readiness, velvet nostrils flared to catch the smell of powder and blood that indicated battle. There were voices raised in anger and confusion, the bellow of a musket. Lord Rutherford eased his mount into the scrub beside the road, dismounted, and crept toward the bend that hid the action from his quickening interest.

A veritable melée met his gaze as he crouched with some discomfort behind a gorse bush. In the darkness, he could make out only a tangle of figures, could hear only a muddle of orders shouted in a variety of voices. One figure caught his eye. Lithe and quick, with the supple speed of youth, the young man was everywhere, a short sword flashing, and slowly Lord Rutherford discerned a pattern. One group of combatants was in uniform, coastguard clearly, the others darkly melting into the night. As he watched, he saw the smugglers reduce in number, fading into the blackness as if by some prearranged plan. Those in uniform tripped over their feet and their swords, following a bungled series of orders that seemed to focus on the dancing stripling and two others—burly and broad as oaks—who kept their opponents fully occupied with a series of tantalizing maneuvers. Above the racket came a light, melodious laugh, taunting the revenuers to yet further futility as their prey vanished into the night.

"Break now, Bart!" The command rang clear and decisive over the general cacophony. The accent was as roughly Cornish as any Lord Rutherford had heard this day, but there was a lightness to it, hardly disguised by a note of assertion, so well entrenched as to defy all opposition. The two burly men were suddenly figments of his imagination, gone heaven only knew where, and for a second only the youth remained, poised on the edge of night, radiating a mocking defiance. The instant before he, too, vanished, the dark sky gave way to a sliver of moonlight that revealed a profile, sharply etched against a tight, knitted cap; a tip-tilted nose with a scattering of freckles, the curve of a well-sculpted mouth, the squared-off side of a small chin, and then the light was doused and the figure was no more.

Damian remained in hiding, as puzzled as the discomfited coastguard by the mysterious disappearance of their foes. It was as if the earth had swallowed them, and that taunting laughter seemed to hang in the air so that the revenue men bickered amongst themselves and threw accusations of stupidity as they gathered themselves together and rode off down the cliff road in the direction of what his lordship rather hoped was the village of Landreth.

Meredith crouched on the narrow ledge just below the cliff overhang, listening to the tumult on the road overhead. The cliff at this point appeared to fall sheer to the rocks beneath, and even in broad daylight the sandy shelf was invisible from above. It was a perch fit only for a goat at the best of times but in an emergency could be a lifesaver. Tonight, when the trap had been sprung, the smugglers had followed the routine they had practiced many times. One by one, they had dropped over the cliff under cover of darkness and the distracting tumult of their fellows. Singly, they had crept along the ledge, hugging the cliff face, until the ledge petered out and they had swung themselves up onto the cliff road a quarter mile from the site of the ambush, to vanish into the scrub and gorse. Now only Meredith and Bart remained, waiting in hiding until the night was still and quiet again after the retreat of their disgruntled opponents.

" 'Tis as well to be forewarned," the burly Cornishman grunted, heaving himself onto the road and stretching an arm down to his companion. Meredith took the proffered hand and scrambled up beside him.

"Indeed it is, Bart." A light chuckle enlivened the night. "They're such addlepates, though, there's little amusement to be had in outwitting them."

"More than enough for me," Bart stated. "I've no

ambition to swing from the gibbet at Hacket's Cross, but there's times when I think you do."

"There's little real danger if we're warned as we were tonight. Had we been surprised with the ponies on the beach, it would have been a different matter. As it is, everyone's away to their beds, the goods and ponies are in the cave. All's right with the world, Bart."

"Until the next time you decide to lock horns with the revenue," the Cornishman muttered. "There was no need to walk into that ambush tonight."

"There was every need, Bart. It was necessary to show them that they do not deal with ill-prepared fools. But we'll not do it again, I promise."

"And with that, I suppose I must be satisfied." Bart peered up at the sky. "We'd best move before the moon finally shows herself. The road's no place to be discovered at this hour of the morning."

His companion nodded agreement, and the two clasped hands briefly before making off across the headland, blissfully ignorant of the watcher hidden in the gorse.

Lord Rutherford retrieved his horse, wondering if he could believe the evidence of his eyes and ears. If so, there were some very strange goings-on in this benighted land. A tiny smile played over his lips, a smile that transformed the somewhat forbidding countenance. It was a smile that had been conspicuously absent in the last six months and one that would have gladdened his mama's heart had she been on that lonely Cornish road to see it.

The smile lasted just as long as it took Lord Rutherford to find Mallory House, outside the village of Landreth in the county of Cornwall. His cousin Matthew had been a reclusive eccentric, not given to the society of his family—or anyone else if rumor were true—and the slate-roofed, gray-stone manor house offered little sign of welcome to the traveler. The driveway was clogged with weeds, the hedges were untrimmed, the paint was peeling on the great door. His lordship's lip curled in distaste as he hammered the tarnished brass knocker and stood back, looking up at the shuttered windows. Cousin Matthew had been dead these two months, but his heir had instructed the servants to remain *in situ* until he came to examine his inheritance and make what provision was necessary. They had also been instructed to prepare for his arrival, but there was little sign that his orders had been obeyed, a dereliction to which Colonel, Lord Rutherford, was not accustomed.

Lord Rutherford regretted yet again that he had yielded to impulse and abandoned Walter and the comforts, however dubious, of the country inn. He pounded the door a second time, the noise reverberating in the still night. Then came the creak of bolts, muttered expletives, and the door groaned wide on its hinges. A bowed figure in cap and nightgown, a horse blanket over his shoulders, held a candle high, peering up at his lordship to demand, "What's all this then? The last trump?"

"I am Rutherford, man," his lordship declared crisply. "Did you not receive my message?"

"Aye," the old man muttered. "But we wasn't expectin' you in the middle o' the night."

"Have someone see to my horse." Lord Rutherford pushed past the servant to stand in the stone-flagged hall lit only by the man's candle.

"There's nobut meself and the missus—not till mornin'."

His eyebrows meeting above gray eyes, Damian stared in cold disbelief at the old retainer. He was not accustomed to being addressed thus by servants, regardless of the time of day or night, and his expression said so with alarming clarity. Under that hard glare, the elderly man shuffled his slippered feet on the cold stone floor. Rutherford's expression did not lighten even as he recognized that the servant was old and frail, and clearly his late master had not been particularly exacting. After what he'd seen this night, little would surprise his lordship about this godforsaken country, but the hour was too advanced for a lesson in conduct toward a peer of the realm and the heir to a dukedom. Time enough tomorrow to bring a little military discipline to bear.

"Show me to the stables, then," he directed. "I'll see to him myself. While I do so, you'll be pleased to fetch brandy and food. I've ridden many miles this night and am exceeding sharp-set."

"What is it, Harry?" A thin voice quavered from the dark oak staircase, and an elderly woman, bearing a lantern, shuffled into the yellow circle of candlelight.

" 'Tis his lordship from London," her husband informed her. "Come to see to his inheritance."

"I'm in need of supper and my bed," Rutherford announced.

"Well, I don't know as 'ow we've much in the way of vittals, m'lord," the woman said with a worried frown. "There's a morsel o' pig's cheek in the pantry

13

left over from Harry's supper . . ."

Damian shuddered. "Bread and cheese will do, woman. Surely you can lay hands on that?"

"I daresay I might," she agreed. "You'll be wantin' sheets on the master's bed, I'll be bound. Hasn't had none on it since they took him away—rest his soul." Muttering, she shuffled off into the nether regions, taking the lantern with her.

"The stables, man!" Rutherford swung impatiently on his heel and strode to the door, Harry following, huddled in the coarse blanket.

It had clearly been some time since the stables at Mallory House had housed an animal of Saracen's caliber, if, indeed, they ever had done so. Two cart horses and a sway-backed nag occupied adjoining stalls. The remainder were empty, bearing odorous signs of their previous occupants. Lord Rutherford decided that he was unequal to the task of mucking out stables in the early hours of a July morning. Saracen would have to endure dirt and discomfort for one night, as his lordship gloomily supposed he must, also. In future, however, he resolved to keep Walter at his side throughout this entire, misbegotten expedition.

The heel of a stale loaf and a chunk of cheese clearly destined for the mousetrap did little to relieve his spirits. The brandy, however, was more than tolerable, a fact that did not surprise his lordship unduly after the scene he had witnessed on the cliff road. The Gentlemen were clearly very active on this part of the Cornish coast and would provide some compensation for discomfort.

Cousin Matthew's bedchamber was as gloomy as if

the corpse still remained. There were sheets on the feather mattress, though, and an oil lamp on the bulky armoire. A pitcher of cold water appeared on request, initial reluctance to fulfilling the request having disappeared miraculously when it had become a sharp order issued in tones more suitable to a barrack square. His lordship was slowly becoming resigned to the idea that London ways had not reached Cornwall. He could have appeared unexpectedly at any one of the establishments owned by the Keighley family, at any time of the night, and been received as if it were mid morning and he had been eagerly awaited. But those establishments were staffed by veritable armies, a far cry from the morose, elderly retainers who had served Cousin Matthew and were now to serve him. Or would do so, if he could bring himself to remain beyond the morrow, Rutherford reflected moodily, dousing the lantern and climbing onto the high mattress. He sniffed suspiciously—the linen was most definitely musty, but at least it didn't feel damp. He'd endured much worse in the Peninsula, of course, but he hadn't had a stiff shoulder then, and what a soldier expected in a war was rather different from what a man expected in his own house in a country at peace.

The small cave was cool, dry, and as bare as Mother Hubbard's cupboard. Meredith moved to the back and then seemed to vanish into the rock face. The entrance to the narrow tunnel, just high and wide enough for a small pony, was concealed behind a jutting boulder in the far corner. The tunnel itself widened as it burrowed into the cliff, eventually opening into a vast cavern where a single lamp burned, sending spectral shadows a-dancing on the rough-hewn walls. The six ponies who had formed the baggage train earlier glanced incuriously at the slim figure, more interested in the contents of their nosebags now that their task was completed. Bundles, boxes, parcels, and casks were stacked against the sides in orderly ranks, and Meredith viewed the results of this night's work with a contented smile. There would be a goodly profit to be had, of which her own share would supply the final mortgage payment on the forty acres of Ducket's Spinney. The process of reclamation was slow but steady, and, at least, sufficient funds were now ensured for the boys' schooling for one more year.

Meredith took the lantern and left the cavern, not the way she had come but by a further passage at the back—a passage that climbed steeply through rock, coming to an abrupt halt at an impenetrable wall. The slight figure did not pause, however, but merely stretched upwards, pushing at a slab of rock in the passage roof. The slab fell back with a dull thud on the thick blanket waiting to muffle the sound of its fall. Meredith hitched herself through the opening with an experienced agility, leaning down to bring up the lantern before replacing the slab. She stood now in a small pantry where slate shelves bore jars of preserves, crocks of butter, and rounds of cheese—the produce of the home farm that kept the household supplied with all but the luxuries.

Merrie removed her boots and, carrying them and the lantern, crept out of the pantry and into a large

16

kitchen, warmed by a black-leaded range, silent but for the ticking of the grandfather clock beside the dresser. It was two-thirty, and the household would not stir for another three hours. On stockinged feet, she made her way out of the kitchen, past the back stairs and through the green-baize door that separated the servants' quarters from the main part of the house.

Sir John Blake, before his untimely demise three years previously, had managed to sell off most of the family heirlooms, and the stone-flagged hallway was bare, where once a rich Turkey carpet would have kept the chill from Merrie's feet. The Jacobean oak table beneath the mullioned windows had escaped the auctioneer's hammer because of its somewhat battered condition, not so the heavy silver tray and the Chinese urns that once had graced its surface. Meredith was now inured to these reminders of her late husband's profligacy, however, and ran soundlessly up the broad, curving staircase, along the minstrel's gallery overlooking the hall, and into a large, front-facing bedchamber.

"Nan!" she exclaimed softly. "What are you thinking of?"

The elderly woman asleep on a chintz-covered chaise longue started up, blinking in the light from Merrie's lantern. "There you are at last, child," she grumbled. " 'Tis most inconsiderate in you to be this late. You know full well I cannot go to my rest until I know you are safe and in your bed."

"That is such nonsense, Nan." Meredith yanked off the knitted cap and sat on the bed to pull off her stockings. "What could possibly happen to me?"

17

Nan raised eyes and hands heavenward. "Why, nothing at all, to be sure." She poured water from a ewer into a matching porcelain basin. " 'Tis but a bit o' smuggling you're about, after all, and the revenue's only desperate to lay hands on you, after all. Why, of course there's nothing to worry about, and I'm a foolish old woman who's only nursed you from your cradle, which gives me no right nor cause for concern . . ."

Meredith made no attempt to interrupt the flow, knowing that only thus would Nan manage to relieve her anxiety. The scolding continued unabated as the elderly maid helped her out of her clothes and into her nightgown, released the dark auburn hair from the tight knot that held the mass confined beneath the cap, and gave it the requisite hundred strokes despite Meredith's pleading that the hour was too advanced for such niceties.

"You'll not go to bed with your hair unbrushed, not while I have anything to say about it," Nan declared. Eventually she released her and turned to pull back the covers on the four-poster bed.

"I cannot imagine the day when you will not have something to say about it," Lady Blake murmured, climbing meekly into bed. It was one thing to command a band of Cornish smugglers or to outwit a troop of revenue men, quite another to stand against Nan Tregaron when she was determined to have her way.

Chapter Two

Lord Rutherford awoke to the rattle of curtain rings being drawn across brass rods. He opened his eyes onto sunlight and onto the wonderful image of Walter.

"Gad, but I'm glad to see you, man." He hitched himself up against the carved headboard with a grimace. Walter regarded his lordship with wary concern, noting the countenance that was, as usual these days, somber, bearing none of its past humor or the signs of pleasurable anticipation in the new day. He also saw the sudden flash of pain in the gray eyes and drew his own conclusions. After yesterday's overlong ride, followed by the damp discomforts of this house, it was no wonder the colonel's shoulder was playing up.

"It was the devil's own work to find this place, m'lord," he said. "We'll be moving on again, I suppose?" It was both question and statement, a technique of his batman's with which Lord Rutherford was well acquainted. It allowed for the expression of Walter's opinion, couched in the discreet language of servant to master.

"You don't care for Mallory House then, Walter?" Damian swung his legs to the floor and looked around the chamber where thick dust coated every surface. "I'm given to understand Cousin Matthew died in this bed," he remarked casually, thumping the pillows. A cloud of feathers rose in the mote-thickened air.

"Can't say it surprises me," Walter intoned. "That couple downstairs don't know their left foot from their right. Beggin' your pardon, m'lord, but this ain't no gentleman's establishment."

"I'm inclined to agree with you," his lordship said with some feeling as he rose from the bed and stretched languidly. "It is always possible, of course, that my esteemed Cousin Matthew was no gentleman himself. Although it seems an unlikely eventuality, given his antecedents which, I am assured, were impeccable. Second cousin to the duke, you understand?"

"Yes, m'lord," said Walter woodenly, turning to open a portmanteau resting on the window seat. "I'll look to your shoulder now, Colonel."

"I received my furlough six months ago," Damian snapped, and there was no disguising the note of bitterness in his voice. "I've no need for that nomenclature now." Shrugging out of his nightshirt, he strode to the open window and looked down at the disordered garden. The lean, powerful frame seemed to vibrate with the pent-up need for action, to radiate an impatient energy.

"You earned it, m'lord, and no wound can take that from you." Walter spoke with resolute determination. If the colonel snapped his head off, so be it. It wouldn't be the first time these days and was unlikely to be the last. "If you'd just sit down, m'lord . . ."

To Walter's relief, the colonel sat on the window seat without a word although his expression was grim as he readied himself to receive the batman's ministrations. The soldier's square hands were incongruously gentle as they moved over the jagged cicatrice carved into Lord Rutherford's shoulder, and massaged ointment into the stiff muscle and joint. "When d'you think we'll be moving along then, m'lord?" Walter returned to the original topic in an effort to divert Lord Rutherford from whatever bleak contemplation was responsible for the present grimness. Such attempts at alleviation were usually unsuccessful but must be tried if Lord Rutherford was not to fall victim to another of the black depressions that had dogged him since his service with the Duke of Wellington in the Peninsula had come to such an abrupt end.

"I'm not sure there's any hurry," Damian returned. "It's not as if more intriguing prospects await elsewhere."

"No, m'lord." Walter sighed. "There's hot water for your shaving on the dresser. If we're to stay here awhile, I'd best see what can be done to make the place habitable. Not to mention the stables," he added. "I doubt Saracen'll recover from the shock in a hurry."

Lord Rutherford gave a somewhat mirthless chuckle as he sharpened his razor on the leather strop. "He's had worse billets, Walter, as have we. Not much worse, I grant you, but I've a mind to improve this one. Such abominable neglect offends me." The image of a slight figure brandishing a small sword flashed unbidden in his mind's eye, and the peal of melodious laughter, rich in enjoyment, rang again in his ear. Unless his lordship much mistook the matter, he had stumbled upon a most intriguing situation last night. The identity of the stripling smuggler would bear some investigation and, while it was hardly appropriate for the heir to the Duke of Keighley to consort with such a band of rascals, it was an infinitely more appealing prospect than listening to his mother's fond solicitude and his father's strictures on the subject of fulfilling the duties of his heir. At some point, Damian supposed, he would take a wife and set up his nursery, but he was still too close to the soldiering that had occupied him to the exclusion of all else since his twentieth year—too close to it, and too bitter at its abrupt cessation to switch easily and swiftly into the role society would have him play.

"I'll see about breakfast, then." Walter moved to the door. "We'll not get much accomplished on an empty belly."

"It's to be hoped you have better luck than I did last night." Damian drew a long swath through the soap on his face and turned to grin at his batman. "Courage, friend. I've a feeling this expedition might turn out to provide some amusement."

Walter's unconvinced sniff hid the pleasure he felt at the sight of that grin and the gleam in the gray eyes. He was quite willing to endure any amount of discomfort if it would restore to his colonel the humor and sunny temper of the past. Ailments of the spirit were a deal harder to cure than those of the body, and, while the colonel's shoulder had healed with the speed of youth and strength, his spirits had remained depressed, seeing only a bleak future of boredom and duty that no diversion could alleviate.

While his lordship completed his ablutions and donned clean linen and his buckskin riding britches, Walter had the elderly couple below stairs scurrying around between henhouse, pantry, and range. Eggs were found, together with a side of bacon, and Walter decreed the ale to be passable. When Lord Rutherford eventually rose from the breakfast table in the hastily dusted parlor, it was with the firm conviction that here, at least, he had found an outlet for his restless energy, a worthwhile task to perform that would provide him with a much-needed sense of purpose. He had not expected to have to put his inheritance to rights when he had set out for Cornwall, and, if he chose to leave it in its present neglected condition, it would make little difference to the long-term fortunes of the future Duke of Keighley, but the soldier's passion for orderliness found the ramshackle condition of his estate quite intolerable.

By early afternoon the village and the surrounding countryside was buzzing with the news. Young Mary Pendragon and little Sally Harper were up at the manor to help old Martha Perry set the place to rights. Messages had been sent, summoning Jonas Williams, the solicitor in Fowey who was executor of Matthew Mallory's estate, to wait on Lord Rutherford. It was said Jonas had been in quite a taking when he'd read the message, so sharp had it been. Bill Wiley, who had had a half-hearted care for the stables at Mallory House, had been given a flea in his ear by his lordship's manservant and had been set to cleaning as if the stables were to house royalty.

Damian, after a morning spent issuing orders and generally instilling the fear of the devil into the slovenly Perrys and anyone else unfortunate enough to earn his disapproval, judged he could safely leave matters to take their course and escaped the hubbub and the clouds of dust being raised by the combined brooms and dusters of the village girls, setting off on Saracen to explore the estate. As he had expected, he found everywhere evidence of wanton neglect: fences broken, fields left fallow, gardens untended. It would take an army to put it to rights and a reliable steward to oversee the work unless he chose to do that himself. It was positively criminal of his cousin to have allowed this devastation, he reflected irritably, pausing by an overgrown stream to water his horse.

A movement in the rushes and a glimpse of red caught his eye. "Who goes there?" he called. Matthew Mallory might have allowed trespassers, and with the estate in its present condition it could hardly matter who wandered over the land, but Mallory House had another owner now and, when fences and fields were in order, there would be no welcome for people without legitimate business. The people of Landreth might as well learn that fact as soon as may be. Silence greeted the question and the rushes became breathlessly still. Lord Rutherford dismounted and walked purposefully toward them.

"I b—beg pardon, sir." A rather small voice spoke, and the rushes parted to reveal a lad of about eleven. "Are you Lord Rutherford?"

"My fame seems to have preceded me," his lordship observed. "And who may you be?"

The lad was dressed like a village boy in a red shirt and worsted britches rolled above his knees, leaving his legs and feet bare. But he spoke in accents as well-bred and educated as Lord Rutherford's own.

"Rob, sir," the boy replied.

"That is somewhat uninformative. Rob who?"

The boy bit his lip, wrinkling a freckled nose, and Lord Rutherford frowned at an elusive memory. "I'm not supposed to be here," Rob offered. "But it's quite the best spot for tickling trout. I've three already." He lifted a catch net from the stream, proudly showing Damian its three brown-speckled occupants. "Merrie doesn't mind," he went on, "but Hugo is so stuffy and prune-faced, and he will prose on forever. I don't see why he should since Merrie is my guardian, not him."

"I am quite at sea, child." Damian sat down on the bank of the stream. "I do understand your difficulties with—uh, Hugo, is it? Prune-faced is most descriptive, but who are these people, and who are you?"

"You won't say you saw me?"

"I'd never betray a poacher," Damian assured him solemnly and Rob chuckled.

"It is poaching, but no one has fished this stream in years. D'you care to try it, sir?"

"Perhaps later. Although, in my case I can hardly be accused of poaching my own trout, Rob—uh?" he prompted.

"Trelawney." Rob shrugged and joined his lordship on the bank. "My parents are dead and there's only Merrie and Hugo and Theo and me left of the Trelawneys, and Merrie's not really a Trelawney anymore. She's supposed to be a Blake, though actually," he dropped his voice confidingly, "she was never a Blake, not even when Sir John was alive. Once a Trelawney always a Trelawney is what Papa used to say and it's true. Except for Hugo. He's not a bit like a Trelawney. He wants to take holy orders although Merrie says it's nonsense for a Trelawney to enter the church, and he's being absurd to think he'll be less of a burden if he accepts Cousin Sybil's living in Dorset. She says a Trelawney could *never* live in Dorset, and she'll not have Hugo sacrificing himself just because our circumstances are a little straitened. She says we'll come about eventually." This last was said in tones of supreme confidence as Damian struggled to separate the threads of this artless recitation.

"Merrie, I take it, is your married sister in addition to being your guardian?"

"Yes, but she's not married anymore. Sir John fell off his horse. It was a real bonebreaker and Merrie says he should never have been on it in the condition he was in. I think she meant he was inebriated, he often was." His lordship was spared the need for response as the boy continued cheerfully. "Anyway, he broke his neck on the hunting field and left Merrie with lots of debts and Hugo and Theo and me to look after. I did say I wouldn't go back to Harrow if it would be easier, but she said it wouldn't," Rob added glumly. "She became quite prune-faced."

"She might well," Rutherford murmured, feeling some sympathy for the mysterious Merrie standing guardian to this ingenuous scapegrace. "Merrie is an unusual name."

"It is really Meredith," Rob explained. "Our mama was a Meredith and it is tradition that the first-born of a Meredith woman bears the name as Christian

26

name. Only usually the first-born is a boy. It is only considered uncommon because Merrie is a girl."

"Quite so," his lordship agreed, much struck by the logic of this. "And Hugo and Theo are your brothers?"

"Yes. Hugo is up at Oxford, and Theo and me are at Harrow. It is because it is such an expense that Hugo says he wants to take orders because, if he does so, Cousin Sybil has offered to provide for him, and when he is ordained she will present him with the living in her gift. He will have to go as curate first because the present incumbent is not dead yet, but he is quite old so Hugo should become the rector quite soon."

"But your sister is opposed to the idea?"

"Yes, indeed." Rob scrambled down the bank, back to the stream where he lay on his stomach, thrusting his arm up to the elbow in the cool water. Silence fell, disturbed only by the indolent droning of a honey bee, as Lord Rutherford watched with amused interest the boy become motionless, concentrating on his battle of wits with the trout. The scene reminded his lordship pleasantly of his own childhood, long summers spent at Rutherford Abbey doing much as that engaging scapegrace was doing now. Rutherford completely forgot his intention to discourage trespassers. The July afternoon had acquired a rather rosy patina, he reflected, feeling pleasantly lazy. Rob's story had created in him a lively desire to make the acquaintance of the rest of the Trelawney family and the oddly named Merrie in particular. She presumably took her place in whatever society the local gentry had to offer unless, of course, she had been recently widowed. But the boy wore no mourning bands, and his manner of speaking of his deceased brother-in-law did not somehow indicate a recent loss—scant respect, certainly. Damian surprised himself with a soft chuckle. He would have liked to ask, but it would be a crime to disturb the lad's concentration, not to mention to alert his intended victim, so he removed himself with due caution, turning Saracen's head for what now passed as home.

A raw-boned bay mare stood in the stableyard, its head held by a distinctly subdued Master Wiley.

"Who does she belong to?" his lordship inquired, swinging from his own mount.

"Squire Barrat, my lord." The answer came promptly. "He's up at the house payin' a call."

"On whom?" Rutherford's eyebrows rose as he handed over Saracen's reins.

"Why—on—on you, m'lord," Bill stammered, nonplussed by such a strange question.

"But I am not there," his lordship pointed out gently.

"I think as how 'e's waitin' on you, m'lord."

"Ah, that makes a little more sense." Lord Rutherford bestowed upon the lad a deceptively benign smile. "Why do you not tether the mare in the barn? Then you may be able to devote your single-minded attention to my horse." With a brisk nod, he turned and strode up to the house.

Sir Algernon Barrat stood in the newly dusted parlor, feeling distinctly awkward. If it had been left to him, he'd not have intruded upon his new neighbor quite so precipitately, but Patience showed little of that quality in her nature and had informed her husband that, as the leading member of the local gentry, it behooved him to make all speed to welcome Lord Rutherford. It was most fortuitous that there was to be a hunt ball on the morrow. It would be a perfect opportunity for his lordship to make the acquaintance of his worthy neighbors, and Sir Algernon was instructed to invite him to dine at South Hill beforehand. Balls and dinners were pesky occasions at the best of times, Sir Algernon reflected gloomily, but they'd be the very devil if a man had this degree of chaos on his hands, and what a man fresh from London society would find to appeal in the countrified company Lady Barrat had to offer quite defeated Sir Algernon's imagination. But his lady was formidable and the commission must be discharged. Sir Algernon was resolved, however, that he would hint gently that of course no one expected Lord Rutherford to attend in the circumstances, and he would be quite happy to tender his lordship's excuses to Lady Barrat.

The squire was surprised, therefore, and Lady Barrat much gratified by Lord Rutherford's prompt and easy acceptance of the invitation. Neither of them, fortunately for good neighborliness, were able to see inside his lordship's head where dread foreboding at the prospect of an evening of cloddish insipidity warred with the knowledge that only thus would he be likely to make the acquaintance of the Trelawneys, and only thus could he make discreet inquiries about the Gentlemen. Sir Algernon, returning to his eager wife, pronounced his lordship to be "a decent sort of fellow, not one to stand on ceremony," and the sherry that had been unearthed from old Mallory's cellars more than met with the squire's approval.

"Why must you always look such a dowd, Merrie?" Rob examined his sister critically the following evening. "You did not do so when Sir John was alive."

"I was a giddy young wife in those days, Rob." Meredith examined her image in the glass above the mantel, tucking a recalcitrant auburn wisp into the severe knot at the nape of her neck. "I am become a sober widow with a host of responsibilities and must dress accordingly."

"Stuff!" Theo looked up from the piece of wood he was whittling. "Rob has the right of it. You do not need to look such a fright. Does she, Hugo?"

His elder brother, thus appealed to, pondered the question. "It would not be proper for Merrie to dress in bright colors or to show signs of frivolity," he pronounced. "And I do not think it polite in you to say she looks a dowd and a fright. She dresses with decorum as suits her position."

"Thank you, Hugo." Meredith smiled at the younger boys who were regarding their brother with unabashed disgust. "I appreciate your concern, my loves, but we must all bow to circumstances on occasion. Anyway," she chuckled, "you must own that there would be little point in looking ravishing this evening. Who am I to charm? Young Peter Foxmoore? He would be a most eligible *parti* if I was inclined to cradle-snatching and willing to hunt every day of my life. Or perhaps Sir Giles? Now there's a thought," she mused. "He cannot be above sixty, and

30

his temper is only a little affected by the gout."

"There is Lord Rutherford," Rob interrupted sturdily. "He is the right age and I like him."

"Now when did you meet Lord Rutherford?" Merrie demanded as her little brother flushed guiltily.

"At Withy Brook," Rob muttered. "I was tickling trout. And you don't need to rip up at me, Hugo, because Lord Rutherford didn't mind a bit and we had a long talk."

"About the Trelawneys, I daresay." Merrie sighed. "I imagine Lord Rutherford is now intimately acquainted with our family history."

"He wanted to know," Rob protested. His predilection for unselective, unsolicited communication to all and sundry was generally frowned upon, but he was determined to defend himself on this occasion.

"Yes, Rob." Merrie shook her head at him in mock exasperation. "I'm sure he was quite fascinated. However, I think it most unlikely that he will deign to grace what modest entertainment we can offer—far too provincial for the heir to the Duke of Keighley. And, if village talk is anything to go by, he has a worse temper than Matthew Mallory, so the less we see of him the happier we shall be."

"He is not at all like Lord Mallory," Rob persisted. "He is young and handsome and—"

"Rich," Theo interrupted with a grin. "A perfect catch for you, Merrie. Just think, all our troubles would be over."

"Your levity is most unedifying, Theodore," Hugo reproved. "It is also quite inappropriate. While I would be the first to agree that the Trelawneys are as ancient and respectable a family as any in the county,

31

it would hardly be considered a suitable match for a Keighley."

His audience burst into peals of laughter at the conclusion of this dignified speech.

"Hugo, you are a nod-cock," Theo gasped. "I was only funning. Can you imagine Merrie as a duchess?"

"Enough, all of you!" Meredith attempted to restore order to the proceedings. "Since I consider the likelihood of my making the acquaintance of Lord Rutherford remote in the extreme, I should be obliged to you if you would drop the subject. I have absolutely no intention of marrying anyone at all and would be much obliged, Rob, if you would refrain from matchmaking." She softened the words with a smile, tugging his hair, but they were all well aware that their sister had spoken in earnest, and it was never wise to arouse her anger.

The double doors to the parlor were opened at this juncture to admit a thick, broad-shouldered figure in britches and baize apron. "The horses have returned from the fields, Lady Merrie. Jem will bring the carriage round in five minutes."

"Thank you, Seecombe." Meredith picked up her cloak from the arm of a sofa. "I do feel a little guilty, expecting the horses to work in the evening when they have spent a hard day in the fields. Perhaps I should tell Jem to bring the carriage back after he has left me at South Hill. I will attempt to procure a ride home with the Abbotts. It is not a great deal out of their way."

"You cannot do that, Merrie," Theo protested. "It is so shabby. It is bad enough that everyone should know we have no carriage horses, but there is no need

32

to draw attention to it."

"Well, if I do not mind, I cannot imagine why you should," his sister retorted. "We cannot overwork the horses in the interests of pretending to a position that we do not have. I shall most definitely send Jem home." With that, Lady Blake swept from the parlor, leaving two of her brothers glaring at the discomfited third.

"If you had not said that, Theo, she would not have decided to send the horses home," Hugo declared.

"No," Rob put in, for once in agreement with his senior. "You know how out-of-reason cross she gets if we seem to complain about being poor."

"Well, I am sorry," Theo said in an unapologetic tone. "But I was not really complaining, I was just stating a fact. Merrie is overly sensitive, sometimes."

"She is not!" Rob, who would never hear a breath of criticism of his sister, flew at Theo, and Hugo, after failing to halt the scrap with the weight of his words, resorted to methods both more effective and more natural.

Meredith sat back against the shabby leather squabs of the heavy, old-fashioned carriage as the two cart horses drew it, bumping and creaking, across the ill-paved roads toward South Hill. Although she had laughed when her brothers had accused her of looking a fright and a dowd, there were moments when she regretted the necessity for her drab disguise, moments when she dreamed again of dressing with the elegance and frivolity of the years before and during her brief marriage. Had she wished, she could still have dressed with a degree of modishness in spite of her straitened circumstances. Silks, satins, and laces were

33

easily available to the smuggler, and Nan was an accomplished seamstress, but the need to appear as a sorrowing, impoverished widow, bravely shouldering her responsibilities, was too important to yield to vanity. No one, not in their wildest fantasies, would suspect that the smuggler who played with the coastguard like a cat with a mouse, who conducted a most efficient business to the satisfaction of all concerned, was also Lady Meredith Blake with her dull, shabby gowns and mouselike manners.

The carriage drew up outside the foursquare solidity of Sir Algernon Barrat's South Hill. Until Sir John's death, the Blakes had been the acknowledged leaders of the community by virtue of family and property. Now the Barrats had that honor, and Lady Barrat was always scrupulous in affording her dethroned neighbor every consideration—a fact that set Merrie's teeth on edge. She could not, however, refuse the charitable attentions without seeming churlish or drawing unwelcome attention to herself. It was for this reason that she formed one of the select group invited to dine at South Hill before the ball.

"Meredith, my dear." Patience Barrat hurried across the drawing room to greet her guest. "How well you are looking." Kindly, she refrained from any hypocritical comment on Merrie's gown of brown bombazine, the old-maidish fichu at her neck, and the obviously darned cotton mittens. She remembered the time when Lady Blake's gowns had been the envy of all, but it was hard to imagine that now. The poor creature was quite ground down by her debt-ridden widowhood and those three great boys.

"All our good friends are here, my dear, so you will

be quite comfortable," she reassured Meredith, drawing her into the room. "We have one excitement though. Lord Rutherford has graciously accepted Sir Algernon's invitation to join us. I do not suppose any of our young ladies will catch his eye, but you can be sure there are some hearts a-flutter in the village."

"Yes, indeed," Merrie murmured, keeping her eyes lowered to hide the unlooked-for flash of chagrin. She had not had to wear the brown bombazine tonight. Her green silk, while it had seen better days, was not nearly so frumpish. Sternly, she told herself not to be so foolish. Rob may have liked the man, but what possible interest could she have in or for a London dandy? Besides, she was hardly in a position to indulge in a flirtation, however harmless.

She was making polite small talk with the elderly Isabelle Carstairs when the butler, in weighty accents, announced Lord Rutherford. There was no denying the quiver of excitement that greeted the arrival of his lordship. Merrie was conscious of a twinge of embarrassment as Patience gushed and twittered and exclaimed at the honor his lordship did her humble abode and how she hoped he would not find the society of simple country folk insipid. Quite how Lord Rutherford could answer that gracefully, Meredith could not imagine. It was a question of the "Have you stopped beating your wife?" order and she watched his reactions with covert interest. He made some deft response, bowing low over his hostess's hand. Meredith was obliged to acknowledge that he was indeed personable.

His evening dress was appropriate to the country: long, black pantaloons strapped under his shoes, a black coat with no adornment but its superb cut, a plain cravat tied with a simple elegance that put to shame the elaborate confections of the young sprigs around him. The dark-brown hair was brushed neatly but without artifice. Meredith revised her opinion. Whatever Lord Rutherford may be, he most definitely did not belong to the dandy set.

She dropped her eyes hastily, turning again to Mrs. Carstairs. Patience was introducing his lordship to those whom she had decided might interest him. It would be Merrie's turn at some point, but the shabby, indigent widow would come low on the list of importance.

Chapter Three

"Meredith, may I present Lord Rutherford." The moment came at last. Merrie turned from Mrs. Carstairs to curtsy, giving him her mittened fingers. The darn on the wrist, though neat, did not escape his lordship's notice.

"Lady Blake," he murmured in response to the introduction. "Servant, ma'am." His lips brushed the air above the small hand in his palm. This drab creature surely could have nothing in common with that young scamp Rob Trelawney. Damian had created an image of Meredith Blake, conjured from her brother's artless prattle. The image most definitely did not match the reality. It was impossible to form an impression of her features since she seemed incapable of raising her eyes from the contemplation of his shoes. Her voice was barely a whisper. Her figure appeared passable in as far as it was possible to judge beneath the voluminous folds of that hideous gown, and her hair, although confined in a most matronly knot, was a promising color, lit as it was by a shaft of evening sunlight piercing the room through an opened casement.

"Mmm—Have you, my lord—I mean, I trust . . ." The meek whisper faltered, her fan fluttered vigorously, and her reticule fell to the floor.

Rutherford bent to pick it up. "You were saying, Lady Blake?" he prompted in a somewhat bored tone. Did she ordinarily behave in this ridiculous fashion? Or was something behind this inordinate display of nervousness? Perhaps she was not accustomed to being spoken to by men? She was like a chicken without a head, gushing her thanks as she received the dropped reticule, bobbing another curtsy, her eyes still riveted to the floor.

"So very kind," Lady Blake murmured. "It was nothing of any importance."

His lordship had little doubt of the truth of this, but the rules of his upbringing obliged a polite disclaimer. Under this encouragement, her ladyship whispered that she hoped he found Cornwall to his liking.

"Uncomfortable, ma'am," he responded dismissively, wondering how best to extricate himself from this painfully stilted exchange.

Arrogant buck! Merrie thought, raising her eyes for the barest second. They were the color of sloes, deep purple, and the flash of indignation quite took his lordship aback. But then her gaze dropped to his shoes again and she murmured something incomprehensible. Rutherford decided that he had been mistaken, this feeble creature was quite incapable of feeling any emotion as positive as indignation. He glanced at Lady Patience in clear appeal, and his hostess came to his rescue with the injunction that he escort her in to dinner.

Meredith, escorted by the very deaf but equally

loud-voiced Admiral Petersham, was left much to her own devices during dinner, a circumstance that suited her very well since it left her free to observe. Lord Rutherford was playing his part manfully, but there was more than a hint of impatience about the firm mouth. There was a good deal of humor about that mouth, though, on the rare occasions that it relaxed, and the gray eyes, set beneath most expressive brows, were remarkably intelligent. While he was not precisely handsome, Meredith thought, if he ever lost that look of barely concealed, impatient boredom, he would have a most pleasing countenance. However, such a possibility was extremely unlikely. Lord Rutherford did not appear as if he could find anything worthy of attention or amusement in his present situation, a circumstance, Meredith decided, for which he had only himself to blame. Effete aristocrats who found country living uncomfortable should stay in the cushioned luxury where they belonged. Merrie was unaware that she was looking directly at the subject of her cogitations. She was so accustomed to being ignored at gatherings of this kind that occasionally, feeling safely invisible, her guard dropped. It proved to be a mistake this time.

Lord Rutherford, raising his gaze from the overcooked venison on his plate, searching desperately for a new topic of conversation, met those sloe eyes again, framed in a luxuriant curly fringe of eyelash. There was no mistaking the critical appraisal of that look or the fact that the owner of those eyes did not like what she saw. His lordship realized with an unpleasant shock what it was that she found so distasteful. He glanced around him, but there was no avoiding the truth. Lady Meredith Blake was looking at him and only him. Still in shock, he noted absently a wide, humorous mouth set above a square, little chin before her head turned to respond to some remark from her neighbor and he heard that nervous little titter again. Surely he'd imagined it? What possible right or justification had that drab little mouse to regard *him* with such patent critical dislike? He wouldn't be surprised if she'd never gone further afield than Fowey! After dinner, he decided grimly, he would seek further speech with the lady, and, if she offered him any impertinence, she would have cause to regret it.

Meredith, unaware of the unfortunate notice she had attracted, was conscious only of her own tedium. It seemed an eternity before the covers were removed and the ladies repaired to the drawing room, leaving the gentlemen to their port. But as she rose from the table, she became conscious of a hard gaze that held more than a hint of puzzlement as well as a distinct flicker of annoyance. For some reason, her chin went up and she returned the look in kind. His lordship frowned, then he turned to his host with a compliment on the port, and Merrie almost scuttled from the room. For a moment she thought of feigning the headache or even a swoon—although she was not sure quite how one accomplished the latter—in order to escape the remainder of the evening, only to remember that she had sent Jem and the horses home and was now dependent on the charity of others. She could not expect anyone to have their horses put to especially to convey her home although she did not doubt that they would do so. They were kindly enough for all their dullness.

The drawing room filled rapidly with those members of the gentry who had received invitations to take tea after dinner. Meredith found it quite possible to blend with the crowd, and when the gentlemen joined them she was engaged in apparently animated conversation with her preferred companions, the matrons whose conversation was always safe and predictable, in whose company she could allow her mind free rein while her tongue trotted along the well-known paths.

Damian watched her whenever it was possible to do so without notice. There was something tantalizingly familiar about the slight figure. Was it simply the familial resemblance to young Rob? The eyes and that splash of freckles across the bridge of the nose were certainly shared by brother and sister. But that was not the reference. He shook his head as if to clear his mind for the elusive memory.

The sound of musicians tuning their instruments, carriage wheels and horses' hooves on the gravel sweep, the excited voices of Landreth's young men and maidens come to enjoy the ball, drew the drawing room party into the ballroom at the rear of the house. Meredith took her place against the wall with the chaperones, mittened hands folded demurely in her lap, slippered feet motionless despite the enticing shiver of the musicians' strings.

"Lady Blake, may I have the honor of this dance?" The soft question took her quite by surprise, and, forgetting her customary caution yet again, Meredith raised her head.

"I am most sensible of the honor, my lord, but I do not dance." Hastily, she dropped her gaze.

"Then let us talk," Lord Rutherford said smoothly.

"Or do you not do that, either?"

Meredith inhaled sharply, then gave a self-deprecating little giggle. "You must forgive my reticence, my lord, but I am so very afraid that you will find my conversation as insipid as you find our county uncomfortable. We are woefully unaccustomed to receiving visits from such august personages and are quite overwhelmed at the honor you have deigned to bestow upon our poor community." Her chicken-skin fan beat the air as she turned to her matronly neighbor. "Is it not so, Mrs. Garfield?"

His lordship, having been made to feel like a thoroughly presumptuous coxcomb, was obliged to listen to Mrs. Garfield's effusive agreement.

"Oh, Patience." Meredith greeted her hostess who had come to ensure her guests were suitably entertained. "We have just been telling Lord Rutherford how he honors us with his illustrious presence." That nerve-grating titter sounded.

"Yes, indeed, dear." Patience smiled kindly at Meredith, patting her hand. It occurred to Lord Rutherford that Lady Blake's inanities were accepted without question amongst her neighbors. Why then was he convinced that appearances were deceiving? He knew nothing of the lady, after all, and was much less qualified to make judgments than her friends. He glanced toward the floor where the set was forming.

"Lady Barrat, I beg you will intercede for me. I am anxious to solicit Lady Blake's hand, but she informs me she does not dance. I would not presume if they were playing a waltz, but the cotillion is quite unexceptionable, is it not, ma'am?" The smile he directed at Patience quite took that lady's breath away, so

42

thoroughly did it transform the rather stern countenance.

"Of course, Lord Rutherford," she concurred. "But
Lady Blake is such a retiring soul, aren't you, my
dear?"

Meredith lowered her head and fluttered her fan,
mumbling in accents of acute distress.

"Come now, Meredith," Patience said in bracing
tones. "A dance will be good for you. You cannot turn
down such a partner, you know."

"I shall be the envy of all eyes," Merrie whispered.

Little hypocrite! Rutherford thought with a surge
of anger. People did not presume to make game of
Colonel, Lord Rutherford, yet this shrinking violet
was playing with him like a cat with a mouse, and
only he seemed to be aware of it. He took one
mittened hand firmly and jerked its owner upright.
The gesture was sufficiently discreet to pass unnoticed
by all save its recipient, who opened her mouth on an
indignant exclamation that was instantly repressed,
but a pink tinge crept into the pale cheeks.

"Come," he said, offering his arm.

As if at the mercy of some puppet master, Merrie
accompanied him onto the floor. She could feel the
surprised looks as they took their places in the set but
was at a loss to know how she could have done
otherwise. Anyway, Patience would vouch for her
reluctance to behave out of character. But why was
Lord Rutherford acting in this manner? Surely she
had conducted herself with sufficient stupidity to give
him more than a little disgust of the widow Blake? Or
had her own instinctive dislike of a man who clearly
considered himself far above his present society re-

vealed itself in some way? There had been that exchange of looks at the end of dinner. . . . No, she was being ridiculous. Even if he did suspect such a thing, it would hardly concern Damian, Lord Rutherford, that a mousy countrified dowd held him in dislike. One thing, Meredith was determined, his lordship would regret his importunity in this matter of dancing.

She was light on her feet, Damian observed, moving with a lithe grace that the folds of bombazine could not hide, moving with a supple grace that he had seen somewhere before, but her knowledge of the steps was apparently nonexistent. She was never where she was supposed to be, bumped into him and their neighbors with blithe unconcern, trod on his toes, exclaiming in embarrassed fulsome apologies until he thought he would shake her. Not once did she raise her eyes from her feet although the scrutiny did not improve their performance in the least, but he became intimately acquainted with her bent neck. It was actually a long, graceful neck, he noted, and the heavy knot of auburn hair at its nape a richly burnished mass.

"Quite clearly you were correct, ma'am, when you said you did not dance," he declared ruthlessly as the measure ended. "My apologies for having importuned you. Allow me to escort you back to your chair."

"Why, Lady Blake, so splendid to see you on the floor again after all these years. Will you do me the honor of this next dance?" Sir Algernon appeared in front of them, beaming jovially.

Meredith inclined her head at Lord Rutherford and placed her hand on Sir Algernon's arm.

44

The following country dance was composed of a series of elaborate figures—all of which Lady Blake performed impeccably. Rutherford stood against the wall, arms folded across his chest, watching incredulously. She was a superb dancer! That ludicrous performance had been entirely for his benefit. Quite obviously, there was a great deal more to Lady Meredith Blake than met the eye, and she was not to be treated with the casual disdain that she invited. Well, whatever game it was she played, she would discover that two could play.

He appeared beside her when supper was announced, ignored the flutterings and fumblings, the expressions of gratitude mixed with apology, as he tucked her hand beneath his arm and moved toward the supper room. Meredith felt a stab of unease as she cast a covert look at the face beside her. The features were set in lines of grim determination almost as if he were resigned to performing a distasteful but necessary task. Had Patience perhaps asked him to take the widow into supper? No, of course she would not have done so. The room was full of much worthier women who would fall over themselves for his lordship's attention.

"I am wondering if this is wise," Lord Rutherford remarked, setting two plates on the supper table. "I have my doubts about Lady Barrat's cook—after the venison, you understand?" He offered her a dry little smile.

Meredith found herself in something of a quandary. On the one hand, she was in wholehearted agreement with him and a bubble of laughter was growing most inconveniently in her chest, but, on the other hand, the contemptuous remark was not one a stranger was entitled to make and seemed entirely in keeping with his previous derisive comments.

"That, my lord, is a Cornish pasty," she informed him with a hesitant smile, playing with her napkin. "They are considered great delicacies in these parts. Our tastes, of course, are not so refined as yours, sir. How could they be? But when one is accustomed to outdoor work and exercise, one develops a hearty appetite."

There was no mistaking the implication. Lady Blake considered Lord Rutherford to be a useless parasite, one who did not know the meaning of hard work and genuine, well-earned hunger.

Rutherford thought bitterly of his years in the Peninsula, years of guerrilla warfare, of forced marches in all weathers, living off an inhospitable land, at the mercy of snipers and treacherous peasants, never sure where one would next lay one's head. Years that he had lived and loved to the full! And this little brown mouse had the unconscionable nerve to imply that he had known nothing but the feather-bedded life of a pampered aristocrat! Except that she was *not* a little brown mouse.

The mittened fingers continued to twist the corner of her napkin, her eyes were resolutely downcast, shoulders hunched.

Damian looked around the crowded dining room. For the moment, their fellow guests seemed absorbed in their supper, and he could detect no inquisitive glances in their direction. Leisurely, almost, he stretched a long forefinger, placed it beneath that square chin, and exerted firm pressure. The face, thus uplifted, expressed infuriated outrage—not a sign of the church mouse. He nodded thoughtfully. "A piece of advice, ma'am. Keep your sword sheathed. It is just possible that I am a more experienced duelist than you."

The long, sable eyelashes dropped, obscuring the challenge in the dark eyes; the full lips began to tremble. "I cannot imagine what you can mean, sir," Lady Blake whispered. The note of distress sounded appallingly genuine. His lordship released her chin instantly, suddenly afraid she was about to weep. What the devil was happening? He seemed to be losing his senses—one minute convinced that he was being made mock of by a consummate actress, the next convinced that he must have been mistaken. Either Merrie Trelawney, sister of Rob Trelawney, alias Lady Meredith Blake, was a most complete fraud, or Lord Rutherford had windmills in his head.

"Let us abandon this repellent pastry and take a turn about the terrace," he suggested in a tone of voice that did not lend itself to suggestion.

"Pasty," Meredith corrected automatically. "I have no desire to leave this room, my lord."

"Fustian! You are in need of a little air. It is abominably stuffy in here." He held out his hand, a polite smile on his lips. "If you argue with me, Lady Blake, it will appear most singular—much more so than a sedate stroll in full view of any interested persons."

"Oh, but my lord, I would never presume to argue with you," she murmured in horror. "But I am at a loss to understand why you should seek out my company in this particular fashion. There are many more interesting persons in the room." Her eyelashes fluttered; her hands twisted in her lap.

"If you say so, ma'am" he concurred equably. "You would know much better than I, of course." His hand remained outstretched in invitation. Meredith looked around them. She could not continue to ignore that invitation without drawing the most unwelcome notice. Except that it was not an invitation—it was an order. Barely controlling a grimace of angry frustration, Meredith laid her mittened fingers in his palm. His own closed over hers, and there was no mistaking the iron grasp that declared her captivity.

The terrace was not deserted, for which Meredith was initially grateful, but their companions were the young and giddy, escaping the eyes of chaperones for a brief interval. Muted giggles came from the shadows, an occasional, hastily suppressed squeal of delighted outrage. It was no suitable place for a respectable widow, Merrie reflected, however sedate their progression.

"I begin to feel a little *de trop*," her companion observed as a young couple separated hastily on seeing them.

"We are certainly spoiling their fun." Meredith, still struggling with her annoyance, was betrayed into tart agreement. Recollecting herself hastily, she tittered again, continuing in a tone of hesitant apology, "You, perhaps, find our country ways a little shocking, sir, but these youngsters have grown up together, and there is little harm in a few minutes of unchaperoned high spirits. They are not often granted the opportunity."

"I have no wish to be a kill-joy. We shall walk on

the lawn." Before Merrie could demur, he had grasped her elbow firmly and proceeded to escort her down the flight of stone steps to the garden where lanterns swung from the trees, casting a soft, enticing glow.

Meredith felt a flicker of panic at the impression the sight of them, strolling in such a romantic setting, would create. "Please, sir, I do not wish to be here," she whispered beseechingly, taking her hand from his arm.

"Oh, but I find it most pleasant," he returned, retrieving her hand and, holding it tightly, guiding her onto a darkened path out of sight of the house. "It is a delightful night. Let us walk in the shrubbery."

"No!" Merrie squeaked, pulling at her hand. "I do not wish to."

"But I do," he replied evenly. "What are you afraid of, Lady Blake? That someone might get the wrong idea about you?"

She would have to be deaf, Meredith decided, to miss the sardonic emphasis to the question. If ever there was a moment for dramatic action, this was it. With a whimper, she went completely limp, sinking to the ground, her skirt settling in a corolla around her.

Rutherford swore violently, dropping in alarm to his knees beside the still figure. Her eyelashes fluttered as he lifted her in his arms. She was amazingly light under those folds of material, he noted even through his dismay at this unexpected turn of events.

"I do beg your pardon," she whispered in a faint voice. "So silly of me, my lord. Pray put me down."

"You are sure you can stand?" he asked anxiously although the last thing he wanted was to have to carry an inert Lady Blake into the house. The fuss that would cause sent shudders of revulsion down his spine, and dimly he realized that somehow or other his attempt to avenge himself on the widow had recoiled.

"Quite sure." Her voice sounded stronger, her eyes opened. Clearly the prospect that dismayed him did not appeal to her either. "If you would just escort me back to the ballroom."

He set her on her feet. "I will take you to Lady Barrat. She will know what to do for you."

"That will not be necessary, sir. I have these turns on occasion. I shall be perfectly all right directly." Meredith gave her companion a hopefully reassuring smile. It was met with a speculative frown.

"They appear to come conveniently, ma'am," Rutherford observed. The sudden flash in the sloe eyes confirmed his suspicion. Lady Blake had just neatly extricated herself from her predicament, and he had no choice but to beat a strategic retreat to plan an attack from another quarter. That he would return to the fight, Lord Rutherford was resolutely determined.

He escorted her back to the ballroom and she disappeared instantly in the direction of the retiring room.

"Will ye join us in the card room, Lord Rutherford?" Sir Algernon appeared at his side. "I've a splendid brandy you'll enjoy. The Gentlemen do us proud."

"Gladly," Damian returned, remembering his other purpose in attending this horrendously cloddish evening. A little information about the Gentlemen

50

might make up for his resounding defeat at the hands of the widow. "In a few minutes, if I may. I've a mind to clear my head in the garden."

"By all means." The squire clapped his lordship's shoulder in a jovial gesture of comprehension. " 'Tis monstrous close in here. Too many bodies and too much exertion to my mind."

"Just so," Lord Rutherford concurred. The atmosphere in the ballroom was indeed becoming a trifle overpowering as the odors of sweat and perfume combined and the breath of the dancers misted the gilt-framed mirrors.

Standing on the terrace, breathing deeply of the fresh night air, the strains of music wafting over his head, he wondered what the devil he was doing here in this barbaric corner of God's earth where heavy pastry crusts enclosing a mélange of root vegetables and chopped meats were considered a delicacy, where young people romped indecorously and unsupervised, where frumpish widows made subtle mock of one of Wellington's colonels and, unless he was much mistaken, made the same mock of her neighbors who seemed to have swallowed the act hook, line and sinker. More fool them! But why? Damian, Lord Rutherford, was determined to find the reason, just as he was determined to teach the widow that one did not play games with him—not with impunity. It was just possible that this excursion into Cornish society was going to prove rather more entertaining than he had imagined.

Chapter Four

Meredith, having dabbed cold water on her wrists and temples and sufficiently recovered her composure, returned to the ballroom, determined to avoid further exchanges with Lord Rutherford at all costs. She had quite forgotten, in the general disturbance of the evening, to ask the Abbots for a place in their carriage. Now she found, to her dismay, that they had been gone a half-hour since. The company in the ballroom was quite depleted, and Merrie was faced with the humiliating prospect of presenting her predicament to Patience.

"My dear Meredith." Patience bustled over to her. "What excitement!" She fanned herself busily, plump, beringed fingers curling around the ivory sticks. "Such attention as he paid you. Quite unlooked for!"

"Quite," Meredith agreed drily, then, seeing the flash of surprise in Lady Barrat's eyes, moderated her tone. "It was a mere kindness on his part, Patience," she fluttered, dropping her gaze, playing with her fan with a fair assumption of embarrassment. "He happened to meet Rob yesterday and was kind enough to say that he found the young scapegrace quite engaging." It was half true, at least!

"Oh, I see." Patience was clearly relieved at such a simple explanation for an extraordinary circumstance. "We are all sensible of your difficulties, my dear." Her voice dropped confidingly. "Sir Algernon, you know, would be most willing to offer advice. A single woman is not equipped to manage growing boys."

"You will thank Sir Algernon for me," Meredith said with a demure smile. "Such consideration quite overwhelms me." Her fan moved rapidly, hiding the flash of irritation in her eyes. Now, more than ever, she was determined not to reveal her carriage-less state to her hostess. Patience was clearly expecting her to make her farewells. It was hardly seemly for the widow to be amongst the last guests, but Meredith smiled blandly, turning toward the terrace. With any luck, Patience would be so occupied with bidding farewell to the others that she would not remember Lady Blake. She had simply to slip through the doors into the garden and make a discreet escape. It was but three miles home, easily walked in less than an hour even in thin slippers and an evening gown. Patience would just assume that she had left in her usual retiring fashion, too shy to intrude with her own farewells. A polite note of thanks on the morrow would satisfy the courtesies.

Her disappearance was simply accomplished for one accustomed to moving with speed and stealth and taking advantage of what cover was available. It was a soft night, heavy with the scent of honeysuckle, and, once clear of the house, Merrie, with a blissful sense of release from captivity, sat on a bank to remove her stockings and slippers, the better to enjoy her solitary walk. She was about to tuck the skirts of the loathed bombazine into the legs of her frilled pantalettes to free her stride when the unmistakable clop of hooves rang from around the corner of the paved road.

Merrie's heart sank as she thought of the picture she must present. There was little hope that the rider would not know her. Strangers were not wont to be abroad at this time of night, and she would be a familiar figure to any resident for miles around. There was nowhere to hide, except the muddy ditch, but, for once, there was nothing illegal about her presence on the road in the middle of the night. Small comfort, perhaps—the sight of her would set the gossips' tongues to running. The sound came closer and she pushed her shoes and stockings behind her on the bank—no time to put them on again. Inspiration would come, it usually did, but the explanation for her plight would depend on the identity of her discoverer. A local farmer would require something less elaborate than a fellow guest at the hunt ball. Tucking her bare feet beneath her skirts, Lady Blake sat upon the bank, a veritable picture of patience-in-waiting, as the horse and rider drew near.

"The deuce take it!" an all-too-familiar voice exclaimed. "If it isn't Lady Blake, taking her ease by the roadside." He sat the most magnificent black Meredith had ever seen, one hand resting casually on his hip, the other holding the reins loosely. Those eyebrows lifted quizzically, and his mouth curved in a smile that contained more than a hint of triumph.

Meredith gnashed her teeth in impotent fury. Anyone else she could have dealt with easily, but she had already developed the unwelcome conviction that, in Lord Rutherford, Merrie Trelawney was in danger of meeting her match. "I am sure you think it a most singular circumstance, Lord Rutherford," she said stiffly.

"Well, yes," he said with due consideration. "I think that I do." He dismounted. "May I join you? You look most comfortable." The gods had decided to smile on him at last, Damian thought complacently. What a stroke of good fortune to catch the deceptive little widow at such a monumental disadvantage. She could feign as many swoons as she wished, out here in the middle of the night, and they would do her not a whit of good.

Maybe an appeal to chivalry would work, Merrie thought rapidly and without much hope. "It is most embarrassing, my lord, to be discovered in this position." A slight shudder shook the slender shoulders. "I cannot tell you how mortifying I find it, but I must beg you to continue on your way." The long eyelashes batted vigorously, the full lips trembled beseechingly. "*Pray* continue on your way, my lord, so that I may continue on mine."

"You cannot expect me to be so unchivalrous as to abandon a lady in such a plight," he remonstrated, spying her shoes and stockings on the bank behind her. Now why the devil was she not wearing them? A bubble of laughter threatened his composure.

Meredith saw the direction of his gaze and bit her lip crossly. There was no possible explanation but the truth for that embarrassment. "I find it easier to walk barefoot," she offered.

"But of course," he responded smoothly. "Quite understandable. I am sure you have a perfectly good reason for nighttime peregrinations, also?"

Merrie, abandoning the masquerade, spoke acidly. "Since you are aware of that fact, sir, I suggest you accept my reasons as both sufficient and not your concern."

It was not a suggestion that suited Lord Rutherford in the least. One did not look gift horses in the mouth and, if ever he had encountered a gift horse, it was now. He shook his head. "No, Lady Blake, I am not to be so easily dismissed. I will escort you home."

Merrie wished she could stand up, straighten her shoulders, and walk away from him. To do so, she would either have to hitch up her skirt and petticoat and put on her stockings or pick up both shoes and stockings and proceed, barefoot and bare-legged. Neither alternative was a remote possibility. "I require no escort, sir. You need have no fears for my safety. I know the road and am well-known in these parts, so I am unlikely to be molested."

Lord Rutherford thought, with an inner chuckle, that he had no fears for her safety. For some reason that he couldn't yet fathom, he was convinced that Merrie Trelawlney was more than capable of taking a care for herself. But that consideration was not the point of this exchange. He was owed a victory and was disinclined to give it up, not when it hung ready for the picking. "I do beg your pardon, Lady Blake, but I find myself quite unable to leave you here." He smiled apologetically. "Some quite ridiculous, and I'm sure unnecessary, notions of propriety prevent me."

"Rules of propriety pertaining in London society, sir, do not apply in the wilds of Cornwall," Meredith snapped. "You will have a miserable time of it during your visit here if you uphold such lofty standards."

"I will remember your advice." Lord Rutherford rose, bowed, picked up her discarded footwear. "You will find it more comfortable to ride if you replace your shoes and stockings," he said, dropping them in her lap.

Meredith blinked, as if to dispel this dreamlike sensation of being quite out of control of the situation. "Lord Rutherford, I do not think you can have heard me correctly—unless your wits are quite addled—by Sir Algernon's brandy, perhaps?" Mobile eyebrows lifted, all thoughts of caution dissipated under an anger that was as much defensive as aggressive.

"Both my wits and my hearing are perfectly sharp," he assured her. "Yours, on the other hand, appear to be a trifle slow this evening." Dropping on one knee in front of her, he took a stocking out of her lap. Even as she sat, transfixed on the bank, he possessed himself of one foot and then, with a skill that bespoke practice, slipped the stocking over the foot, smoothing out the wrinkles as he eased it over both ankle and calf, calmly pushing up her skirt to facilitate his progress. Meredith, after a moment's frozen horror when she watched his fingers sliding up her bare leg, feeling the stroking warmth smoothing over her skin, lashed out. Her flat palm, powered with the full force of her arm, cracked against his cheek.

The gray eyes closed for an instant, his head falling back under the blow, but the hands remained on her leg. "You would do well to remember, Merrie Trelawney, that that is the one and only time you will do such a thing without my permission." The voice was level, his face, seared with the scarlet mark of her hand, quite expressionless. And the top of her stocking reached her thigh.

She wanted to hit him again more than she had ever wanted to do anything in her life but, to her utter fury, found that she did not dare. The note of chill certainty in his voice was one she had never heard before although it would have been familiar enough to any man under the command of Colonel, Lord Rutherford. Desperately, she tugged at her imprisoned leg, bracing herself with her hands on the bank beside her. The maneuver achieved nothing, and her garter slipped over the top of her stocking before her unlikely maid turned his attention to her other leg.

"I could *kill* you," she declared in a choked whisper. "How *dare* you do this to me?"

"You gave me little option," he said coolly, "having refused to do it for yourself. There now." Her slippers slid over her feet, her skirt and petticoat were pulled down to her ankles, and Lord Rutherford stood up, extending his hand. "On your feet, Lady Blake." His fingers snapped imperatively.

Quivering with temper, Merrie turned her head away from him in mute defiance. "Dear me," he said, shaking his head in mild exasperation. "You do not appear to be an apt pupil at all." He bent and, before she had time to realize his intention, scooped her up into his arms. Forgetting his unspoken warning, Merrie slapped him again. There was an instant of dreadful silence during which she fancied she could still hear the resounding crack of her flat palm. Then he spoke very softly. "I repeat, Merrie Trelawney, you are not an apt pupil. You will not, I trust, deny my right to retaliate." Meredith was speechless, shaking now with fright rather than rage as he set her down, standing her against the trunk of an oak tree. Both of her wrists were seized in one large hand, and she stood sandwiched between the tree and what suddenly seemed to be an alarmingly broad, sinewy body, radiating strength and determination.

Merrie forced herself to meet his eyes. She could not begin to imagine what form the retaliation would take, but she would not give him the satisfaction of seeing her fear. A long-fingered hand encircled the slender column of her neck, the thumb feeling the wildly beating pulse at the base of her throat. "Mmmm," he murmured, smiling slightly. Meredith did not, however, find the smile reassuring. "What exactly *are* you, Merrie Trelawney?" It was clearly a rhetorical question since, before she could reply, she found herself unable to do so. His mouth came down on hers, the pressure bending her head back, holding her immobile against the tree, the grip on her wrists tightening as she fought back in a wash of panic. Meredith thought she would suffocate under the bruising punishment of a kiss that pressed her lips against her teeth, her body against his length so close she could feel the rapid thud of his heart against her breast, the power of his thighs forcing her to be still. Then abruptly the pressure ceased although he continued to hold her. The lips on hers softened, the hand at her throat stroked gently before moving downward, gliding over the swell of her breasts beneath the stiff material of her gown. Merrie felt herself tremble deep within her at some core she had not known she possessed. She trembled, not with anger or fear this time, but with some sensation previously unknown to her. His tongue ran over her lips gently, then more insistently, demanding entrance. The hand at her bosom traced the outline of her breasts, circled their tips with knowing urgency until her nipples peaked hard and her lips parted to receive the exploration of a muscular tongue.

After what seemed an eternity of sensation, Rutherford straightened slowly, raising his head to look down at the stunned, heart-shaped face below. The sloe eyes were bemused, the full lips kiss-reddened, the ivory complexion tinged with pink. What had started out as retribution had taken a most definite turn in the reverse direction, he reflected, absentmindedly running a finger over the bridge of her freckled nose. "I think that perhaps you had better make a habit of slapping me," he said with a smile. "I found the consequences most pleasant."

"*I* did not," Merrie denied in a stifled voice, turning her head away.

"Liar," he accused, gently and without rancor. "But I'll not prove it to you again tonight, much as I would like to. Let us go." Taking her elbow, he turned her toward Saracen. "Do you prefer to ride pillion or before me?"

Meredith swallowed. "I prefer to walk—alone!"

"I should find it easier to have you before me," Lord Rutherford continued as if she had not spoken. "Up with you." Catching her by the waist, he lifted her onto the saddle with the firm injunction to hold the pommel. The black stood at least twenty hands,

Merrie thought, looking down at the distant ground, wondering if she dared leap from her perch. "If you do, I shall simply put you back again," her companion said, reading her thoughts with infuriating accuracy. He then swung up behind, reaching around her for the reins, asking with formal solicitude, "Are you quite comfortable, Lady Blake?"

Meredith, who did not think she had ever been less comfortable in her life, did not deign to reply. Chuckling, Damian nudged Saracen's flanks and the horse moved forward, clearly unperturbed by his double burden.

Meredith found an arm at her waist. While common sense told her that it was necessary for her safety, all the sweet reason in the world could not slow her heartbeat or dissolve the goose bumps prickling her back at the inevitable close contact with Lord Rutherford's broad chest.

Her companion coughed apologetically. "Could you furnish me with directions, Lady Blake? I am not familiar with the neighborhood, I am afraid."

With a supreme effort, Merrie pulled herself together. "It would be both quicker and less conspicuous, sir, if we were to leave the road and travel as the crow flies. I do not care to be discovered in this enforced and compromising position."

"Oh, but surely no one in this county would think anything of it," he said blandly. "Now, if it were London . . . But you were kind enough to advise me that rules of propriety in the wilds of Cornwall are considerably less strict."

Meredith bit her lip. Would she ever have the last word? "If you will take the next gap in the hedge to

61

your left, we may follow the bridle path."

"As you command, ma'am." Rutherford, for his part, was no stranger to the contours of the female frame, but he was finding the proximity of Lady Blake both disconcerting and distracting. There was a lithe suppleness to her, a vibrant tension in her body where it touched his, a muscular vibrancy rarely found in the fair sex, and his hands still carried the memory of her breasts, small and shapely beneath that hideous bodice.

Such thoughts did not allow for conversation. Once they had attained the bridle path, complete silence reigned until they broke through a small copse of young birch trees onto a gravel driveway leading to a long, low building, dark and silent under the moon.

Damian drew in Saracen, and into the silence came the unmistakable roar and crash of breakers. The salt tang of the sea filled the air, the night breeze was fresher, tipped with moisture. "Where is the sea?" he asked, frowning into the gloom.

"Beyond the house," Meredith replied. "Pendennis stands atop the cliff, its back to the sea. We have approached it from inland." It had been a civil enough question, deserving of a civil response, but now her voice sharpened. "If you will allow me to dismount here, Lord Rutherford, I may make my own way to the house in complete safety as you can see."

"Indeed," he agreed, swinging promptly to the ground. "I should be sorry to think I was the only one to enjoy our ride." Reaching up, he took her by the waist again.

Meredith, to her annoyance, felt herself blush as he lifted her down, felt her body tense in anticipation as he held onto her after her feet touched ground. Then he was bowing to her with impeccable formality, and, thoroughly flustered, she returned a curtsy.

Knowing laughter gleamed in the gray eyes. "Would you perhaps have preferred another kiss, my lady?"

Merrie's jaw dropped. "You are insufferable, Lord Rutherford." Swinging on her heel, she walked away toward the house.

Damian stood, watching until she had disappeared around the side of the building. What an intriguing kettle of fish he had stumbled upon. A lively, attractive, unconventional young woman who, for reasons known only to herself, pretended to be a reclusive dowd. But, unless he was much mistaken, beneath that prim exterior ran a well of passion as yet barely touched. He had scratched the surface just a little tonight. What would be revealed if he persevered? Of one thing Lord Rutherford was convinced, there would be much pleasure in the persevering.

Yes, the cultivation of Lady Blake was going to provide considerable entertainment, he decided as he remounted and turned his horse back to the copse. His lordship was in sore need of diversion these days to keep the bleak sense of futility at bay, the sense that his usefulness was over, that life held only the prospect of the annual society round, the Season, marriage, succession to his father's title, producing his own heirs, overseeing his estates, engaging in combat with nothing more dangerous than hand-reared pheasants. His lips curled. No, for a while he would remain in Cornwall amusing himself with the widow. He had ended this night the victor, well revenged for her earlier insults. Tomorrow, he would approach from another quarter. He could afford a little placation, a little softness, and, if conscience reared its ugly head, it could be quietened with the reminder that the widow had begun the game. She would receive only what she had invited. Whistling cheerfully, Lord Rutherford went home to his bed.

Chapter Five

Meredith was rarely troubled by sleeplessness, but her dreams that night were confused, and she slept later into the morning than was her custom.

Nan woke her eventually with the reminder that the steward was waiting in the library for his monthly discussion of estate business.

"Oh, Nan, why did you not wake me earlier?" Meredith sprang from bed. "I cannot imagine how I could have been such a slug-a-bed."

Nan, looking at her erstwhile nursling's heavy eyes, sniffed but refrained from comment. While Meredith sponged herself with water from the ewer, she laid out a simple day dress of faded muslin, knowing that Meredith would be out and about on the estate once her interview with Mr. Farquarson was over.

"I suppose the boys have breakfasted already." Merrie fumbled with the buttons on her sleeves in her haste. Nan, tutting, pushed her hands away and did the task herself.

"Hours ago," she said. "Master Hugo's with his

books, Master Theo's off to the village, and the good Lord only knows what that young rapscallion Rob is about."

Merrie laughed, knowing full well Nan's great fondness for Rob. "He'll be back when he's hungry," she declared, twisting the thick, auburn braid into a coronet around her head. "Having first regaled every available pair of ears with the most intimate details of the household."

That thought gave her pause; her forehead puckered as the image of Damian, Lord Rutherford, rose with alarming clarity. She had already come to the conclusion that she would avoid any further encounter even if it meant immuring herself in Pendennis until the charms of Cornwall palled on the London buck and he decided to return whence he came. He was quite the most detestable creature it had ever been her misfortune to meet—so arrogantly certain of his superiority, so devastatingly assured of achieving his own ends, so appallingly powerful. Meredith gulped as her eyes met their reflection in the glass. It was the consciousness of that power that frightened her. It was not simply that he was physically so much stronger than herself although she had ample reason for knowing that, but there was something else, something indefinable about the aura of authority he carried—a feeling she had that once he set his mind to something, nothing and no one could stand in his way. And if he set his mind to something concerning Merrie Trelawney . . . ?

She shivered. Why did he call her that? She was known as Merrie only to her most intimate friends, family, and household, and it had been five years since she had legitimately been known as Merrie Trelawney. Yet, Lord Rutherford used that name as if he had the right—as if it carried some special significance, just for him.

She gave herself a vigorous mental shake. There was a busy day's work to be accomplished, a household and estate to manage, decisions to be made. Thoughts of domineering noblemen who didn't recognize when they were unwelcome had no place in the scheme of things.

Meredith went downstairs. "Seecombe, would you be good enough to bring coffee to the library? I am behindhand this morning and have no time for breakfast."

"Certainly, Lady Merrie." Seecombe inclined his head, determined that he would take rather more than just coffee to the library. Her ladyship needed to keep up her strength. The entire household was aware of the struggles Lady Blake had to keep her head above water as they were also aware that, while their wages were occasionally late in coming, they were always paid as the first priority. Sir John had had a fine time gambling away his fortune, and it was a crying shame that, young as she was, his widow should be reduced to such desperate straits. A lesser woman, they all knew, would have sunk beneath the burdens, but her ladyship refused to surrender. The boys were kept in school, no member of the household had been turned away, the pensions and gratuities to retired retainers were maintained. How she did it was the puzzle and a subject for considerable speculation in the kitchens of the neighboring manor houses, if not in the drawing rooms.

Meredith greeted her steward with a warm smile. "Are you come to depress me, Stuart? You are looking uncommon grave."

" 'Tis the matter of the Longwood cottages, Lady Blake," Farquarson said ponderously, laying his hands on plump thighs in worsted britches. "The expenditures cannot be delayed any longer. The roofs must be repaired and the alley repaved before winter. The tenants have been understanding, but I fear they will begin to grumble before long and with good reason."

Meredith sucked the tip of her thumb in the unconscious manner she had had since a child whenever she was troubled. She had intended to pay off the final mortgage payment on Ducket's Spinney with the profits from the last run. Now, it would have to be delayed. Reclaiming the estate had so often to take second place to necessary maintenance, and the latter was so much less satisfying than sitting in solicitor Donne's office in Fowey, handing over a banker's draft, and receiving in exchange the deeds to whatever part of the estate she had managed to buy back. The solicitor had no more idea than anyone else where the money came from but assumed that extraordinary thrift was responsible. One had only to look at Lady Blake herself to see one area of strict economy.

"Very well, Stuart. Set the repairs in motion." Having bowed to necessity, there was no point repining. She poured coffee, nibbled a piece of bread and butter, and, in typical fashion, put the disappointment out of mind as she and the steward went over the accounts.

After Farquarson had left, however, Merrie sat at

the chipped oak desk that had also escaped the auctioneer's hammer, staring out of the long windows facing the sea. The sea . . . two runs a month would solve all her problems. She could pay off debts *and* maintain the estate. But doubling the profits meant doubling the risk, particularly with the revenue become so active. While Jacques, she knew, would agree to the proposal, would Bart and the others be willing to accept the increased risk? Well, she would not find out unless she asked, and there was work to be done that would not be done if she sat like a dressmaker's dummy gazing out of the window.

"Seecombe, I shall be in the stables until nuncheon. The farrier comes this morning and I must talk with him."

"Very well, my lady." The manservant held the side door for her and she went out into the warm, summer day. It was such a relief to be outside, after the gloomy confines of the library, that she skipped a little on her way to the stableyard. It would not matter who saw her here where she was surrounded only by friends.

It was nearing noon when Lord Rutherford's stallion trotted up to the front door of Pendennis. The doors stood open on the balmy air, and a rather ancient red setter cocked an ear at the new arrival before resuming her nap in the sun. There was a pleasantly somnolent, relaxed atmosphere about the gracious, mellow stone house standing as it had done for two hundred years amidst well-tended, flower-filled gardens, hedges and shrubs neatly trimmed. Rutherford examined his surroundings appreciatively before hitching Saracen's bridle over the stone knob of the balustrade, mounting the short flight of steps, and pausing in the doorway to look for something with which to herald his presence. There appeared to be neither door knocker nor bellpull. Cornish habits were most singular. Where else would one find front doors standing open to all comers? He took a tentative step into the dim light of the hall. As if on cue, the baize door at the rear swung open to reveal a substantial, gray-haired figure, his britches and waistcoat covered by a green apron, who trod towards him.

"Sir?" Seecombe managed to convey disapproval in the very inflection. Strange gentlemen at Pendennis were not to be encouraged in this manservant's opinion.

Damian was not amused. This covert incivility seemed to be a characteristic of Cornish servants. "Is Lady Blake at home?" he inquired, directing a flinty stare at this most unbutlerlike figure.

"She is not, sir," he was informed.

"When do you expect her?"

"I couldn't say, sir."

There seemed to be nothing for it but to leave his card, something he had hoped to avoid, having a strong suspicion that his quarry, once alerted, would attempt to elude him.

"It's Lord Rutherford! I told you it was his horse, Theo." Rob, preceded by a cocker spaniel pup with flying ears, catapulted into the hall. "Good day, sir. How do you do? This is my brother, Theo. We have been in the village, you know, down by the quay," he added, as if the information were eagerly sought. "Have you come to call?"

"That was my intention," Damian agreed. "But I understand your sister is not at home." He nodded at

70

Theo, who was gazing wide-eyed at his lordship's cravat, the set of his coat, the snug fit of the buckskin britches across powerful thighs.

"Is—is your coat made by Weston, sir?" Theo stammered.

"As it happens. But you should not stare so. It shows a sad lack of sophistication." Lord Rutherford did not consider the snub to be particularly severe, but clearly its recipient was unaccustomed to any form of set-down for he flushed with mortification and began to stammer an apology.

"Oh, do not be in such a taking, Theo," Rob advised. "It only makes you look silly. His lordship did not mean to be unkind, did you, sir?"

Damian found himself hastening to assure them both that nothing had been further from his mind. He had not, in fact, intended to be unkind but had responded automatically to what at first sight struck him as ill-bred scrutiny. He looked again at the two boys, noting their resemblance to their sister and the very clear fragility of the older's dignity. It brought a stab of youthful remembrance and, anxious to make amends, he smiled. The smile was returned with instant trust and warmth, and his lordship felt absurdly relieved that his flash of irritation had not irretrievably blotted his copybook.

"Merrie is only in the stables," Rob was saying. "She will be back soon, will she not, Seecombe?"

"I couldn't say, Master Rob," the manservant replied repressively. "Not being party to her ladyship's plans." With that, he returned to the servants' quarters.

"That's such fustian!" Rob looked after him indig-

71

nantly. "Merrie always tells Seecombe when she is coming back and where she is going. Do you think he can think Merrie would not care to see you, Lord Rutherford?"

"I wish you would learn to hold your tongue occasionally." Theo, his composure recovered, rebuked his young brother sharply. "I cannot imagine what Lord Rutherford must think. Will you step into the parlor, sir? I will send someone to fetch my sister."

"But she will be back shortly," Rob protested. "And who will you send?"

"You," Theo hissed in an undertone.

Damian stepped through the door Theo held for him, wondering if at any minute he would be required to separate the warring brothers.

"Go and tell Merrie that Lord Rutherford is here, Rob," Theo instructed.

"But she is probably on her way back. She only went to talk to the farrier about Jen's canker, and I saw him leave above ten minutes ago."

"She will like to know that she has a visitor," his brother said, looking daggers.

"Oh." Comprehension dawned on Rob's open countenance. "You mean that she might wish to change her dress when she knows that Lord Rutherford has come to pay a call?"

Rutherford began to examine his surroundings with an appearance of overpowering interest, ignoring the hissing behind him. He could not help but near Rob whisper, "I do not care what you say. Merrie does not care a jot for such things." There was a muffled squeak, sounds of a scuffle, then silence. Rutherford turned from his contemplation of the only pieces of

72

any note in the shabby, yet cheerful room—a pretty, japanned workbox resting on a small satinwood table beneath the window—to find himself alone. It was with a measure of relief that he sallied forth, unaccompanied, in the direction of the stableyard. His reception had been sufficiently unconventional for him to feel justified in going in search of the lady of the house; besides, he strongly suspected that in the heat of their squabble Masters Theo and Rob had quite forgotten any intention of alerting their sister to the visitor if, indeed, they remembered his presence in the first place.

The stables, as he had expected, were to be found on the westerly, sheltered side of the house. They were clean and orderly, bearing all the marks of good management, unlike his own at Mallory House. Of Merrie Trelawney, there was no sign.

A lad was sitting on an upturned pail, a hunk of bread and cheese in one hand, a tankard of ale in the other. He vouchsafed the information that he'd last seen the mistress in the barn. Damian accordingly made his way to the red-roofed building. It was dim and dusty within, and he stood for a moment, inhaling the rich fragrance of the hay, noting the orderly stacks of bales. This was one establishment that would not go short in the winter months. The signs of good husbandry were everywhere, in the clean, dull gleam of forks and rakes, the swept yard, the full rainwater barrels.

"Lady Blake?" he called into the dimness. Silence greeted him.

Meredith, up in the hayloft, froze. What the devil was he? Some kind of nemesis pursuing her even into the safety of her own sanctum? Perhaps if she kept quiet, he would go away again. Booted footsteps sounded on the stone floor of the barn below.

"It's been some years since I played hide-and-seek so you may have to remind me of the rules," he said, and there was a distinct note of amusement in the voice. Merrie reviewed her options rapidly. She could continue to cower like a hunted rabbit behind the hay bales, she could demand in self-righteous panic that he leave her property instantly, or she could declare her presence. Only the latter option allowed any dignity, but, even as she hesitated, Lord Rutherford's neat brown head appeared at the head of the ladder rising to the loft. "Ah, there you are," he announced with calm pleasure. "I have been calling you, but I expect you didn't hear."

"I am rather occupied, sir," she replied in a definitely muffled voice, turning her head away abruptly back to her task. "To what do I owe this pleasure?"

"Pleasure? Somehow, the word doesn't carry a ring of truth," Rutherford mused, hitching himself into the loft. In the dim, dusty light, he saw her crouched in a corner under the eaves where a round window let in a smidgen of light. "Perhaps I may be of help," he offered.

"I do not think so, sir." Resolutely, Merrie kept her back to him, trying not to react as she heard and felt his approach. The devil take the man! Why did he always catch her at a disadvantage? She was dressed like a milkmaid with straw in her hair, grubbing around in the dust. She could not even play the horror-struck, prim, matronly widow in these circumstances—not with any conviction, at least. But then, after last night, that role would carry little credibility with this audience. "If you wish to be of help, Lord Rutherford, you will leave as quietly as you can. They are frightened enough as it is, and I am afraid they will die of heart failure. They are such fragile little creatures."

Rather than ask what she was talking about, Rutherford decided he would do best to find out for himself. Crossing the rafters, he came to stand behind her. The sunlight in the round window gave the crown of auburn hair a rich luster that distracted him for a moment from his mission. Her simple print gown of faded muslin was an immeasurable improvement on the previous evening's bombazine, clinging as it did to the supple curves of a deliciously slender frame. Slender, but again he noticed that tautness that had so struck him last night. She held herself almost like a soldier as if her body was a machine under her control. What could she possibly have done in this retiring life she seemed to lead to have taught her that? It was a fascinating question and one to which he would soon find an answer. But unless he could overcome the very clear hostility radiating in his direction, he might as well return to Mallory House.

He saw that she held in her lap a bird's nest, perfectly formed, containing three fledgling house martins. Instinctively, he dropped onto his haunches beside her, asking softly, "what's to do with these babies?"

"The mother has abandoned them," Merrie heard herself explain in the same soft tones, "because they would not fly. I have been watching these last few days, and she has been quite frantic trying to teach them. They are too frightened, the sillies, although they are quite big enough. I have it in mind to take the nest below and put it on the lower window. Perhaps they would be willing to try from there."

"More like the cat will get them," Rutherford observed.

"Well, it is that or starvation up here," she declared matter-of-factly. "I intend to try. If you will go back down the ladder, I will pass the nest to you. The ladder is a trifle unsteady, you understand. I am unwilling to climb down in these skirts with only one hand."

"A wise decision," he murmured. "Had you not been wearing skirts, the matter would have been different."

Damn the man! He was laughing at her again. Then it occurred to her that her statement had sounded a little peculiar. It only made sense if she was in the habit of not wearing skirts, as his lordship had just gently pointed out. Why the devil did he have to be so sharp? Or she so careless? She had meant exactly that. In her britches, she wouldn't have thought twice about descending the ladder encumbered with a nest of chicks.

The only safe course was to ignore his observation. "Would you be kind enough to take the nest, my lord, while I stand up?" She spoke with creditable dignity, holding the nest up to him. The fledglings twittered in distress as he received their home in cupped palms. Rescuing baby birds was not an activity the soldier had experienced before. He had rescued comrades on a battlefield, women and children from marauding armies, and he'd done his share of killing, too. So what was he doing concerning himself in the fate of these pathetic, fragile, little creatures whose chances of survival were minimal at best?

Rutherford shrugged mentally and accepted whatever direction fate and whim chose to take him. Such abdication made a refreshing change, and he clucked comfortingly at the fledglings, who, sadly, were not to be comforted.

Merrie stood up, shook out her skirts, brushing off dust and straw impatiently. Wisps of hay clung in the shining auburn coronet. Such an opportunity was not to be missed, his lordship decided with an almost apologetic sigh.

"Pray take the nest for a minute." She received it automatically and with lamentable lack of caution. "You are very untidy," he explained, "and, since you do not have a mirror, it will be best if I put you to rights." Merrie stood rigid under his hands as they moved over her hair, picking out straw, fluff, and feathers. Hampered by the nest of baby birds, she had no choice but to keep still as he dusted down her skirt, straightened her linen collar, and retied her sash. "There, that is much better." Standing back, he nodded with approval. "Now, if you give me back the nest, you may hit me again. Since you have my permission, I will not retaliate this time—unless you should wish it, of course."

How could anyone be so insufferable! Meredith's eyes narrowed, a chilly smile touched her lips. "Why would I want to hit you, Lord Rutherford? I am grateful for your assistance. If you will be good enough to go down the ladder, I will pass you the nest."

Rutherford grinned ruefully, raising his hand in the gesture of a fencer acknowledging a hit. "Touché, Merrie Trelawney. A thousand pardons for such a clumsy piece of swordplay. I crave your indulgence."

Why did she want to laugh? A moment before, she could cheerfully have shot him through the heart! All the cynicism had left the gray eyes, the bored, disdainful curl of the lip was gone, even the arrogance appeared mitigated by his seemingly genuine acknowledgment of defeat. He was almost a different person. And that was a most disturbing thought. Meredith turned abruptly toward the ladder, looking for a new and safer topic of conversation.

"How did you know where to find me? Seecombe would not have said, I'll lay odds."

"No," he agreed. "Seecombe would have cut his tongue out first. Fortunately, as I was being turned from the door, young Rob bounced in."

"Ah, that would indeed explain all." Merrie chuckled inadvertently. "Why did he not accompany you?"

"He and Theo had a falling out," Damian said carefully, "and—uh—appeared to forget all about me."

"Oh, dear." Meredith sighed, continuing for some reason as if her companion was in some way a family intimate. "Poor Theo finds Rob such a trial. I suppose, when one is fifteen and trying to be dignified, eleven-year-old brothers *are* a sore trial. I had thought to send Rob to Eton rather than to Harrow in order to spare Theo embarrassment, but Trelawneys and Merediths have always gone to Harrow and none of them would hear of such a thing."

"I do not think you need concern yourself. If

memory serves me right, Theo will have ample support in keeping his brother in his place, and I'm convinced Rob has already learned that first years do not know fourth years. What goes on at home will not be repeated at school." He offered the truth with a degree of impatience. Schoolboys were hardly the most fascinating of topics. When her troubled expression cleared miraculously, he instantly regretted his brusqueness.

"That is such a comfort," Merrie said. "I was so afraid Theo was being made miserable at school. But you would know about such things, after all."

Damian nodded, marveling at the extraordinary sense of warmth he felt at having reassured this unconventional woman who, for a moment, had looked as if she were carrying the burdens of the world upon those slender shoulders.

Merrie saw the strange darkening in those gray eyes and felt suddenly uneasy. The disdainful cynic was much easier to deal with than a Lord Rutherford with humor and compassion in his eyes. At least, when they were engaged in a battle of wits, she was sure of her ground, sure of her feelings. For a moment, tension tautened like string stretched between them, then Rutherford, to Merrie's relieved annoyance, returned their relationship to its normal footing. "If you will give me the nest, I will carry it down. Since I am not hampered by petticoats, I may do so with ease."

Meredith set her lips in a thin line but meekly handed over her charges, unable to think of any logical objection to this modification of her plan. She followed him nimbly down the rickety ladder, clearly needing no chivalrous assistance, and Damian placed the nest on the broad sill of the only window.

"I hope you were not right about the cat," she muttered with a worried frown. "If you will but stay here and watch over them, I will dig up some worms. I am sure they must be starving."

"You will do *what*?" Rutherford exclaimed. Then his shoulders began to shake. "Oh, Merrie Trelawney, you are too much! You really would go grubbing for worms as if you were a grimy little boy with a stick and a bent pin for fishing!" Leaning against the barn wall for support, he gave himself up to the rich laughter rippling through him. He hadn't laughed like this for many many months, and his entire body seemed to open with the pleasure of it.

Meredith stood nonplussed for the moment it took her to realize why he was laughing. The suggestion had seemed perfectly reasonable when she had made it, but now, remembering the masquerade she had played for his benefit last night—prim, proper widow Blake, murmuring idiocies, dropping her possessions in her fluster—she could hardly wonder at his hilarity. Her cheeks warmed with a mixture of indignation and discomfiture. "Oh, do stop," she said crossly. "It is not *that* amusing."

"Oh, but it is," he gasped. "It is utterly delicious. *You* are utterly delicious, Merrie Trelawney—a wondrous conundrum that I have to solve."

Cold fingers marched down her spine at these words and she found refuge and diversion in anger. One sandaled foot stamped vigorously. "Stop it, I say! I will not have you laughing at me. You are trespassing on my land, or, at least, you are here without invitation, and I will not tolerate further discourtesy."

Rutherford stopped laughing although merriment still lurked in the depths of his eyes. "Then I should perhaps make amends—with a little civility," he said softly, placing his hands on her shoulders. Meredith stepped back, a strange fluttering sensation in her belly, but she could not evade his hold drawing her against him. "There is a passion in you, Merrie Trelawney. One that I would delve," he whispered, moving one hand to palm her scalp as he brought his head down until his lips covered hers. Merrie's eyes closed as she inhaled deeply of the fragrance of his skin, a sun-warmed scent that seemed one with the taste of him as his tongue explored the soft cavern of her mouth. His hands ran down her back, feeling her skin, warm and pliant beneath the thin material of her dress, stroked over the curve of her hips, kneaded her buttocks as she reached against him with a low moan wrenched from some place deep within herself.

"Sweet heaven!" Rutherford murmured in a tone of awe, raising his head slowly. "What *are* you, Merrie Trelawney? I think I am bewitched."

Meredith stood in a shaft of sunlight, the back of her hand pressed to her warmed, tingling lips as the world steadied again on its axis, and she saw her predicament in all its dreadful truth. She could not now deny her response to this man, either to herself or to him. But if she could not deny it, what *could* she do about it?

"Merrie? Merrie? Where are you?" Rob's imperative yells shivered the tension like a stone on crystal.

"In the barn," she called back, moving swiftly to the door, her eyes slipping past those of her compan-

81

ion.

"Oh, you found Lord Rutherford," Rob announced, appearing in the doorway. "That's good because Theo and I forgot all about him for a minute. Seecombe says it's time for nuncheon, and if you don't come quickly the oysters will go cold. They are cook's special recipe," he informed Rutherford solemnly. "She will be as cross as two sticks if they spoil. Won't she, Merrie? Of course, if I hadn't come to find you, Hugo and Theo and me could have had them all to ourselves." He beamed at his elders. "I hope you like scalloped oysters, Lord Rutherford."

Meredith blinked in a bemused fashion. Had Rob just invited his lordship to nuncheon?

"One of my favorite dishes," Rutherford was saying, smiling at the boy.

"Oh, that is good. There is plenty for everyone, and Hugo is most anxious to meet you." With that, he slipped a hand into Rutherford's larger one just as if they were the oldest of friends and proceeded to lead him back to the house.

There was nothing to be done but follow with a good grace. At least the company of her brothers would ensure a thoroughly domestic, undramatic atmosphere.

Nuncheon at Pendennis, his lordship discovered, was far from a light meal. The refectory table in the dining room bore both sirloin and ham, a tureen of rich vegetable soup, the promised scalloped oysters, cheeses, and fruit—a repast clearly designed to satisfy the appetites of growing boys. Rob and Theo did ample justice to it, their earlier quarrel apparently forgotten. Hugo Trelawney, a rather pale, spindly young man with an overly serious expression, responded politely when introduced to Lord Rutherford and toyed with his food. Or at least, Damian qualified silently, gave the appearance of toying with it. A substantial quantity of meat nevertheless found its way onto his plate and subsequently disappeared. Meredith drank tea, the boys lemonade, Lord Rutherford was presented with a foaming tankard of ale that Hugo informed him solemnly was their own brew.

Meredith apologized for the fact that she could not offer him claret but explained nonchalantly that any bottle from their cellars would require an hour to breathe if it were to be appreciated. Since they had not been expecting guests, they were unprepared. "You will find that to be the case in most houses in the neighborhood," she said. "We pride ourselves on our cellars."

"Yes, it is thanks to the Gentlemen," Rob put in. "They make deliveries every month, but no one ever sees them, and you cannot hear them coming either, because they muffle the ponies' hooves. Is it not so, Merrie?"

"That is what is said, certainly," she replied without a flicker. It was a relatively innocuous topic of conversation and a fairly absorbing one. "It is a major business in these parts, Lord Rutherford. Have you yet had a chance to examine Lord Mallory's cellars? I dare swear you will find them well stocked."

"I have sampled the brandy and found it to be more than superior," he said. "I must confess to an abiding interest in these Gentlemen." He looked up from his plate, surprising a sudden, sharp glance from his hostess.

"Only outsiders find the idea of smuggling romantic, sir," Meredith said with a light shrug. "For
Cornishmen, it is a simple fact of life—dangerous and
dirty more often than not."

That remark was clearly designed to put him firmly
in his place—an impractical outsider with romantic
notions about a serious business. "I did not say I
found it romantic," he countered gently. " 'Interesting' was the word. I happened to run into them, you
see."

Meredith dropped her fork with a tinny clatter on
her plate. "How could you have done such a thing?"
she demanded. "No one sees them."

"But I did," he replied as gently as before, wondering what on earth was the matter with her. She looked
as uncomfortable as if she were sitting on an ants'
nest.

"Where, sir?" Rob bounced up and down on his
seat, and even Hugo had stopped his methodical
chewing.

"On the cliff road the night I arrived." He helped
himself to another slice of sirloin. "They were engaged in a skirmish with the coastguard as far as I
could see."

"Who won?" Theo was staring again, the Trelawney eyes wide open.

Damian chuckled. "Oh, the smugglers without a
doubt. They disappeared, you see, right under the
revenue's noses. It was fascinating."

"Where were you when you saw this?" Meredith
asked, having herself well in hand again.

"Hiding behind a gorse bush." He laughed again.
"It was devilishly uncomfortable, not to mention

undignified, but well worth it. Their leader intrigued me."

"How? Why?" Rob, unable to keep his seat, began to dance on his toes. "I have never ever talked to anyone who's seen the Gentlemen!"

"Sit down, Robin!" his sister said sharply. "It is hardly earth-shattering news."

"Why were you intrigued, sir?" Hugo asked as his brother resumed his seat with a pout.

"He seemed little more than a lad," Damian explained. "Incredibly young to be commanding such a group but clearly very competent." He wondered whether to tell them of his other suspicion, but Meredith was looking distinctly discouraging, and he decided to keep it to himself. She would probably accuse him of being fanciful. Obviously, for some reason, she did not consider the topic suitable for a family dinner table.

"If you wish to trade with the Gentlemen yourself, sir, you must pass them a message," Rob said, having recovered from his momentary discomfiture. "Must he not, Merrie?"

"I do not imagine Lord Rutherford's stay in these parts will be long enough to warrant that, Rob," his sister returned, the note in her voice clearly indicating that the subject should now be closed.

"But I have not yet decided how long I shall remain," Damian said mischievously, seeing the flash of annoyance before she dropped her eyes to the apple she was peeling.

"We have little enough amusement to offer," Meredith said. "I should imagine you will soon be bored and anxious for the pleasures of London society."

"Now I wonder what could have given you that impression," his lordship mused. "I did not think I appeared unamused by last night's entertainments and, in truth, look forward to a repetition."

Meredith bit her lip. He was teasing her shamelessly, and in the presence of her brothers she was quite unable to respond as she would like.

"Besides, Merrie, there is lots to do," Rob put in. "Riding and shooting and fishing. And then there are the soirées and Fowey is a sizeable town—"

"It is not," Theo interrupted. "Compared with London or Brighton, Fowey is no larger than a village. Is that not right, Hugo?"

"Quite right. Even compared with Oxford it is tiny," the eldest Trelawney pronounced.

"But I was not comparing it," Rob protested sturdily. "I have seen bigger towns on the journey to school; I am not such a bumpkin! But it is a big town in *these* parts."

"That is self-evident," Theo said crushingly, and Rob, crestfallen, was again momentarily silenced.

"How would one pass a message to the Gentlemen?" Lord Rutherford asked casually, diverting the subject to give the lad time to recover, wondering vaguely why he should feel the need to do so.

"That is not a piece of information vouchsafed to women and minors, my lord," Meredith said. "If you are, indeed, serious, you could do no better than to ask Sir Algernon Barrat. He will be able to advise you, I am convinced." She gave him a smile as bland as milk pudding, but the razor's edge to her voice could not be ignored. For all her innocent, correct appearance with her demure coiffure and the plain

86

simplicity of her muslin gown, Lady Meredith Blake, presiding so decorously over a family nuncheon, was a force to be reckoned with. She had just given him a most direct order to drop the subject, and he did so although he could not imagine why it should be taboo. Probably some strange Cornish custom known only to insiders!

He took his leave soon after. His hostess he found to be both dignified and withdrawn as she escorted him to his horse. Saracen had clearly been cared for during his stay, and Rutherford offered his thanks as he stood on the gravel sweep before the house.

"We are not such barbarians, sir, as to ignore our guests or their mounts," she said coldly.

"Now in what way have I offended you?" Frowning, he took her hands.

Meredith withdrew them with a jerk. "If you do not know, then you are even more obtuse than I had thought."

"And you are most impolite," he said curtly. "You will not talk to me in that fashion if you please."

"A thousand pardons," she said sarcastically. "I had not the intention of offending your so delicate sensibilities although you clearly consider you have the right to ride roughshod over mine."

"With a kiss?" he hazarded, eyebrows raised.

Merrie flushed angrily. "As it happens, that was not what I was referring to."

"I wonder why not," he mused. "You would certainly be entitled to take exception to such a liberty."

"You are intolerable!" she hissed. "How could you taunt me in that manner?"

Damian sighed, taking Saracen's reins. "You are

87

capable of bringing out the worst in me, Merrie Trelawney. But I asked you a simple question: how have I offended you? Your response deserved a similar discourtesy."

"A gentleman would have turned the other cheek," she shot back, unwilling to admit that he was right.

"Yes, I expect he would have done," Damian agreed placidly, laying his booted foot in the stirrup and swinging into the saddle.

"It was unsporting in me to object to being made game of in front of my brothers when I am not in a position to retaliate, I suppose," she demanded furiously.

"Ah, so that is what has annoyed you," he nodded his head thoughtfully. "Yes, you are quite right. It was an unpardonable way to return your hospitality. I will endeavor to make amends, ma'am, when next we meet." Wheeling his horse, he waved and trotted down the drive.

Merrie watched the black horse out of sight. What was happening to her? Some thoroughly disagreeable man marches into her well-ordered existence and turns it completely topsy-turvy, and the only responses she can produce are childish petulance or a most definitely adult passion! And he'd seen her on the cliff road. To her knowledge, no one in Landreth or the surrounding village had ever seen the smugglers. It was an unspoken rule that, when the band was abroad, the local inhabitants kept their faces to the wall. But then, Merrie was beginning to fear that Damian, Lord Rutherford, was a law unto himself. She, of course, was a law unto *her*self and always had been, but that was no reason why others should have the same privilege—particularly foreigners who did not understand Cornwall and Cornishmen, who despised what they saw and thought they could do exactly as they pleased.

Chapter Six

The following morning, Meredith donned her riding habit, had her angular, but always reliable, mare saddled, and set off for the village. Landreth was a fishing village where little business was transacted unless it be over the lobster pots at the quay or in the taproom of the Falcon. She walked the mare down the cobbled street between the whitewashed cottages, looking for Bart, knowing full well that, of those who saw her, at least half of them knew her for their leader. No one but Nan, Jacques, and these fisherfolk who plied the same trade knew the truth, and they were all content to keep it so. Only in secrecy and still tongues was there safety.

"Lad!" She beckoned to a child of around six, barefoot and in torn britches and a grimy shirt. He pulled his forelock and crossed the narrow street.

"Yes'm."

"A penny for you, if you'll go into the Falcon and tell Bart I'd like a word."

The boy scampered off, disappearing through the

blackened oak door of the tavern. It was only mid morning but the taproom was doing a roaring trade, the fishermen having returned from the dawn setting of the lobster pots, with little to look forward to but the tedious business of mending nets and pots.

The atmosphere was more subdued than usual, however, the talk less ribald, the laughter less raucous. On one or two faces, the expression was downright sullen. The boy, looking around through the smoke of many pipes, saw the reason. Young as he was, he spat on the sawdust of the floor. The presence in the Falcon of the hated coastguard from Fowey was an unforgivable intrusion. No one knew what they hoped to gain by it. They'd not hear anything to their advantage, that was for sure. Indeed, the two men lounging against the bar looked as uncomfortable and out of place as they felt. They were not in uniform, but the homespun britches and leather waistcoats did little to disguise them, and they were morosely cursing the stupidity of those dolts in Fowey who knew nothing of Cornishmen and thought spying on them was a simple matter. The fact was, the very sight of a stranger, be he the epitome of innocence, was enough to make them clam up, and some of the fishermen in the taproom had an ugly look to them. You'd not want to meet them in a dark alley on a moonless night.

The appearance of a small boy, wriggling like an eel through the throng, drew little remark. When he whispered to Bart, only a few took notice. As far as the revenue men were concerned, the lad had probably been sent by his mother to fetch home her errant husband. Amongst those few who could make an informed guess as to the child's business, a ripple communicated itself. If Merrie was in the village in search of Bart, then something important was afoot. It was also reasonable to assume she did not know of the revenue spies in the taproom.

Bart listened, cuffed the lad in a friendly fashion, sending him about his business. All perfectly ordinary, nothing at all untoward. But it was not he who left the inn on the boy's heels. Bart remained to down another tankard and make several derogatory remarks as to the strangers' attire, remarks that they struggled to ignore even as they found themselves surrounded by a mocking circle of bearded men. Thus occupied, they did not remark Luke Trewatha's exit.

Luke sauntered past Merrie as she sat her horse across from the tavern. They exchanged no words, but Meredith immediately continued on her way down the village street, out along the coast road. Something had kept Bart in the tavern, and Luke had made it clear she had best hasten her own departure. Bart knew now that she wanted to speak with him, though, and would make the agreed rendezvous in the cave beneath the house, two hours after nightfall. She would find out then what was amiss in the tavern.

It was as much by accident as design that she came to the low stone wall surrounding Mallory House and its gardens. Lord Mallory had not encouraged visitors, and there were few in the community familiar with either house or property. Now, however, Merrie reined in her mare at the gate to look with undisguised curiosity at the activity. Men were at work in the gardens, weeding, trimming, and scything. They swarmed over the outside of the house, repointing chimneys, replacing roof tiles, repainting the wood-work. The sounds of hammers and saws rang in the morning air. Lord Rutherford appeared to have em-ployed every available pair of hands in the neighbor-hood, she thought. He must, then, be planning an extended stay unless he did not feel the need to oversee the work himself.

"Good morning, Lady Blake. This is indeed a delightful surprise. Have you come to return my call?"

The voice came from behind her. Merrie realized that she had been so absorbed in her reflections that she had lost awareness of her surroundings and had not heard his footsteps on the grass verge. A little shiver ran down her spine as she determined that this exchange should be pleasantly dignified. Her position on horseback gave her some advantage over the foot soldier and certainly ensured that there could be no physical contact. She turned slightly in the saddle, smiling graciously down at him.

"We are not quite so unconventional, sir, that an unmarried lady may pay a call on an unmarried gentlemen with impunity."

"But it is considered quite proper for a young lady to go abroad unattended?" he queried with raised eyebrows.

"Not for young ladies, sir, no. But I do not fall into that category. Only the highest sticklers would see anything to censure in a widow of advanced years going about unescorted," she responded sweetly.

Lord Rutherford pursed his lips, examining her. Her riding habit of rust-colored cloth was serviceable rather than elegant, but it was well cut, and the color complimented her hair, tendrils of which escaped from beneath the brim of her tall hat. Her muslin stock was pristine and beautifully starched, lifting that square little chin, and no expense had been spared on her boots. Although the scuffs on the leather were visible through the high polish, the boots were clearly of the highest quality.

"A widow of advanced years," he mused. "I can only assume, ma'am, that you are fishing for a compliment. I cannot decide whether to oblige you or not." The smile he gave her quite took her breath away. Warm and conspiratorial, it invited a light, flirtatious response.

"Oh, but think how unkind it would be to disappoint me," she countered before she had time to question the wisdom of accepting the invitation. "You must realize how few compliments come my way."

"Well, if you will go about dressed as you were the other evening, it is hardly surprising," he retorted. "And, by the by, I intend to discover your reasons for that absurd masquerade. They are presumably part and parcel of the whole conundrum."

Merrie felt a stab of panic. There was no knowing what this man would find out if he put his mind to it. "There is no conundrum, sir. Merely an impoverished widow who cannot afford the frills of fashion."

"I beg your pardon, ma'am, but that is really doing it a little too brown." His eyebrows lifted quizzically. "Pray do not insult my intelligence with such tarradiddles. You may be able to pull the wool over the eyes of your neighbors, but I am not so easily deceived."

Meredith chewed her lip in frustration. "I fail to see what business it is of yours, my lord, how I choose to dress."

"Strictly speaking, of course, it is none of my business," he said thoughtfully. "But I am in sore need of occupation these days, and a little mystery to unravel will fill my idle hours quite nicely."

"I am flattered, sir, that I should be considered worthy of such attention. It is a signal honor to be able to serve your lordship in such a manner." She clipped her words, incensed at the cool arrogance of the statement that quite destroyed her resolution to avoid undignified sparring.

He bowed. "The honor is all mine, my lady."

"I am certain the activity will soon pall, sir." She gave him a shark's smile. "Small-town mysteries will not be able to compensate you for the absence of those luxuries and comforts to which I know you must be accustomed. You know the tale of the princess and the pea, of course? I am forcibly reminded of it when I think of you tossing and turning on Matthew Mallory's bed."

The barb seemed even more successful than she had hoped, and Merrie suddenly found herself very glad that she had the advantage of the mare's back. Lord Rutherford's face went ominously still, and the gray eyes became as cold as the winter sea. "I do not find the comparison amusing. You seem to be in the habit of making such remarks. You would be advised to cease them forthwith."

Meredith decided that she was not going to be intimidated although some inner caution told her to take the advice. "Lord Rutherford, you may find our quaint ways moderately diverting at the moment, but you'd not survive the tedious ordeal of a Cornish winter." She made no attempt to disguise the note of mockery in her laugh. It was a statement in which she believed wholeheartedly, anyway. No London buck would survive more than a week of winter in these parts when the roads became impassable, the sea grew wild under the lash of winter gales, and folks kept to themselves within doors for weeks at a time. There was little social intercourse, and even the parish church bore empty pews of a Sunday.

"It pleases you to think me such a poor-spirited creature, then, ma'am? I can assure you I have suffered many greater hardships than any Cornish winter could impose." He spoke harshly, his bitterness exacerbated by the realization that he sounded like a schoolboy defending an accusation of cowardice. He had no desire to boast of his army career or to repine over its loss to anyone, and now he found himself on the verge of doing both to this infuriating, mocking creature who seemed to delight in nettling him and stood in sore need of a lesson in manners.

"I must bid you good day. There are matters requiring my attention." With a curt bow, he walked off through the gate, pausing to talk to one of the gardeners, never once looking back as Merrie returned to the road and her way home. Curiously, her clear victory in that exchange brought her little satisfaction.

Later that afternoon, Walter looked despondently at the colonel's black expression. The batman had begun to hope that this Cornish expedition had finally done the trick, so cheerful as his lordship had been. But now he was staring morosely into the empty grate, holding a glass of port, his fourth so far in the last hour, as if it were a lifeline.

It wasn't that the colonel couldn't hold his wine, Walter thought. No one would ever know when he was foxed except for the eyes that became shuttered and expressionless. But it seemed to increase his depression rather than alleviate it. The simple luncheon produced by Martha Perry lay neglected on the sideboard, and Walter had too much regard for his head to risk having it bitten off if he suggested again that the colonel eat.

"Have you nothing better to do, Walter, than stand there sighing like a virgin on St. Agnes's Eve?" Rutherford snapped.

"Beggin' your pardon, sir," Walter said woodenly. He did not change his position and the colonel appeared to forget his presence again.

The sounds of commotion outside at first did not penetrate his melancholy although Walter moved swiftly to the open French doors. "What the devil?" the batman exclaimed, staring at a knot of workmen shouting and gesticulating at something on the roof.

"What's that infernal racket?" Lord Rutherford's eyes snapped into focus.

"Dunno, Colonel, something on the roof, it looks."

Damian gave vent to an ill-tempered oath, striding past Walter into the garden up to the workmen. "What in Hades is going on?" he demanded.

"Village lads, m'lord." The foreman tugged his forelock. "Young devils've found the ladders, but those tiles are loose . . ."

Looking up, Rutherford saw a group of grimy, impish faces, and one that he recognized as having no place with the village lads. His heart missed a beat as

97

he bellowed, "Rob, come down here, this instant!"

At the sound of his lordship's voice the boys disappeared over the crown of the roof in a slithering, squealing mass, all except for Rob who hesitated, clearly wondering if obedience or flight was his best course. As he wavered, his foot slipped, dislodging a tile. Damian watched, transfixed, as the boy lost his footing and sat with a thump to slide inexorably down the steep pitch of the roof, his arms flailing wildly. Rutherford moved, running to the spot beneath the roof where Rob was bound to land. He could only cushion the fall as the boy was catapulted in a tangle of limbs. Knocking Rutherford off his feet, Rob landed awkwardly, his body largely protected by Damian's, but his arm was twisted beneath him, and he gave an anguished scream as his would-be rescuer tried to disentangle himself.

"Easy now." Damian gentled the boy as he helped him to sit up, took one look at the greenish cast to the white face, and held Rob's head as he crouched, retching miserably into an overgrown flower bed, his arm hanging limply at his side. When the spasms ceased, Lord Rutherford lifted him easily and carried him into the house.

"I b—beg your pardon, sir," Rob whispered. "I d—d—did not mean to be such a milksop." He blinked rapidly to dispel the tears filling the large purple-black eyes that seemed to be the Trelawney hallmark.

"That, young man, is not a word I would apply to you," Damian declared brusquely although his eyes softened. "There is nothing cowardly about feeling pain although trespassing on roofs is foolish beyond permission!" He laid the boy on the sofa in the library. "Walter will look at your arm."

"Is—is it broken, do you think?" Rob asked and bit his lip hard as Walter, with those incongruously gentle hands, began to feel the injured limb.

"You had best pray that it is," Lord Rutherford said grimly. "Otherwise, my friend, by the time I've finished with you, you'll be eating your dinner off the mantelpiece!"

The threat had the desired effect; the small face set, the shoulders stiffened as Rob determined to endure Walter's examination in silence. Damian turned back to the French doors, hiding his smile. "You there!" He summoned one of the workmen. "Can you find someone to go to Pendennis and tell Lady Blake what has occurred? There is nothing to concern her unduly, and I will convey the lad home myself as soon as he has rested."

"Aye, I'll go meself, m'lord. She'll be in a right taking, I'll be bound. Thinks the world of those boys, Lady Merrie does." The man went off at a run and Damian returned to the library. So, she was Lady Merrie to the villagers—still a Trelawney for them, presumably, although they gave her the Blake courtesy title. It was all most interesting: Lady Blake, Merrie Trelawney, Lady Merrie. What other facets of her personality were there?

Walter looked up from his examination of Rob's arm as his lordship came into the room. "Is it broken, Walter?"

The batman shook his head. "No, it's not broken as far as I can see. Just a severe sprain and painful enough, Colonel, and it needs a splint. He's a game lad, though. I haven't heard a whimper."

"Of course you haven't." Rutherford smiled at the white-faced Rob. "He's a Trelawney when all's said and done." He·poured a tot of brandy from the decanter on the sideboard and brought it over to the sofa. "Drink this, Rob. It'll blur the edges a little when Walter fixes the splint."

Rob obediently swallowed, choked, and swallowed again. A little color crept back in his face. "I should go home, sir. Merrie will be worried if I am late for dinner."

"I have sent a message to her so she will not worry. When you have rested, I will take you home." He watched the lad with considerable compassion. Walter was as gentle as it was possible to be, but Rob was in great discomfort as the soldier fastened splints and a tight bandage.

"That's the ticket," Walter said after what seemed to poor Rob an eternity. "If there is any possibility of a fracture, that'll see to it. You'd best keep away from roofs in future, my lad."

The sound of voices in the hall saved Rob from further strictures. "Where is his lordship, Harry?" It was Meredith's voice, clear and brisk, but the edge of anxiety was unmistakable.

Damian strode from the room immediately. The chances of old Harry Perry having any notion of the drama that had been enacted was fairly remote. Both he and his wife seemed blind and deaf to the outside world. "I am here, Lady Blake. But there was no need for you to come yourself. Did the messenger not tell you that I would convey Rob home?"

"Yes, yes, indeed he did." Meredith drew off her gloves with hands that shook slightly. "But you must know, my lord, that I could not put you to such inconvenience. I am so sorry for the trouble you have already been caused. Is—is he truly unharmed?" The sloe eyes were enormous in her pale face and Rutherford took her hands, frowning at their coldness.

"My dear girl, do not be in such a fret," he enjoined her, chafing her fingers. "The boy's had the devil of a shock and has sprained his arm badly. He's lucky it were no worse, but I think he has been punished sufficiently for his recklessness."

"Rob is quite incapable of associating cause and effect," said Hugo forcefully, coming into the hall at this point. "I am always telling him he should not go about with the village boys, but much notice he takes. Perhaps this time, Merrie, you will insist he pay heed, or you can be sure that, as soon as his arm is better, he will have quite forgot the lesson and be hip deep in trouble again. I hope you do not mind, sir"—he turned punctiliously to Rutherford—"but I charged your stable lad with the care of the gig."

"That is what he is there for," Damian observed drily. "I think, if you will take my advice, Hugo, that you would do well not to lecture Rob at present. He is not feeling quite the thing, for all that he's a game little bantam."

"Where is he?" Merrie asked, tossing her gloves onto the hall table and untying the ribbons of her chip hat. "In the library?"

Damian held the door for her. She almost ran past him to the sofa where Rob was struggling to sit up against the cushions. What happened next surprised Lord Rutherford. He had expected her to fall all over the boy, fussing and scolding in true female fashion, achieving nothing but the relief of her own feelings and the exacerbation of the patient's. Instead, with no indication of her earlier distress, she examined Rob's face carefully, looked closely into his eyes, nodding her satisfaction before scrutinizing Walter's handiwork.

"You did not send for the doctor, Lord Rutherford?"

His lordship shook his head. "Walter is more skilled than any country sawbones, ma'am. His expertise once saved me from the surgeon's knife in a field hospital. I'd trust him with a deal more than a sprain."

A frown appeared in her eyes and she gave him an interested, speculative look as if she would like to pursue the subject, but then turned back to Rob, saying matter-of-factly, "So, you managed not to break it this time."

Her brother grinned weakly. "I would have broke *all* of my bones if Lord Rutherford had not caught me."

"I fear that 'caught' is not quite the right word," his lordship observed, turning from the sideboard where he was pouring two glasses of port. "Lady Blake?" He handed one to her. "You will find it restorative," he said, seeing the look of refusal in her eyes. "I think you are in need of it."

There was a firmness behind the polite tone, but Merrie had the unmistakable impression that it arose simply out of concern for her. His expression bore none of the signs of annoyance, superiority, sarcasm that so offended her. And young Rob was regarding his lordship with worshipful, trusting eyes. He was a most puzzling man, one minute so odious she would be glad never to see him again, the next warm and compassionate. And when he smiled or laughed with genuine pleasure, it was as if the sun had come out on a rainy day. Her calm front with Rob had clearly not deceived him, and she could not deny the sense of relief that came from having a fellow adult concerning himself with her brother's well-being, not to mention her own.

Meredith took the wine with a word of thanks, having the strong suspicion that her host would not take no for an answer. "We appear to owe you a great deal, my lord," she said. "Not only does my brother trespass on your property, but you are then obliged to pick up the pieces. I do not know how to apologize."

"It is a great deal too bad of you, Rob," Hugo put in. "You have been told, I don't know how many times, not to run with the village boys, but you do not care a jot for Merrie's feelings. You have put her in a monstrous uncomfortable position. The story will be around the houses in no time and then she will have to listen to the old cats—"

"That is enough, Hugo," Merrie said quietly. "I know you mean well." She patted his arm, fully sensible of the truth of his words, although wishing, as always, that he could be a little more tactful. "But it will not help Rob to hear those things at present."

"I hate Hugo!" Rob declared on a choked sob. "He's always prosing on. I know I shouldn't have done it, but I'd sooner have a thrashing than listen to Hugo going on about it for the next year!"

Meredith raised her eyes to the ceiling. It occurred to Rutherford that she had probably had about as much as she could bear for one day. "We will leave these two to their own devices," he said in accents that brooked no argument. "Let us take a turn about the garden."

"But I must take Rob home," Merrie protested.

"You shall do so shortly and I will escort you. For the moment, you are going to take a turn about the garden. I would like your advice on one or two matters." Cupping her elbow, he propelled her with an almost indecent haste through the French doors and into the air.

For some reason, Merrie found that she had no desire to argue with this decisive action. There was something most appealing about leaving decisions up to someone else for once. She smiled ruefully. "It is not at all kind to desert Rob. Hugo is determined to have his say."

"And it will do that young scamp no harm to hear it," Rutherford declared forcefully. "Besides, I do not care to see you looking harassed. You are far too young to carry the burdens of the world upon your shoulders, Merrie Trelawney, for all your talk about widows of advanced years." This last was said with sardonic emphasis. "It seems to me that, if you are not concerning yourself with the plight of baby birds, you are being plagued to death by those quarrelsome youngsters. I should inform you, ma'am, that I intend to do something about it."

Meredith was for a moment too taken aback by this forthright statement to reply. While it was a declaration of intent that ought to have enraged her with its cool assumption of command, his motives for making it could only be interpreted as friendly and concerned.

104

Her elbow was still held in a firm clasp, so her feet were obliged to follow the direction dictated by her companion.

"Has the cat run away with your tongue, Lady Blake?" he teased when the silence continued.

"I think you delight in putting me at a disadvantage, sir," she retorted. "You are quite sensible of the obligation I am under. I have no choice but to keep silent, for, if I replied to you, I fear I should be most impolite, and I cannot repay your kindness in such a manner."

"I have never heard such a Banbury story," his lordship scoffed. "Nothing would prevent your saying whatever you wished to me, as well you know. The fact is, my lady, you cannot come up with a suitable reply."

"Oh, you are quite odious," Merrie grumbled, unable to refute the charge. "But I *am* determined not to quarrel with you this afternoon. Your kindness to Rob forbids it. However, it will be much easier if you do not provoke me, as you seem to take so much pleasure in doing."

"I had rather thought it was the other way around," Rutherford said evenly. "From the very first, you have never lost an opportunity to make some derogatory remark—by innuendo, I grant you, but I am neither deaf nor obtuse."

Merrie's jaw dropped and she stopped in her tracks. "How can you possibly say that? I have merely been responding to intolerable . . ." Memory of those kisses rose with unwelcome clarity. She bit her lip. "It is time I returned home, Lord Rutherford."

"Presently you shall. We will not pursue this topic

for the moment, interesting though it is. I wish you to relax a little, and I do not think that that discussion will help you to do so," he replied blandly. "Now, will you tell me what should be planted in this border? I know little of such things, but I was much struck by your flower garden at Pendennis."

There seemed little option but obedience. And in all truth, Meredith was loath to continue with the subject herself. There were some distinctly uncomfortable implications lurking in its depth, ones she would prefer to examine in privacy. She turned her attention to the noncombative matter of flowers and a good twenty minutes passed in this pleasant fashion until she recalled Rob.

"I *must* return to Pendennis." She turned back to the house. "I shall put Rob in Nan's charge for the evening, which she will enjoy a great deal more than he, I daresay."

"Who is Nan?" his lordship inquired, keeping pace with her.

"Oh, she was our nurse but now devotes most of her care to me." Merrie laughed. "She is a veritable bully and my knees knock whenever she frowns, but I could not manage without her, and Rob will mind her."

"That is, indeed, fortunate," his lordship observed and Merrie looked at him sharply.

"It is only high spirits," she said. "There is not an ounce of—"

"Hush. I do not recall saying that there was." Lord Rutherford, smiling, placed a long finger on her lips. "There is no call to rip up at me this time. I meant no criticism of Rob. He is neither better nor worse than any other boy his age. But do not tell me he is not a handful."

Since his finger remained pressed to her lips, Merrie was unable to tell him anything. Besides, when he smiled at her like that, all acerbity left her. He waited until the fire died in the sloe eyes before removing the finger, which he then placed beneath her chin.

"No," Merrie whispered, knowing what he was about to do. Her eyes darted wildly from side to side. "Not here."

"Somewhere else, then?" he asked gently, the gray eyes glinting.

"No!" she almost shouted although she knew she had invited the mischievous question. With a little, choked gasp, she jerked herself away from the finger, turning back to the house almost at a run.

Rutherford followed, chuckling to himself. Perhaps it was not gentlemanly to play with her in that manner, but it was quite irresistible—as irresistible as the urge to kiss her again, to feel that supple pliancy reaching against him.

They reentered the library where the atmosphere was thick enough to cut with a knife. Rob glowered resentfully at his sister. Hugo bore the mien of one who has satisfactorily discharged an unpleasant duty, and Lord Rutherford was hard pressed to keep a straight face. He dispatched Hugo to fetch the gig and tell the stable lad to saddle Saracen, then suggested briskly to the younger boy that he try his legs.

Rob appeared much recovered. When his reproachful looks bore no fruit from either of the adults, he seemed to forget his grievance. He was soon installed in the gig beside Merrie who took the pony's reins. Hugo, who was on horseback, rode ahead at his

107

sister's request, to alert the household to their impending arrival.

"It is kind in you to escort us, Lord Rutherford, but I am sure you must have more pressing matters to attend to." Merrie flicked the reins and the dappled pony shook its head with a chink of the bridle, snuffling disgustedly as she hauled her burden down the drive.

"None that comes to mind," Lord Rutherford replied with another of his bland smiles.

"I shall become quite puffed up, sir, if you continue to favor me with such attention," Merrie murmured demurely, her eyes resolutely on the road ahead.

"Have no fear, ma'am. Should that happen, I will not hesitate to deflate your self-consequence."

"My gratitude exceeds all bounds," she returned.

Lord Rutherford chuckled. "You are a worthy opponent, Merrie Trelawney. Shall we agree to fence in the future only with the foils buttoned?"

"If you are able to be so restrained, sir, I am sure that I can," she replied swiftly.

"I do not understand what you are talking about." Rob spoke up, an unusually petulant note in his voice. Merrie turned to him with instant comprehension.

"Does your arm pain you, love?"

"Yes, and my head aches."

"We shall be home soon," she reassured him, patting his grubby hand comfortingly. "Then you shall go to bed and Nan will make you a posset."

Lord Rutherford, excluded from the family exchange and seeing again the pucker of her brow, resolved to separate Meredith Blake from her brothers whenever possible. He preferred her undivided attention just as he preferred to see her without that nagging frown. It was almost as bad as the lowered head, twisting hands, and slumped shoulders of the widow Blake, but at least he knew that was an act. The maternal role she played with her brothers was genuine enough and, in his lordship's opinion, a totally unreasonable burden. He found himself smiling again as he realized that for the first time in many months his own concerns seemed remarkably unimportant. In fact, since he'd met this extraordinary creature, he had experienced a good many firsts, and this afternoon's black mood had become a total irrelevancy.

"Forgive my curiosity, Lord Rutherford." Meredith unexpectedly broke into his reverie. "But did you say you were in the army?"

"Did I?" He frowned. "I do not recall saying any such thing."

"I did not mean to pry," she said stiffly, hearing the note of reluctance in his voice. "You said something about Walter saving you from a field hospital. I am sorry if it is a subject you prefer to keep to yourself."

Damian sighed. "I do not, in general, care to talk about it. But, yes. I was with Wellington in the Peninsula, until a shoulder wound earned me my furlough, some six months ago."

"Hence the hardships you referred to this morning," Merrie said reflectively.

"Just so," he concurred in a voice as dry as dust.

"Well, I suppose I must beg your pardon," Merrie said matter-of-factly. "I had thought you to be an effete London buck."

"An opinion you did not scruple to hide," he

109

replied.

"Attack is frequently the best form of defense, my lord. Did your soldiering not teach you that?"

"It taught me many things but clearly not the best way of handling sharp-tongued widows," he retorted.

Merrie decided to side-step that. She was too interested in this new information to be diverted into another argumentative exchange. "You found it difficult to leave the army?" It was a guess, but somehow she knew it to be accurate.

"Damnably!" His mouth twisted in the travesty of a smile. "I am a soldier and always have been. I cannot abide kicking my heels about town. But what's a man to do if he's fit for nothing but idle small talk, the gaming tables, and squiring the ladies?"

"It must be quite dreadful," she said. He looked at her, amazed at this instant recognition of a problem that no one else except Walter had begun to comprehend. Merrie was thinking how dreadfully dull she would find her own life if she were forced to give up her smuggling. That activity served two purposes. It brought much needed funds to swell her purse, but it also provided her with the excitement and satisfaction of using skills, physical and intellectual. Without that outlet, she would shrivel and fade in this ritual-bound, inbred backwater.

"You must find something else to do," she said briskly. "We must all have a purpose, a reason for existing."

"I think that perhaps I have found one," Rutherford said softly.

That premonitory shiver ran down her spine. Was he referring to unraveling conundrums again? "What is that?" she asked hesitantly.

He smiled. "Restoring my inheritance."

Meredith considered this as they reached the driveway to Pendennis. Whether she believed him or not, it were best to respond blandly. "That is a worthy cause, sir, albeit a little limited. But it is a start."

"Oh, yes," he agreed. "Most definitely a start."

Chapter Seven

"What think you, Bart?" Merrie nibbled her thumb as she posed the question to the fisherman who sat on a rock in a corner of the cavern, puffing thoughtfully on a clay pipe.

"I don't like it," he said with his usual directness. "It's asking for trouble with the revenue the way they are now. Two runs a month means two deliveries. That's four nights in a month we'll be running the gauntlet."

"There's those in Fowey who'd be glad of regular deliveries," Merrie said. "What if we were to deliver to one place where those who are buying know to go? There is less risk than in making individual calls as we do around here."

"What place?" Bart's eyes narrowed against the blue curl of pipe smoke. He knew Merrie well enough to be sure that this was no vague, unthought-out idea she was presenting.

"The Eagle and Child in Fowey. I hear the landlord would be willing to receive and dispense the goods in exchange for a—a consideration, shall we say?"

"Who tells you that?"

"Jacques." Merrie chuckled. "He was in there two months ago, sampling mine host's brew. You know Jacques, my friend! They fell into conversation about brandy and . . ." She shrugged expressively.

Bart cradled the warm bowl of his pipe in a cupped hand, considering in silence. Merrie made no attempt to disturb his cogitations. Bart could never be hurried and without his support she'd do well to forget the idea.

"I'll talk to the others," he said finally. "They're family men for the most part, Merrie. The money comes in handy enough, but they'd as lief keep their necks the length they are now."

"I also," she agreed.

"Sometimes I wonder." Bart snorted, then tamped down the glowing tobacco with a callused thumb before getting to his feet. "We'll be delivering that lot tomorrow night, then?" He jerked his head toward the casks and bundles ranged against the wall.

"Unless our friend in the custom house can give us a reason not to," Merrie replied.

Bart grinned. "We struck lucky there. Fancy Luke's brother-in-law clerking for the revenue." He shook his head in mock wonder. "There'll be something extra special in there for him, I'll be bound."

Merrie nodded. "Jacques recommends the madeira. I have it in mind to broach a case for our friend. If we had not had warning of that last ambush, we'd be in a pretty pickle now."

"Aye. Well, I'll be off then. Unless we get a cautionary word from Greg, we'll have the ponies here by eleven tomorrow night."

"Don't forget to pass the word in the village," Merrie reminded him. "We'll want no watchers from windows or accidental meetings on the roads." That had already happened once too often, but she was not about to alarm Bart with that piece of information.

" 'Tis done already," Bart replied laconically, going into the narrow tunnel leading to the smaller cave, Merrie following. The village grapevine was amazingly efficient. A servant in one of the great houses would happen to hear on the wind that the Gentlemen would be riding on a certain night and the word would spread, always via the kitchens and stables, so that all remained within doors, and, if a dog barked for any reason, it was ignored. In the morning, in barn or stableyard, would be found a cask, a well-wrapped parcel, a case of the finest burgundy in exchange for the small packet that had gone out with the cat when the household retired. It was all most satisfactory. No one was compromised, no one knew anything, and no one ventured to ask the questions for which they would receive no truthful answers.

Meredith waited in the outside cave until Bart had had a ten-minute start, then sauntered out onto the path that led downward to the beach, upward to the cliff top at the rear of Pendennis. She had not used the secret passage because the household had been still awake when she had left for the rendezvous. Besides, she could not make the scramble in petticoats, and the sight of their mistress in britches would have certainly given the servants cause for speculation.

It was a balmy evening and she decided to wander down to the beach before returning to the house and bed. All in all, it had been an aggravating day: coastguard spying in the Falcon, Rob's adventures, Hugo's lectures, Lord Rutherford. What was she to do about Lord Rutherford? If only she still found him utterly dislikeable as she had done the night of the ball, there would be no problem. He was still possessed of disagreeable traits, certainly. He seemed to delight in teasing her, but there was little teasing in his manner when he issued directives or pronouncements of intention. And there was nothing remotely amusing, either, about the way she seemed obliged to follow the directives or about the alarming way in which he managed to fulfill his intentions.

But those would just be irritations if she could judge the man with calm objectivity. How could she be objective about someone who turned her insides to a *blanc-manger*? It was quite ridiculous! Merrie kicked irritably at the sand and only succeeded in filling her shoe with the damp, scratchy stuff. She was far too wise and experienced to respond like some starstruck debutante to an interesting new face. Except that she wasn't reacting like a star-struck debutante, she was responding with all the maturity and experience of a woman who had known a disillusioning marriage, who knew what it was to wrestle with an unkind fate until some peace and acceptance could be gained, who had a set of goals and a clear plan to achieve those goals, and who had three dependents to care and provide for. Damnation! Merrie swore aloud at the night sky as her arms crossed themselves over her breast, hugging her shoulders. She *wanted* Da-

115

mian, Lord Rutherford, with all the aching maturity of her twenty-three years. Her neglected body throbbed at the thought, and a mutinous spirit demanded to know why she could not have him. It was a thoroughly shocking thought, of course. Or, at least, it would be to anyone but Merrie Trelawney, who seemed to have been forgotten when notions of propriety and decorum had been handed out.

Picking up a small, round pebble, she sent it skimming across the dark water. Furthering her acquaintance with Lord Rutherford was undoubtedly a dangerous prospect. His eyes were too sharp for comfort; he already knew more than he should about her double life; he had seen her on the cliff road. So he didn't know that he had, but he had made no bones about his interest in the youth who led the smugglers. Her only safety lay in avoiding him whether she wanted to or not. Of course, if Rutherford refused to be avoided, as seemed highly likely . . . ? But since when had a little danger been anything but exciting? And this was, after all, self-limiting. Whatever he might say about the tedium of London pleasures, he would find out soon enough that the capital was a whirl of excitement compared to the daily social round of this quiet little backwater. The depression caused by his premature furlough would lift in the fullness of time, and he would see matters clearly again. In the meantime, if she kept her wits about her, surely she could enjoy the spice of a flirtation that he seemed determined to pursue? No more than that, of course, and that discreetly, she told herself, turning back to the path leading to the cliff top. Lord Rutherford's kindly interest in her brothers would provide ample excuse for her neighbors. When she was with him in company, the widow's mask would be firmly in place.

Those blithe plans suffered something of a setback the following morning when Meredith was honored with a visit from Lady Barrat, Miss Elizabeth Ansby and her mama, and Lady Collier.

"My dear Meredith." Lady Barrat clasped her hostess's hands in a firm squeeze. "You poor girl! What an unfortunate thing to have happened! So dreadfully embarrassing for you, and to be obliged to enter the house quite unchaperoned!" Meredith's hands, much to her relief, were released in order for Lady Barrat to throw her own into the air in a gesture of inarticulate horror.

"Could you not have sent Hugo, my dear Lady Blake?" Miss Ansby inquired. "Mama was so deeply shocked when she heard, I was afraid she would have one of her turns, and I was about to send for Dr. Higgins, but fortunately a little hartshorn in water . . ."

"Please," Meredith begged. "You must think me very stupid, but I am afraid that I have no idea what has caused you this alarm. Will you take some lemonade to refresh you after your journey? It is such a hot morning."

"Meredith, you must know what we mean. We refer of course to the visit you paid to Lord Rutherford's house yesterday," Patience explained. "A single lady alone in a bachelor's establishments. What can you have been thinking of, dear?"

So the crows have come home to roost, Merrie thought wearily. "I was hardly alone," she said,

117

ringing the bell for Seecombe. "Both Rob and Hugo were there. Rob had an accident and injured his arm."

"Oh, yes. We heard all about that," Mrs. Ansby of the delicate sensibilities put in, dabbing at her forehead with her handkerchief. "And we are all of the opinion that something must be done about that boy."

"Seecombe, would you bring lemonade for my guests?" Merrie requested as the manservant appeared, giving her a few seconds to control her rising temper.

"You are all too kind," she whispered, wringing her hands as she turned back to her visitors. "It was, of course, most uncomfortable for me, but his lordship was all consideration."

"And escorted you home," Lady Collier announced in damning accents. "Hardly necessary if you had your brothers' escort."

"No, but Lord Rutherford was most kind. Rob was in great pain, you understand. And his lordship was a most calming influence."

"Meredith, pray do not distress yourself," Patience said soothingly, patting Merrie's hand. "It is quite understandable that you forgot the proprieties in your anxiety over your brother, and, if Hugo was with you, then it was not so very dreadful. But, my dear, do consider. Is it wise to encourage Lord Rutherford's visits to your house? I understand he was here two days ago, and you were seen talking to him in a most friendly fashion outside Mallory House yesterday morning."

"Oh, dear," Merrie murmured, quite overcome. "I did not think there was anything wrong in it—oh, Seecombe, thank you." She smiled as Seecombe placed a tray on the table. With an impassive countenance, he poured lemonade from the pitcher, handing round the glasses before stationing himself at the door as if prepared to wait on the ladies. It was all too clear to him what was going on in the parlor. Lady Merrie was under attack from the village cats, something that wasn't going to continue if he could help it.

Meredith, realizing his intention of remaining in the room and recognizing, with an internal smile, the reasons for it, said quietly, "Thank you, Seecombe. I'll ring if I need you again."

"As you wish, my lady." With a stiff bow, he left the parlor. Merrie resigned herself to some hurt sniffs ad reproachful glances from her self-appointed protector once the visitors had left.

"You would surely not expect me to cut Lord Rutherford?" she asked innocently. "He has been so kind as to take an interest in the boys. Hugo, you know, so needs a man to talk to. He wishes to take holy orders, you see. It is such a big decision, but he will not take the advice of a mere sister. And Theo and Rob look up so to Lord Rutherford. He has promised to take them under his wing." The fibs appeared with disgraceful ease, but their perpetrator cared not a jot. "I, myself, barely know Lord Rutherford, but I understand from Rob that he was with Wellington in the Peninsula until a shoulder wound forced him to take his furlough and now he needs some occupation." She smiled with pathetic helplessness. "His lordship appears to wish to occupy himself with my brothers and I can only be grateful."

"Sir Algernon would willingly help you in this," Patience said with a degree of severity. "I do not know

119

how many times he has offered his advice."

"And I am always most grateful," Merrie assured her hastily. "But you know how difficult boys can be? They are not always willing to be advised by those who are willing to advise them." It was the nearest to a barb that she dared allow herself; fortunately it appeared to pass without notice.

The parlor door opened abruptly. "Lord Rutherford, my lady," Seecombe announced, standing aside to allow the subject of discussion to stride into the sudden hush. Merrie's expression for the barest instant was one of guilt and consternation before her face was wiped clean of all vibrancy and her hands fluttered like the wings of a dismayed bird.

Little wretch! Lord Rutherford thought. What had she been up to to cause her to look at him like a child caught in mischief?

She was fluttering around him, stammering an inarticulate greeting, introducing him to her guests, then recollecting that he must already know them and smiling in self-denigration as she scolded herself for being such a silly goose. Damian wanted to take her by the shoulders and shake her. He strongly suspected that she derived considerable amusement from this game, but he found it annoying in the extreme. In particular, he found irritating the patronizing, compassionate attitude of Lady Barrat; yet, looking at Meredith, twittering like a half-witted maiden, he could hardly blame Patience.

"I am come to inquire after that young scamp, Rob, ma'am," he said, brusquely interrupting her in the middle of some interminable apologia that had no apparent substance. "He has taken no great harm, I trust."

"Oh, you are too kind, sir. Did I not say how kind his lordship has been?" Merrie's hands worked, her head bobbed as she addressed the ladies. "So—so kind in you, sir, to take such an interest—"

"How *is* the lad, ma'am?" he interrupted again, little realizing how reassuring was his curtness to Meredith's well-wishers, how splendidly it reinforced her tissue of half-truths.

"He does indeed appear to have taken little harm, sir. I did, of course, suggest that he keep to his bed with a little gruel to avert any excitation of the nerves—That was wise, do you not think, Lady Collier? You have so much experience in these matters— Will you take a glass of lemonade, my lord?" She turned to his lordship, a brittle smile on her lips, and encountered a look that brought the bright prattle to a full stop.

"No, I thank you," he said icily. "I will, if I may, visit the patient. I am sure you ladies have much to discuss." He bowed to the company in general, accorded Merrie a curt nod, and left the parlor.

Merrie had absolutely no idea where Rob was to be found, not in his bed with a bowl of gruel that was for sure. She wondered a little nervously if Rutherford would return to confront her with her lie. He had looked furious enough to be capable of anything, but surely he must realize she had had a particularly good reason for involving him in that exaggerated display of idiocy? Of course, if he thought she was just playing games with him again, their accord of last evening would be in some danger.

"Well, I will say, my dear, Lord Rutherford's taking

an interest in your brothers must be most gratifying," Patience declared, gathering up her reticule. "It may be a little unusual, but I see no harm in it. It is quite clear that he has no ulterior motives. You may rest assured that I will put all malicious rumors to rest."

"Oh, Patience!" Meredith gazed in wide-eyed horror at her visitor. "Whatever can you mean? Ulterior motives—rumors. You could not be suggesting that people might think . . . ? Oh, dear me, I feel quite faint." Sinking onto the couch, she began fanning herself frantically with one hand. "Such a dreadful possibility had never crossed my mind."

"You are such a sweet innocent, Meredith," Patience bent solicitously over her. "It is because we know you to be so that we have your interests so much at heart. When poor Sir John passed away, Sir Algernon said that we must all take a care for the little widow. His very words." She looked at her companions with a complacent nod. "Sir Algernon is such a sympathetic soul, and he always knows exactly what is to be done."

"You are all so kind. I am quite overwhelmed," Meredith murmured, wondering desperately whether a quick recovery would ensure their departure or whether she should feign a complete collapse and summon Seecombe to convey her to her bedchamber.

"Take heart, now, Lady Blake." Lady Collier spoke briskly. "We must be thankful that Sir John made adequate provision for your brothers' schooling. It is a great deal more than many a gentleman would make for his wife's family, as my dear Sir Peter was saying only the other night. I dread to think what would have become of them had you been obliged to educate them

122

at home. There would have been no steadying outside influence, no true discipline." She gave Merrie a condescending smile. "We know you do your best, my dear Lady Blake, but a young woman, unsupported by the rock of a husband, cannot hope to influence children in the correct paths."

Meredith pressed a handkerchief to her eyes. "My dear, dear husband was such a rock." Her voice was choked. "Such a splendid example to the boys." She dabbed at her nose and blinked rapidly. "Ladies—dear friends—I must ask you to excuse me."

"Yes, of course. Do not trouble yourself to see us out, my dear." Patience patted a limp hand again. "Have a good cry, now. It will make you feel much more the thing."

"I hope to see you at Lavender Hill tomorrow evening, Lady Blake," Mrs. Ansby said, drawing on her gloves. "Tea and cards, and a little music. Vicar and Mrs. Elsbury will be joining us. We shall play only for counters, of course, as it is Sunday. I do not think the vicar will object to that." She conveyed the benediction of what its recipient supposed was a smile. "Come, Elizabeth." Miss Ansby, in her turn, stroked the afflicted widow's shoulder, tutted sympathetically, and followed her mama.

It remained only for Lady Collier to pat Merrie's shoulder condescendingly and make her farewells; then Merrie was alone. With quiet deliberation, she picked up the empty pitcher and hurled it across the room where it smashed against the wainscot in a thoroughly satisfying cascade of glass.

"Bravo!" Lord Rutherford applauded softly from the door. "So the little widow shows her teeth." He closed the door behind him and lounged against it with folded arms as the glasses, one by one, joined the shattered pitcher.

"It is insufferable!" Meredith raged, pacing the room in a manner that spoke more clearly than anything else the agitation of her spirits. "Adequate provision for the boys' education, indeed! A rock of support! A perfect example of manhood. Oh, there are times when I cannot bear the hypocrisy! Everyone is aware of the truth."

"I fear, Lady Blake, that I am not. Will you not enlighten me?"

Meredith paused in her restless pacing and sighed. "What an abominable display of temper, sir. Pray accept my apologies."

Rutherford chuckled. "No need. You forget that I have been on the receiving end of your tantrums before. At least *that* one didn't seem to be directed at me personally. I would like an explanation for it, though."

She stood for a moment nibbling the tip of her thumb, deep frown lines between her eyebrows.

"Meredith," Lord Rutherford said. "I am reluctant to appear importunate, but I must repeat, I would like an explanation."

"Why?" Meredith demanded. "It is actually no business of yours, my lord. You are not of these parts. If you were, you would have no need of explanation."

"And I am going to take my pampered aristocratic body back to London at the first sign of a mud puddle," he said amiably. "You've said that so many times, it does not bear further repetition. Obviously, I must demonstrate why your business is to some extent

124

mine also."

He strolled forward, eyes glinting. Merrie backed away swiftly. A large cabinet prevented her from retreating further and, Rutherford coolly following, she found herself cornered. He stood in front of her, looking down into her face with a tiny smile. She could not take her gaze from his, could not hide the anticipation quivering in the purple depths of her eyes, could not control the strange spreading sensation starting in her belly and creeping down over her thighs as if sinew and muscle were losing all substance.

For a long moment, the charged silence continued, the suddenly his smile broadened. "You shall have your kiss, Merrie Trelawney, when you have told me what I wish to know. It does not seem a sensible tactic to reward obstinacy."

"Why you pompous, complacent bastard!" Meredith yelped. "Leave my house this instant!"

"Do not be missish," he advised gently, selecting an apple from the fruit bowl on the table, crunching into it with every appearance of pleasure. "I want to kiss you as much as you want to be kissed, and once we have disposed of this tedious procrastination of yours, we shall both be able to enjoy ourselves."

"Do you make it a habit to offer insult to respectable widows, sir?" Meredith glared at him as she wondered if she would ever be in control of this encounter.

"Indeed not, ma'am!" he declared with every appearance of outraged horror. "Whatever could have given you such an idea?" His eyes twinkled. "Unless, of course, you consider yourself to be respectable, Merrie Trelawney. If so, I beg leave to inform you that you are the least respectable widow it has been my good fortune to meet."

It was quite hopeless. She looked merely silly attempting to stand on a dignity that she did not have. Merrie sighed in frustration, making no attempt to refute the charge they both knew to be true. "I do wish you had not come into Cornwall. It is making everything most awkward."

"You are wholly adorable," Lord Rutherford declared, not a whit put out by this statement. "Except when you are playing a half-witted nincompoop," he added. "Those displays arouse in me nothing more than the desire to shake you soundly."

"You do not understand." Merrie moved restlessly around the room, straightening ornaments and cushions with impatient fingers.

"Unless my memory fails me, I have been begging for enlightenment for the past half an hour," Rutherford said.

"My neighbors called upon me this morning to express their shock and dismay at my boldness—the dreadful impropriety I showed in going to your house yesterday. I cannot even be seen talking to you in the public street, it would seem, without giving rise to malicious rumor. They had only my best interests at heart, you understand?" Her lips twisted in a sardonic travesty of a smile and her listener nodded without comment.

"I played the shocked innocent," Merrie explained. "I was obliged to—uh—to tell some small untruths." She gave him that guilty look again.

"Pray continue," he prompted, keeping his face expressionless although his eyes danced.

"Well, I said that you had been kind enough to interest yourself in my brothers because you had told Rob you were in need of occupation after your experiences in the Peninsula." The look she gave him this time was half rueful, half defiant. "I am sorry if you do not like it, sir, but I had to think of something. I did not mean to betray a confidence."

"You are thoroughly unprincipled," he said with mock severity. "But I will reserve my wrath since I feel sure you have not yet made a clean breast."

"I was obliged to demonstrate, sir, that you could have no possible interest in me, that—that no sensible man could. And I said also that you were willing to advise Hugo where I could not in the matter of his taking orders." This last was said in a rush as if only thus could the full disclosure be made.

"I am to advise Hugo on—Oh, no, Meredith! That is the outside of enough! The rest I will go along with, will even allow that on the spur of the moment it was an understandable fabrication, but that is gilding the lily beyond what is permissible."

"I beg your pardon, Lord Rutherford." Meredith began to rub at a smudge on the sleeve of her print gown.

"I do not think you have ever been repentant in your life," Damian pronounced, lifting her chin again. "What did those cats say to bring about that tantrum? Something to do with hypocrisy, as I recall."

"It pleases this society to remember my late husband as a pillar of the community, a generous man who undertook to provide for his wife's orphaned brothers, who gave them wise counsel and exhibited all the qualities they should emulate. A man, in short, whose death was a tragedy for all who knew him." Her voice was bitter, her eyes filled with cold distaste. "The truth, my lord, was far from that as they are all aware."

"What was the truth?" He still held her chin but, when she pulled away, released it immediately.

Meredith sighed and went over to the open window. "It was my father's wish that I marry Sir John. Father knew he was dying, our mother had passed away some two years previously and we were none of us of age. The only possible guardian in Cornwall was an elderly relative of my mother's, but my father had never got on with the Merediths. I was not unduly averse to the idea. Sir John was personable enough, his Cornish lineage was almost as old as mine, he lived the life I was used to, and Father would die easy." She shrugged but kept her back toward her audience.

Damian would have found nothing unusual in this story if it had been anyone but Merrie Trelawney telling it. This blind acceptance of a mediocre fate at the command of her father did not sit right with what he knew of the woman.

"My inheritance, and that of my brothers', was placed, as is customary, in the hands of my husband who was also the boys' guardian." She swung round to face him, resting her hands on the window sill at her back. "It is not a pretty story, Lord Rutherford, but a sufficiently familiar one for you to be able to guess at its conclusion. Had my husband not died when he did, we would have been completely destitute. As it was, all furniture and possessions of any value, be they Blake, Meredith, or Trelawney, were sold, and the proceeds managed to cover the outstanding gaming debts. The house and estate are heavily mortgaged, but with stringent economies we are able to keep our independence."

Rutherford frowned. It was not a pretty story, as she had said, and neither was it unusual except for the personality of one of the chief protagonists. "Forgive me, Merrie, but I do not think you married a man to whom you were basically indifferent just to please your father."

Meredith decided that Lord Rutherford was a great deal too perspicacious for comfort. But then that was not an unexpected revelation. "No," she agreed, in her customary forthright fashion. "But had I not done so, the boys would have been separated, sent to live with different relatives out of Cornwall, and it would have been quite dreadful for them. Besides, I daresay I should have been obliged to live with Aunt Mary in Helston." She pulled a face. "If you had met my Aunt Mary, Lord Rutherford, you would understand why I chose as I did. She has an abominable little pug which must be walked three times a day, and she does not keep enough servants so someone must polish the silverware and do the mending—"

"Enough!" Rutherford gazed at her in undisguised horror. "I quite see that Aunt Mary's establishment would not do at all."

"No, but had I been aware that my husband would run through my brothers' fortunes, I daresay I would have bowed to necessity," she said grimly. "As it is, I must do what I can to ensure that they do not suffer too much from my mistaken decision."

"And how do you propose doing that?" Rutherford

asked with considerable interest. The statement had been made with such confidence, she must have a definite plan, he decided. Although what an impoverished widow could possibly do to repair such a catastrophe, he could not begin to imagine.

Merrie had her answer ready. "With thrift," she replied easily. "I know of no other way. Theo would have me marry a rich husband." She chuckled. "Poor Theo finds poverty most degrading. But I know of no eligible candidates and, in order to avoid the attention of the matchmakers, play my little game of reclusive, sorrowing, soft-headed widow."

How neatly she had satisfied his curiosity as to the masquerade she played for the benefit of her neighbors. It was perfectly reasonable to suppose that a young widow would be the target of matchmakers in such an inbred community. Pendennis was still intact, if mortgaged, and could be considered adequate compensation for relieving the widow of her single state. And it was perfectly reasonable that she should wish to avoid unpleasantness in whatever manner she chose. Lord Rutherford should have no further need to puzzle over conundrums. She did, however, feel just a prick of guilt as the truths, half-truths, and downright lies tripped off her tongue with such consummate artistry. That in itself was rather strange. Her conscience was rarely troubled by the deceptions she practiced. Did it perhaps have something to do with the fact that it was Rutherford she was deceiving so cleverly? Meredith decided that she did not want to pursue that avenue and was saved from further uncomfortable reflection by an interruption that proceeded to create more problems than it solved.

"Merrie! Do you know what Seecombe has just told me?" Rob burst into the room, his usual impetuousness not at all impaired by his bandaged arm. "Oh, good day, sir. Are you come to inquire after me? I am quite well, as you see, and the arm does not pain in the slightest."

"That is indeed good news," Rutherford responded with creditable gravity. "You have quite put my mind at rest."

"Yes, I thought it would do so." Rob's eye fell on the heap of broken glass against the wainscot. "What happened?"

"An accident," Meredith said smoothly. "Pray ring the bell for Eliza."

Rob's curiosity about the glass was fortunately easily satisfied, and he pulled the bell rope. "I was about to tell you what Seecombe has just said."

"So you were," Merrie agreed. "Lord Rutherford and I are all agog."

Rob, who had a remarkably unsuspicious nature, saw only genuine interest on the faces of his elders. "He says the Gentlemen will ride tonight."

"Really," said Merrie in a bored tone. "I had thought you were about to tell me that the world was coming to an end. Yes—it is the glass, Eliza. An accident, I am afraid." The maid bobbed a curtsy and busied herself removing the evidence of her mistress's outburst.

Damnation! Merrie cursed silently. She had been hoping that news of tonight's delivery would escape Rutherford. As a stranger, he would not normally have been apprised of it, and to her certain knowledge there was nothing to be delivered to Mallory House.

"Well, I think it monstrous exciting," Rob declared. "And I shall stay awake and watch for them."

"Much good will it do you," his sister said in dampening tones. "Pendennis, as it happens, does not expect a delivery this night. Our cellars are full."

The boy's face fell. Even Damian, in spite of his own interest in the news, was obliged to laugh. Rob looked at him reproachfully. "I do not know what is amusing, sir."

"No, of course you do not," Rutherford agreed. "If you are able to ride with one arm and care to do so, you may accompany me home. Harry has unearthed a deal of fishing tackle in the attics. If any of it is any use to you, you may have it with pleasure."

"May Theo come too?" Rob asked, hopping from one foot to the other. "He is a more serious fisherman even than I am, sir. He actually thinks tickling trout unsportsmanlike!"

"An opinion that I am sure he shares with the trout," Rutherford said solemnly. "By all means fetch him, but I should warn you that I leave in ten minutes—with or without you."

Rob scampered off and Lord Rutherford said, "I play the part assigned to me, as you can see, Lady Blake."

"I did not intend that you take it seriously, Lord Rutherford. You surely cannot wish to saddle yourself with two schoolboys for the afternoon."

"No," he agreed, "there is nothing I wish less. Walter shall have the charge of them."

Merrie laughed. "Well, if you are not very careful, Rob will develop a lasting passion and will be forever on your doorstep. He is a most faithful friend."

"I will bear the warning in mind, ma'am." For a moment there was silence between them, then Lord Rutherford held out his hand. "Come here, Merrie," he instructed quietly.

She moved toward him even as the sensible, lucid part of her mind told her to remain where she was, safely at arm's length.

"You have a reward to claim," he said softly, taking her hands. "It is one I cannot resist awarding. I had not expected, when I made this foray into Cornwall, to be so diverted, Merrie Trelawney."

"As I said before, sir, I am happy to be of service." Somehow, the intended sardonic note was lamentably absent and she knew the vulnerability of her wanting was like an open book. Merrie tugged at her imprisoned hands. "Are not ten minutes passed, sir? Theo and Rob will be waiting for you."

Damian smiled. "So, you will not claim your due. But that is perhaps wise, in the circumstances. It will certainly be more satisfactory when we can be assured of privacy." With that, he raised her hands to his lips, then very gently kissed the corner of her mouth. "I will not forget what is owed you, Merrie Trelawney."

He left her then, standing alone in the parlor, shivering as if the sun had just gone behind a cloud. She could not possibly indulge in a flirtation with Lord Rutherford. She had been mad to think it feasible. Such a thing was only possible if one was carefree, heart-free, had nothing to lose. One could not flirt lightly with a man who aroused such imperative longings, particularly when the man in question was more than aware of the effect he had and had too little delicacy to hide that knowledge!

133

What a pickle it all was! But there was a delivery to be made tonight. Thoughts of Damian, Lord Rutherford, had best be buried deep if she were to have her wits about her. On those wits hung the safety of more people than herself.

Chapter Eight

Lord Rutherford kept his impatience well in check as the day wore on. The soldier, after all, was well accustomed to biding his time, watching and waiting for the optimal moment for attack. Rob and Theo afforded some distraction, and, whenever he could do so discreetly, he encouraged them to talk of their past, their parents, life with Sir John Blake, and in particular of their sister. Rob required no encouragement. Theo was more careful until he realized that his interlocuter already knew a great deal, information that he could only have gleaned from Merrie.

Damian sent them home in time for dinner and prepared to pass a long, solitary evening. At what hour did the Gentlemen ride? Not before midnight, surely. Walter, watching anxiously, saw no signs of the dreaded depression in his lordship's preoccupation. He drank but two glasses of claret with the mutton chop and boiled potato provided by Mrs. Perry and, instead of settling over the brandy bottle for the night, informed Walter that he was going to take a stroll in

135

the evening air.

He walked through the village, keeping ears and eyes alert for a sign that something out of the ordinary was going to take place. But everything seemed as usual. The taproom at the Falcon rang with customary merriment, and judging by the crowds, every man in the village was there. He had little doubt but that the smugglers were amongst the noisy drinkers. They would have to be villagers and fishermen from the immediate area, but it would be foolish of them to jeopardize their mission and their safety by dulling their wits with mine host's home brew.

They wouldn't be doing so, of course. These men knew what they were about, as he had seen that first night. They'd hardly arouse suspicions by behaving in an unusually abstemious manner on the night of the delivery, not when there was the possibility of a revenue spy in the village. But where did their leader come from? He had seen no one in the village remotely resembling that lithe stripling, but, if his suspicions were correct and the youth was most definitely *not* a youth, then that was hardly surprising. None of his enquiries had yielded any information of note. No one he spoke to had ever seen the Gentlemen—it was not considered wise to pry, such indiscretion might lead to a reduction in supply, and that fate was clearly viewed as one to be avoided at all costs by the bucolic squirearchy. However, since he himself had no vested interested in discretion, his lordship decided to pursue his investigation in person. He had it in mind to track down the Gentlemen this evening—not a difficult task, surely, since they would be out and about the village, and it was hard to imagine how they could make a delivery without being in some way visible.

One hour before midnight, he took to the cliff road on foot, looking again for the spot where he had come across the skirmish. The conversation between the youth and the man called Bart had made clear that the goods had been safely stowed before the ambush. It was to be assumed that the hiding place was somewhere near the cliff road and that the smugglers would begin tonight's ride from there.

When he first heard the sounds—a chink of a bridle, a whispered exclamation—he was hard put to place them, so disembodied and disoriented they sounded in the darkness. Then he realized that they came from immediately below him. He inched forward until he was lying prone, gazing down over the edge of the cliff at a narrow trail snaking against the cliff face. The ponies were dark shapes, the figures of men like specters, all moving in an eerie silence. The youth was easy to distinguish by his size. He seemed tiny beside the others, yet, as before, the slender figure riding astride the lead pony was invested with that indefinable aura of authority. The watcher on the cliff blinked, shook his head in disbelief, crept even closer to the cliff edge until his shoulders were suspended in mid air. But even this added proximity could not alter the facts. There was no denying the evidence of his eyes. The set of her shoulders beneath the dark jacket, the tilt of her head in the tight knitted cap, that square little chin were all unmistakable. Damian wondered why he had not guessed. With hindsight it seemed obvious. It explained that unusual muscular, supple vibrancy that so intrigued and excited him. It explained all the games she played; it explained that sense of déjà vu he had constantly in her presence.

Rutherford watched the train out of sight along the path. His original plan to follow them now seemed unnecessary. He had solved the major mystery—the identity of that competent stripling who laughed in the face of danger and handled a small sword with the best. What he was to do with the knowledge was a problem for another day. He decided, in the absence of the band, to retrace their steps, find out, if he could, where this operation had its headquarters. That piece of information could well stand him in good stead at some point.

A few yards along the road, he found a narrow path leading down to the trail below. Following the tracks of the pony train, he came to a point on the trail just below the cliff where stood Pendennis. What he found there at first puzzled him mightily. There was a cave set into the cliff, but it appeared far too small to serve any useful purpose. Yet it was clearly the one they had used, judging by the prints of man and beast scuffed into the sand. It took ten minutes of minute exploration before he found the concealed opening behind the boulder at the rear of the cave. Half an hour later, he stood again on the cliff path, in no doubt at all that the tunnel from the central cavern led directly to Pendennis. Its origin definitely predated Meredith's arrival as bride of Sir John Blake. How had she discovered it? And, even more to the point, how had she prevented Rob from discovering it? Presumably she would return to the house via the cave once this night's work was accomplished—always assuming that it would be accomplished safely. Ruth-erford decided that speculation on the outcome of Merrie's mission would be fruitless. He found the way up to the cliff above, there to await her return.

The soldier was accustomed to keeping vigil, as he was accustomed to discomfort, but the hours dragged nevertheless, the muscles in his shoulders stiffening. Although it was high summer, the dew was heavy, striking a chill through the cloth of his britches as he crouched in the scrub. But the chill was nothing compared to his anxiety as he strained his ears for a telltale sound, peering at the sky for the first gray streaks of dawn. The delivery was taking an uncon-scionably long time unless he had been mistaken and she had returned some other way and was now safely abed and asleep. Should that prove to be the case, Damian, Lord Rutherford, shivering in abominable discomfort and with an anxiety akin to fear, decided that Merrie Trelawney had best have a care for her skin when next they met!

He was about to call a halt to his watch and return home for what was left of the night when he heard a soft whistling from the path below. Looking down he saw the familiar, slender figure, hands thrust into the pockets of her britches, kicking up sand in a manner that expressed the total lack of a care in the world as she whistled cheerfully, if somewhat tunelessly. With relief came anger. How dared she return so noncha-lantly while he had been kicking his heels in cold and trepidation for hours! As he watched, she suddenly broke into a little dance, pulling off the knitted cap, tossing it into the air with a soft, exultant laugh. His anger faded, admiration and more than a touch of envy taking its place. He knew the wonderful feeling that followed danger and tension, the sense of a job well done, of well-earned peace and relaxation. It required considerable restraint to refrain from calling down to her as he shared vicariously in the youthful, carefree high spirits she was exhibiting.

Merrie was indeed feeling very satisfied with the night's work, the proceeds of which were contained in a bulky leather pouch in her back pocket. Tomorrow, she would divide them up and Bart would see to the distribution of the shares. Next month, it had been unanimously agreed, there would be two runs. The first they would make to the Eagle and Child in Fowey. If all went well, there would be others. Still whistling, she fetched a straw besom from the back of the cave and began to swerep the sand of cave and path, obscuring the prints of men and ponies. It was a small precaution, probably unnecessary since few people came this way, but one could never be too careful, she thought with a smug little smile. As she retreated into the cave, she swept the sand clean behind her, and, when Merrie Trelawney disappeared behind the jutting boulder, there were no signs of any activity other than that of the wheeling gulls and the breaking surf.

Damian rose stiffly to his feet. For this time, at least, she was away to her bed in safety, so he could seek his own with a peaceful heart. He was, however, uncertain how many more such nights he could endure and keep silent. During the long hours of his vigil, he had had ample time to look at the extraordinary revelation that had hit him between the eyes when he'd recognized the figure, sitting so straight, tall, and indomitable astride the pony loaded with contraband. What had begun as a game informed by the need for a little revenge had taken a dramatically serious turn. He was in love, for the first time in his thirty years, and with just about the most unsuitable creature imaginable. It was not hard to picture his mother's reactions—or those of the gouty duke. Strangely, the thought made him laugh. One thing was clear. While he might just possibly be able to take an indigent Cornish widow into the bosom of his family, an active smuggler was out of the question. Somehow or other he was going to have to persuade Merrie Trelawney to join the ranks of the law-abiding.

When next he saw her, it was some six hours later. The bells of St. James's had been pealing joyously for half an hour, summoning the faithful and not-so-faithful to matins. One would need to be on one's deathbed to be excused attendance at the village ritual and Damian, after three hours of dreamless sleep, a substantial breakfast, and twenty minutes of Walter's skilled massage, rode across the fields, divided between the desire to see Meredith and the dread at the company picture he knew she would present and the part she would oblige him to play.

Merrie, with Hugo, Rob, and Theo in attendance, stood beneath the lych gate in conversation with an elderly couple whom Damian recognized as Admiral and Lady Petersham. Tethering Saracen to the railing, and drawing off his gloves, he walked toward the group.

"Ah, Lord Rutherford." Lady Petersham greeted

his approach with her vague smile.

"Rutherford, morning," the admiral boomed, presenting his good ear to his lordship in order to catch the reply.

"Good morning." Rutherford bowed punctiliously before turning to acknowledge Lady Blake. "Ma'am, your servant."

"Oh, dear, Lord Rutherford. You do me too much honor," she fluttered, attempting to curtsy, extend her hand, and keep hold of her prayer book at one and the same time. The prayer book proved to be the last straw and fell to the ground. Damian, expressionless, bent to pick it up. As he handed it to her, she gave him an up-from-under look, brimming with mischief. His lordship resolved to inform her at the earliest possible moment that, if she desired his cooperation in this deception she practiced for the benefit of her neighbors, it was encumbent upon her to play fair. Cutting short her babble of thanks, he turned to the boys, all of whom appeared quite unaffected by their sister's extraordinary behavior. Hugo was sober-suited and solemn, Theo resigned, but Rob, Rutherford noticed, bore a suspiciously innocent expression belied by the suppressed excitement in the Trelawney eyes.

The bells ceased their chiming and the group moved swiftly up the path to the heavy oaken doors. Mr. Grantham, the verger, was well known for his insistence on punctuality, and it was a brave soul who would creep in once he had closed the doors.

Damian walked behind the Trelawneys, his eyes fixed on the youngest member. As they approached the door, Rob put his hand in his back pocket, which pocket seemed at once to come alive. Rutherford's hand closed over the boy's shoulder

"Take it out, my friend, whatever it is, *before* you go inside."

Meredith turned, giving them both a startled look that changed to exasperation as she saw her brother's guilty expression. "What *have* you got this time?"

Seeing little hope for it, Rob drew from his coat pocket a tiny field mouse. Under the inplacable stares of his elders, he released the creature on the path. "Is that all?" his sister inquired sharply, and when Rob nodded dispiritedly, pushed him in front of her. The organ had begun to play and Mr. Grantham was glowering impatiently, so she had little time to exchange more than a speaking look with Lord Rutherford before hurrying to the Blake pew, where she firmly placed Rob between herself and the wall. Lord Rutherford followed the sidesman to the Mallory pew and the service began.

Damian's pew was across the aisle from the Trelawney's, one row behind, so he found it possible to observe them covertly throughout what seemed an interminable two hours. Hugo wore an expression of complete devotion, attending to Vicar Elsbury's monotonous sermon as if his life depended on it. Theo and Meredith produced responses, sang, prayed and appeared to listen with impeccable duty. Rob ridgeted and made no attempt to disguise his boredom although otherwise he behaved himself.

Meredith, Rutherford decided, even allowing for his partiality, looked positively hagged. She wore a satinet gown of unrelieved black. The color would have done little for her even when her complexion bore its usual vibrant tones and her eyes their customary brilliance. As it was, she was as pale and heavy-eyed as one would expect of someone who had not gained her bed before dawn. While what little of her hair he could see still retained its luster, most of it was hidden beneath a hideous widow's cap—a monstrosity that he had not seen her affect before.

At long last the benediction brought release, and the congregation rose to engage in the other purpose of the morning's exercise in devotion—the opportunity to gather with their neighbors and talk over the events of the week. The vicar beamed at the Trelawneys as he stood in the sunshine, greeting his flock. "Lady Blake, how well you look." Damian, a few paces behind, shuddered at this shameless hypocrisy on the tongue of a man of the cloth. "And the boys. Splendid, splendid. Such a splendid family! As for you, young man." He bent a stern look on Rob. "Climbing on roofs, I hear. Roofs that don't belong to you, either."

Rob, responding to a pinch from Hugo, mumbled something and lowered his head.

"You know what they say, vicar, about boys being boys." Lord Rutherford stepped into the circle.

"Ah, Lord Rutherford. Delighted to see you. I did call upon you yesterday. Perhaps Harry Perry informed you? You were not at home, but I do like to welcome new parishioners as soon as may be. We are always so excited at the prospect of fresh blood." He smiled benignly. "Is it not so, Lady Blake? We are such a small community as a rule and know each other so well."

"Yes, indeed, vicar." Lady Blake twittered and

played with the fringe of her shawl. "We do all seem to know each other *so* well. There are no secrets in *this* village, Lord Rutherford."

"I can readily believe it, ma'am," he said in a voice as dry as dust.

"Ah, vicar, such an inspiring sermon. I do find that text from Leviticus most uplifting." Mrs. Ansby billowed down the path toward them. "We are expecting you and dear Mrs. Elsbury this evening, you know. And Lady Blake, of course." Meredith received a condescending smile to which she responded with stammered thanks and fluttering eyelashes. "Lord Rutherford, we would be most honored if you would join us." Mrs. Ansby's gargoyle smile embraced his lordship. "A simple country evening, to be sure, but you will be glad of something a little more delicate than one of Martha Perry's suppers, I'll be bound, and Ansby has a fine port."

Rutherford bowed his thanks and grateful acceptance. It was a prospect that offered little amusement except that he would have Meredith under his eye for the evening. She had moved away already, pausing to exchange a few obligatory words with the Barrats. Of her brothers, there was no sign until he passed through the lych gate and onto the street where he found Theo and Rob engaged in adoration of Saracen.

"I wish I could ride him," Rob said wistfully. "Theo says Walter said he was Mameluke-trained."

"So he is." Rutherford lifted the boy into the saddle, much as he had done his sister a few nights past. "I will lead you since you still have only one good arm."

"Oh, there you are." Meredith appeared behind them. "Has Hugo gone home?"

"No," Theo told her disgustedly. "He is talking to the curate and, I'm certain, hopes to wangle an invitation to nuncheon at the vicarage so he can discuss this morning's text."

"Well, at least he will not then discuss it at home," Rob piped from atop Saracen.

"It would be as well for all of us if you shared a few of your brother's virtues," Meredith said severely. "What are you doing on Lord Rutherford's horse?"

"He said I might," Rob said defensively. "He put me up here himself."

"He would hardly be up there had I not done so," Damian pointed out gently. "Theo, do you care to lead Saracen?" He handed the reins over to the eager Theo, then fell into step beside Meredith who could not think of one good reason why she should object to his companionship on the walk home.

"I must thank you for your timely intervention with the mouse." She shook her head in a gesture of resignation. "I am in the habit of checking his pockets before we leave, but for some reason this morning it slipped my mind."

"You were perhaps a little fatigued," he suggested, swishing at the hedgerow with his riding crop.

"Yes, as it happens." She directed a puzzled frown toward him. "But I cannot imagine how you could know such a thing."

"If I may be brutally frank," he replied, "one has only to look at you. You look the very devil, Merrie."

"That is not very polite, sir."

"No," he agreed calmly. "But then you have gone to

such pains to appear at your worst, you would hardly be gratified if I denied you had succeeded in your object."

"I beg leave to inform you, my lord, that I am wearing my Sunday-best gown," she said loftily, unable to resist the invitation to a little light banter. It was perfectly safe, after all, out in the sunshine on a Sunday morning, along a country lane, with her brothers just a few paces ahead. And it was such incredible relief to be in the company of one who knew the masquerade she played and had an acceptable reason for it, one he would not question.

"You have rendered me speechless, ma'am."

At that she chuckled, and he could not help his own responding smile even as he said, "I must beg one small boon though."

"And what is that, sir?"

"The cap," he said with a visible shudder. "I very much fear that, if I have to see it again, I shall run quite mad." They had reached the boundary of Pendennis by this time, and Meredith found that she was obliged to halt as his lordship stopped, catching her upper arm. Experience having taught her that resistance would be as undignified as it would be fruitless, she stood still, thankful that Saracen and the boys had vanished around the corner ahead and hoping that the lane would remain empty. Holding her thus with one hand, he untied the strings of the cap with the other, pulling it off her head. "Do you wish to put this in your reticule, or shall I toss it over the hedge?"

"Oh, pray give it to me!" Meredith took the offending garment, stuffing it into her reticule. "I have not worn it before, but I thought it most appropriate."

"If you are wise, you will refrain from wearing it again." There was a familiar note of warning in his voice and Meredith's eyes flashed.

"And just what does that mean, sir?"

"It means simply that, if I should see you wearing it again, this evening for instance, I shall remove it again."

Meredith sucked in her lower lip, regarding him speculatively. "I wonder if you would," she said thoughtfully.

"You could always put it to the test," he observed, smiling.

It was a perfectly pleasant smile, but Merrie was not to be fooled. "I think not."

"You are not wholly without wisdom."

"I do not think that what I choose to wear is any of your business, Lord Rutherford." It was simply a token protest, necessary if she were not to feel that she had submitted without a murmur. Clearly his lordship realized this since he made no attempt to respond.

An imperative shout from ahead drew the exchange to a halt, rather to Merrie's relief. Lord Rutherford refused Rob's insistent invitation that he come up to the house for nuncheon and set the boy firmly on his feet again.

"Until this evening, Lady Blake." He remounted, looking down at her. "May I suggest you try to rest a little this afternoon? Sleepless nights play havoc with the complexion."

Meredith flushed indignantly. "I did not say I spent a sleepless night, sir. And I find your remarks impertinent beyond bearing."

148

"Then I most humbly beg your forgiveness. They are quite true, nevertheless." With a casual wave, he wheeled Saracen and cantered off down the drive, leaving Meredith both indignant and chagrinned. Regardless of the necessity for the game she played, her vanity was deeply wounded by Rutherford's unflattering truths, and she determined to spend the afternoon upon her bed, with pads soaked in witch hazel to soothe her eyes. Maybe she would wear the green silk this evening. It was hardly a thing of beauty but was a distinct improvement on her present attire or on the brown bombazine, which were her only alternatives.

As she dressed that evening, she found herself wondering if it would cause comment were she to wear her hair a little more softly, enliven the green silk with the elegant shawl of Norwich silk and the Meredith pearls, whose magnificence was known the length and breadth of Cornwall. But she could not do so. It would look most peculiar, particularly on such a modest occasion. Lady Barrat might get away with a degree of overdressing, but the downtrodden Lady Blake, never. She was obliged to be satisfied with what gifts nature had bestowed upon her. A restful afternoon and several hours of sleep had brought the color back into her cheeks and the sparkle to her eyes. Nan had washed her hair so that it glistened rich auburn under the candlelight although it remained confined in a matronly knot at the nape of her neck.

Meredith drove herself to the Ansbys' in the gig, taking Tommy as a gesture toward the proprieties. The young stable lad was not averse to spending the evening in the Ansby stables with his cronies, so

Meredith was relieved of guilt at keeping him from his bed.

She found herself in a strange state of paradox. Normally, the prospect of the evening that lay ahead would have had her yawning with boredom; tonight she was looking forward to it. She did not have to look far for the reason, either. And there lay the paradox. The prospect of an evening in Lord Rutherford's company set her toes tapping with pleasure even as she knew the face of the danger to which she was exposing herself—the danger that she could not keep her own reactions, needs, the nakedness of her wanting under control if she found herself alone with him again and if, again, he took advantage of their privacy.

There was every reason to suppose that he would do so if the opportunity arose. But why? Initially perhaps, because she had angered and challenged him just as he had angered her. The colonel was unaccustomed to challenge or to being bested, and Merrie had certainly succeeded in doing both on more than one occasion. She had paid as a result, but the penalty had backfired as they were both aware. Anything so thoroughly enjoyable could hardly be called punishment!

Besides, how could she possibly hold at a distance someone who treated her brothers with such gently humorous understanding? Since his arrival in Landreth, her days had somehow not seemed complete without an encounter of some kind. This morning, in the churchyard, she could not deny that she had been waiting for him, every nerve seemingly strained to catch sight or sound of his approach. No doubt he found the game amusing, a welcome diversion from the bleak boredom that had brought him to Cornwall. Flirting to the point of danger with an unconventional widow was certainly one way to occupy the idle hours. That he was an accomplished flirt, Merrie was in little doubt. How else had he succeeded in capturing her attentions so thoroughly?

Well, she must remember that she was the author of her own fate. If she was unable to handle the combination of herself and Lord Rutherford, then she could immure herself in Pendennis until he decided to return to London. But how wretchedly poor-spirited that would be! She came to the conclusion she had known all along she would, however many times she rode the carousel. It was the same conclusion she had reached on the beach. Maybe it was dangerous, but to the devil with it.

In this spirit of reckless determination, Lady Blake entered the Ansbys' drawing room to be conscious of instant disappointment when the broad shoulders and teasing eyes of Lord Rutherford were not in evidence. He appeared some twenty minutes later, however, and Meredith had ample opportunity to observe him since he moved around the room, greeting his fellow guests punctiliously, and was clearly not in a hurry to reach the corner where Lady Blake was seated, timidly shrinking behind a tapestry screen. With that delicacy she had noticed before, his dress was simple to the point of being unassuming: plain, dark-gray pantaloons and a blue coat of superfine with modest buttons. He wore neither lace nor jewels, only a perfect cravat with folds of deceptive simplicity. He still stood out amongst his country peers though,

Meredith reflected, for all his efforts to appear unremarkable. There was little he could do to disguise the superb tailoring that seemed to accentuate the noble bearing, the air of wealth and privilege that went hand in hand with the soldier's certainty of command.

"Good evening, Lady Blake." With the slightest lift of his eyebrows, he moved the screen to one side. "You must not hide your light under a bushel," he said gently. "I was about to miss you altogether."

Merrie bit her quivering lip. "I would have thought, sir, after your earlier remarks as to my appearance, that you would be glad to have missed me."

His lordship frowned, one hand resting negligently on his hip. "Hardly the first style of elegance, I grant you, but some improvement on this morning. You do not look quite so fatigued at least."

Her eyes flashed a warning suddenly and her hands fluttered in her lap. He responded instantly. "Your servant, ma'am." Bowing, he turned away just as Mr. Ansby, wreathed in smiles, came within earshot. "Lord Rutherford, the young people are desirous of engaging in a game of lottery, but doubtless you'd prefer something a little more stimulating. We are setting up a whist table, y'know—"

His lordship bowed, but before he could offer an opinion on the arrangement, his hostess, in full sail, her lavender skirts billowing around her, joined them. "You will be glad of a game of whist, my lord," she announced in a tone that admitted no dissent. "I am sure you have had little enough civilized entertainment since you arrived in these parts. And few of life's little elegancies, either, I'll be bound. Martha Perry is not known for her housekeeping. Your cousin, if you'll forgive my bluntness, was not overly concerned with such things so she had little encouragement."

His lordship appeared momentarily dumbstruck by this forceful speech. Out of the corner of his eye he saw Merrie drop her head abruptly, but not before he'd caught the laughter on her face.

"Lady Blake shall partner you," Mrs. Ansby proclaimed. "It will do you good, my dear, to come out of your corner for once. You are a deal too reclusive, y'know. It must be months since you made a four."

"It is indeed," Merrie murmured tremulously. "But it does not seem kind to inflict on Lord Rutherford a partner so lamentably out of practice."

"I am certain his lordship's skill will make up for any you lack, Lady Blake," Mr. Ansby boomed kindly in ample support of his wife's happy notion.

Damian's face bore witness to his dismay at the prospect, then all emotion was politely extinguished as he hastened to express his delight in the arrangement. He offered Lady Blake his arm and, with much tutting and twittering at his kindness, she took it.

"Stop it!" he hissed, escorting her to the card room. "It is bad enough to be obliged to partner a half-wit without having to listen to that nonsense."

Merrie's shoulders shook imperceptibly to all but her companion, who stood arm to arm with her. His lordship began to wonder how he was to survive the evening without yielding to the temptation to wring her neck.

At the end of the bidding, he thought that he had possibly misjudged her. When she led to his singleton heart, he was convinced. What did interest him was why, when it came to cards, she was prepared to reveal her true colors. True, she continued to flutter, dropped her fan and her gloves with irritating regularity, and laughed in that self-deprecating way whenever she won a trick, but she played with a cool calculation that left them clear winners at the end of the rubber.

"Ah, Lady Blake, I had quite forgot how you and Sir John used to trounce us all." Mr. Ansby laughed, then his already florid complexion reddened, and he coughed awkwardly. "So sorry, m'dear, didn't intend to bring back unwelcome . . . "

"Pray, Mr. Ansby, do not trouble yourself," Meredith said hastily although a scrap of lace appeared from her reticule, and she dabbed at her eyes.

Lord Rutherford rose from the table, unable to bear the affecting spectacle a minute longer. How he had fallen in love with a mischievous, consummate liar, actress, hypocrite, and lawbreaker would forever remain a mystery. He wanted to shake her as often as he wanted to kiss her and, at the moment, could not decide which desire was uppermost. One thing was clear, she had drawn him into her game and with every outrageous sally invited his laugher. It was high time he laid some other cards upon the table.

There was little opportunity for conversation of any kind as the evening progressed through some indifferent playing and singing by aspiring daughters of the gentry, all of whom his lordship was obliged to applaud and compliment with indiscriminate evenhandedness. At the end of an excruciating harp performance, he heard Meredith's voice raised in exaggerated praise, requesting an encore.

"Will you not play for us, Lady Blake?" he enquired in silken tones.

"Oh, dear me, no." Meredith flapped her hands in distress. "I am such a poor player, my lord, and have no voice at all. Why it would put me to shame in front of these accomplished young ladies." She smiled in nervous appeal around the room.

"Perhaps Lady Blake will honor us after supper." Patience came to her rescue with the smile of kindly condescension that set his lordship's teeth on edge, but Meredith gave her a look brimming with gratitude and fluttered to her side.

"Do you again intend returning home on foot, Lady Blake?" his lordship enquired in her ear, catching up with her as she left the supper room.

"Thank you, but I have the gig," she replied as if he had made some offer of transport.

"Then you must allow me to escort you," he said.

"You are too kind, my lord. But my groom is here to accompany me."

"Send him home beforehand."

The instruction was delivered in the colonel's incisive accents and Meredith inhaled sharply. "I have some things I wish to say to you," he went on quietly. "You will prefer to hear them alone." He moved away from her then and showed no inclination to talk again with her for the remainder of the evening.

Meredith found this most disconcerting. Not only was he so sure of her obedience that he would offer no further explanation or inducement, but there had been a note of deadly seriousness in his voice as if the time for games playing had passed. Intrigued, in spite of the distant pealing of alarm bells, she went into the hall where the butler stood at the door.

"Jacobson, would you have a message conveyed to the stables, please? Tommy should return to Pendennis immediately. He will have to be up betimes in the morning and I'll not keep him overlong from his bed."

"Yes, my lady." Jacobson was not unduly surprised at the instruction. Lady Blake was well known for the care she took of her servants, particularly of the young ones. It was not like her ladyship to keep late hours herself though, but she seemed in little hurry to make her farewells this evening.

When she did leave, it was at the instigation of Lord Rutherford. "May I fetch your cloak?" he inquired pleasantly as she stood talking to Lady Collier. "Your carriage has been brought round."

It was on the tip of her tongue to say that she had not ordered her gig and had no intention of leaving just yet, but to do so would look most singular. Smiling compliance seemed the only choice. To her relief, Rutherford made no attempt to accompany her publicly. She was allowed to make her farewells and drive the gig out of sight of the house before the black stallion caught up with her.

"You are learning to be an apt pupil, it would seem," Lord Rutherford said with approval, drawing up alongside.

"Indeed, my lord? You, I presume, were never taught to be gracious in victory." She held the reins loosely in her lap. Even had she wished to outrun him, the prospect of the dappled mare and gig against the black was merely amusing.

"I might become so, were I ever to be certain that a victory over you would not turn out to be Pyrrhic," he retorted, looping Saracen's reins around the pommel before, with a deft movement, swinging himself into the gig beside her.

"You have something you wish to say to me, my lord?" Merrie kept her eyes on the road ahead.

"First, there is something I must do. Something I owe you if you recall." He removed the reins from her hand. "Does this animal know its own way home?"

"Probably. Oh, what are you doing?"

"I hope that was a rhetorical question," he said, slipping an arm around her and drawing her across his lap. Merrie, in sudden panic, struggled in good earnest, but the muscular thighs beneath her squirming body tautened, both arms encircled her, turning her sideways and cradling her against his chest. The hold was quite invincible and with that realization her struggles momentarily subsided. The skirmish had been fought in silence. Now, with her head pressed to his chest, she could hear the steady thud of his heart against her ear, in the crimson-shot darkness behind her closed eyes. "That's better." His voice, that infuriatingly carried a note of laughter mingled with undeniable satisfaction, brought her back to a sense of reality.

"Let me go!" She pushed against his chest, anger, not panic motivating her now. Damian chuckled, reveling in the feel of that lithe body twisting against him. His new knowledge of how and why Merrie Trelawney possessed such strength and muscular control merely added to his guilt-free determination to ignore all the rules of chivalry in the pursuit of his purpose. This mischievous little smuggler in the crook of his arm broke more than enough rules of her own to make her fair game in the battle of love he must wage. And he was in no doubt that the strongest card he held was his recognition of her deep well of passion that, he was convinced, had not yet been fully drawn by anyone.

He loosened his grip sufficiently to give her room to wriggle, although not to escape, and, having no desire to be used as a punchball, prudently took possession of her hands in one of his. "Why do you fight me, little one? You know I will not hurt you, just as you know that you are fighting yourself as much as me."

"I am not!" she denied even as the urge to fight became something else, as her body shivered like a sapling in a gale against the hardness of his, and desire shimmered, unmistakable and undeniable.

"You are such a little liar," he said softly, catching her chin with his free hand. "Do you think I cannot feel that longing in you? Do you think I cannot see it in your eyes?"

Meredith instinctively closed her eyes as if, by doing so, she could deny the truth. Damian released her wrists and touched the tip of her nose with a long finger. "Answer me, Merrie Trelawney," he commanded, bending to press his lips to the quivering, blue-veined eyelids. The tip of his tongue ran hotly over the thinly covered orbs before dancing across her cheek to her ear. Merrie moaned as he nipped the tender lobe, and then his tongue moved in and around, tracing the whorls and contours of that vulnerable shell that she could never have believed could be so sensitive. The hand left her chin, ran down over the open column of her throat, moved to the gentle swell of her bosom. She arched against him, half in protest, half in joy, and heard his own groan, felt his pleasure in hard evidence against her silk-covered thighs. Her nipple pressed urgently into his caressing palm, burning against the constraints of camisole and bodice. His mouth moved to hers in a tantalizing butterfly kiss until she made her own demand, sucking on his lower lip as if it were a ripe plum, and then her tongue pushed into the sweet, warm cavern where, for some unaccountable reason, it seemed to belong.

Then the dappled pony stumbled in a pothole and the gig lurched. Damian's arm tightened in immediate, instinctive support around the body across his knees, his head lifting as he reached for the reins and steadied the animal. Meredith found that she was unable to move, to take advantage of the break in his hold that a few minutes ago she would have welcomed. Having lost all sense of perspective, she just lay still in the circle of his arm, waiting in patient subjugation until he would come back to her.

"For such a little liar, you have the most honest eyes." He touched the tip of her nose with a long finger. The finger moved to her mouth, tracing the full curve of her lips; her tongue darted between them, dampening his fingertip even as she drew it between her teeth, nipping in a movement that was as mischievous as it was sensuous. His breath whistled in the still night air as, urgently, he raised her body, catching her chin again with his free hand, bringing his lips to hers.

Nothing existed but this wondrous joining of lips and tongues, the hot moistness of his breath against her throat as he kissed the pulsing hollow, the liquid weakness in the recesses of her body preparing itself for the inevitable conclusion of this wanting. Fingers caressed her ankle, circling the sharp bone, before pitpatting up her calf, pushing aside the layers of silk and cotton, reaching her thigh and the bare skin above her garter.

Maybe it was the intimacy of that skin contact, maybe it was the light breeze springing up to fan her cheeks, to brush her exposed leg, that brought the real world crashing in on this sensate dream. Whatever it was, Merrie abruptly pulled herself out of his hold, pushing frantically at the invading hand.

"No, this is madness. You do not understand."

"What do I not understand?" He held her tightly for a minute, staring into her eyes where the truth of desire still lingered behind a film of confusion and fear. Then the sloe eyes seemed to glaze, blanking out the candor.

"You do not understand that I must live in this place with as much comfort as I can. There will be precious little of that if I am found behaving in this disgraceful fashion with a man whose reputation does not depend on Cornishmen. You may go home whenever you please, sir, and escape what censure comes your way. I *am* home."

Her words carried the conviction of truth, but he knew that it was yet another of her convenient half-truths to obscure the real issue, whatever that might be. The fear was real enough, though, whatever caused it. She was shivering—and not with the passion of the last moments.

Deciding he had nothing to lose by taking the bull by the horns, he spoke with gentle determination.

"Meredith, my world, my home can be yours."

"Whatever do you mean?" She looked at him, uncomprehending.

"I wish you to marry me," he said simply.

She stared at him blankly for a minute, then produced the only explanation for such a ludicrous statement that she could think of. "I fear, my lord, that you are become moon mad! It is quite unchivalrous to make mock of me in that manner." Merrie caught up the reins, flicking them against the mare's rump. The pony broke into an indignant trot.

"It is you who make mock of me," Rutherford countered. "I am in earnest, Meredith. I do not know how or why it should have happened, but I love you."

Meredith spoke slowly, as if to a half-witted child. "Lord Rutherford on your own admission you came into Cornwall at a loose end, depressed and unhappy. You met a woman unlike those you are accustomed to. I challenge you, perhaps; amuse you, perhaps. What—what has just taken place between us is . . ." her voice faded.

"Unconventional, certainly," he completed for her in level tones. "Was that what you were going to say?"

"It should not have happened." Her voice sounded small and unconvincing. "I do not know how or why—"

"Don't talk nonsense! You know perfectly well how and why, just as I do. You are no schoolroom miss, Merrie Trelawney." He spoke harshly although he had not wanted to, but somehow her denial of the passion that had informed her responses angered him almost as much as did her casual dismissal of his declaration—angered him but did not alarm him. Deny it as she would, the passion of that response went far deeper than the transitory desire of a neglected widow. He would just have to teach her that, if she could not learn it for herself. Time was one commodity he had in great supply, and patience was a quality he had learned the hard way.

Chapter Nine

Try as she would that night, Meredith could not hold down the panic. It floated around her, an amorphous, swirling haze, eluding her comprehension. If she could but understand it, she could control it, but it had come upon her with such startling force. For one minute, she had been lost in the glorious sensation of their contact, her senses and emotions turned in on the warm blackness that contained only the two of them, her only desire that the moment would stretch to infinity. Then the panic had exploded, a violent red ball in the cloaking darkness behind her eyes. She was in danger of losing something, something fundamental, integral to her sense of self and the purpose that informed her life.

It was dawn before she was able to look clearly at what had happened to her. She had fallen in love with the Duke of Keighley's heir. Merrie Trelawney, who earned her living as a smuggler, who lived under the shadow of the hangman's noose, was in love with a future duke. And the future duke had said he loved her, had actually asked her to marry him. But, of course, his madness was easily explained; she had done so quite satisfactorily last night, after all. It was

163

her own that was the mystery. Her reckless self-indulgence had landed her hip deep in waters hotter than she had ever before encountered. She fell asleep eventually to the sounds of the crowing cock, her mind slightly eased by resolution. A resolution she would put into effect at the earliest opportunity.

"Put out my riding habit, Nan, if you please. I have business with Mr. Donne in Fowey." Meredith pushed aside the bedclothes and stood on the oak floor where the boards were warmed by the morning sun. She stretched, yawned, firmly put aside the strange feeling of emptiness, and drew her nightgown over her head. She was rarely conscious of her body, there being little time and even less reason to be so in her busy, chaste existence, but this morning, as she sponged herself with cool water, she became aware of the length and firmness of her limbs, the softness of her skin. As she touched her breasts, their nipples peaked, hard and rosy, as they had done last night under hands other than her own.

Curiously, she stood in front of the pier glass, heedless of Nan's puzzled disapproval. Did she have the sort of body that would attract a man? She had not been entirely to her husband's taste as he had told her often enough. Boy's hips, he had said, breasts like little lemons, nothing a man could get a hold of. Not like Georgiana Collier, who at seventeen had the voluptuous curves of a Rubens nude.

"Just what are you thinking of? Staring at yourself like that without a stitch on! It's not decent, Meredith!" Nan pushed her chemise into her hands. "You've the body God gave you, and there's naught you can do about it."

"No," Merrie agreed sadly. "I had come to the same conclusion."

"Now, what's brought all this on?" Nan's intelligent old eyes sharpened, and she stared at her erstwhile nursling as if Merrie were again in the schoolroom, harboring an unhappy secret.

"Oh, 'tis nothing at all." Meredith turned away from the mirror and began to dress hastily.

Nan humphed her disbelief but, to Merrie's relief, did not pursue the matter. In fact, the elderly nurse had her own ideas as to the reasons for this out-of-character behavior, but she was too wise to reveal them, being confident that they would be overhastily denied.

Meredith had reached the foot of the stairs when she heard the unmistakable voice coming from the breakfast parlor. Rob's excited prattle mingled with the clatter of dishes, Hugo's solemn tones, and Lord Rutherford's light but steady ones. She half-turned, hand on the newel post, intending to flee back to her chamber, but Seecombe, bearing a coffee pot, appeared from backstairs.

"Good morning, Lady Merrie. I have just this minute made your coffee, so it is nice and fresh."

"Thank you, Seecombe. You are most thoughtful." Resigned, she smiled warmly and preceded him into the breakfast parlor. "Good morning, Lord Rutherford, you are up and visiting betimes. What a delightful surprise."

His eyes narrowed at her cool tone, but he rose, bowed, and held a chair for her. "I did not intend inviting myself to breakfast, Lady Blake, but I have a passion for deviled kidneys, and Mrs. Perry does not seem able to provide them."

"You are most welcome, sir," she said, taking her seat. "Thank you, Seecombe." The servant placed the coffee pot at her elbow. "Do you care for coffee, Lord Rutherford?"

"Thank you, ma'am, but no. This excellent ale will more than satisfy me."

"Only think, Merrie!" Rob was bouncing in his seat. "Lord Rutherford has come to invite us all to a picnic. He says we will take horses and a big hamper and go to Yellan Falls."

"That is most kind of Lord Rutherford," Merrie responded. "I am sure you will have a most enjoyable day."

"The invitation included you." Damian sat back in the carved oak chair at the table's head, one leg crossed negligently over the other, regarding her steadily.

"I fear I do not have the time for pleasure excursions, sir. I must ride into Fowey after breakfast."

"Then perhaps we should turn a business excursion into a pleasure trip," he said smoothly. "I passed through Fowey on my way to Landreth and it seemed an agreeable enough town. I am sure the inn can provide us with a tolerable meal. While you conduct your business, perhaps Rob and Theo, Hugo, too, if he can spare the time, will show me the sights."

"That is a capital idea, sir." Theo sprang to his feet. "We have not been to Fowey this holiday. Shall we ride, Merrie, or take the gig?"

Rob was cavorting around the parlor in a state of high excitement, and even Hugo's expression had lightened at the prospect of the treat. Merrie knew she could not disappoint them without good reason, and the only reason she had, while it was sufficient, was not one she could reveal to her brothers. The dawn resolution would have to be put into effect another time unless she was afforded the opportunity to be alone with Rutherford during the day and could inform him of her decision.

The sight of the four Trelawneys and Lord Rutherford taking the Fowey road on this Monday morning at the end of July caused some considerable interest. Lady Collier, giving instruction to her gardener pruning the climbing rose around the garden gate, saw them first. The cavalcade politely drew rein so that greetings could be exchanged. Once they were on their way again, Lady Collier hastened indoors to change her dress and give orders for the barouche to be brought around. It would be most diverting to be, for once, ahead of Patience Barrat with such a tidbit. While there could be nothing improper exactly about Meredith's riding with Lord Rutherford in the company of her brothers, it was a most singular circumstance. The little widow was hardly known for her extrovert nature.

If Meredith had expected any special attention, any speaking looks from soulful eyes, she was disappointed. Lord Rutherford rode alongside her, talking the merest commonplace when he was not engaged with one of the others. There was not even opportunity to exhibit a frosty withdrawal since there was nothing from which to withdraw. He was behaving as if last night had never happened, as if he had never said the things he had said, and Meredith could almost believe that she had imagined the whole.

Except for the curious, inconvenient sense of excitement she felt in his proximity, the way her eyes kept sliding to his hands, remembering the way they had felt as he held her, and then she would see his mouth, smiling, and her lips tingled with memory.

They reached Fowey just before noon. The town, at the head of the Fowey river, gleamed in whitewashed freshness, bustling with noise and life. "Which inn do you recommend, ma'am?" Rutherford turned to his companion with a polite smile.

"The Royal is more accustomed to Quality than the Eagle and Child," she replied, "but I dare swear neither will provide what you are accustomed to."

"I think I told you once before that my tastes are not overly refined," he responded evenly. "I will bespeak a parlor and nuncheon at the Royal. You will join us there when your business is completed."

"I should not be above half an hour with Mr. Donne." Merrie, to her annoyance, found herself offering a conciliatory smile.

In return, his lordship leaned over to give her cheek a careless pat. "I shall await your return most eagerly." His eyes twinkled conspiratorially and Meredith could not help but respond. Mumbling something incoherently, she directed her mare across the street to the lawyer's office. Mr. Donne's clerk bellowed for an apprentice, who appeared and held Lady Blake's horse while the clerk ushered the client into the lawyer's sanctum.

"Ah, Lady Blake, good morning." Mr. Donne was a jovial man with the portly belly and ruddy complexion of one who enjoyed the good things of life. "It is always such a pleasure to see you."

Meredith greeted him with genuine warmth. The lawyer had stood her friend in the years since her husband's death, negotiating the redemption of the estate with the utmost discretion, never once questioning her as to how she achieved the miracles. He had also offered sound advice as to which portions of the estate she would do well to buy back as priorities, treating his female client with all the deference he would have accorded her husband. More, in fact, as he was in the habit of telling Mrs. Donne, since her ladyship had a shrewd head on her shoulders and a tight hand to the purse strings, unlike the profligate Sir John.

Now, he waved her ladyship to a chair with an expansive hand and offered sherry. Meredith accepted both, then came straight to the point. "I had hoped to be in a position to redeem Ducket's Spinney this morning, Mr. Donne, but, unfortunately, there are other claims on the money."

The lawyer shook his head. "That is a pity. I have the papers ready for you since you had said it would be your intention."

"Next month," she said with confidence. "For the moment, I have half of the sum." Reaching into the deep pocket of her riding habit, she drew out a leather pouch, laid a fold of bills on the desk. "I realize that the bank will not deal piecemeal, but I would be glad if you would keep this until I may lay hands on the rest."

"May I make a suggestion?" The lawyer crossed his hands over an ample paunch and, when she inclined her head in agreement, went on. "The interest payment falls due next month on the substantial loan Sir John took out just before his death. Were you to use this sum to pay the interest ahead of time, you would save a month of six percent." His head nodded sagaciously. "The money would be better employed in that manner, d'ye not think, Lady Blake?"

She sighed. "You are right, of course. It is just that I hate to send good money after bad. Without those interest payments, I would have Pendennis free and clear by now."

"Why do you not pay off the loan first, then? The mortgages will hold." He looked at her with shrewd sympathy. The suggestion had been made before, but Meredith had needed the concrete satisfaction of gaining back the land, and he had understood her need.

"It will take at least a year. Five thousand pounds is no trifle. There remains only Ducket's Spinney and the Lower Forty. I must have those first, Mr. Donne."

"It is, of course, for you to decide." Taking the bills, he went over to the iron safe in the corner of the room. "I shall keep these for you until next month."

"No." Merrie stood up, drawing on her riding gloves. "Pay the interest on the loan, if you please. I shall hope to have sufficient for the spinney next month."

"Your husbandry is most amazing," he observed.

"Yes," Meredith agreed calmly. "It is extraordinary what one can do if one counts the pennies."

"Just so, my lady." He stroked his chin thoughtfully, seemed about to say something further, but, when she moved toward the door, made haste to accompany her out to the street where the apprentice assisted her to mount.

"Good day, Mr. Donne. I thank you again for your trouble." She leant down to give him her hand. The lawyer reached up to grasp it firmly.

"My pleasure, your ladyship."

Mr. Donne watched the horse and rider down the street, still stroking his chin. Lady Blake had some other source of income, of that he was convinced. All the penny counting in the world could not achieve the sums she had laid out in the last two and a half years. But some inner voice of caution told him to keep this surmise to himself, even from his dear wife who would find it most fascinating. Shaking his head, he returned to his office for his coat. It was time he went upstairs in search of the midday meal that that excellent lady would have waiting for him.

Merrie made her way to the Royal feeling a stab of unease at the latter part of her exchange with the lawyer. He was obviously aware that simple economy could not achieve the sums she brought in, but he had never commented on it before, never looked so thoughtful. It was not as if he could guess the truth in a millennium, but, if he shared his thoughts, speculation would be rife in Fowey, and it would not be long before it reached Landreth. Merrie had been aware of the risk since the beginning, but she had had to have an agent in the business, and she trusted the lawyer who had never been less than honest and sympathetic about her financial situation. What would he think when she came up with twice as much money in the future? She would not be able to do so, Merrie decided reluctantly. She could not escalate the redemption without legitimate questions from the lawyer. In spite of her natural impatience, she would have to proceed with caution.

She was still frowning, however, as she left the mare in the yard of the Royal and went into the inn. "Lady Blake." The landlord bowed low, rubbing pudgy hands together, expressive of some degree of contentment. "His lordship awaits you in the parlor above stairs."

"Thank you, Jud." She followed him upstairs and was surprised, on being shown with considerable flourish into the only private parlor the Royal possessed, that it contained only Lord Rutherford and a laden table.

"I did not expect to find you alone, sir." She drew off her gloves and removed her hat, tossing both onto the window seat. "Where are the boys?"

"Rob heard tell of a traveling circus." Rutherford smiled and poured her a glass of sherry. "Also a fair, as I understand. Even Hugo was induced to go to see if they would be worth an extended visit this afternoon."

"Then I daresay we shall not see them for hours." She took the sherry and went to the mullioned window, looking down onto the street. "Had I known, I would have given Theo and Rob some money. They would never ask for it, but a fair can provide little amusement if one is penniless."

Her companion cleared his throat and said somewhat hesitantly, "I—uh—took the liberty of . . ."

She whirled from the window. "Thank you. It is what I would have expected of you, to think of such a thing." She spoke with completely natural warmth. There had never been any constraint between them when it came to dealings with the Trelawney brothers.

172

"How much do I owe you?"

"You would not, I suppose, allow me to make a present of it to my young friends?"

"No," she said definitely. "I could not possibly."

"Very well then—half a sovereign apiece. Hugo did not see any need for funds."

Merrie laughed. "No, he would not." She handed him a sovereign which he pocketed with appropriate solemnity.

"How was your business?" Lord Rutherford inquired politely. "Successful, I trust."

"Yes, thank you. Quite successful." The accompanying smile was, however, distinctly preoccupied.

"That is not an entirely honest answer," he declared, leaning broad shoulders against the mantel. "I am intrigued. In general, when you lie you do so with such consummate artistry that it is near impossible to detect. You have made little attempt to disguise that particular untruth. I wonder why."

"Perhaps, sir, because with you there would be little point." She took a slow sip of sherry. "I beg your pardon if I appear a trifle distrait, but there are matters that concern me at present, and I had not intended to take on social obligations in addition to my business."

Lord Rutherford whistled softly. "So, I am a social obligation. That is something of a facer, I confess. I have never to my knowledge been viewed in quite such an unflattering light before, particularly by my guests."

Meredith flushed to the roots of her hair. "I must apologize if I sounded impolite, my lord. It was not my intention."

"Liar," he said without rancor or emphasis.

"I wish you would stop accusing me of lying." Meredith gave up the pretense of formality.

"When you stop, so will I also. It is a very bad habit, you know," he informed her rather in the manner of a kindly schoolmaster addressing an erring pupil.

Her lips quivered at the absurdity, and with two long strides he stood in front of her. One hand removed her glass while the other lifted her chin.

"No . . ." she managed to say, the instant before he kissed her. "You must not," she completed when his mouth released hers.

"Why must I not, Merrie?" He smiled, the warm, glowing, all-embracing smile that fuzzed the edges of reality and seemed to make nonsense of her fears. But they were not nonsense, and she was no naive maiden to be swept foolishly off her feet by an engaging countenance, a beguiling smile, and a pair of sparkling eyes. Widows in their twenty-fourth year, with debts and brothers to raise and provide for, could not afford to lose touch with the ground beneath their serviceable shoes.

"Lord Rutherford," she began, stepping backward away from his hand. "I must ask you, please, to—to cease your visits to Pendennis and to refrain from singling me out in any way. I do not wish for your company—although, of course, I am deeply honored by your attentions," she added with the self-deprecating smile she reserved for her neighbors.

"You dare do that to me!" he exclaimed, all humor vanishing from his expression. Taking her by the shoulders, he gave her a vigorous shake, ignoring her

174

gasp of outrage. "Never smile at me like that again! Now, what is all this nonsense?"

"A gentleman, my lord, does not require an explanation when a lady says she does not wish for his company," she said icily.

"You lack many of the definitive qualities of a lady, Merrie Trelawney," he retorted. "It is hardly surprising that I should act accordingly."

"You are insufferable!" Snatching up her gloves and hat, she marched to the door, but Rutherford reached it before she did. A long arm in a maroon velvet jacket barred her progress.

"I will beg your pardon for that remark, Merrie, if you insist that it is necessary," he said. "But will you not acknowledge the truth? What has passed between us from the first has had little in common with the veneer of propriety."

"That may be so," she said in a low voice, keeping her eyes fixed on a hairline crack in the door's paneling. "But that does not mean that I forfeit my right to make my wishes known or to have them granted."

"Yesterday, I said that I loved you, that I wished you to be my wife. You were kind enough to tell me that I was quite mistaken, that I was merely amused and challenged by you, found you a diversion from my boredom. Those observations, I beg to inform you, were insulting. If you have the right to make your wishes known, I have the right to be believed in what I say. Do you not think me more likely to know how and what I feel than you?"

Meredith remained silent. If she could fall in love with Rutherford, why should he not have fallen in love with her? It did not alter the facts, however. Talk of marriage between them was as chimeric as believing in fairies. If he had not been in such a strange state of mind, dissatisfied and unhappy, he would see that as clearly as she did.

"I await an answer, Meredith. And I would like you to look at me when you give it."

She waited for him to turn up her face in his accustomed fashion and, when he did not, was obliged to look up of her own accord—an action that uncomfortably implied obedience. "I will grant, sir, that you know your own feelings best."

He pursed his lips, continuing to scrutinize her expression in silence, then the sounds of hasty footsteps on the stairs and the voices of Rob and Theo engaged in argument came from outside. With one mind, they both moved away from the door. When the boys burst in, their elders were to be found sipping sherry, Merrie by the window, Lord Rutherford leaning casually against the carved mantel.

"Merrie, there is a famous fair!" Rob babbled. "The circus is nothing, just a mangy tiger and a parrot, but the fair has a Fat Lady. She is enormous! Sir, you would not believe . . ." He turned shining eyes to his lordship whose rather hard expression softened.

"I think I can imagine, Rob," he said. "What did you think of it, Theo?"

"Not a great deal." With the wisdom and experience of his fifteen years, Theo shrugged in blasé indifference. "It's nothing compared to the one that comes to Harrow in September. But Rob hasn't seen that yet, and he won't be able to until he's in the third year and allowed to visit the town."

"Well, I do not care," Rob said stoutly. "And as soon as I have had nuncheon, I am going back. I am starved!"

"I cannot think how you can be," Hugo declared. "You have been eating humbugs and gingerbread all morning."

"Peace," their sister implored. "I cannot see what possible fun there would be in a fair if one did not stuff oneself with sweetmeats. Do you not agree, Lord Rutherford?" For a moment forgetting their quarrel, she turned naturally to him as an ally.

"Absolutely," he concurred without the blink of an eyelid. "Shall we address ourselves to this more than adequate repast?" He drew out a chair for her, and, as she took her seat, his fingertips brushed the back of her neck.

Meredith shivered at the contact, knowing that he had felt the reaction. She passed a dish of Cornish pasties to Rob and made some inconsequential remark about the weather.

"May I carve you some ham, Lady Blake?" Rutherford inquired with sardonic courtesy. "Or perhaps you would prefer the game pie?"

"Some ham, thank you."

"Very wise." Carving wafer-thin slices, he laid them on her plate. "This Cornish predilection for pastry is something of an acquired taste unless one has the appetite of extreme youth."

"Or one earned by labor in the fields or with the lobster pots," she countered. "I would have thought that as a soldier you would sympathize with the hunger resulting from physical exercise in the open air."

"Were you a soldier, sir?" Theo's attention was instantly caught. "In the Peninsula?"

Meredith held her breath, wondering if he would snap the boy's head off. There was a short pause, then Rutherford said easily, "Yes, as it happens."

"Oh, famous!" Theo's eyes shone. "I wish of all things for a pair of colors when I am old enough. But Merrie is as difficult about that as she is about Hugo's taking orders."

"I am not difficult," Merrie protested. "I merely said that we would wait until you were older before we discussed it. And if Hugo is still of the same mind when he comes down from Oxford, then I will not stand in his way."

"You are well served, I think," his lordship said softly, placing a piece of bread and butter on her plate. She did not pretend to misunderstand him. Having brought up the subject of his army experience to annoy him, she had only herself to blame if the tables had been turned.

Theo, however, continued to question Rutherford eagerly and, after only the barest hesitation, his lordship responded, leaving Merrie free to retreat into her own thoughts without further interruption.

After the meal, at Rob's insistence, they repaired to the fair where Merrie was induced to shy for coconuts, and in the ensuing competition she found it impossible to maintain her air of hauteur with Rutherford. The Fat Lady was pronounced to be truly prodigious, and it was generally agreed that, if Rob's consumption of toffee apples continued at its present rate, she would soon have a rival.

At the end of the afternoon, Merrie found herself in possession of a number of trinkets representing presents from her brothers and their combined winnings at the stalls where the prizes seemed exclusively designed to appeal to the fairer sex. "What am I to do with them?" Laughing she laid out the trumpery bracelets and rings, the little bone fan, and a colorful scrap of material intended as a scarf. "There must be many a girl in the village who'd be glad of them."

"Keep them." Rutherford gathered up the fairings, tying them in the scarf. "One day, when you are old and gray, you will find them in a storeroom and wonder for a moment where they came from. Then you'll remember a sunny afternoon in Fowey when the world lay at your feet."

Meredith frowned as a finger of cold touched her between the shoulders. "That is a most depressing thought, Lord Rutherford."

"It is depressing to have the world at your feet?" he inquired with an unreadable smile. "Surely it will only be depressing if you kick it away?"

There was no mistaking his meaning and, with a definitive gesture of refusal, Meredith turned away from him, calling to the boys. "It is time we were returning home. Cook will not be best pleased if her dinner is kept waiting."

Lord Rutherford's visits to Pendennis continued during the following two weeks, and Meredith avoided him as and when she could. But she could not avoid the thrill of eagerness when she heard his voice in conversation with the boys or the pang of disappointment when, on returning from some errand around the estate, she did not see the black patiently awaiting his master. He did not deliberately seek her out on these visits, but she was aware of his gaze, shrewd and just a little amused as if he could read her mind, whenever they were in the same room.

One afternoon in August, four nights into the new moon, he noticed something different about her, an air of suppressed excitement, an absent-minded preoccupation. She seemed not to hear what was said to her or, if she did, to forget to respond.

Lord Rutherford could think of only one explanation. It had been just over a month since that night of his arrival on the cliff road. Was there to be another run tonight? If so, would there be another ambush? He remembered hearing her say that they had been warned of the last one, and, from what Bart had said, they had walked deliberately into the trap. Surely she would not take such a risk again? She had promised Bart, had she not? He could not help the thought, though, that perhaps Meredith treated promises with the same insouciance that she treated the truth. Having twice seen how much pleasure the danger afforded her, Rutherford had developed the shrewd suspicion that the excitement of smuggling, combined with the mischievous amusement she took in hoodwinking her neighbors, was the breath of life for Merrie, the only compensations for an imprisonment that such a free spirit could not help but find intolerable.

He was waiting on the cliff top when she emerged from the cave beneath just before midnight. She was alone, and tonight there was no whistling tune, no skipping dance. She moved along the path with the stealth of a hunter—or of the hunted—and, even from that distance, he could sense the tension in the wire-sprung frame.

Damian followed at a considerable distance, having the conviction that even a conventionally safe gap would be too close for those sharp ears, the senses alerted to a hint of anything out of the ordinary. At one point she halted, standing motionless, staring into the darkness ahead. After a minute he saw it too. A light flashing so briefly and intermittently that it would escape a casual watcher. As far as he could deduce, it came from the spot on the headland known as Devil's Point for the treacherous reef of jagged rock below.

Merrie moved on, then quite suddenly disappeared as she had done that other night. Damian swore softly, afraid to move in case she had stopped in hiding for some reason and he should run up against her. After five minutes, he crept forward again. At the point where she had vanished, he peered cautiously over the cliff. A thin, steep trail more suited to a goat than a human snaked down the almost sheer cliff. The beach below was invisible, but he could hear the roar of surf that even on a calm night rose high. It was clear that, if he wanted to continue his observation, down the path he must go.

Cursing the ill luck that had catapulted him into love with a creature who treated goal trails in the pitch dark as if they were the post road from London to Dover, Rutherford lowered himself over the cliff. It would be interesting, he reflected dourly, to see how his shoulder bore up under the strain of this night's activities. The descent would have been difficult enough in ideal circumstances, but the need for silence presented a devilish complication, that and his fear that he would dislodge a stone or a shower of sand to alert anyone below.

Meanwhile Meredith, blissfully unaware of her follower, stood on the beach with the others. They were a silent, but not anxious, group. Anxiety was an emotion that tended to impair efficiency. They were alert, however, ears and eyes straining in the darkness for the sound and sight of Jacques's boat.

"Here she comes." Bart discerned the dark shape riding high on the white crest of surf. "That wave'll run her direct to the beach."

Merrie ran to the shore with the rest, kicking off her shoes to wade thigh high into the waves to catch and steady the boat. Damian's incredulous ears caught that unmistakable chuckle of exhilaration as the surf slapped against her. Sweet heavens! What kind of duchess would she make? But he had a long row to hoe before that became a possibility, his lordship reminded himself, settling into the sandy hollow behind a jutting boulder. It was not particularly comfortable but provided him with an unobstructed view of the goings-on in the cove while at the same time afforded him a fair degree of protection against casual eyes.

He stiffened, however, when Merrie, in conversation with a short, stocky man from the French boat, moved away from the activity and came up the beach toward his boulder. To his relief, they stopped just short of his hiding place, providing him with the added bonus of ears as well as eyes.

"Jacques, I intend to deliver this run to the Eagle and Child in Fowey." Merrie spoke in a brisk, businesslike manner, but there was a hint of excitement in her voice.

"Ah, *magnifique*!" The Frenchman clapped her on the shoulder with a hearty camaraderie that made the watcher wince with annoyance. "I wondered if you would take the bait, *mon amie*."

"You knew well I would, you old devil!" Merrie chuckled. "But I will need another run within the month for our regular customers. They'll not take kindly to being ousted."

"In three weeks," Jacques promised. "After the full moon."

"Aye." Merrie nodded with satisfaction. "We'll be waiting. I think 'twill be safe enough to use Devil's Point for the signal again. We'll change the position next month."

"You'll need to be charging a bit extra for the brandy," Jacques said, pulling a flask from his hip pocket, offering it to Merrie. When she shook her head, he took a long pull, wiping his mouth with the back of his hand. "My contact's become a little greedy." His eyes narrowed. "This time he will get away with it. It will make him feel secure, you understand? It will not happen again, you can be sure, Merrie. But—uh—I must pass on the cost. *Vous comprenez?*"

"I would rather continue to pay the extra, Jacques, than that you should . . ." Meredith paused, then continued with resolution, "than that you should eliminate your contact."

"Tsk-tsk." Jacques shook his head. "So brutally

frank, Merrie. You must leave these matters to me. They do not concern you. You complete your end of the business; I will complete mine."

Damian felt a cold shiver as he watched Merrie's face in the moonlight. The usually vibrant features were cold, set, wiped clean of all emotion, telling him more clearly than anything else how affected she was by the exchange. Smuggling was no prank, for all that she seemed to treat it as such. Then, suddenly, she shrugged, turned back to the beach, and Rutherford heard no more.

The contraband was loaded onto the ponies, the French boat departed, and the train started up the broad cliff path running diagonal to the beach. The goat trail was clearly a shortcut, not one that could be taken by laden ponies. Rutherford, now knowing the smugglers' destination, was in no hurry as he scrambled back up the trail. His only concern was to be sure that Meredith reached Pendennis safely. If she did not, he had no idea what he could do about it, but he did know that he would not sleep this night if he was uncertain of the outcome of the enterprise.

All went well, however, without scent or sight of the revenue. Ponies, contraband, and Merrie disappeared into the cave beneath Pendennis. The rest of the group vanished into the night.

Damian, Lord Rutherford, went home to his bed, more than ever convinced that smuggling was no activity for the future Duchess of Keighley, however proficient at it she might be.

Chapter Ten

It was in a mood of strong determination that Lord Rutherford set out for Pendennis three days later. It was the first time he had ridden over since the day of the smugglers' run, and his absence had been deliberate. He did not think he had mistaken Merrie's pleasure in his visits, however hard she had concealed it beneath a mask of indifference. If she had missed him at all in the last three days, then it was possible she might be more receptive to what he had to say when he appeared unheralded. Receptive or no, his lordship was resolved that Merrie Trelawney would at least hear him out. Extricating her from her brothers would be the major problem.

As it happened, this proved less arduous than he had expected. Upon being shown into the morning room where he found the three brothers, he was instantly struck by their subdued, disconsolate mien. "What's to do?" he inquired cheerfully, laying whip and gloves on the sofa table. "You all look as if you have lost a sovereign and found a penny."

"Hugo and Merrie have quarreled," Rob informed him glumly. "And now Merrie is as cross as two sticks. It is quite horrid when she is."

185

"Oh, I see." His lordship glanced at the eldest Trelawney. "D'ye care to tell me about it, Hugo?"

Hugo flushed a dull crimson. "She treats me like a baby as if I do not know my own mind," he blurted out. "I am almost twenty and only wish to help, but she will not allow anyone to do so."

"Well, you ought to have known she would not allow you to come down from Oxford before you are finished," Theo put in. "If you must waste your life as a poor-relation curate making up to Cousin Sybil in Dorset, then you may as well have some amusement first."

"Merrie said Hugo likes to be a martyr," Rob explained helpfully. "And Hugo said she was a—a—"

"Hold your tongue!" Hugo exploded, advancing on his brother, fists clenched, definite menace in his eyes.

Lord Rutherford stepped between them. "I think I have heard enough. Where is your sister?"

"Riding on the beach, I expect," Theo said, absently shuffling a pack of cards. "It's what she usually does when she's out of sorts."

His lordship retrieved his whip and gloves. "Rob, I would recommend that you make yourself scarce," he suggested. "I am certain you do not intend to exacerbate raw nerves, but I fear that you do, nevertheless."

He left the morning room without waiting to see if his advice was followed and went to reclaim Saracen. Ten minutes later he found Meredith, as Theo had said, riding on the beach below the house. She heard the thud of hooves on the sand behind her and reined in the mare, turning to look over her shoulder.

"Good morning, Lord Rutherford. You had best continue on your way, for I should warn you that I am

186

"out-of-reason cross."

"Yes, so I have been informed," he responded placidly, drawing up alongside her. "But that does not scare me off."

Merrie, who, much as she hated to acknowledge it, had been racking her brains for the last three days to find a reason for his absence, made no comment.

"What was it that Hugo said when you accused him of martyrdom?" his lordship inquired with a quizzical lift of his brows. "Rob was about to tell me, but Hugo became somewhat annoyed."

"I am a petticoat dictator, it seems." Meredith found that she had no hesitation in pouring out her woes to this, the one person she somehow trusted to hear them with a sympathetic, if objective, ear. Neither did she stop to consider why this should be so. "I am in love with power and wish to keep my brothers in leading strings to gratify myself." She gave a short laugh, nudging the mare into a trot. "If Hugo is set upon entering the church, then of course I will not prevent him. But I am not yet convinced of that, and he is too young to be making such a decision for the wrong reasons."

"He is but three years younger than yourself," Rutherford reminded gently. "You have been making decisions as important since you were younger than he."

"And not always the correct ones," she flashed. "Sacrifice appeals to Hugo at the present. It is but a stage he is going through. In a year's time, there will be no need for his sacrifice."

"What do you mean?" Convinced that she had let slip the statement, he waited breathlessly to see how

187

she would answer him.

"Why, simply that by then I shall hope to have saved sufficient funds to ease matters a little," she responded with an airy wave, but he had not missed the hesitation, the sudden biting of her lower lip.

"You are not telling the truth again." It was worth trying, he thought, although it might be considered unchivalrous to push so hard when she was already vulnerable. But it was the best opportunity he had had.

Meredith flushed, and there was no mistaking either the appeal, or the anger, in the glorious purple eyes as she looked across at him. "My affairs are mine to manage," she said curtly.

"I expect it is that attitude that annoys Hugo," Rutherford replied with a bland smile.

Meredith's heels pressed into the mare's flanks and the animal took off along the sand, swerving abruptly into the waves. Damian, taken by surprise, watched for a minute as horse and rider galloped along the edge of the breaking surf. She would be drenched in a minute! But what would that matter to such an impulsive, headstrong creature? Urging the stallion into a canter, he rode parallel with Meredith and the mare but well away from the water, keeping pace with her until, with her headlong gallop, she had exorcised the demons possessing her.

When she rejoined him, the bottom of her habit was dark with water and her hair, escaping from her hat, was whipped into a tangle. Her expression, however, was calm, her eyes swept clean of anger.

"Saltwater will not do your boots much good," he remarked casually.

She laughed. "But it is good for my temper."

"That is fortunate as there is something I wish to discuss with you, and in the past the subject has tended to lead to acrimony." Leaning over, Rutherford took hold of the mare's bridle at the bit, bringing her to a halt. "I wish you to hear me out," he explained, "so we will stay still for the moment."

"What is it you wish to talk about, my lord, that necessitates this degree of compulsion?"

"You know full well, Merrie, so let us dispense with games if you please. I have already told you twice that I am in love with you, so will not bore you with a repetition. What I wish to hear from you is a statement of how you feel. So far, I have heard nothing but a tangle of half-truths blanketed with confusion."

"How dare you talk to me in this manner!" It was fear that fueled the resurgence of anger, panic that led her to encourage the mare forward.

"No, my dear girl, you will not run from me." His lordship tightened his grip on the bridle. "I will have the truth. Do you—could you—return my affections?"

Anger was a futile emotion, an inappropriate reaction to the reasonable but determined question, and in its absence she had no defense but the truth. "It cannot be."

"Look at me, Meredith, and tell me that you feel nothing for me."

She tried and failed. The color came and went in her face; there was an almost wild desperation in her eyes. "It cannot be," she repeated eventually, whispering the words as if they were dragged from her with screw and rack.

To her astonishment, he smiled, straightened, and released the mare's bridle. "Very well. We will say no more about it. Let us return to the house. You will wish to change your dress, wet as it is, and make peace with Hugo."

"Yes," she murmured, considerably taken aback by this calm, matter-of-fact manner of treating her rejection.

Back in the stableyard, he assisted her in dismounting with a light hand at her waist. "If my presence will be of any assistance in this business with Hugo, I shall gladly accompany you into the house."

"You are too kind, sir." Her lips seemed strangely stiff as she attempted a smile. "But I would not trouble you."

The was laughter in his eyes, skimming across a gravity that he was obviously struggling to maintain. Merrie could not for the life of her understand what he should find amusing. One minute he was demanding an answer to what was surely an important question for him. Then, when he received the wrong answer, he behaved as if the weight of the universe had been removed from his shoulders.

"I will bid you good day, then." Solemnly, he bowed over her hand, remounted, and horse and rider left, the black's hooves clattering on the cobbles of the yard.

In fact, Lord Rutherford was well pleased with his morning's work. He would have preferred Merrie to confide in him, but it was as obvious that she would not as it was that she had struggled to hide her true feelings. He was clearly going to have to take matters into his own hands in a suitably dramatic fashion, confident that, caught off guard, her innate honesty would reveal itself. She had never, after all, attempted to dissemble when confronted with an accurate charge.

He had satisfied himself the previous evening that the contraband still lay in the secret cavern. She had said to the Frenchman that this run was to be delivered to the Eagle and Child in Fowey, so it was reasonable to assume that Landreth would not be made aware of the day, as it was when its inhabitants were to be the recipients. That being the case, he would have to watch and wait.

For two evenings, he kept vigil on the cliff and was rewarded on the third. It was a black, moonless night, obviously carefully chosen. The scene was similar to the one he had watched before, the same silent order and efficiency on the cliff path below as the ponies were loaded. Merrie took the lead again, and he watched them go with his heart in his mouth. It was a six-mile journey into Fowey, six miles of open road, and the coastguard headquarters were in the town. It was a mad, wild risk that she took, but, short of pulling her from the pony and imprisoning her in his arms, there was nothing Rutherford could do to prevent her. Not yet, not until he had established some claim.

While Lord Rutherford hid in the inner cave to await her return, closing his mind to the possibility that she might not return, Meredith, imbued with an even greater recklessness than usual, was playing tricks on the revenue. When Bart and the others were engaged in unloading the goods in the hushed yard behind the inn, she slipped through the dark streets, passed shuttered houses holding their sleeping inhabitants, passed the smithy and the tailor and the apothecary, and up the whitewashed steps to the door of the custom house. Carefully, without so much as a chink of glass on stone, she placed two bottles of the finest madeira against the door. There was a note attached, *With heartfelt gratitude*, written in bold black script. That would have them gnashing their teeth in the morning! Chuckling, she returned as stealthily as she had come. It was an unnecessary risk, and Bart would disapprove mightily if she told him, but it was too good a joke to pass up. Merrie did not stop to wonder why she felt so reckless or to connect it with the nagging emptiness that had plagued her over the last several days.

They rode the now unburdened ponies to the outskirts of Landreth where they went their separate ways. Meredith, freed of her companions and of danger for one more night, felt the usual rush of exultation as she made her way, on foot, back to the cave. They had succeeded in making a large delivery right under the noses of the coastguard. It was too delicious, and she wished, as she sometimes did, that there was someone with whom she could share the exhilaration. But she had chosen the lonely road; there was little point in repining.

Merrie performed her customary task with the broom, sweeping clean the path and outer cave before going into the inner cavern where the welcoming lantern burned as usual. This time, the cave was empty of boxes, crates, and parcels. The ponies were gone to their own stables, and the space seemed suddenly vast, echoing like a cathedral or a deserted theater. Meredith, on sudden impulse, began to dance around the cavern, singing at the top of her voice, secure in the knowledge that there was no one to see or to hear this absurd display of high spirits released from tension.

"I am delighted you found your evening amusing." Rutherford stepped into the cavern from the narrow tunnel at the rear. "I found mine somewhat nerve-racking."

Meredith stopped in mid-step, the color fading from her face as she stared as if she were seeing a ghoul.

Cursing his stupidity for startling her so violently, he moved swiftly, afraid that she would swoon. But even as he reached her, her eyes focused again, the color returned to her cheeks. He should have known she was made of sterner stuff, Rutherford thought ruefully, finding the support he wished to offer unneeded.

"You knew," Merrie said simply, speaking from a sudden calm space that contained only relief and inevitability. If this, the last secret, was known and accepted, then was she freed of all chains. There could be no question of marriage between them, of course, but they could love and the aching void could be filled.

"Yes," he agreed.

"How? It is important that you tell me." In spite of her sense of peace, her voice as she asked this all-important question was low and tense.

"As you know, I saw you, the night I arrived in Landreth, on the cliff path engaged in battle with the coastguard." He smiled. "I knew there was something familiar about Lady Blake but didn't guess the truth until I went out hunting smugglers and saw you again. On that occasion, blessed with hindsight, there was no mistaking the identity of that mysterious young man! But I would not else have seen through your masquerade."

Merrie sighed with relief. "Well, that is all right then."

"It is?" His eyebrows shot up at this matter-of-fact statement. He hadn't known quite what to expect when he confronted her. Shock, denial, embarrassment, anger, fear—a combination of them all. But definitely not this calm acceptance. She was quite unperturbed that he should know of her disreputable activities, her only concern being that she had not given herself away inadvertently.

Merrie's eyes danced as she read his expression. "You are, of course, shocked. But it is a most entertaining business, you understand, and lucrative enough to enable—"

"Yes, I have pieced all that together," he interrupted. "It is also dangerous and against the law."

"Quite so, my lord." She seemed to be brimming over with mischief and elation. "But it would not be nearly so entertaining if it were not."

"What am I to do with you?" He pulled her into his arms with a violence to equal the exclamation. Merrie gasped, lifted her face before his hand caught her chin. Rutherford looked down into the sloe eyes where recklessness and passion shone clear and true. The lithe, muscular body in his arms seemed to vibrate against him. He could feel the warmth of her skin beneath the thin shirt, the press of her breasts

194

against his chest, the taut curve of her hips. In the shirt and britches, her frame was as clearly outlined as if she were naked, yet the covering tantalized and invited.

Taking hold of the knitted cap, he tossed it to the floor. His hands moved to the pins in her hair; her eyes widened but she made no move to stop him as he released the shining mass to tumble down her back in a luxuriant, auburn cascade.

"Even more magnificent than I had thought," Rutherford murmured, burying his fingers in the fragrant mass. "I do not know what you deserve for keeping it hidden in that abominable fashion."

"It is necessary," she whispered through a constricted throat.

He shook his head in denial and reproof before cupping her face. He kissed her as he had done that evening in the gig and Merrie responded in the same way. Alone in the cave, safe from all eyes, hidden from the world's knowledge, reality ceased to exist for either of them. Merrie's hands slid beneath his coat, running over the broad rippling back as her tongue fenced with the muscular presence inside her mouth, a presence that explored the whorls and contours of her mouth, stroked over her teeth, pillaged with a rapacious hunger that created a deep tension in her belly, brought her body hard and urgent against his length.

As she reached against him, he seized her hips, his fingers biting into the firm curves outlined by the britches as he held her in place. Now there was no deception between them, only truth, hard and shining as enamel. Merrie tugged at the fine lawn of his shirt, drawing it free of the constraint of his waistband; her fingers slipped inside. At the feel of his bare skin beneath her touch, a sibilant sigh of satisfaction whispered against his mouth.

Damian raised his head slowly, without moving his body away from her exploration. His eyes were hooded, concentrated pools of passion as he unbuttoned her shirt, opened it, and unfastened the tiny buttons of the camisole beneath. Merrie's breath came fast now, her hands moving under his shirt to his chest, palming the hard points of his nipples as he drew out her breasts, globing them in cupped hands. The flickering glow of the lantern illuminated the ivory damask of her skin, the rosy crowns of her breasts, small and erect with desire. His gaze held a question, one answered by her own gaze, the flick of her tongue across her lips, the arch of her back that thrust her breasts against his palms. His mouth enclosed the hard nipples, tongue lifting and tantalizing so that she moaned, caressing the bent head, savoring the slight rasp of his cheeks, rough with late-night stubble, against her tender flesh.

Damian straightened, slipped his hands beneath her shirt, pushing both shirt and camisole off her shoulders to slide unheeded to the sandy floor. Unconsciously almost, Merrie drew back her shoulders, facing him, proud in her nakedness. He smiled, shrugged out of his coat and shirt, eyes never leaving hers. Not a word had passed between them and the silence continued, but it was the silence of tongues only; eyes and bodies were speaking—shouting, rather—their message. With a long, delicate finger Merrie traced the jagged white scar carved into his shoulder, then, standing on tiptoe, pressed her lips against it.

When she stood back, he knelt to pull off her shoes and stockings, lifting each foot in turn, running his hand over the high arches, the narrow soles. His hands moved to her waist; for an instant, Merrie tensed, drawing in her breath. His fingers paused at the fastening of her britches, stroked over the skin of her midriff, traced the delineation of her ribs until, with a soft exhalation, she relaxed again, renewing her permission. The fastening opened, the garment was pushed slowly over her hips and then stopped as he kissed the softness of her stomach, his tongue flicking in the tight shell of her navel. Merrie knew only the deep coil of tension spiraling within her, the moistness of her soft petaled center that seemed to swell and part in eager preparation. Her hands gripped his bare shoulders with a fierceness that brought a low groan to his lips. Her britches slipped to her ankles, were drawn over her feet, and tossed aside.

Damian sat back on his heels and ran a long, leisurely look up and down the slight figure, the bared skin glowing in the lamplight.

"Oh, but you are so beautiful," he whispered, and Merrie smiled tremulously, thrilled at the sincerity in his voice. He began to touch her, a small frown of concentration between the gray eyes, a slight smile on his lips that broadened as he felt her quiver under his hands. "So passionate," he said softly. "Such a wild, reckless, passionate little smuggler you are, Merrie Trelawney." He kissed her belly again, and she moaned under the intensity of her pleasure as he steadied her with one hand on her bottom, the other sliding between her thighs to touch deeply and intimately.

She had never been touched in that way, never before felt this hot rush of a desire that could not be denied, coursing like molten lava along her veins. Coupling with her husband had been an infrequent and perfunctory business, neither pleasurable nor particularly distasteful. Nothing had prepared her for this breathtaking glory that misted her skin with a fine sheen of sweat and sent waves of heat and icy cold crashing over her like the Atlantic breakers. Urgent words were on her lips, words of passion and appeal as her thighs parted under the questing fingers, and she clung to his shoulders like a drowning man clings to a piece of driftwood.

Damian drew her down to the sandy floor of the cave, spreading his coat and shirt beneath her as she lay, shuddering with her longing, eyes heavy with wonder. He found that his own powerful excitement was in check, allowing him to play on that taut, wire-sprung, lean little body until she vibrated, thrummed, and was lost in the maelstrom of sensation. Somehow, he knew that this was new for her, that she had never before attained the heights of ecstasy, and to take her with his love to that peak became his sole purpose, his own gratification now unimportant.

Merrie was incapable of anything but the responses drawn from her by his hands and mouth, incapable of questioning, of taking any initiative of her own, of controlling what was happening to her, and, as her lover possessed himself of every curve, every millimeter of skin, every entrance to her body, she knew that nothing but response was expected of her. When it seemed that there could be no further peaks to conquer, when she lay spread-eagled and suffused with joy, Damian stripped off his remaining clothes and took her with his body. She was weeping with a pleasure so intense that it was almost pain, reaching new peaks as he stroked within her, paused on the very edge of her body, sheathed himself with exquisite slowness. And then, when she knew she could bear it no longer, he drove deep to her very core, and she lost touch with herself, with the world, knew only the fusion of their selves as his own completion throbbed and filled her.

They lay still fused for many long minutes until reality returned and Merrie became aware of the hard floor of the cave pressing into her shoulder blades, the heaviness of the body crushing her breasts. She moved infinitesimally, but it was enough. Damian, with a tender word of apology, disengaged, rolling sideways to prop himself on one elbow, looking down at her. A long finger wiped the smudge of tears on her cheeks. Smiling, he bent and kissed the tip of her nose. The lamplight flickered, deepening the translucent radiance of her skin, the glow of fulfillment in the sloe eyes. Merrie smiled back, ran a languid caress over his chest shining with the sweat of ecstatic effort.

"I love you, Merrie Trelawney," he said.

She nodded. "And I you."

Damian sighed with satisfaction. "At last we begin to touch truth. You will marry me, my little smuggler, and become a law-abiding citizen forthwith." He regretted the words instantly as the light left her eyes and her mouth set in a determined line.

"It cannot be," she said as she had done once

before.

He gave her the answer he had given before. "Very well. We will say no more about it."

Both relief and puzzlement flickered over her mobile features, but he simply kissed her before standing up and pulling her to her feet. "It is not that I object to making love in a smuggler's cave," he remarked, turning her around to brush the sand from her back where the protection of his shirt and coat had failed. "But if it is to be our fate, I think we must contrive a more comfortable bed in the future."

"That is easily done." The sloe eyes danced again with the familiar mischief. "I will arrange matters quite satisfactorily. No one comes here except on the nights of a run or a delivery, so it will belong just to us. I do not expect Jacques for another three weeks. Until then, we shall set up house in a most pleasing manner."

He loved her and, watching the deft movements as she dressed herself, his loins stirred as desire rose again, but the anger of frustration also rose. He was powerless to stop her madness unless she gave him the right to do so. Instead, she had simply incorporated the fact of their loving into the dangerous, duplicitous framework of her existence. They would conduct their clandestine affair by way of secret passages and hidden caves because Meredith chose not to make it legitimate. He had no choice but to accept her wishes for the moment; it was that or lose her altogether, but Damian, Lord Rutherford, was prepared to play only a waiting game.

"Pray do not look so stern, Damian." Her voice was soft, concerned, as she came over to him, putting her

200

arms around his waist, nuzzling against his chest. "We must accept what we have. To wish for more than is possible can only bring unhappiness."

"Is it not possible to wish for your safety?" he asked, stroking through the auburn hair massed against his chest.

"You must not worry about that." Her tongue ran delicately over the scar on his shoulder. "I have been quite safe for three years, and there is no reason why that should change. The operation is most efficient, you should know."

"I am sure that it is." He could not conceal the dryness of his tone. "I will endeavor to calm my fears, ma'am."

Merrie chuckled. "You have much in common with Nan, Lord Rutherford. She will be waiting up for me. She always does so on these occasions and scolds me unmercifully until I am in bed."

"Then I will leave the scolding to Nan." Cupping her buttocks, he pulled her against him. "You will promise me one thing."

"If I am able." The mischief had left her expression, which was now quiet and grave.

"You will not go off on these insane flights without first telling me."

"They are not insane, Damian, my love. They are the only way I may keep body and soul together."

He shook his head. "It is more than that. You enjoy the danger and the risks."

Meredith thought of the bottles of madeira and the note left on the steps of the custom house. That was something she should perhaps keep to herself. "A little, mayhap. It enlivens an otherwise dull existence."

Damian caught her chin, examining her face carefully. "You have not answered me."

"I will tell you when there is to be a run or a delivery," she agreed. "But perhaps you would be easier if you did not know."

"Your promise," he demanded.

"You have it."

"Then I must be satisfied for the moment." Releasing her, he picked up his britches, pulling them on roughly before shrugging into his shirt. "Do not, however, imagine that the matter rests permanently."

"It cannot be otherwise." Her voice was low but nonetheless determined.

Rutherford simply smiled and tweaked her nose. "There are still things you need to learn, my little smuggler, for all that you think you know all there is to know. Come, I will escort you to your door and, since I do not wish to see you looking fagged tomorrow, you will oblige me by sleeping late in the morning."

That made her laugh. "You, sir, are responsible for the lateness of the hour. It is already morning."

"So it is." He eased her ahead of him into the passage that climbed to the house. "Tomorrow night we shall be a little earlier, I think."

"And a little more comfortable," she whispered, turning to face him in the narrow space as they reached the tunnel's end. "Do not let us spoil this. I have never been so happy, so at peace. Can you not also be content?"

He could not resist the appeal. Meredith had known little enough happiness in her adult life, and it was his intention to increase what she had, not to reduce it. "I am content," he said. "Kiss me goodnight, my love."

She did so, her lips lingering sweetly on his, her hands palming his scalp before she broke away and reached up to the stone slab. It fell back with a muffled thud and Rutherford lifted her through the opening. As he made to hand her the lantern, she shook her head. "No, I have no further need of it, but it will lighten your way. Leave it in the cave."

He kissed his fingertips to her, waiting until the slab fell back into place before returning to the cave. Were he not so afraid for her safety, he would have drawn considerable amusement from this game she insisted they play. It was so utterly absurd that a former colonel in Wellington's army should be aiding and abetting a flagrant lawbreaker, conducting a love affair subterranean in more ways than one, hoisting his mistress through secret trap doors. Lord Rutherford shook his head helplessly as he emerged into the gray dawn of the cliff path. He had come into Cornwell looking for distraction. It were foolish to complain when he found it far greater than his wildest dreams.

Nan, starting up from the day bed where she had been dozing, blinked at her nursling. "Land sakes! What have you been up to?"

Meredith closed the door softly. "Smuggling, Nan." Her eyes twinkled.

"Look at your hair!" Nan stared. "And your clothes! Where are your stockings? And your shirt is not buttoned right."

"Oh, hush," Meredith begged. "If you ask no

questions, love, you will be told no lies."

"If your mother could see you now!" the old woman muttered, but to Merrie's relief she said no more. Nan was too shrewd and knew Meredith far too well to pursue the subject of her disarray. She formed her own opinions, drew her own conclusions as she put Merrie to bed, tucking her in briskly. There was a look in the sloe eyes that gladdened her heart, a look she hadn't seen in years. The girl was happy and Nan was not going to throw any obstacle in the way of that happiness. Blowing out the candle, she left her and went off to seek her own bed.

Merrie lay in bed, her head turned toward the window, watching the gray streaks in the sky turn to roseate dawn. It was going to be a beautiful day. Her heart skipped and, if she hadn't been filled with the most wonderful, satisfied lethargy, she would have left her bed to skip along the shore as the day grew full. She loved and was loved in return; the night's business had gone well and Ducket's Spinney would soon be in her hands again. In another year, she would have paid off the five-thousand-pound loan. Life was good if one learned to take what was offered and not to ask for more. She would be satisfied with what she had for as long as it was vouchsafed her. When Damian had to return to his family and the life to which he was born and bred, she would accept that also, giving thanks for what she had had. It was a glory that few women experienced, after all, and she would make the memories last a lifetime.

Chapter Eleven

"I heard a monstrous amusing story in Fowey this morning." Sir Algernon Barrat beamed around the circle of guests in his wife's drawing room. He was a hospitable soul, always delighted to find his wife entertained by callers, and it was thus that he thought of it. The caller entertained Patience rather than the reverse. There was quite a party of them this afternoon, and he made haste to offer the gentlemen a more spirited alternative to the teapot.

" 'Tis a story to shock the ladies, I dare swear, but a little shock to the delicate sensibilities does not always come amiss." He chuckled, refilling Lord Rutherford's glass with claret. "In fact, I think, for all their protests, the ladies enjoy it. What think ye, Rutherford?"

"Not being a married man, Barrat, I wouldn't dare venture an opinion," his lordship demurred. "My knowledge of the fair sex is far from extensive."

"As befits a soldier, my lord," Lady Blake murmured demurely, her fingers picking nervously at her glove.

"Just so, ma'am," he concurred with a solemn bow.

"Now, do tell us your story, Algernon," Patience broke in. "I am sure we shall not be subject to a fit of the vapors. For all you gentlemen like to think of us as hothouse plants, we are not so delicate." She smiled and nodded complacently around the room.

"Well, 'tis a story of the Gentlemen," her husband announced, reposing his large bulk in a delicate Chippendale chair, twirling the stem of his wine glass between meaty fingers. "Not a subject generally mentioned in front of the ladies, Rutherford," he informed his lordship. "In fact, the least said about them in society the better, but this story is too rich, so we'll break the rules for once."

"Oh, do make haste and reach the point, husband," Lady Barrat said impatiently. "We are like to die of anticipation."

"Very well, m'dear, very well. I had it from Dr. Forrest that the Gentlemen made a delivery to Fowey two nights ago, right under the noses of the revenue *and*—" he paused for dramatic effect "—played such a trick that has the coastguard hopping mad as fire. 'Tis the talk of Fowey that this time whoever leads the Gentlemen has gone too far in his audacity."

"Oh, dear," Meredith said, her teacup chattering in the saucer. "I am so sorry, but talk of those rough men makes me so nervous. Why, Sir John used to say that they had no compunction in dealing with spies and informants, and any knowledge that one had of them was a dangerous thing. Pray do not let us speak of them further."

"Oh, you must not worry, my dear." Patience patted her hand as she adroitly removed the shivering teacup. "There is no need to be nervous about what is said in this room. You are amongst friends. It is not as if any of us would even know a smuggler, so what is said here could hardly reach their ears."

"You are right, of course, dear Lady Barrat," Meredith murmured. "I am just being foolish."

"If Lady Blake's fears are sufficiently quietened, Barrat, we're all eager to hear the cream of the jest," Lord Rutherford prompted, his eyes on Meredith. He was in little doubt that her interruption had been a diversionary tactic designed to prevent his hearing the end of the story. Her head was lowered, but there was a pink tinge to her cheeks that would pass unnoticed by all save himself, who was learning to read her like a book.

"It is said that when the officers arrived at headquarters the next morning, they found two bottles of madeira and a note of thanks up against the door." Sir Algernon roared with laughter, slapping his corduroy-clad thigh. "Is it not rich? Such a nerve to issue the challenge direct. Why, 'tis as good as a glove in the face. They'll be bound to answer it."

"Perhaps not," Meredith said hesitantly in her low voice. "Perhaps, if the madeira were of a particularly fine vintage, they will simply be grateful for it."

The remark was sufficiently asinine to render the group speechless for a moment until Sir Algernon coughed and said, "Just so, just so, dear lady. A nice thought, very nice, but I do not think the world is as pleasant a place as you would have it, my lady."

"It would be a pity to destroy Lady Blake's illusions," Damian said, with a smile at Meredith that came nowhere near his eyes. "Such a refreshingly charitable view of human nature is rare indeed."

"Dear me," Meredith fluttered. "You are too kind, my lord. But it is true that there is so much unpleasantness, we must do all possible to mitigate it." She offered her nervous smile to the room at large.

"On occasion," his lordship observed meaningfully, "a degree of unpleasantness is both necessary and good for the soul."

"Do you think that perhaps the coastguard will succeed in stopping the Gentlemen, Sir Algernon?" Mrs. Ansby asked.

"It's to be hoped not," the squire declared in fervent accents. "I cannot imagine how we'd go on without them. But I dare swear the officers will be a deal more watchful in the future."

Meredith gathered up her recticule and stood, smoothing down the skirts of the dull, brown round gown she wore for afternoon visiting. "Dear Patience, thank you so much for your hospitality. And Sir Algernon." She dropped a small curtsy in his direction. "Your story was most entertaining, sir, and you must not regard my foolishness." A small titter that grated on Rutherford's already raw nerves accompanied the statement. As she curtsied, giving him her hand in farewell, Damian squeezed her fingers hard enough to draw from her a slight grimace of pained protest.

"I must make my farewells, also, Lady Barrat," he said smoothly. "If you will but wait a moment, Lady Blake, I will escort you to your carriage."

Meredith could not refuse his offer without appearing appallingly impolite and so was obliged to stand to one side as he punctiliously made his bows to the ladies, shook his host's hand, and then held the door for Merrie.

The gig stood before the front door in the charge of young Tommy. Lord Rutherford handed her up, saying in tones as soft as silk, "I look forward to our next meeting, Lady Blake. There is much I would say to you."

"Is there, my lord?" The square chin went up. "I cannot imagine what you mean."

"I am certain that, if you allow your powers of imagination full rein, ma'am, you will come up with the answer." He stood back as she flicked the reins and the inelegant equippage moved away down the drive.

"I cannot imagine why, at some point in your lamentably neglected childhood, someone did not trouble to beat some common sense into you!" Lord Rutherford raged, as he had been doing for the best part of ten minutes.

Merrie, who had maintained a prudent and defenseless silence throughout his peroration, continued to sit upon a rock, hands folded in her lap, eyes firmly riveted to the sandy floor of the cave.

"*Why?*" Damian demanded. "Give me one good reason why you should add to what are already intolerable risks by such a piece of self-indulgent foolishness."

"I did not think of it as such at the time," she offered with a hopefully placating smile. "It is done now and there is nothing to be gained by complaint although you are most eloquent." Her lips twitched impishly. "Shall we not have a glass of burgundy—it is quite excellent, I promise you—and a little of the supper that I have been at such pains to prepare?"

Supper was laid out on an upturned box covered with a gaily checkered cloth. A dusty, crusted wine bottle stood open beside a platter of dressed crabs, a basket of new baked bread, a crock of golden butter, and a bowl of cherries.

"The crabs are fresh caught and dressed with my own hands," she said, pouring the rich ruby wine into two glasses. "A toast, my lord?"

He took the glass, reluctant to give up his righteous wrath, yet incapable of maintaining it in the face of that smile. "To what, Merrie Trelawney?"

"Truce?" she suggested. "Love, perhaps?" Her hair hung loose to her shoulders, and she wore one of the simple dimity print gowns that he found infinitely preferable to the stuffy formality of the hideous bombazines, satinets, and merinos that she affected for her public persona. The gown was modestly cut at the neck, had long, tight sleeves buttoning to the wrists, and was caught at the waist with a broad sash. Beneath it, her feet were bare. She presented an image almost virginal in its country simplicity except for those wicked eyes and the grin that tugged at the corners of her mouth. She was quite clearly totally unabashed by the recriminations just now heaped upon her head.

Rutherford sighed in resignation. "In the name of love, then, Merrie, will you not give up this wildness?"

"I cannot," she said quietly. "And it were wildness only if it were unnecessary. But only thus can I achieve my goals. I must have Pendennis back in my hands. I must be free of debt and then do what I can to provide for my brothers. I cannot send them penniless into the world."

"Then marry me," he said fiercely, putting his glass down on the makeshift table, reaching for her hands.

Meredith shook her head. "That is not an answer, Damian. I'll not marry anyone to escape my difficulties."

"That is not what I am suggesting." He took away her glass and put it with his own. "Marry me for love, the love I have for you and that you say you have for me."

"Only in the novels of Mrs. Radclyffe, my dear, does love conquer all." She smiled, trying to soften what she was saying. "What we have is an adventure, and it can never be more than that. Only consider our positions: Keighleys do not marry Trelawneys, but, more than that, they most certainly do not marry smugglers."

"You would not be a smuggler when I married you, and this modesty about your birth is nonsense. I have neither the need nor the inclination to make a brilliant match, and the only disreputable part of you, Merrie Trelawney, is this passion for illegal adventuring."

"I am an adventuress and I shall always be so." Meredith was unsure how true that was, but she knew only that for Rutherford's sake she must convince him of the futility of his arguments. "You have been unhappy, bored—"

"That is enough!" He released her hands abruptly. "You insult me, ma'am. I'll not stand to hear you tell me again that my feelings for you arise solely out of boredom and anger over my interrupted military career." Swinging on his heel, he made for the passage leading to the cliff path.

Meredith looked sadly around the cavern. The little table, the colorful bed of bright cushions stolen from the gazebo, that elegant little supper, all the preparations that she had made with such a light heart informed by passion now seemed just what they were—the pathetic evidence of a little girl playing house in fantasy land. It had been foolish to think Damian would be her playmate without asking for more. He didn't live in the land of make-believe as she did, was not accustomed to playing so many parts that sometimes one was not sure quite which part was the true one. She had seen this love affair as an extension of her theatricals, another play within the play. Only by seeing it in those terms could she distance the reality and, thus, the pain of the knowledge of its inevitable transitory nature.

"Very well, my little adventuress, if that is what you want, then that is what you shall have."

Meredith spun around at the suddenly harsh voice. Damian stood in the tunnel's entrance, hands on hips, and there was little of the lover about the grim set of his jaw, the determination in the gray eyes. "If risks and adventure are necessary for you, then I am happy to supply them."

Her mouth opened and closed rather in the manner of one of Rob's trout. Before she could form any words, let alone articulate them, he had picked her up as if she weighed no more than a kitten, which she knew she did not, and was striding with her into the tunnel.

They had emerged into the soft air of late evening before Merrie found her voice. "Put me down! Are you quite mad?"

"Indubitably," Rutherford replied. "It appears to be an infectious condition." He walked down the path to the beach. "I've a mind to swim," he informed her conversationally. "You will join me."

It was statement rather than question. Meredith, torn between indignation and laughter, found herself on her feet and then, rather rapidly, found herself naked under the stars. She had been undressed with a deft efficiency that bore no resemblance to the lingering unpeeling that had hitherto been his habit. In similar fashion, he removed his own clothing, then drew her into a hard embrace, hands and lips making a fierce statement as he held her immobile against his length.

The night air on her bare skin, the roughness of his hands moving intimately over her body, his growing hardness against her thigh combined to send Meredith into a world of sensation shot through with the sparks of their recklessness. Her toes scrunched into the sand, her nipples rose against the wiry mat of chest hair, her buttocks tightened as he pressed her to him as if she would become an extension of his body. She moaned against his mouth, moved her hand down to cup the twin globes of promise, adapting her limbs to accommodate him, her guiding hand leading him within.

"Put your arms around my neck," he whispered. When she obeyed eagerly, he caught her behind the knees, lifting her off the sand as he joined with her.

Merrie's legs curled around his back. She kissed him, sucking in his lower lip with all the desperate thirst of a lost wanderer in the Sahara. Nothing existed but this moment on the beach when two naked lovers were clearly to be seen by any stroller in search of the balmy night air, any fisherman visiting his lobster pots. It was as wild as anything she had ever done, but this time *she* had not initiated the madness.

"Is this reckless enough for you, my hotheaded little adventuress?" Damian demanded, suddenly loosening his hold so that she slipped down his length until her feet touched sand again. "Come, we are going to swim."

Merrie let out an involuntary wail of protest as he seized her hands and hauled her down the beach. "I do not wish to swim. Why must we stop?"

"If you have not yet learned the pleasures of anticipation, little hothead, I look forward to teaching you," Rutherford announced, striding into the waves, Merrie, perforce, following. "There is much to be gained from prolonging one's pleasures, my love."

When the water reached the top of her thighs, he stopped and drew her close against him, one hand encircling her waist while the other tilted her chin. He was smiling, but something lurked in his eyes that she struggled to read—a combination of desire, hurt, determination. Then her own eyes closed under his kiss, and his hand left her chin to trace the outline of her breasts, rising clear of the water that cooled and stroked her lower body. Gently, he rolled her hardening nipples between thumb and forefinger, increasing the pressure until she moaned and shivered, the throbbing heat of her body in sharp contrast to the cold, lapping sea. Damian bent her backward slightly over his encircling arm as his other hand drifted downward over her belly where his fingers lost themselves in the soft dark triangle at its base. His knee nudged her thighs apart to receive the cold caress of the sea even as his fingers followed the water, probing deeply, insistently until her moans became little sobbing cries of delight. The sea became as much an instrument of her pleasure as his hand, and he used it, drawing her backward into deeper water where she floated against his arm, her body drifting free and open for exploration. When she was mindless, only a sensate being at one with the watery element that held and caressed her indivisible from the man, he carried her to the water's edge and laid her down in the shallow, creaming surf. The sand shifted beneath her under the rhythmic progression and retreat of the little waves as he possessed her with the fierce urgency of his own pent-up passion kept waiting during the long moments of her joy. And that earlier joy was as nothing compared to the wonder that now flooded her, caught between his body and the shifting sand and sea.

Spent, they lay, each enclosing the other, allowing the sea to slap and stroke them, until finally Damian moved his mouth from hers and drew them both upright. Dreamily, as if still entranced, they washed the sand off each other. Meredith shivered suddenly and Damian, torn back to the reality of night air and cold water on overheated bodies, seized her hand.

"You must run, love," he commanded. "You will catch your death of cold!" He began to run along the beach, pulling her along behind him. Merrie stumbled and at first protested this rude interruption of bewitchment, then, as the blood began to flow fast in her veins and the salt sea to dry on her skin, she

215

laughed exultantly, lengthening her stride to keep pace with him, her hair streaming in the breeze.

Only when he was satisfied that they were both dry and relatively warm did Damian stop running. Laughing and touching, they dressed hastily and returned to the lamplit cave where the burgundy awaited its welcome.

"You are as mad for risks as I am myself." Meredith chuckled, rising on her toes to kiss him. "More so, I think."

"Since I must compete with smuggling to provide sufficient excitement for you, I have little choice, it seems."

Meredith stepped back, wincing as if he had struck her. "That, then, was done out of anger?" she asked in a low voice.

Rutherford frowned, pressing a thumb and forefinger against his temples. "Initially," he said slowly. "I was angry, but my anger did not survive beyond the first touch." He regarded her gravely for a moment, then his lips curved in a tiny smile. "It shall be as you wish, Merrie Trelawney—an adventure. I am not fool enough to give up what little I have because it cannot be as much as I would like."

For some reason, the statement gave her little comfort. It was as if he were upbraiding her for a niggardly offering in exchange for his own largesse. Yet Merrie knew she was right. She had too much pride to accept the world he held out for her, the simple, magnanimous solution to all her difficulties. It was not possible for two such different people from such vastly different realms of society to deal together in marriage. Rutherford was not behaving like the son

216

and heir to the Duke of Keighley at present, and there were reasons aplenty for this step out of character. But someone had to prevent a hideous mistake that could ruin both their lives. Both? Meredith laughed mirthlessly to herself. It would ruin Damian's as surely as the sun would rise tomorrow. She, on the other hand, would simply collapse into the lap of luxury, her future and that of the boys secure for the rest of their lives. Rutherford would never go back on his word, however disastrous his error of judgment. And when he discovered that an unconventional Cornishwoman was not the wife he needed or really wanted, then he would face a most disastrous error of judgment. No, clearly Meredith must think for them both.

She found, however, that she had no further need to think. In the following days, the subject of marriage was never again referred to. At night in the cave, they loved gloriously and free of care or conflict. Their days were enlivened by their shared secret, and Damian found his talents for the stage improving by the hour. Merrie was outrageous with her innuendos, spoken in dulcet tones, so that he had often great difficulty maintaining a sober countenance. And while she was not engaged in smuggling, he was unafraid for her safety.

This happy state of affairs, unfortunately, was short-lived.

Chapter Twelve

It was in Fowey that Meredith first made the acquaintance of Lt. Richard Oliver. She had satisfactorily completed her business with lawyer Donne and was in a cheerful mood as she ordered a bolt of gray worsted of the finest quality to be made up into suits for Theo and Rob before they returned to Harrow next month. It was most pleasing to find no need to stint on this expenditure, and she ordered three new shirts apiece in addition.

"Ye'll be bringing the young gentlemen in for fittings, Lady Blake?" Sam Helford, the tailor, bowed her to the door, every bit as pleased as his customer at this substantial piece of business.

"Next week," Meredith agreed, drawing on her gloves. "I'll probably have to tie Rob down in order to do so, though."

Sam chuckled. He'd been doing business with the Trelawneys, like his father before him, since he'd first taken over the shop. His laughter died, however, as he peered out into the street. He spat contemptuously into the dust. "Demmed coastguard! Look at that fine fellow they've brought down from Bodmin."

Meredith looked. An immaculate gentleman in scarlet coat with epaulets, dark-blue britches, and cocked hat stood on the steps of the custom house. "Who is he, Sam?"

"From the regiment in Bodmin." Sam spat again. "Sent to kick this dozy lot in the backside, beggin' your pardon, m'lady. That last delivery and the madeira on the steps finished 'em off. Can't have it said a passle o' smugglers got the revenue on the run!"

"No, indeed not," Meredith agreed thoughtfully. Bart had told her of this new arrival, but she could not reveal her prior knowledge to Sam. "I had not heard of this. When did he arrive?"

"Two days ago," her informant supplied. " 'Tis said he's been creating somethin' dreadful in the custom house. Thinks he'll make soldiers outta them." Sam's sardonic laugh showed what he thought of this hope.

Meredith shrugged with a fair assumption of indifference. "He'll have scant welcome from the folks here abouts, I'll be bound." Then she frowned. Lord Rutherford had appeared around the corner of the street and was riding purposefully towards the custom house and the soldier on the steps.

"Not from foreigners, it seems," Sam grunted, watching as the two men greeted each other. "But what else can you expect of a Londoner? 'Tis time that lord went back where he came from."

Meredith couldn't help her smile. Strangers, or foreigners as they were called, were regarded with deep suspicion by the locals. Not even his connection with Matthew Mallory could win Rutherford acceptance in the villages. And he would certainly not endear himself if he were to be seen on amiable terms with the detested revenue.

Bidding farewell to Sam, she crossed the street toward the two men. It would not be considered strange in her to acknowledge Lord Rutherford. They were known to be acquainted, and he was seen often enough in the company of her brothers for an exchange of greetings to be thought necessary.

"Good morning, Lord Rutherford." She held up her hand, squinting in the bright sunlight reflected off the smooth flat waters of the River Fowey.

"Lady Blake. Your servant, ma'am." Reaching down, he took her hand, exerting special but invisible pressure. Their eyes locked in mischief and memory for the barest instant before he said, "You have not, I think, met Lieutenant Oliver, ma'am. He is but newly arrived from Bodmin to take the revenue forces in hand."

"Indeed," she said coldly. "A pleasure, Lieutenant."

The soldier clicked his heels together and bowed. "Your ladyship, an honor."

"You are come, then, to engage in battle with this audacious smuggler who leaves presents for the coastguard?" Her smile was silky and did nothing to hide the note of derision in her voice.

The lieutenant flushed a dull red. It was a note he had heard in the voice of every one he had so far met in Fowey except for Lord Rutherford. "That particular gentleman will find himself at the end of a rope in

Bodmin jail, ma'am," he said stiffly. "We'll not put up with it any longer. He'll find that under *my* command, the forces of law and order will be something to be reckoned with."

"I commend your confidence, Lieutenant," Meredith said sweetly. "Good day, gentlemen." She dropped a small curtsy before going back across the street to where her mare waited.

"Cornishmen!" the lieutenant muttered viciously. "Two years I've been in Bodmin and I still don't understand them. They don't have a civil word for strangers, and no respect for the law. But I'll have that smuggler despite 'em!"

"I wish you luck, Lieutenant." Rutherford sounded genuinely sympathetic, and the other man's grim expression softened slightly.

"Of course, my lord, being a foreigner in these parts yourself, you know just what I mean."

"On the contrary, I have met with a deal of civility," Damian replied. "But then, I am not bent on halting the supply of contraband." He laughed, nodded farewell, and turned Saracen to follow Merrie, who was proceeding on her mare along the quay in the direction of the Landreth road.

He caught her up easily enough. "May I bear you company, Lady Blake? We are fellow travelers, it would seem."

"By all means, sir." She smiled but looked thoroughly distracted, he decided.

"What think you of our friend, Lieutenant Oliver?" he enquired casually.

"A pompous ass with an overweaning conceit," she condemned roundly.

221

"Do not underestimate him, Merrie," Damian warned softly. "I have gone to some pains to discover a little about him. You may treat him with the contempt of your fellow Cornishmen, but you will do so at your peril."

Meredith was silent, but a deep frown drew arched brows together over the purple eyes. "I'll not underestimate him," she said eventually. "Indeed, I shall enjoy a worthy opponent, I think. Tell me what you know of him." The frown had vanished, and she turned on him eyes that were alight with mischievous curiosity. It was a look that filled her companion with foreboding.

"He is a career soldier of some repute, Merrie. A man who has fought with Wellington before his regiment was withdrawn to serve its country at home. You will find him both intelligent and energetic."

"All the better. The challenge will add spice to the enterprise." She nudged the mare into a trot. With a sigh, Rutherford followed suit.

"You will surely take additional precautions?" he demanded.

"But of course." She smiled a reassurance that quite failed to satisfy him. "We have our own spy amongst their ranks. He has not failed us yet."

"And if he is discovered?"

She shrugged. "That is a bridge we will cross when we reach it, sir."

"Would it not be sensible to lie low for a while?" he asked, trying to sound reasonable and detached, to keep the panicky plea from his voice.

"But think how poor-spirited," Merrie protested. "Besides, everything is arranged." She put the mare to a canter and Damian, after a shocked moment as the words sunk in, thundered after her.

"*What* is arranged?"

"The next run. It is for tomorrow night." She waved an airy hand. "I was going to tell you when next we met."

Forgetting that they were on a public highway, Rutherford leant over, seized the mare's bridle, and pulled her to a halt. "Am I supposed to believe that you would have told me if we had not chanced to have this conversation?" The gray eyes were mere slits.

"Yes, of course. I promised that I would tell you, did I not?" She was a picture of innocence. "I had just thought that it would be easier for you if you did not know until the last minute. You would have less time to worry, you understand."

Flabbergasted at this blithe statement, Damian was struck dumb for a moment. Then he said savagely, "One of these days, Meredith, I am convinced I shall wring your neck if the law has not done the job for me!"

"Oh, do not get on your high ropes," Merrie begged. "It will be quite safe, I assure you. I do not think Lieutenant Oliver will expect anything quite so soon after his arrival. He will think that the smugglers must run from the fire he breathes at least until they have had time to weigh up his mighty powers."

"If you believe that, then you are a fool," Damian said curtly.

"I do believe it, and I am no fool," she retorted. "There seems little point in riding together if we are to quarrel, Lord Rutherford."

"For once we find ourselves in agreement," he

replied furiously, releasing the mare's bridle. "Continue on your way, Lady Blake."

She went ahead for a few paces, then reined in the mare, turning back to him. "I am sorry. You are frightened and I have no right to make light of your fears. It is easier for me because I am active. I understand how difficult it must be for you, having to sit and wait."

"It is the very devil!" he exploded. "If you understand that, why must you do it?"

"You know the answer, love." Smiling, she laid her hand over his. "I am committed to the run tomorrow night. It has been arranged this age and too many people are involved for a change of plan. After tomorrow, I will talk with Bart."

Rutherford sighed. "I suppose I must be satisfied with that."

Could he have been a fly on the wall of the custom house later that day, he would have been far from satisfied, would probably have hauled Meredith from her horse, placed her across his own saddle, and removed her forthwith from both temptation and danger.

Experience with Cornishmen had taught Lieutenant Oliver caution. It had occurred to him that the presence in the custom house of certain local employees who were not members of His Majesty's coastguard was inviting a wider disclosure of his plans than was perhaps wise. As a result, Luke's brother-in-law had gone home for the night before the lieutenant gathered his men together and proceeded to outline his plan. It was a plan beautiful and comprehensive in its simplicity. Instead of making random raids along the coast, they would be on the watch *every* night. They did not know which beach was used, but they did know that it was one along the short stretch of coast between Fowey and Mevagissey. It was reasonable to assume that a signal of some kind would be given from the shore. They would simply post watchers.

The men grumbled, muttered at the waste of time and energy. To be on the alert every night meant less time in the taprooms. The grousing died under the steely stare of their commanding officer. Since the only brush the coastguard had had so far with the smugglers had been on the road near Landreth, they would concentrate their activities there for the first few days, but they would do so discreetly.

Lieutenant Oliver glared at the circle of sullen faces. "Discreetly," he repeated. "Keep out of the taverns and away from the villages. You'll learn nothing by being visible. We catch them when they don't know we're there. We need the advantage of surprise only once." This last was said with such quiet, confident emphasis that a flicker of enthusiasm showed on the hitherto unresponsive faces of his audience. "Just once," he said again, "and the man who makes a mockery of His Majesty's laws will be yours."

A low rumble ran around the room and the lieutenant nodded his satisfaction. "It'll be some time before we can transport him to Bodmin. You'll have him in custody here some days, I shouldn't wonder."

That thought was more than sufficient inducement to give the lieutenant a willing and eager force to hand. "We start tonight," he said briskly, unrolling a detailed map of the immediate area.

That night, there were men deployed at significant positions along the headland between Fowey and Mevagissey, and, if a light had been shown from Devil's Point, it would not have escaped notice. All was quiet, however, as those that they sought went about their legitimate business.

Lord Rutherford, leaving the lovers' nest in the cliff just before midnight, wore a preoccupied frown. Meredith had been as gay and loving as ever, and he had held his tongue on the subjects of marriage and smuggling. He had helped her dismantle their playhouse in preparation for the following night's arrivals, and the grimly serious nature of the business had stood out in stark contrast to the flippant gauze of their play. On parting, she had clung to him just a little longer and tighter than usual, and he had known full well that, for all her appearance of carefree insouciance, she was fully sensible of the dangers. If only she were not so blindly obstinate, he thought with the now familiar sense of helpless frustration.

Saracen whinnied a soft greeting as Rutherford gained the copse where the black had become accustomed to his nightly stable under the trees. Deciding for a change to take the cliff road rather than the fields back to Mallory House, Damian turned his mount toward the dark sea where white-tipped breakers gleamed in the moonlight. It was a magnificent coastline of craggy cliffs rising sheer from foaming surf, long sandy beaches in quiet coves, its treachery hard to believe on a quiet night; yet only the most skilled sailor, well-versed in the ways of these waters, would venture beyond the headland.

A movement on the field side of the path set the hairs aprickle on the nape of his neck. Who else would be abroad at this hour? Unless there were other clandestine lovers returning from the trysting place. A remote possibility! Rutherford realized that foolishly he was unarmed except for his riding whip. Somehow, the presence of footpads in this small, close-knit community had not occurred to him. Saracen tossed his head, the skin of his long sinewy neck rippling. He, too, was alerted to the possibility of danger, the sense of someone close by.

Whoever it was did not show himself, but throughout the ride, Rutherford could almost feel disembodied eyes on his back. His scalp tingled with the knowledge of hidden watchers, and his sense of foreboding increased.

The next morning he rode over to Pendennis.

"You will find Lady Merrie in the library, m'lord," Seecombe said. Rutherford nodded his thanks. He was never sure whether the manservant accepted his visits with equanimity. He was certainly not accorded any especial courtesies, but Seecombe's countenance was a little less forbidding than it had been in earlier days.

"Good morning, sir." Rob appeared at the head of the stairs and threw one sturdy leg over the banisters.

"Don't you dare, Master Rob," Seecombe expostulated. "Those banisters're not made to carry great lumps of boys!"

"Oh, pshaw!" Rob scoffed, sliding with a high-pitched squeal of delight down the shiny rail to come to a sharp halt at the newel post.

His beam faded under a withering look from his

lordship, who said nothing, merely drew off his gloves, laying them and his crop on the hall table before following Seecombe to the library. The chastened Rob decided not to follow and returned upstairs.

"Lord Rutherford, this is a surprise." Meredith looked up from the pile of ledgers on the desk.

"A pleasant one, I trust." He bowed.

Seecombe closed the door and Meredith said, "What's to do, love? I thought you were to leave me free of distractions, today. I do find your presence *most* distracting." It was said with a suggestive smile, a sensual narrowing of the sloe eyes.

"I'll not keep you long," he replied, without responding to the invitation. "I would not have disturbed you except that it may be a matter of some importance."

Meredith frowned at his gravity. "You appear a little annoyed, sir. Have I done something to offend you?"

"It is anxiety, not annoyance," he answered. "Although, in my dealings with you, the two become somewhat enmeshed, I'll confess."

The door opened to admit Seecombe with the sherry decanter. Merrie offered some casual remark about the weather. Damian accepted a glass of sherry and responded punctiliously. Seecombe left once more.

"Has something happened to cause more than your usual anxiety?" Merrie asked directly.

"Not exactly." He told her about his experience the previous night and was relieved that she did not dismiss it as a figment of an overanxious imagination.

"There is an alternative plan for emergencies," she said slowly. "We have never had cause to use it before, but it would seem a wise precaution in this instance. If our friend Oliver is indeed on the watch, then we will give him a little activity of the wrong kind." Her eyes gleamed and the tip of her thumb disappeared between her teeth in that telltale gesture of excitement.

"What do you mean?" Rutherford asked.

"I mean, my love, that there will be no run to the cove this night," she replied cheerfully. "The lieutenant will be disappointed, and I do not think his men will happily cool their heels night after night for very long."

"You will cancel the run?" He looked at her closely.

"Well, not exactly," Merrie said evasively, wishing she could lie to him as easily as she could to everyone else.

"What exactly?" he demanded.

"We will not make the run to the cove as I have just said. While the coastguard look here, the goods will be delivered to another destination, near Polruan, the other side of Fowey. We do not use it as a rule because it is not so convenient for delivery afterward. The lieutenant will not suspect, and we shall provide a little diversion for him here just to maintain his interest in this part of the world." She smiled with kindly reassurance as she stood up. "I am grateful to you for the warning; you may be sure I shall act upon it. But I must ask you to excuse me now. There are people I must talk to if we are to change plans at such short notice."

"There will come a time, Merrie Trelawney, when you will not dismiss me so easily," Damian stated. "Be warned of that." He placed his sherry glass on the table, inclined his head in curt farewell, and left.

Meredith looked unhappily at the sharply closed door. She *had* sounded brusque and dismissive; no doubt his pride was hurt. But it was near impossible to play the sweet, loving kitten when all her thoughts and energies were concentrated on the formation and implementation of a daring plan that would achieve the confusion of the coastguard *and* the safe landing of the contraband. It was yet further indication of the impossibility of a marriage between a Lord Rutherford and a Merrie Trelawney. Perhaps Damian was beginning to see this. He had not brought up the subject in an age. What had he meant by that last warning though? Probably it had meant nothing. Shrugging, she put the question to one side and went to change into her habit. She must ride into the village and speak with Bart. He would pass the message and instruction to the others.

Thus it was that a fishing boat left Landreth harbor at sunset, sailing beyond the headland and treacherous reefs. In the open sea, it hove to, lights at bow and stern. The French boat, sailing without lights, changed course at the sight. When the fishing boat turned toward Polruan, extinguishing its own lights, Jacques sucked in his bottom lip, nodding his comprehension. Something was amiss, but Merrie was not willing to give up the run. The alternate destination involved Jacques in no more danger, but it exposed the Cornishmen to greater risk. They had further to go afterward to reach the safety of home and many extra miles to cover when it came to delivery. However, that was not Jacques's concern. Merrie would have made the decision, and, if her men were prepared to follow their leader, then they presumably knew what they were doing.

Meredith, herself, was not in the fishing boat or one of the party waiting on the beach near Polruan. With three others, she was in the cave beneath Pendennis.

"It is agreed then. Luke, you will signal with the beacon from the beach. It will draw our quarry like moths to a candle. Tod, you will be there with the ponies. When the coastguard come, you will scare the beasts so that they create a great confusion in the dark. The revenue will be expecting ponies and will think they have surprised the men who go with them." She chuckled, her teeth gleaming white in a face blackened with burnt cork. "They will find no one since, in the confusion, you two will have made off up the trail. Joss and I will do our part then. Hares to their hounds. We'll lead them a merry chase, I swear. And while they're busy with us, they'll not be looking toward Polruan."

Her companions were men of few words and signified understanding and agreement by moving toward the entrance of the cave.

Lieutenant Oliver and his men, strung out along the coast road, stamping their feet and picking their teeth in expectation of another wasted vigil, saw the unmistakable flash of a signal—a light showing for an instant, then doused. The signal was repeated often enough for them to pinpoint it, much to the lieutenant's amusement. Cornishmen were fools for all their suspicious hostility. It took nearly an hour before they were all gathered together at the cliff head above the beach from where the beacon had shown. The delay did not concern Lieutenant Oliver. He intended to catch the smugglers redhanded, and it was to be assumed that it would take at least an hour for the signaled boat to make landfall. When he peered over the cliff, the sight that met his eyes would have gladdened the heart of a corpse. Dark shapes milled on the sand, men and ponies. A dinghy, smaller than he had expected but a boat nevertheless, was pulled clear of the surf. It was enough. He fired his flintlock pistol in the air—a dramatic warning for those on the beach, but they had no avenue of escape, and a fearsome signal for his own men who leapt down the path after their commanding officer.

The ponies, already scared by the shot, needed little further encouragement from the prodding thorn twigs wielded by Tod. They milled around snorting and stamping, and, when the horde of men brandishing swords and muskets leapt amongst them, they went wild. Tod and Luke amused themselves for a short while, adding to the confusion by popping up amongst the ponies to offer encouragement to the coastguard, who were no longer sure where the enemy was or if, indeed, they had one. Every time they saw a dark figure, seemingly faceless except for the occasional white flash of teeth or the glint of an eye, their confidence in the enterprise was renewed.

Tod and Luke had left the melée and were safe on the narrow trail when another pistol shot rang out and Merrie's voice rose above the cacophony, adding fuel to the revenue's enthusiasm. "Run for it lads. It's every man for himself!"

Lieutenant Oliver saw a figure on the beach, brandishing a small sword, a smoking firearm in his other hand. Another figure ran for the cliff path. The soldier had no idea what had happened on the beach, but he did know that he wanted something to show for this night's work. If he had been made to look a fool, he wanted the prankster. A few hours in his hands, and the man would be more than happy to give Lieutenant Oliver all the information he needed.

He bellowed a command, and his scattered force disentangled themselves from the ponies and each other. Two figures streaked up the path to the cliff top with their pursuers close behind. At the head of the path, they separated, and the lieutenant paused for a second. He only needed one of them. Should he split his forces or throw all his eggs into one basket? The smaller of the two runaways suddenly turned. A laugh, rich in enjoyment, imbued with a mocking challenge, filled the night air, shivering the soldier to the soles of his feet. He was being laughed at and so, therefore, was His Majesty's army and the forces of law and order. He sprang at the figure, sword in hand.

Merrie was ready for him. She caught his blade with her own, lunged, felt the resistance of flesh against the sword point, heard the rip of material, knew that if she tarried the rest would be upon her, pivoted on the balls of her feet, and ran. The pain in her thigh caught her by surprise. It stung like the smarting of a severe cut. When she put her hand to the spot, her fingers came away warm with a wet stickiness. In the instant of her turn, the wounded lieutenant had struck out wildly in his desperation to make his own mark. Merrie had not felt the sword cut at the moment of impact but a minute later realized what had happened. The stinging became real pain, and the warm, wet stickiness ran down her leg, soaking through her britches. The faster she ran, the faster the wound would bleed. She veered off the road into the fields, clamping her hand to her thigh in a makeshift but ineffectual tourniquet. They were still behind her. How many she did not know; nor did she know if any had gone in pursuit of Joss or if they were all hounds to her single hare. Unwounded, she would have had no difficulty. She knew the terrain like the back of her hand and had planned her route. She could have lost them any time she pleased, but now her path was marked by the bright splodges of her life blood welling up between her fingers. The bullrushes of Withy Brook waved ahead. Only in water could she disguise her trail. Dropping to her belly, she wriggled through the rushes and into the cold, muddy waters where Rob tickled his trout. She could hear her pursuers crackling through the rushes, muttered curses and shouted expletives ringing in the air, but only her head was visible above the water and that just for the seconds necessary for her to draw breath before sinking below again.

When the voices receded somewhat, Merrie surfaced and took stock. The muddy waters around her leg were tinged with red, her thigh felt strangely numb, and there was a faint buzzing in her ears. Half a mile away across the brook, lay Mallory House.

If she crossed the brook, the trail of blood would be broken, and it would perhaps take her pursuers a while to pick it up again. They had not given up, that much was sure. Damian was her only chance unless

234

she chose to bleed to death in Withy Brook. Not an appealing alternative! A certain grim humor came to her aid as she dragged herself across the brook and into the rushes on the far side. There she abandoned the pistol and small sword. They were little good to her now. The sounds of pursuit came from further away. The lieutenant had obviously set his men to beating the fields running beside the brook. If they found no trace, it would not be long before the soldier, if he was as intelligent as Damian maintained, would put two and two together and cross the brook. They would pick up her trail again easily enough there. She had gained perhaps five or ten minutes, minutes to be used to reach Mallory House. How she was to wake Damian was a problem to be faced when she arrived.

Rutherford, however, was far from sleep. For an hour he had lain in Cousin Matthew's poster bed, gazing fixedly at the faded pattern of dragons and other serpentine shapes on the brocade tester overhead. Nothing would induce the blissful, anxiety-free state of unconsciousness. With a muttered oath, he flung himself from bed, struck a flint, and lit the tapers on the carved mantelpiece. For all he knew, that infuriating little wretch was safely abed by now while he paced the chamber a prey to every terror both real and imagined.

A stone flew through the open casement, struck the bedpost with a harmless crack, and fell to the threadbare carpet. Picking it up, he went to the window and peered down at the dark garden below.

"Who goes there?"

"Hush," came Merrie's unmistakable voice. "Please . . ."

Her voice seemed to fade, and his heart began to pound, sweat to form on his palms. "Wait there!" Dragging a robe over his nightshirt, he took the stairs three at a time, hauled on the bolts of the great front door, for once thankful that the Perrys were both blind and deaf to what went on around them. The house could burn down about their ears, and they would sleep through it.

He found Merrie crouched in the shrubs beneath his window. For a moment, he thought she was in a dead faint, then she opened her eyes and whispered, "the coastguard . . . they will be here soon . . . following the blood . . ."

"Dear God!" he muttered fiercely, lifting the soaked, shivering little body into his arms. "Damnation, Meredith! You are half-drowned!"

"I had to swim." She sounded a little stronger. "To break the trail, you understand."

"I understand nothing!" He strode with her into the house, feeling the stickiness of blood beneath his hand.

"What's amiss, Colonel?" Walter appeared at the head of the stairs, tucking his shirt into his britches.

"Check there's no blood leading to the door, Walter, then lock and bolt it. We'll be having visitors soon. They must find the house asleep," Rutherford commanded with clear-cut decision.

The soldier, as always, obeyed his commander's orders without question. The body in the colonel's arms was quite unrecognizable to Walter, and the instructions unfathomable, but clearly his lordship had his reasons.

Damian carried Merrie to his own chamber, kicking the door shut behind him. "How long do we have?" he asked, depositing his bundle on the wooden window seat where water, mud, and blood could be easily removed.

"Five, maybe ten, minutes," she whispered clutching her thigh.

"I can do little for you in that time," Rutherford gritted, pulling a towel from the polished wooden rail beneath the dresser. "Move your hand." He bound the towel tightly around her bloody thigh. "That will help to staunch the blood for the moment. We will deal with it properly anon." He tugged off her boots, dragged three blankets from the bed, and swaddled her shivering frame before putting her on the bed, piling the remaining covers over her. "It's to be hoped the damp of your clothes will not seep through those blankets and soak the mattress. I've no desire to sleep in a wet bed," he remarked as if such a pragmatic consideration were all important in this matter of life and death. That it was a matter of such grave import, neither of them were in any doubt. If Merrie were discovered, there would be no alibi for her condition, and Lord Rutherford would stand convicted of harboring a fugitive from the law.

He blew out the tapers on the mantel and went to the window, listening. The sounds were faint but unmistakably drawing closer. Mallory House was now dark and quiet, however. Walter had returned to his own room, and Damian hastily took off his robe that bore streaks of mud and blood amidst the wet patches where he had held Merrie against him. Bundling up the garment, he tossed it to the back of the wardrobe, commenting with a resigned sigh that it had always

237

been one of his favorite robes and, he assumed, that it was now quite ruined.

Meredith said nothing, but her shivering had ceased, and the tightness of the towel bandage around her wound was strangely comforting as if it held back the pumping blood. Damian's prosaic concerns about damp mattresses and ruined dressing gowns had the effect of returning perspective to the nightmare of the last hour. More than anything, with the need to make decisions removed, she felt safe. There was little reason to do so except that she trusted this man, who had taken command without once faltering in his stride, to pull the irons out of this fire of her stoking.

The voices were now close by. To Meredith they sounded like the baying of hounds. There was a grim excitement about them. "Damian," she whispered as a stab of cold fear shot through her. "I am certain I wounded the lieutenant. I do not know how badly, but I drew blood. They will be all the more determined . . ."

"Doubtless," he returned evenly, shrugging into another dressing gown. "It is to be hoped you stopped short of murder. I've no desire to swing beside you."

"It finishes here," a voice called from the lawn. "He's around here somewhere. He's been bleeding like a stuck pig; 'tis not far he'll get."

"What the devil is going on?" Damian bellowed suddenly through the open window. "Is a man to be granted no peace in his own house?"

"Lord Rutherford?" It was the lieutenant in strong voice, and Meredith heaved a sigh of relief. His wound was clearly not even disabling. "I beg your pardon, my lord, but I need to search your property."

"What?" his lordship exclaimed. "What the deuce are you talking about, man?"

The lieutenant peered up at the window. He could hardly blame Lord Rutherford for his irascibility at being hauled from his bed at this ungodly hour, but the forces of law and order had to be served. "Could I have speech with you, m'lord?"

"I was under the impression you were," said his lordship irritably.

Meredith, to her amazement, heard herself give a choked giggle. An imperative gesture from Rutherford silenced her.

"Would you come down, sir?" the lieutenant requested, struggling to hide his impatience. While he bandied words with Lord Rutherford, the smuggler could be increasing the distance between them, but he had no warrant to search the property and could not do so without permission. If he offended his lordship, it would not be granted, and, by the time they'd woken a justice and obtained the necessary authorization, the fugitive would either have bled to death or holed up somewhere.

"Just a minute," Rutherford said grudgingly. Shutting the casement, he left the room, closing the door carefully behind him.

"You need me, Colonel?" Walter reappeared.

"Not for the moment. I shall when I have rid us of our visitors." Rutherford strode to the door and for the second time that night drew back the bolts.

Lieutenant Oliver saw a sleepy, disheveled man, clearly just dragged from his bed, tying the girdle of a brocade dressing gown. "You've an explanation for this, I hope," Rutherford demanded, peering blearily

239

at the circle of faces behind the lieutenant.

"Smugglers, sir," the soldier said briskly. "We surprised them on the beach, but they eluded us, all but one. He's sorely wounded, my lord, and we have followed his trail to that bush." A hand gestured dramatically to the shrubbery.

"Then it's to be assumed this desperado is hidden beneath it." Rutherford yawned. "Have you looked?"

The lieutenant ground his teeth. "There is no sign of him, my lord, but he could not have been more than five minutes in front of us. Bleeding as he is, he cannot make much speed. I would like your permission to search the grounds."

"Have you a warrant?" Lord Rutherford covered his mouth to hide a second, prodigious yawn. "It is customary in these cases, is it not?"

"Yes, my lord," the lieutenant said unhappily. "But in the circumstances, I was hoping . . ."

"Oh, very well." Rutherford cut him off with a careless gesture. "Go where you wish but have a care for my horse in the stables. He is of nervous disposition and no more fond than I of having his rest disturbed."

Lieutenant Oliver hardly waited to express his gratitude before issuing sharp orders to his men. Rutherford watched through eyes carefully hooded to hide their sharpness. The soldier's tunic was ripped from arm to waist, and he wore his sash, bloodstained and twisted, around his midriff.

"You appear to be wounded, lieutenant."

The soldier shrugged. "Just a graze, sir, but I'll have my revenge for it."

"No doubt, no doubt," his lordship murmured,

turning within doors.

Upstairs, he changed into britches and shirt, remarking to the shrouded figure on the bed that he would later give her some instruction in the use of the small sword since merely pinking one's opponent did little but arouse ire and a desire for vengeance.

"It was a little difficult," she said apologetically. "I could not take them all on single-handed, so could not tarry to employ proper science."

"Excuses," he declared, making for the door. "I've a mind to join the search for this desperate smuggler."

Merrie lay alone, listening to the quiet. The closed casement muffled the sounds from outside, and the house was as silent as the grave. The earlier numbness in her leg had been replaced by a savage, fiery pain. But the pain was welcome; at least she knew she was still alive, still in possession of her leg. In spite of her wet clothes, she was now quite warm, so well wrapped was she beneath the nesting covers. There was nothing to be done but wait until the hue and cry took off again.

"Found anything, yet?" Rutherford inquired of the lieutenant with an expression of polite interest. The soldier's men appeared to be taking the barn apart.

"Only rats," Oliver replied disgustedly. "He's here somewhere, my lord, I can feel it."

"Well, you must leave no stone unturned," said his lordship. "I do not want some wild and desperate creature on my land, but I am convinced that such a large and active force cannot help but prevail against one wounded smuggler." His smile somehow did not allay the lieutenant's suspicions that he was in some way being made mock of. He marched angrily into the barn, bellowing at his men scurrying around amidst the hay bales.

The stables and outhouses yielded nothing. No further spots of blood were to be found, and the orchard and herb garden offered only their produce. "Perhaps he contrived to find a way into the house," Rutherford suggested to the frustrated lieutenant.

"How could he have done so?" Oliver stared at his lordship, who shrugged easily.

"I have no idea, my dear fellow, but, since you remain convinced he is here somewhere and he is not to be found outside, it seems the only alternative."

The soldier chewed his lip, "Through a scullery window, perhaps?"

"Most certainly," concurred his lordship. "I suggest you take your search within doors."

"You are most helpful, my lord." The lieutenant, though, could not reject the unworthy suspicion that there was a catch in this unlooked-for cooperation.

"Far be it from me to impede the law," Rutherford replied smoothly. "Besides, I'll sleep easier knowing there is no desperado, with a cutlass between his teeth, hiding beneath my bed."

Looking at the speaker's powerful frame where the muscles rippled beneath the thin cambric shirt, Lieutenant Oliver could not take this statement seriously. However, at the repeat of the invitation, he called over a group of his men and followed Lord Rutherford into the house.

They were escorted solemnly from room to room on the ground floor; pantries and sculleries were examined, yet none revealed an open window. The lieutenant began to feel rather uncomfortable and ran his fingers around the inexplicably constricting neck of his tunic. The aristocratic owner of Mallory House appeared to be all consideration, opening doors, peering behind curtains, moving screens. There was nothing in his demeanor to indicate anything but a desire to be helpful. When he moved to the stairs, Oliver muttered that perhaps it wasn't necessary to disturb his lordship further.

"Nonsense, dear boy," Rutherford expostulated. "Having come so far, it were foolish not to complete the task." He preceded Oliver and his men up the stairs. "There'll be no need to disturb the servants. We would have heard from them by now, had there been an intruder in their quarters."

"Yes, indeed, my lord," the lieutenant made haste to agree and accorded the succession of bedrooms opened for his scrutiny only the barest glance.

Outside his own door, Lord Rutherford paused, turned the knob, opening the door a crack. "My chamber," he said with a pleasant smile. "By all means feel free to inspect it although I suspect I would have noticed if—"

"Lawks-a-mercy, me lord! Don't let no one come in 'ere!" From behind the door interrupted the shrill accents of a village girl. Rutherford's lips tightened at this indication that Meredith had decided to take a totally unnecessary hand in the business.

The lieutenant coughed, shuffling his feet. His men tried with lamentable lack of success to hide their grins.

"Well, thank you very much, my lord. Sorry to have disturbed you." Oliver turned back to the stairs, glaring at his smirking men.

Lord Rutherford, appearing not a whit discomposed, accompanied them to the front door, offering his condolences on the unsuccessful search and expressing his hopes for a happier outcome on the next occasion.

Upstairs, Merrie struggled free of her wrappings and sat on the edge of the bed. The towel around her thigh was stained red, but the stain appeared not to be spreading. She found her boots beneath the bed and was in the process of dragging them over her sodden stockings when the door opened and Rutherford appeared.

"What in the devil's name do you think you're doing?" He had been torn between amusement and annoyance at her unlooked-for intervention, but all amusement left him now.

"They have gone," said Merrie through teeth clenched against pain and exhaustion. "They will not search further tonight. I can be back at Pendennis in an hour even if I must crawl—"

"Get back on that bed this instant!" He pushed her backward onto the heap of discarded blankets, lifting her legs into a horizontal position once again. "Now, you will listen to me, my girl, because I am going to give you a warning that may not come amiss." As she lay, for the moment silenced by this sudden harshness, he dipped a cloth into the ewer, took her face between his hands, and began to scrub it clean of the streaks of burnt cork.

"When you came here tonight asking for my help, you put the reins in my hands," he went on with clipped determination. "I still hold those reins, and, while I continue to do so, ma'am, you will run as I choose."

The meekness with which she received this uncompromising statement should have gratified his lordship, but instead it furnished him with some alarm. The face revealed under the blacking was milk white, the purple eyes huge and overbright.

There came a knock at the door. At Rutherford's invitation, Walter entered, bearing a jug of hot water, rolls of gauze and linen, and a box containing various salves and ointments.

Meredith swallowed uncomfortably. It was one thing to be lying here in her present disreputable condition under Damian's gaze, quite another to be seen by his batman. She waited for Damian to dismiss him, but she waited in vain.

Walter set his burden on a small table beside the bed and brought over the candles, positioning them to provide the greatest light. Meredith closed her eyes under a wash of embarrassment as she realized what was going to happen. Walter was the one skilled at doctoring, and it was Walter who would tend to her injury. Rutherford untied the makeshift bandage, easing it away from the wound, which still bled, but sluggishly now. Taking the sword rent in her britches with both hands, he ripped the cloth apart, exposing the length of her thigh from hip to knee. Slipping a hand beneath her hip, he turned her slightly on her side so that the cut, running to the back of her leg, was easily accessible.

Meredith thought she would drown in mortification and squeezed her eyelids tightly on the welling tears. Her only comfort lay in the fact that both men ignored her, whether out of delicacy, she knew not. There was certainly no delicacy in the matter-of-fact way that Walter cleansed the wound. Although she knew that he was being as gentle as he could, the hurt scorched her torn flesh.

"She'll do, Colonel," Walter pronounced when the sword cut was finally revealed, cleansed of river mud and dried blood. " 'Tis long, but not deep. A flesh wound only."

Meredith opened her eyes at this, embarrassment forgotten under the rush of relief. There had been moments when she had had to fight panic, feeling the hot blood pumping between her fingers.

"Lost a deal of blood, though," Walter continued calmly as if reading her mind. He smeared something cool over the jagged cut before laying a strip of gauze along its length. "Best keep off it for a few days. Don't want it opening up again." The advice was delivered in the general direction of the wall as if Walter were unsure whether his patient or his master were the appropriate recipient. "Laudanum for the pain," he added casually, deft hands twisting a linen bandage in overlapping strips over the gauze. "Will that be all, Colonel?" He straightened, picking up the basin of red-dyed, scummy water.

"Thank you, Walter." Rutherford nodded his satisfaction. "I'll leave you to deal with that other matter then. Good-night."

" 'Night, sir—ma'am." For the first time, the batman met Meredith's eye.

"Good-night, Walter, and thank you." The smile was feeble, but it was a smile.

The door closed behind Walter. "Let us see what we can do to clean you up." Rutherford pulled off her

246

stockings, unfastened the ripped britches, and carefully eased them down over the neat but thick bandage. "It is to be hoped that you do not fall victim to the ague," he remarked, unbuttoning her shirt. "On some other occasion you shall explain to me exactly why it was necessary to immerse your entire body in the brook." Shirt and camisole joined the britches and socks on the floor. Damian plucked a strand of green weed from between her breasts, his eyebrows raised in a question mark. "I wonder where else you have attracted samples of plant life?"

"You seem to find my predicament monstrous amusing, sir," Meredith stated with an assumption of dignity.

"Well, at least for the moment you are not on your way to Bodmin and the hangman's noose," he retorted with unwonted callousness, Merrie thought. "As it happens, I cannot remember when I have been less amused." A cloth soaked in warm water was drawn over her body, rinsed, and reapplied.

"That is the best I can do for the moment," Rutherford said. "You should really be put in the bath, but it is too late for that tonight."

Merrie thought she should do or say something about going home, but her head was suddenly lost in the fragrant folds of a voluminous linen nightshirt. Her arms were thrust into long sleeves that were expertly rolled back to her wrists, a flat palm beneath her bottom lifted her as the gown was pulled down to her ankles and beyond.

The pile of blankets that had protected the mattress and bedding from her soaked clothing was pulled out from beneath her and Merrie found herself ensconced between the sheets of Matthew Mallory's deathbed, enveloped in one of Rutherford's nightshirts, her throbbing leg stretched out stiffly and her aching head resting mercifully on a plump pillow. She swallowed the laudanum without protest, all too aware of her need for it. When he kissed her good-night, preparing to leave her alone and gently stroking the still damp tendrils of hair from her brow, Merrie whispered her request. Damian smiled, stripped off his clothes, and slipped in beside her. She cuddled against him as the opiate began to take effect. He held the suddenly fragile, little body, her head cradled in the crook of his arm until the first gray streaks of dawn appeared in the sky. They had reached a turning point in their affair, and it was one Damian, Lord Rutherford, was determined to put to good use.

Chapter Thirteen

Bright sunshine filled the room when Merrie next opened her eyes. Everything was unfamiliar from the contours of the mattress beneath her to the throb of her thigh. She lay for a moment, blinking as if to dispel the disorientation. Memory returned in a rush, and with it the forlorn sense that something was lacking. It took but a minute to realize that her body was missing the warmth of the arms that had held her throughout sleep. She was alone in the big bed but not in the room as she realized when she struggled to sit up.

"Nan!" Meredith stared at the familiar figure who had no business in *this* bedchamber.

Nan turned from the armoire where she appeared to be hanging what looked like one of Merrie's gowns, only, of course, it couldn't be. "So, you're awake, are you?" She bustled over to the bed, her lips set in a disapproving line. "You've really gone and done it this time, girl. If his lordship has saved you from the consequences of that piece of folly, then you are luckier than you deserve."

"What do you do here, Nan?" Meredith made no attempt to defend herself, needing what energy she had for enterprises that might hold out hope for success.

"I am here to look after you, of course. Although, to be sure, I don't know why I should take the trouble. I'll fetch you some tea. That nice Sergeant Walter just brought up a tray."

Meredith began to wonder if she were going quite mad. How could she and Nan take up residence in Rutherford's bedchamber, needing tea and food and hot water, without the Perrys knowing about it? And if they knew . . . The opening door interrupted this confusing chain of thought.

"How is she, Nan?" It was Rutherford's voice, light and charming, addressing the elderly woman as if he had known her all his life.

"Take a look for yourself, my lord. She's awake at least," Nan replied with easy familiarity.

Damian came over to the bed, smiling. "Good morning, my little adventuress." He laid a hand on her brow, then looked anxiously at Nan. The skin beneath his fingers was hot.

"Don't you put yourself in a pucker, my lord," Nan reassured. "It's only to be expected. A quiet day in bed and it'll be down by this evening, you mark my words."

"But I cannot stay here in bed all day!" Merrie wailed, pushing the covers away impatiently. "I must go home at once—"

Damian caught her hards in a hard grip, silencing with a stern look the voice that was beginning to rise

250

alarmingly. "I told you last night that I hold the reins," he said evenly. "If you attempt to take the bit between your teeth, Merrie Trelawney, you will answer to me."

Meredith, to her own disgust and Damian's consternation, burst into tears.

"Let her cry it out," Nan advised placidly. "Overwrought she is, and more than a little weak, I'll be bound. But that doesn't mean you're to give in to her, my lord. She's a deal too hot to hand, and who'd know better than me, nursing her from her cradle?"

Damian seriously doubted the wisdom of talking in this fashion in front of the subject, whose head at the moment was clasped to his chest.

"But I do not understand what is happening." Merrie snuffled plaintively. "Why is Nan here and how did she come? Everyone at Pendennis will be wondering where I am, and the Perrys—"

"The Perrys, my love, have not the slightest idea that you are here." Rutherford broke into the catalogue of dismay. "They have no interest in anything that is not directly related to their own well-being. Now, sit up and drink your tea. See, Nan has it here." He coaxed her back against the pillows and held the cup to her lips.

"I am not a baby," Meredith sniffed, taking the cup for herself, "although I could not blame you for thinking it. Neither am I in the way of enacting Cheltenham tragedies."

Damian laughed. "I do not doubt it. You are weak and overwrought as Nan said." Had he been tempted to repeat the third item in Nan's description, a certain glint in Merrie's eye would have warned him to be silent. "Now, Nan is going to help you with your bath, then you may put on your own nightgown, which I am sure you will find more comfortable than the one you wear now." His eyes twinkled. "When you have had some breakfast and are back in bed, there are some things we must talk about, I will then answer all your questions."

The invalid offered no further protests, having the strong conviction that they would be of little use. With as good a grace as she could muster, she submitted to Nan's ministrations. The bath was an awkward process since she must keep the bandaged leg dry, and nothing was helped by Nan's dire mutterings.

It was as plain to Nan as the nose on her face that her nursling was engaged in a degree of intimacy with Lord Rutherford that transgressed all the rules. She did not scruple to say as much, all the while scrubbing, soaping, and rinsing. Meredith, however, was aware that this scandalous aspect of her behavior concerned Nan much less than did last night's narrow escape. Nan was a country woman with feet firmly planted on the ground. Young girls, widowed when they stood on the threshold of life, should not be doomed to chastity for their remaining years. Those same young girls, however, had no right to risk life and limb to satisfy an unnatural urge for adventure. It was one thing to join discreetly with the Gentlemen in the interests of repairing the damage done by her late husband, quite another to court danger as if there were no one in the world to be affected by it. She hadn't given a thought to those boys, of course. What would have happened to them, the brothers of a hanged smuggler?

It was a most downcast and subdued Meredith, neat and clean in a demure white nightgown, hair freshly washed, that Damian found half an hour later. She gave him a speaking look and put out her tongue at Nan's averted back. Rutherford grinned. "Would you mind leaving us for a while, Nan?" he asked politely. "You will find the next-door chamber quite comfortable, I believe. Walter has made some preparations."

"I can do my mending there as easily as here." Placidly, Nan gathered up a sewing box.

Meredith heaved a sigh of relief as the door closed behind her nurse. "It was most unkind in you to leave me alone with Nan, my lord. I have been so scolded and scrubbed that I swear my spirit is scraped as raw as my skin."

"I confess that I had rather hoped to find you sufficiently chastened to hear me out without interruption." Frowning, he touched the tip of her nose with a long forefinger. "It has to stop now, Merrie. You know that, do you not?"

"If the run was successful last night, then there will be a delivery to be made," she objected.

"You are deliberately trying to anger me! You *know* this smuggling must stop—at least until Lieutenant Oliver loses his enthusiasm for a lost cause. You cannot expose your partners to further danger even if you will not take common-sense precautions for yourself." He stood up abruptly. "Do not force me to lose all patience with you, Meredith. I am well aware that you are not stupid, for all that you are reckless and obstinate. Will you now admit the truth?"

253

Merrie sighed, plucking restlessly at the coverlet. "It is so hard to give it up. I am so close, Damian. You cannot understand what torment it will be to have the means within my grasp and be unable to use them. Another six months—a year at the outside— and I shall have redeemed all the mortgages, paid off the last debt." When he said nothing and simply looked at her in weary patience, Merrie finally gave in. The nod of her head was barely perceptible, but it was enough to flood Rutherford with relief.

"I do not know how I shall pass the time, though," she said somewhat pettishly. "I shall die of ennui."

"I have a solution for that," he responded quietly. "Marry me, and I will promise you all the excitement you could wish for."

"Yes, I can imagine," she countered swiftly. "Learning to force myself into the mold of a duchess would be monstrous exciting, I am sure—much enlivened by running the gauntlet of your family. And only think how exciting it will be when you discover that a wayward Cornishwoman is an impossible wife for a Keighley."

"A wayward Cornishwoman is the only wife I want," he said in level tones that belied the hurt frustration in the gray eyes.

Meredith looked at him with a sudden speculative gleam. "I have always wished to visit London," she mused, pushing back the cuticles of her left hand with a frown of concentration. "The boys will return to school at the beginning of September. Time will hang heavy on my hands for three months without Rob and Theo to plague me and with no other diversions."

"What is it that you are suggesting?" Something

about the sudden tension in her body, the mischief lurking behind the innocent-seeming voice, the way she kept her eyes fixed on her fingernails sent ripples of unease down his back.

"Why, sir, only that if you were to offer me a carte blanche until—Christmas, shall we say?—I might well be induced to accept your protection."

He kept his hands off her with the exercise of supreme self-control. She dared to suggest that he set her up in London as his mistress so that she could while away the idle autumn months! She would not be his wife, but she would agree to be his mistress! Then, through his anger a thought glimmered. Maybe he could play it her way and beat her at her own game. She was such a duplicitous little wretch, she should not complain if her own weapons were used against her.

"What say you, my lord?" He thought he could detect just the hint of laughter behind the demure accents. "Or perhaps you already have a mistress in London?"

"No, as it happens, I do not," he said drily. "Your suggestion has some merit, I think." He was amply rewarded when her head shot up and the sloe eyes stared, wide with amazement. "I have but one stipulation."

Meredith moistened her lips, recognizing how adroitly he had turned the tables. Wicked impulse had prompted her suggestion, that and the desire to end all further talk of marriage. Not for one minute had she expected agreement. "What is that, sir?" she bravely asked.

"Simply that you agree to accept without question

255

the arrangements I shall make and the conditions I lay down for conducting this matter. I shall make every effort to ensure your comfort as is customary in these affairs." His accompanying smile carried the worldly wisdom of one well up to snuff in such a business.

Meredith bit her lip. "I would not wish to be a charge upon you, Rutherford."

"Oh, come now," he said dismissively. "It was a carte blanche you suggested, my dear girl. And it is a carte blanche that I will agree to, subject to that single stipulation."

Merrie was out of her depth and had only herself to blame. There had been no need to jump into such deep waters, but then she was always doing so. Accepting a carte blanche meant, by definition, that she accept Rutherford's protection and that included his paying all her expenditures. She would not, though, need to be expensive. Some little house in an unfashionable part of town would be quite appropriate and surely very cheap. She could take Nan, and they could manage perfectly well with one servant girl and a man for the heavy work. Entertainment would not be costly; she would be quite happy with simple things like exploring the town that she had always had an ambition to see. Besides, if she were to fulfill her obligations of the carte blanche, most of her entertainment would be at home. That thought brought a saucy gleam to her eye. Three months with Damian and no distractions. No need to hide from prying eyes, to creep around by secret passages, making love in caves. There had been much pleasure and excitement in their clandestine assignations and the hoodwinking of her neighbors, but it would be wonderful to love openly. No one would know who she was in London, and she could use an assumed name to be doubly certain. Taking her as his mistress would do Damian no social harm, unlike marriage.

She had nothing to lose and everything to gain. Merrie was under no illusions as to what her long-term future held—marriage to some local squire once the smuggling had achieved its purpose and she could again become a law-abiding citizen; or a reclusive widowhood where she must live on her memories. What was there to prevent her taking three months and living them illicitly but to the full? She loved Damian, Lord Rutherford, as she knew she would never love again. Since she could not, for his sake, be his wife, then she would be his mistress for as long as the opportunity was there.

Damian watched her closely during the long moments of cogitation. He could make a fairly accurate guess at the trend of her thoughts and could not help an internal smile at the thought of how she would react to *his* plans. But by then she would be committed to a promise to which he would hold her as ruthlessly as necessary.

"Well, Lady Blake," he prompted. "How do you answer me?"

She raised her eyes and he saw then the roguish gleam. "Why, sir, most gratefully. I will accept both your protection and your stipulation. I can only hope that I prove worthy of such an honor."

"I wonder if we shall manage three months without my committing murder," Damian said in a considered serious tone. "My hand in marriage you reject, yet you doubt your worthiness to accept my protection."

"Ah, but one is a business contract with clear obligations on both sides," she informed him. "The other confers upon you the honor of giving while allowing me only to accept."

"I do not think I shall manage one month, let alone three," Damian observed equably. "But it would perhaps be a fitting irony if it were *I* who swung from the hangman's rope for the untimely demise of a smuggler."

Meredith's peal of laughter was hastily suppressed at the thought of the Perrys, but she rocked with bitten-back giggles as he wrapped her in his arms, sealing their bargain with a kiss that made her regret her wounded leg more than anything had done so far.

When he released her, she reverted to her earlier anxieties. "How am I to remain here all day without everyone at Pendennis sounding the alarm? And how is Nan here? In London I may do as I please, I will be known to no one, but can you begin to imagine what my presence in your house—?"

"Yes, I can," he interrupted. "And I should be glad if you would give me credit for some ingenuity. You are not the only one with a fertile imagination and a certain talent for developing and implementing strategies."

Rebuked, Merrie kept silent, rearranging herself against the pillows and fixing meekly trusting eyes on his face. "Wretch!" His lips quivered. "You are not at all penitent."

"I am trying," she protested. "Only do tell me."

Damian sighed. "It was not difficult for Walter to gain entrance to Pendennis by way of the secret passage or to locate your chamber by the light burning. You had told me that Nan waited up for you." Meredith nodded. "Nan deemed it sensible and necessary to take Seecombe into her, or rather your, confidence." Damian saw the flicker of uncertainty cross her expression and went on calmly. "I gather that Seecombe was not greatly surprised."

"No, perhaps not," Merrie agreed. "But I could wish it had not been necessary."

"Consider who made it necessary." The reminder was gentle but nonetheless uncomfortable. Satisfied that the point had been well taken, Rutherford continued. "Seecombe will have told the boys that you are not feeling at all the thing and wish to keep to your room, undisturbed for today. Nan will attend you."

"But I never take to my bed," Merrie objected. "The boys will never believe it."

"And why not?" he inquired. "They have no reason to doubt Seecombe's word. You will open your chamber door to them tomorrow, and, since you will be obliged to remain abed for several more days, they will accept your unusual indisposition as fact."

Merrie sucked the tip of her thumb, examining the plan from every angle. It was simple but it would certainly work. Rob might be alarmed and puzzled, but he would not attempt to defy the interdiction, and if it were only for today . . . "How do I return to the house?"

"I shall convey you and Nan home once your household, except for Seecombe, is asleep. Seecombe will open the side door."

The plan worked like a charm. Meredith, dressed in her own gown and cloak, was carried by Lord

Rutherford to the ancient barouche that had once belonged to Cousin Matthew. Nan accepted Walter's assistance in taking her place beside Meredith. Damian drove the carriage down the deserted lanes, trying not to think of the possible reaction of his Four Horse Club cronies, could they see him with a dozy cart horse in hand. Seecombe was waiting for them, and the door opened to the crunch of hooves on gravel. Rutherford scooped Merrie off the seat, carried her into the house and up to her chamber, his booted feet making hardly a sound on the oak floors.

"I shall not see you for several days." He laid her on the bed, smiling softly. "It would look most singular were I to visit your sickbed, and you may not leave it until Nan considers it wise." Glancing over his shoulder, he received a short, affirmative nod of the gray head.

"You cannot know to what you condemn me," Meredith murmured in mock horror. "I shall be a wreck after just a few hours' imprisonment at the hands of such a jailer."

"She stands in my stead." He pinched the freckled nose. "Only remember that you will answer to me."

"I tremble at the thought, my lord."

"You could well have cause."

Merrie reached for him, ignoring Nan's presence as she pulled him down with a fierce hunger that expressed both her gratitude for what he had done in the last twenty-four hours and the aching promise of what was to come. Damian, guessing at this turmoil, controlled the passion of his own response even as he held her, thankful that she was now safe, that he had until Christmas, a veritable age in which to rid her of

260

an obstinate pride, to draw from her, once and for all, the acknowledgment of the truth.

"Sleep now, my love," he whispered against her mouth. "You must regain your strength for we have much to look forward to, and you will need your wits about you when you make your plans."

"I have made them already." She swallowed an involuntary yawn, saying wistfully, "I wish we could sleep as we did last night."

"When next we do so, love, you will not be hampered by the exhaustion of the hunted or a wounded thigh." He kissed her in brisk farewell, deciding that the moment for loving murmurs and tender kisses was past. Meredith needed sleep and it were incumbent upon him to make his departure with due speed and stealth.

"You will send for me, Nan, should your patient prove recalcitrant," he teased, hand on the doorknob. Nan's derisory sniff dismissed such a possibility out of hand. He blew Merrie a kiss and closed the door softly behind him.

"There is really nothing to fret about, loves." Merrie looked at the three anxious faces crowding around her bedside. "I shall be up and about again before you know it."

"But you are never ill," Rob said. "When you would not let us visit you, yesterday, I though perhaps you were dying!"

"Well, as you can see, I am not," she reassured him briskly. "Yesterday, I was tired and I wished to sleep. Today, I shall be very happy if you will bear me

261

company."

"Lord Rutherford came to call yesterday afternoon," Theo informed her, helping himself to a plum from the bowl of fruit that the brothers had picked for the invalid. "He was very sorry to hear you were indisposed."

"That was indeed kind of him," Merrie replied. Presumably he had made the visit while she was sleeping. It was a clever although surely unnecessary precaution. No one could have suspected her true whereabouts. Then it occurred to her that he had probably been satisfying himself as to the well-being of the boys in her absence, checking to be sure that Seecombe's story was holding together. That would be very like him.

"Here he is now," Rob said, running to the open window at the sound of hooves on the driveway. "Good morning, sir!" he called down excitedly. "Merrie is really feeling much more the thing today, but she says she cannot get up yet."

Damian, remaining astride Saracen, responded suitably to this information. "Would you tell your sister that I must ride into Fowey, and ask her if she has any commissions she would like me to execute?"

"His lordship wants to know if—"

"Yes, Rob, I heard," Merrie broke into this faithful repetition. "The only business I have in Fowey is with you and Theo and Sam Helford. You must go for your fittings this week, or the suits will not be ready before you return to school. But I do not think I can ask Lord Rutherford to discharge such a business."

"Oh, fustian!" Rob declared and, before she could prevent him, was hanging out of the window again, explaining to Rutherford how Merrie would like him to take himself and Theo to the tailor for their fitting.

"Rob, I said no such thing!" Merrie called, wishing she could get out of bed and to the window without revealing that there was something the matter with her leg. "Lord Rutherford, pray disregard his nonsense. Of course I would not ask such a thing."

Damian was shaking with laughter, imagining correctly Merrie's frustration at this telegraph system. "Do not concern yourself, ma'am. I shall be pleased to take them. Only tell me if there is anything further. Do they perhaps need boots, stockings?"

"No," Merrie choked. "I am most sensible of your kindness, sir, but I cannot possibly allow you to undertake such an errand."

"Now, you are making a great piece of work out of a trivial matter," he called, still laughing. "You must not exacerbate your nerves, you know, if you are already unwell. Rob, tell your brother to get ready. I will wait here for you both. No more than ten minutes, mind."

The boys vanished, exhibiting much more enthusiasm for the excursion in Rutherford's company than they would have with their sister as escort.

"Hugo," Merrie addressed her remaining brother. "Would you send a message to the stables for the boys' horses. I do not wish them to keep his lordship waiting, and they must change their clothes."

Hugo went willingly enough. With a sigh of relief, she swung herself gingerly to the floor, hobbling over to the window seat. Both horse and rider were a magnificent sight, both well-groomed and gleaming in the sunlight, both powerful, muscular creatures who seemed to communicate with each other in their stillness. "My lord?"

He looked up instantly, his eyes warming at the sight of her face framed in the loose auburn mass, looking so much younger and more vulnerable than usual. "What do you do out of bed?" he demanded with feigned severity.

"It is quite all right. There is no one here," she assured him. "You cannot wish to do this."

He shook his head in exasperation. "I have said that I am more than happy with the arrangement."

"But Rob is always quite impossible and fidgets so," Merrie insisted. "It is such a long and tedious business."

"He'll not fidget with me." Damian chuckled and lowered his voice. "Be a good girl and get back into bed. I find the sight of you so far out of my reach most tantalizing."

That made her laugh. She blew him a kiss before maneuvering herself back between the sheets.

The next week Merrie found most tedious. She was obliged to keep to her bed until she could walk almost freely but even then found her movements severely restricted and was reduced to lying on a sofa in the parlor, playing cat's cradle or solitaire when one or other of her brothers was not available to entertain her. One unlooked-for but most satisfying consequence of her forced inactivity was that Hugo took over all aspects of estate business that required her presence outside the house.

"He shows some considerable talent when it comes to dealing with the tenants," Meredith remarked to Lord Rutherford one afternoon, moving her knight to fork his bishop and rook.

"Then you should perhaps ensure that he has the opportunity to exercise it on a regular basis." Resigned to losing the bishop, Rutherford retreated his rook. "You play a devilish game of chess, Merrie. As good as your play with the cards."

"My late husband expected to be well partnered," she informed him, serenely removing his bishop from the board. "You think, then, that I should employ Hugo on the estate during the holidays?"

"Most certainly. The lad needs to feel useful. You are so damnably competent, he has little opportunity to prove himself."

"If he proves himself, then mayhap he will not feel the need for self-sacrifice." Meredith sat back, shifting her leg on the footstool and frowned. "I begin to rely on your wisdom, Damian. I am sure I do not know how I shall go on when you are no longer here to offer it."

Damian looked at her sharply but could read no hidden meaning in either voice or expression. She behaved as if the impossibility of their marriage was now an agreed and accepted fact between them. It was fortunate he was prepared for the inevitable fireworks when she realized her mistake.

"How will you explain your absence for three months? Have you given the matter any thought?"

"But of course." She smiled. "Check, my lord."

He examined his options on the board with a rueful grimace. "And mate in two. There seems little I can do to avoid it." A long, elegant finger toppled the black king and he held out his hand. "So, how will you explain it?"

She left her hand in his for a moment. These casually acceptable contacts were all they had these days, Merrie not being in a fit condition to scramble through secret passages. "I have received a letter from a distant cousin in Kensington inviting me to go to her for a visit. Maybe she will find me a respectable husband."

Damian shuddered. "Kensington! Must it be Kensington?"

"But is that area not perfectly respectable?" Her eyebrows lifted in surprise.

"Genteel," he pronounced with a disdainful curl of the lip.

"I have no greater pretensions, sir!" Her eyes flashed.

"I do beg your pardon." Rutherford made haste to apologize. "If it must be Kensington, then so be it."

She looked at him suspiciously. There appeared nothing in the bland expression to justify suspicion. "I will need to furnish the boys with an address so that they may write to me. And Farquarson, also."

Damian frowned. Somehow he had overlooked that complication. "I leave for London in two days. I will make the necessary arrangements and send you the requisite information before you leave. You will travel by hired post chaise until Okehampton where my own chaise and postilions will meet you. At that point, my love, our contract becomes binding." His eyes held hers. A shiver, part apprehension, part anticipation, ran down Merrie's spine, seeming to stroke each vertebra to sensitivity.

"I will be ready to leave by the third week of September," she said slowly. "It will take little more than a day to reach Okehampton."

"My people will be waiting for you."

"And you?"

"In London," he promised. "Straining at the leash."

"It will be an adventure of another kind." Merrie smiled. "I am most eager also."

"You will not be disappointed," he vowed. Surprised and furious most probably; disappointed, never!

Chapter Fourteen

"How could you imagine that I would not help you, Damian?" The Marchioness of Beaumont clasped her hands dramatically and gazed at her brother, making the most of a particularly fine pair of deep-gray eyes.

"I did not imagine any such thing, Bella," Rutherford demurred, regarding his twin with some amusement. "There is no need for you to look at me in that fashion, m'dear. I am not one of your *cicisbeos* to be charmed into performing some tiresome favor, nor am I poor George to be teased for some indulgence."

"George is never here to tease," Arabella said with a pout. "Most of the time, I think he is quite oblivious to the fact that he has a wife."

"Now there you are quite out." Rutherford rose from the scroll-ended couch and went over to one of the tall windows giving on to Cavendish Square. "Beaumont is well aware of his wife. But he is more interested in politics than in society. Many a wife faces worse competition."

"You are so unsympathetic," Bella grumbled. "You have not a drop of romance in your soul. I am to be glad my husband spends his days giving speeches in the Lords and his nights writing those speeches rather than setting up mistresses and gambling away his fortune—"

"Exactly so," her brother concurred, turning back from the window. "Pragmatic and unromantic it may be, Bella, but it is the plain truth, nevertheless."

Arabella was silent for a moment, plaiting the fringe of her silk shawl. "Well, I cannot think, Rutherford, that your sole intention in calling upon me was to give me one of your odious lectures," she said eventually. "Did you not mention something about a favor?"

Smiling, he crossed the Axminster carpet to take her hands. "Yes, indeed I did. And I did not mean to lecture you. As it happens, the favor I am going to ask may well benefit you, also. You are in sore need of occupation, I think, Bella."

"Occupation! Whatever can you mean? Why I dare swear I have not a moment to myself. If it is not a ridotto or a card party or an excursion to the Botanical Gardens or a balloon ascension, then there is—"

"Just so, Bella," Rutherford interrupted. "And you are as bored of the round as I am myself."

Under the relentless gaze, Bella shook her head in candid resignation. "Yes, you are right. But I cannot disappear to Cornwall in search of diversions." She cast a shrewd look at her twin's countenance. "Unless I much mistake, brother, you have found some diversion in the wilderness."

"It is that obvious?"

"According to Mama, you are a changed man. Or, at least," Bella qualified, "you are changed back to what you were before your wound."

Rutherford nodded, a little smile playing over his lips. "The answer, I was told, is to find a purpose, a reason for existing. It is something at which my informant is amazingly adept. I learned the lesson well."

"This—uh—person," Bella inquired, moving to the fireplace to pull the tasseled bell cord, "is a lady?"

"Sometimes," her brother replied. "When it suits her."

The appearance of a footman to draw the blue and crimson curtains and light the lamps against the gathering dusk put a period to the conversation. Lady Beaumont waited impatiently, intrigued by her brother's wordplay. He had, indeed, returned from Cornwall a different man as the Duchess of Keighley had pronounced with such satisfaction. He had still as little enthusiasm for the Season's squeezes as ever but considerably greater patience than previously. His old friends, who had stood by him when irascible and depressed, now welcomed with relief the return of one who was again willing to participate in the Corinthian pursuits even if he avoided social events. Cribb's parlor knew him again; White's and Watier's and the Four Horse also welcomed the prodigal who smiled and joked with the ease of earlier days and proved that he had lost none of his former skills.

The footman left at last and Lady Beaumont was able to give vent to her curiosity. "Whatever can you mean, Damian? A lady when it suits her."

"Exactly that, my dear." Rutherford poured himself a glass of claret from the decanter on the satinwood sofa table. "Merrie Trelawney, Lady Blake, Lady Merrie is a woman of many parts." He grinned at his sister's bemused expression. "Most of the time she is not at all respectable even when she pretends to be."

"Damian, whatever will Mama say?" Bella breathed, needing no further statement from her twin to underline the look in his eye. Rutherford was clearly head over heels in love. "And to think I said you had not a drop of romance in your soul." She sank down upon one of the gilt-and-crimson couches, arranging herself artistically. "Perhaps you will pour me a glass of sherry. I suspect I may have need of some fortification."

Her brother obliged. "To answer your question, Bella, Mama will know only what I decide is fit for her ears. You, on the other hand, will know everything since I must enlist your aid. You will, however, not breathe a word of what passes between us—not even to George, you understand?" The laughter had died out of his eyes and he looked both stern and forbidding.

"Have I ever betrayed you?" she exclaimed indignantly. "Not even when you threw me into the fish pond."

He laughed and sat opposite her in a deep chair with earpieces, crossing one top-booted leg over the other. "Then listen to my tale, sister, and my plan and tell me if I may count upon you."

271

Arabella listened intently, only her wide eyes betraying her amazement. Rutherford had decided that he must take his sister absolutely into his confidence if his plan was to work. Merrie must have neither the need nor the opportunity to concoct some play when she was with Arabella.

"It is quite scandalous," Lady Beaumont pronounced in remarkably matter-of-fact accents. "A carte blanche, you say? And *she* suggested it."

"As an alternative to marriage," he concurred calmly. "My Merrie is a most obstinate creature."

Arabella's eyes began to dance. "But you do not accept her objections?"

"Absolutely not. Will you help me?"

"Of course." His sister put down her sherry glass, rising gracefully. "It will be monstrous amusing, and, if it will make you happy—"

"It will," he corroborated quietly. "Unimaginably happy."

"Is she a beauty?" Bella asked curiously.

Damian frowned, considering this. "No," he said slowly. "Not a beauty, but with the right wardrobe and some time spent with your hairdresser she will cause quite a stir, I fancy."

"And if she is not willing?"

He laughed. "She will not be, make no mistake, Bella. But we have an agreement which she will honor, and I think that, once Merrie has accepted the necessity, she will take much pleasure in the adventure."

"And—uh—" Belle hesitated, then took the plunge. "The carte blanche. Will it be a part of this

272

arrangement?"

"But of course," he replied levelly. "If it were not, then Meredith would consider there to be no contract. She is also quite unable to fund herself in such an enterprise, so I must oblige her to accept my purse."

Arabella paced the long saloon, the embroidered flounce of her gown of jaconet muslin swinging against yellow kid Roman boots. "You know, brother, if Lady Blake is as proud and independent as you maintain, I foresee some obstacles to this plan. I am delighted to attempt it, but, if she should really dislike it and be unhappy—"

"You may safely leave that to me, Bella. I will not permit Merrie's unhappiness. Just play your part. That is all I ask."

"Most willingly, Damian. I can hardly wait to meet her."

Meredith stood in the cobbled yard of the Bell at Okehampton surveying the well-sprung coach bearing Lord Rutherford's arms emblazoned on the panels. It had been here when she had arrived the preceding evening exactly in accordance with Damian's promise.

Now, it was early on the morning of September twenty-fifth, and she had spent a restless night in one of the Bell's best bedchambers. The departure from Landreth had gone so smoothly that she had been deprived of any anxieties to take her mind off the unknown into which she was so blithely leaping. Her neighbors had congratulated her on her good fortune. Hardly a malicious remark had come her way although Patience in particular had been full of good advice and many warnings as to the perils in London waiting to trap the innocent and unwary. Patience, who had once spent three days in the capital when she was eighteen, considered herself something of an expert. Meredith had received advice, good wishes, and warnings with her customary humble gratitude. Stuart Farquarson had exhibited no concern about being required to act for her in all matters concerning the estate, lawyer Donne had sufficient funds for all emergencies, and Seecombe was perfectly happy to hold the reins of the household in his more-than-capable hands.

Nan, of course, accompanied Meredith, as did a trunk containing several new gowns and a riding habit that Nan, an expert seamstress, had produced with some satisfaction. Merrie, herself, was well pleased with the results. They were not of the first style of elegance, certainly, but for genteel Kensington would be surely more than appropriate.

That thought drew her eyebrows together in a perplexed frown. Damian had sent her a poste restante address for her mail, but he had not furnished her with her exact destination. It seemed a strange oversight, but presumably the address was known to the coachman, postilions, and outriders, who were gathering around the coach in preparation for an imminent departure.

Remembering that she had not yet paid her reckoning, Merrie turned back to the inn in search of the landlord. With many bows and smiles, he informed her that the coachman had taken care of everything.

That was the way it would be from now on, of course. Damian had said that once she met up with his people at Okehampton their contract would become binding. What was she getting herself into? It was one thing to have Lord Rutherford as a lover on her own territory, quite another to go into his world where she had already agreed to relinquish all control. Oh, it was ridiculous to feel this panicky fluttering of apprehension! If she could trust anyone, she could trust Rutherford. He had saved her life, had taught her the inexpressible delight of bodies joined in love; for the moment, he loved her. And for the last three weeks, she had been lonelier than ever before.

With renewed determination, Meredith walked to the coach where a postilion handed her into the luxurious, leather-squabbèd interior. Nan settled herself on the seat opposite, expressing her satisfaction in this improved mode of travel with pursed lips and a short nod. She was grimly resigned to this mad excursion into foreign parts where she was convinced evil awaited around every corner. Merrie's tentative suggestion that she might prefer to remain in Cornwall had resulted in a tirade worse than any Merrie had experienced since she was discovered on the back of her father's hunter at the age of ten. So now, the lesson well learned, Meredith began to chat cheerfully as the coach passed through increasingly unfamiliar territory.

They crossed Dartmoor that day, passed through Exeter, and spent the night at Honiton. From then on, as they left Devon and came into Somerset, everything familiar vanished. Merrie was conscious first of the absence of the sea. She had lived all her life on the narrow peninsula that was Cornwall, where nowhere was far from the water. Now, she found herself fighting an uneasy, bereft feeling as she saw all around her only pretty country villages, peaceful lanes, orchards, neat enclosed fields, and thatched-roof cottages. It seemed tame beside the wild magnificence of her native land, and the people, rosy-cheeked and smiling, seemed overly friendly and ingratiating. Cornishmen only gave their smiles and friendship where they considered it deserved and Merrie could not help suspecting hypocrisy in this easy warmth and acceptance.

By the fifth day, however, she had become accustomed to it just as she had become accustomed to the civil attention accorded the passengers in Lord Rutherford's coach. There was always a private parlor, always the best bedchamber, and dinner was uniformly excellent. These things appeared miraculously without her once having to give an order just as the teams harnessed to the coach at the frequent changing posts appeared miraculously and were always prime animals.

They reached the outskirts of London by early afternoon of the seventh day. By this time, Merrie was heartily sick of the carriage, and, judging by her companion's steadfast silence, Nan also would be glad to be rid of enforced idleness. It was dusk when they reached the city itself. Merrie's heart beat faster at the thought of what awaited her. Surely Damian would be there to welcome her in whatever accommodation he had hired. Would it be a house? Or perhaps, since it was just Nan and herself, he would consider two or three rooms to be sufficient with a landlady to take care of the cooking and housekeeping.

They were passing through wide, elegant streets lined with tall, gracious houses, their long windows already lamplit. Once or twice, Merrie glimpsed an open front door as some supremely elegant creature passed through, bowed inside by liveried footmen. Light town carriages, preceded by link boys carrying torches, frequently passed the heavier vehicle conveying Merrie and Nan. They turned into a quiet square formed by large, imposing houses. A pretty, iron-railed garden stood in the center. The carriage drew up before the sweep of white-honed steps leading to an enormous oak door, yellow light showing through the fanlight above. The door opened on the instant before the postilion, hand raised to grasp the gleaming brass knocker, could reach the top step. A large, black-suited figure stood outlined in the doorway, then another in blue livery came down the steps, opened the carriage door, and pulled down the footstep.

"Lady Blake," he said in neutral tones, extending a hand to assist her to alight. Meredith felt as if the breath had been knocked from her body, but she retained sufficient presence of mind to accept the proffered hand with a gracious smile. Nan followed suit although she cast the footman a darkling look which he blandly ignored.

Meredith's thoughts were racing as she did what was clearly expected of her and mounted the steps. Was this Rutherford's house? Surely he would not have her staying under his roof? The conventions of a carte blanche were something of a mystery, but such an arrangement had to be unthinkable. Perhaps this was to be a temporary halt from where he would accompany her to her final destination.

"Welcome, your ladyship." The black-clad figure bowed low. He was dressed with such elegance that Meredith became unpleasantly conscious of her travel-stained condition, her dress that bore all the hallmarks of country tailoring and style.

"My dear Lady Blake, you are most welcome." A warm voice, a rustle of skirts, a lingering fragrance was all she was aware of at first, then her gloved hands were taken in a firmly friendly clasp, and she found herself looking at a vision in turquoise crape lavishly trimmed with lace. Particularly fine diamonds hung from the vision's ears and enclosed a creamy throat. Dark hair, cut stylishly short, shone under the lamplight, and Rutherford's large gray eyes smiled with genuine pleasure. This, however, did nothing for Merrie's confidence. That the woman was the spitting image of Damian was her first thought, that she must appear hopelessly shabby her second and, shamefully, more important.

"You must be dreadfully tired," the woman said quickly, taking her arm as she still stood searching for words. "Come into the drawing room. Grantly will have your maid taken to your apartments where she will be quite comfortable."

Meredith found herself eased willy-nilly into a most noble apartment hung with a delicate blue paper, furnished in blue and crimson. The door closed and her mysterious hostess clasped her hands again, saying compassionately, "You poor thing. You have no idea what is happening. The servants, you must understand, do not know that you were not expecting to come here. That is why I brought you into the saloon so quickly."

"Who are you?" Merrie found her voice in the blunt question, not caring if it sounded rude.

"Arabella, Damian's twin sister." Bella's eyes twinkled. "We are much alike, I think."

"Yes," Merrie agreed. "Very much. Where is your brother?"

"First you must take off your pelisse and hat and have some refreshment. I will explain everything when you are comfortable."

"I beg your pardon, ma'am," Merrie said quietly. "But I think you are evading my question."

Bella gave her a rueful smile. "You are just as Damian said you would be."

"And how was that?"

"Cross and determined."

Meredith's jaw dropped, then she burst into a peal of laughter. It was all too absurd; besides, she could not help feeling drawn to this woman who was extending such a genuine welcome. Her quarrel was with Rutherford, not with his sister. "I do beg your pardon," she said again. "If I may, I *will* take off my things. I begin to feel that they are growing on me, so long have I worn them."

"Yes, indeed you must." Bella pulled the bell rope. When the footman appeared immediately, he took Meredith's outdoor garments, acknowledging with a low bow the request to bring tea.

"I take it your brother is not here?" Meredith raised her eyebrows. "When do you expect him?"

"He will come tomorrow morning," Bella replied hesitantly. It occurred to her that she would not wish to face her guest's wrath. For all her travel-stained appearance and outmoded gown, there was an air of authority and confidence about Meredith Blake that crossed their six-year-age difference. "He has left you a letter," she went on, going swiftly to a secretaire with a cylinder front.

Meredith took the paper with a smile of thanks and walked over to the window, turning her back on her hostess before breaking the heavy seal and unfolding the sheet. She read: Welcome to your new adventure, my love. You may ring a peal over my head tomorrow, but for tonight oblige me by accepting Bella's hospitality with a good grace. She is most anxious to make your acquaintance and knows all there is to know, so you will have no need to play one of your parts with her. She will explain to you the part you will play for the rest of the world unless you prefer to hear it from me. Sleep well, little one. Until tomorrow.

A scrawled signature completed this bewildering missive that, except for the salutations, smacked more of a series of orders than a love letter. Meredith folded it carefully, turning back to Rutherford's sister, who was looking at her anxiously.

"I cannot help feeling it most cowardly of your brother to leave the full burden of my reception at your door," Merrie said. "But I am enjoined to accept your hospitality with good grace and, indeed, it would be discourteous in me to do otherwise."

"You are very angry, are you not?" Bella observed, pouring tea into a delicate, fluted cup, which she handed to her guest.

"With your brother? Furious," Meredith concurred, accepting the tea gratefully. "Will you tell me what plans he has for me? I understand that you are completely in his confidence."

"We have always been close," Bella said apologetically. "I hope you do not mind that I know your story."

"It would profit me little if I did," Merrie responded with a shrug. "Will you not enlighten me?"

She listened incredulously. The background concocted for her was as near to her own as possible except for one or two major differences. She was still Lady Blake, widow of Sir John Blake. But some vague connections had been established between Matthew, Lord Mallory, and the Blakes. Lord Rutherford, on discovering this distant connection, had offered the aegis of his family to the *rich* young widow in her introduction to London society. Merrie learned that the Duchess of Keighley was delighted that her son had shown such consideration and was looking forward to extending her own welcome. The duke had no opinion on the matter, but that was not unusual.

"I see," Meredith said thoughtfully at the end of the exposition. "And where, pray, has Lord Rutherford determined that I should lodge for the duration of this deception?"

Arabella stared. "Oh, but I thought you understood. Here. You will live here with me, and I shall sponsor you."

"That is outrageous!" Meredith sprang to her feet, heedless of the effect her explosion had upon her hostess. "How *dare* he!"

"Oh, please." Bella also rose in great distress. "If it is so repugnant to you, then of course you must not. Only I had hoped that we would deal extremely. I was so looking forward to having your company, and everything will be so much more pleasant if we do it together. I have become so wearied of the Season, and George is always in Parliament, and now that Georgy had gone to Eton I am quite alone."

Meredith watched in horror as two large tears rolled down Lady Beaumont's damask cheeks. "Oh, dear, Lady Beaumont I did not mean to be unkind."

"Oh, you must call me Bella." A winsome smile trembled on the rosebud mouth, but the tears still gleamed. "And I may call you Merrie, may I not? You will stay? Say you will."

This affair, Meredith decided, was considerably more complex than she had immediately perceived. It was clear that she would not be the only benefactor of Damian's plans; it was also clear that that explained his absence this evening. His sister's appeal would carry greater weight than anything he might say at this point.

"I can decide nothing until I have seen Rutherford," she said gently. "But of course I would not find staying with you repugnant. Your husband might look a little askance, though."

"Oh, not George." Arabella's tears dried miraculously. "If he notices you at all, it will be in the vaguest way. But he will be perfectly happy, you may rest assured."

Meredith smiled an acknowledgment, no other suitable response occurring to her.

"You must be greatly fatigued." Arabella was suddenly the charming hostess again, in complete command of the situation. "Let me show you to your apartments and I will have a tray sent up. I am sure you will be glad of something."

Meredith owned that she would welcome a little supper, having partaken of dinner near Staines, at around five o'clock, with an appetite reduced by excitement. Accordingly, she followed her hostess upstairs where she was shown into a boudoir of rose and cream. A Wilton carpet of deep rose pink cushioned the floor, cream curtains draped the windows, silken tassels attached to their thick cords. A pretty Sheraton secretaire of rich rosewood stood against the wall, a leather blotter, inkstand, and set of quills lying ready to invite the eager correspondent. A chaise lounge of cream satin stood beneath the windows, and several dainty Sheraton chairs on delicately carved legs were scattered over the carpet.

"How very pretty," Meredith said appreciatively.

"I am so glad you like it." Bella moved to a door in the far wall. "Your bedchamber is here."

The bedchamber was in every respect as tasteful and welcoming as the boudoir. In addition to the poster bed with rich, rose silk hangings, it also contained Nan, who was supervising a girl unpacking Meredith's trunk.

Merrie opened her mouth to tell Nan to cease the unpacking since it was unlikely they would be here above one night, then she closed it again. It would not be appropriate to express doubts in front of Bella's servant, however freely she might do so with Nan.

"Charming," she said instead to her hostess. "I am most sensible of your kindness, Lady Beaumont."

"I had thought we had agreed to dispense with formality," Bella smiled, turning back to the boudoir.

"If that is what you wish, Bella." Merrie returned the smile warmly. "You will understand if I bid you good-night now. It has been a tiring seven days, and I have had some shocks this evening."

"Yes, of course." Bella made haste to assure Merrie of her understanding. "And I expect you will wish to be at your best in the morning when you confront Damian." Her eyes danced, and the smile she directed at Meredith was most definitely conspiratorial. "I own I would like to see my brother meet his match."

"After this night's work, Bella, I begin to doubt he will meet it in me." Merrie shook her head in a degree of disbelief. "Seldom have I been so outplayed. However, I shall come about, make no mistake."

Much later, lying in the unfamiliar, yet most comfortable bed, in her unfamiliar, but ineffably luxurious surroundings, Meredith admitted to herself some doubts as to that confident statement. Rutherford would have more than one trick up his sleeve, of that she had no doubt. He would not have brought her this far without the certainty that he could override all the objections he must have known she would make.

Nan had not offered any support either. She had decided that Cavendish Square would suit her very well, having been given a most comfortable room next

284

to the housekeeper's apartments. That lady was proclaimed remarkably sensible and not at all like a Londoner. In fact, she was a very good sort indeed and had invited Nan to share her sitting room since it was clear Nan would not wish to mix with the riffraff in the servant's hall. Grantly, the butler, had condescended to bid her welcome, saying she should direct her complaints and desires to him and he would see all was right for her.

Quite clearly, this exceptional courtesy to the elderly maid of an unknown and hardly impressive guest had its roots in some shenanigans of Damian and Bella. Meredith was not to know—although Nan had already realized the fact—that her supposed fortune had assumed nabob proportions belowstairs, and her unfashionable country dress thereby found ample excuse as a mere eccentricity.

Nan, having put two and two together, was quite prepared to play along with the charade. It had clearly been initiated by Lord Rutherford in whom she reposed the most complete trust where Meredith's affairs were concerned.

Meredith woke to sunshine, sinfully late, the following morning. For once there had been no crack-of-dawn knock at the door heralding the arrival of hot water, no need to be on the road after an early, rushed breakfast. She slept dreamlessly and deeply, stretching with languid, pleasurable relaxation as her body swam upward to greet the new day.

"I was beginning to wonder if you intended to sleep the day away." Nan pulled aside the bed curtains and placed a silver tray on the coverlet. "There's hot chocolate for you. Seems to be a custom in these parts," she remarked with a sniff. "Encourages idleness, I'd say."

"Maybe there is no great urgency to be up betimes," Merrie murmured, propping herself up on the mound of fluffy pillows at her back and examining the steaming silver pot and plate of sweet biscuits with a degree of enthusiasm. Such a bedside arrival at home would be considered rampant self-indulgence leading inevitably to the wages of sin.

Nan just grunted. "Lady Beaumont's maid said as how her ladyship would await you in the breakfast parlor at your convenience," she informed Meredith. "You'll be wanting to wear one of the new gowns."

"Yes, the figured muslin," Merrie agreed, her mouth full of biscuit. Her new gowns, while they might do very well in Kensington, were going to be lamentably unmodish in Cavendish Square, but they were all she had, and Meredith had never been one to complain over things she could not undo. Anyway, since she had absolutely no intention of going into society, however well-laid Damian's plans, it would hardly matter.

That thought brought her out of bed with a surge of energy. His promised visit this morning must not find her unprepared. Her stomach fluttered at the thought. Even quarreling with Damian was better than the long weeks of his absence. But she did not want to quarrel with him, she wanted to hold him and be held by him, to feel the press of his lips on hers, the intimate, knowing brush of his fingers, the long hard length of him moving in possession as he bore her captured body and spirit to that plane where only sensation existed.

"I will bathe, Nan," she declared energetically. "I am as dirty as a swineherd after all those days of travel. And I would like you to dress my hair as you used to. Do you remember how?"

Nan nodded. "Aye," she said gruffly. "I remember well."

An hour later, Meredith surveyed herself in the long pier glass. For the first time in three years she was dressed simply for the pleasure of it. There was no estate business that required one of her simple working gowns of faded print, no social event that necessitated one of her deliberately hideous outfits. The figured muslin might not rival one of Lady Beaumont's, but it was very pretty with a russet-colored pattern that complemented the rich auburn hair drawn into a soft knot on top of her head, a few side curls framing her face. A sash of the same russet outlined a waist whose smallness was one of her best features. All in all, Meredith decided, the effect was quite satisfactory. Bending, she dropped a grateful kiss on Nan's wizened cheek, receiving a gruff, "Go along with you, now," in return.

An attentive footman escorted her to the breakfast parlor, a small room at the back of the house. A lean ascetic-looking gentleman was its only occupant. He looked up from his perusal of the *Gazette* at Merrie's entrance and rose swiftly. "Lady Blake, I must bid you welcome. I was unable to receive you last evening—a late debate in the House, you understand."

"Yes, of course." Meredith took the proffered

hand, then the chair he pulled out for her. "I am delighted to make your acquaintance, Lord Beaumont. It is most kind in you to let me come to you."

"Oh, not at all, not at all," he demurred. "Arabella will be most happy to entertain you." A slight frown crossed his countenance. "To be quite frank, Lady Blake, she has been in a blue megrim since Georgy went to school, but the news of your arrival quite cheered her. I think it a capital scheme and hope that you will be as happy here as we are to have you."

In the face of such a wholehearted statement, Meredith could do little but express her own pleasure in the arrangement. She was now dug in so deeply, it seemed, it would take an act of appalling discourtesy to extricate herself. For which, of course, she had only Rutherford to thank.

Seeing her host's eyes sliding surreptitiously to the newspaper beside his plate even as he attempted polite conversation, she said with a smile. "Pray do not feel you must entertain me, Lord Beaumont. I shall be very happy for you to read your paper. I have always felt conversation at the breakfast table to be an imposition."

The marquis's relief was patent, and his guest went up even further in his estimation. A companionable silence fell between them as Meredith consumed an ample breakfast, wondering when she would be vouchsafed sight of her hostess. It was nearly ten o'clock before Arabella appeared, radiant in jonquil muslin, causing Meredith instantly to feel the country cousin.

Bella's greeting was so warm that Merrie put such

disconsolate thoughts behind her. "George, you have not been reading the *Gazette* all the while Merrie has been here." Bella took her husband to task as she received his morning salute on her cheek.

"Lady Blake said she preferred not to talk at the breakfast table," her husband defended himself, looking in appeal at their guest.

She laughed. "Indeed I did, Bella. I would never come between a man and his newspaper before noon."

"Well, my dear, I must be going." The marquis moved to the door. "I shall be in my book room with Arnold if you should need me. I have a most important speech to write on the corn tax."

"Yes, dear," his wife replied tranquilly, pouring tea. "I do not suppose I shall need to disturb you." She dipped a finger of toast into the tea and smiled a little sadly at Merrie. "Damian insists that George is not neglectful, and I daresay he has no intention of being so. He is very clever, you see, and is much relied upon by the Government." The finger of toast disappeared between rosy lips. "It is most unfashionable in me to be always wanting my husband's company." She sighed. "But love is not to be ruled by fashion."

"No, I suppose it is not." Merrie watched Bella's languid consumption of tea and toast with fascinated awe. "But then I know very little of the fashionable world, and I think, in such an instance, I would probably care not a jot for its dictates."

Bella looked startled at this novel idea, then remembered what she knew of Merrie's history. "I do trust that you will take, my dear," she said rather doubtfully. "You are most definitely out of the com-

289

mon way, but you cannot be *too* unconventional."

"Take what?" Merrie asked, more than a little puzzled by this speech.

"Why, in society, of course." Bella put down her teacup and rested her chin on an elbow-propped palm. "Do not be offended, Merrie, but while your gown may do very well in Cornwall, and, indeed, I think it quite fetching, you cannot be introduced until you have a new wardrobe."

Meredith, having reached the same conclusion herself, was not offended. "I do not intend to be introduced, Bella, so it does not signify."

Bella said carefully, "I do not think that will suit Damian."

"What will not suit him?" There was a laugh in the voice coming from the door that had opened so quietly neither of them had heard.

A battalion of moths found a candle in Merrie's stomach. She looked at him and, in spite of her anger, felt herself opening like a crocus under the spring sun.

"Good morning, my little adventuress," said he, softly.

"Good morning, Lord Rutherford." He wore a many-caped driving coat that she would later learn signified his membership in the exclusive Four Horse Club. This he now removed, laying it with his gloves and a curly-brimmed beaver hat on a couch in the corner of the parlor.

"Sister." He greeted Bella with a light kiss, observing, "you persist in maudling your insides with that slop, I see."

"You are always so charming, brother," Bella responded sweetly. "Do you care to join us?"

"Thank you, no. I breakfasted hours ago. But I will bear you company until Meredith is done with hers."

He had not so much as shaken her hand, yet Merrie felt as weak and fluttery as a star-struck maiden. "I am quite finished," she said with icy dignity.

"Then let us go and quarrel in private," he responded amiably. "You will excuse us, Bella?"

"Yes, of course." His sister looked anxiously at them. "Oh, dear. I do hope you will be able to resolve this. Why do you not go into the morning room and tell Grantly that you do not wish to be disturbed?"

Damian nodded, opening the door for Meredith, offering a small mock bow as she swept passed him. "To your right." A warm palm fitted into the small of her back and the hairs on the nape of her neck lifted. He felt her quiver and smiled—a satisfied smile that Merrie, fortunately, did not see.

She found herself eased into another elegant apartment where the hangings and furnishings were of cheerful sunshine yellow. Appropriate enough for a morning room, she thought distractedly. The door clicked shut behind her and, with strange trepidation, Merrie turned to face the powerful figure behind her.

"I have missed you so much," Damian said softly. "I did not know it was possible to miss anyone that much." He shook his head thoughtfully. "No—no, I do not think that I shall permit you to quarrel with me." It was an unequivocal statement, followed immediately with action as he swept her into his arms. Merrie had time for only a squeak of protest before all breath seemed to leave her under a relentless kiss that demanded, then enforced a response. Then all desire to protest vanished together with her will to resist the hands and body that, as always, felt so right in their proximity.

Still holding her against him, he moved backward to a chair. Releasing her tingling mouth, he let his hands drift slowly down her body as he sat in the chair, drawing her between his knees. Holding her hips lightly, he smiled up at her. "You look quite adorable with your hair like that. How is your leg?"

Without waiting for the reply that she seemed to be having difficulty making anyway, Damian very deliberately drew her muslin skirts and embroidered petticoat up to her hips.

"You *must* not!" she protested in a shocked whisper. "Supposing someone should come in."

"A little reckless, is it not?" he agreed. "But I have vowed to satisfy your craving for danger whenever possible. Hold up your skirts. I must roll down your stocking if I am to look at your thigh."

As if in a trance, Meredith found herself obeying, taking the soft bunched material at the front of her gown in her own hands as he untied her garter, laying it carefully on the arm of the chair before very slowly and delicately unrolling the thin silk stocking to her ankle. Meredith shivered as she stood, feeling the air on the bared, warm skin of her leg. Without a word, he pushed up the cuff of her white ruffled pantalettes. A manicured finger traced the long thin red line drawn toward the back of her thigh. "You will bear the scar," he stated matter-of-factly. "It will serve as a reminder to you to act in future with reasonable caution."

Meredith gaped at this cool audacity. "*You* cannot talk of reasonable caution—"

"Hush," he directed, pressing his lips to the scar, his hands sliding behind, beneath her skirts, to grasp her bottom firmly. She swallowed, a heat wave gathering momentum in her belly. His lips moved upward, scorched through the thin lawn of her pantalettes as his hands gripped tighter and that most sensitive core of her vulnerability pulsed through the material under his lips. She was drifting on that curling wave of sensation, now so familiar, as he held her with one hand, the other slipping into the moist furrow where the secrets of desire opened to his touch. The sensation of being touched, yet not being touched as the protection of her undergarments prevented the contact of his skin on hers, drove Meredith into a state resembling frenzy. Unable to do anything but stand between his knees that pressed against her thighs, holding up her skirt, mutely offering herself to the invader who knew so well how to draw from her the notes of perfection, she shivered and shook as the curling wave carried her, ever higher on the crest of surf, finally to roll in on itself at the moment of her drowning.

"There now. You are not going to quarrel with me, are you, Meredith?" Rutherford inquired softly once the paroxysms had passed and she could stand without his support.

"The devil take you, Damian!" Merrie muttered weakly and without conviction.

He just laughed and rolled up her stocking, retying the garter with a deftness that bespoke practice. Her skirt slid back to her ankles and was smoothed carefully, lingeringly over her hips.

"Now, my love, to business." The brisk tones added to Merrie's feeling of unreality. Dimly she realized that he was playing a clever game. By keeping her constantly disoriented, he ensured that she was unable to formulate, let alone to express, her anger at the blatant manipulation that had brought her to Cavendish Square. For the moment, she could not even think why she did not wish to be here. "Bella explained the plan to you?" Damian went on, watching her shrewdly, well satisfied with what he saw. In dealing with such a formidable opponent, one was obliged to put aside a strict code of honor. He was all too well aware of how few scruples she would have had if their roles were reversed.

"It is an outrageous plan and you know it." Meredith found her voice at last. "This was not what we agreed."

"And to what exactly did we agree, my little adventuress?" Sure of his ground, Rutherford lounged in his chair, flicking at the snowy-white tops of his riding boots with his handkerchief.

Merrie thought and saw the trap. When she remained silent, he said quietly, "a contract that became binding at Okehampton as I recall. Do I have it right?" His eyes fixed her like a worm on a hook, and she nodded, cursing her stupidity. "Tell me about the contract, Merrie?" he pressed gently.

"Oh, you are quite insufferable!" Swinging on her

heel, she began to pace the room. He watched her with a slight smile, wondering whether her temper would find an outlet in hurling Arabella's possessions against the wall. "Utterly unscrupulous!" she declared almost breathlessly, striding across to him.

"Exactly so," Rutherford agreed, possessing himself of her right hand, which he doubled into a fist. "You may hit me if it will make you feel better. Keep your thumb down so, and hit like that. Aim for the eye, or the nose if you prefer. Not my chin, you might hurt your hand."

"Ohhh!" cried Meredith. "There are no words for what you are! You know you have me because I will not renege on an agreement. There is no need to be odious about it."

Laughing, he pulled her down onto his knee. "Cry peace, my love. When you are accustomed to the idea, I promise that you will enjoy this adventure. You could not possibly have wished to live in seclusion in a genteel backwater. It would be a criminal waste of your talents. I predict that within the month, if you will put yourself unreservedly into Bella's hands, you will be all the rage."

Meredith sighed, snuggling into the encircling arms, surrendering the battle she had known all along she would lose. At the beginning of this enterprise, she had agreed to accept Rutherford's terms unconditionally. They were not what she had expected, but her position in the Beaumont household would clearly not be one of pensioner. She could be of service to Arabella, thus discharging any sense of obligation. She knew, as she nestled against his chest, listened to

295

the rhythmic thud of his heart beneath the gray coat, felt his hands stroking her cheek, that she could not forgo the opportunity to be with him for the time that was left to them. Besides, the prospect of taking an unwarranted place amongst the haut ton set the actress's toes tapping. The indigent, law-breaking widow of a Cornish baronet accepted by the highest sticklers; vouchers for Almack's, maybe. No, most certainly, if she were under the aegis of the house of Keighley.

Meredith chuckled and Damian hugged her with delight. "You begin to see the possibilities, my darling?"

"Indeed, I do. I would not have countenanced deceiving your sister, but, since she seems to derive some amusement from the plan—and, if *you* do not feel guilty about hoodwinking your mother, I fail to see why I should—then I will play the game."

One crucial question they both forgot to discuss in the ensuing moments, and, since Rutherford then took Meredith on a sightseeing tour that included the wild beasts at the Exeter Exchange, Whitehall, and Westminster Abbey, Merrie was so absorbed in new experiences and Damian equally absorbed in her delight that they talked only of love and trivia.

Chapter Fifteen

"As soon as we have finished breakfast, Merrie, we must go shopping." Arabella came into the breakfast parlor, infused with energy the following morning. "I have ordered the barouche. We will go directly to Bond Street."

Meredith, after some anguished soul-searching, had decided that she could afford the indulgence of one or maybe even two London gowns. Having agreed to play her part in this game, it would be self-defeating to quibble at detail. She therefore agreed to the excursion cheerfully and went for her pelisse and hat.

The Bond Street establishment that enjoyed the patronage of the Marchioness of Beaumont bore little overt sign of a place of business. The ladies were ushered into a sitting room where they were encouraged to repose themselves on little gilt chairs. Refreshments were brought, and with them arrived a most elegant lady of ample proportions, who greeted Lady Beaumont with a mixture of deference and familiarity that irritated Meredith as much as it puzzled her. Arabella, however, seemed not to notice.

"Madame Bernice, my cousin is but newly arrived from Cornwall and has need of certain things."

Madame Bernice, running an appraising eye over the cousin's cloth pelisse and chip hat, agreed wholeheartedly with this statement as she made haste to assure her customers of her pleasure in being able to serve them. A discussion then took place, in which Meredith bore little part as much because the terms were unfamiliar as because her companions rarely referred to her.

There was much talk of the relative merits of gauze and muslin, of the new French cambrics that were becoming so popular. A variety of gowns was paraded before them. Merrie agreed with Arabella's comments since she was too bewildered, initially, to formulate her own opinions and, indeed, found all of the gowns quite delightful. She presumed that, once she had seen all that Madame Bernice had to offer, she would be permitted to make her selection although how she was to choose from the array of promenade gowns, morning and afternoon dresses, driving dresses, and evening gowns became a monumental question.

She had just decided that her wardrobe lacked an evening gown and that a promenade gown might be an interesting possession since she had never owned one, not being in the habit of promenading, when Arabella stunned her into stupefaction.

"We are agreed then, my love." Lady Beaumont drew on her gloves and stood up. "Since you must have gowns you may wear immediately, we will take the yellow craped-muslin promenade gown, that very pretty sprigged muslin, and also the cream cambric. It will look so well with your hair. The lavender silk for evening because it is so perfect with your eyes. We will visit the warehouses and choose materials to be made up for the rest of your wardrobe. Madame Bernice will go through patterns that we may examine. You must trust her, my dear. She has never yet failed in knowing exactly what style will suit."

Madame smiled complacently and said that she rather thought the more classic styles would exactly suit Lady Blake's face and form. It would be a great pleasure to dress one of her ladyship's trim figure.

Meredith found her voice at last. "There is some misunderstanding. I beg your pardon, Bella, I am entirely at fault. I should have explained my situation before we came here; I did not realize you did not know it."

Arabella was looking at her aghast and the modiste's sharp eyes narrowed. The Marchioness of Beaumont was one of her best customers, and madame was far from averse to the prospect of dressing the country cousin. But, unless she was much mistaken, a word that was never mentioned was about to rear its ugly head. The cousin was going to discuss money.

"Madame Bernice, would you leave us for a minute?" Arabella recollected herself. The modiste inclined her head, smiled with only her lips, and sailed from the room.

"I am so sorry to have embarrassed you, Bella," Meredith apologized hastily. "I am not in a position to buy more than two gowns, and, to be candid, if the price is as high as I fear, then I must settle for only one. We may certainly look at materials and patterns that Nan may make up for me. But that is the extent of my ability."

"But my love, Damian will—"

"He will not!"

Arabella flinched at the flashing eyes, the sharp crackle in the previously modulated voice. "I do not know what you have concocted between you," Meredith went on, "but I can assure you that I and only I am responsible for expenses of this nature. I have accepted your hospitality most gratefully, but that is as far as it goes."

Arabella pulled a rueful grimace. This stumbling block had not occurred to her, but it was a major one. Merrie could not enter society in gowns made up by her maid. And the gowns were only the beginning. There were hats and shoes of every description, shawls and scarves, gloves and mittens and stockings, cloaks and wraps. The list was endless. Her brother had said to spare no expense. Had he not envisaged his mistress's reaction? Or had he hoped Arabella would succeed in persuading her? Well, his sister decided firmly, he was going to have pull the coals out of this fire himself. Even for a beloved twin, he had laid too much upon her shoulders already.

"It must be as you say, of course." She smiled amicably at Merrie. "Do you wish to choose one of the gowns we have seen? I would suggest either the yellow craped muslin or the cream cambric."

Disarmed by this easy capitulation and guiltily

conscious of how she must have embarrassed her hostess in front of the modiste, Merrie agreed to take both gowns. If necessary, she would have to send to lawyer Donne for more funds. The money was earmarked for the estate; however, once she was back in Cornwall and had resumed her customary activities, she would replace it easily enough. But she was only at the beginning of this adventure, Merrie reminded herself. It were far too soon to think of its conclusion.

Bella had a few words with Madame Bernice who, as a result, beamed and congratulated Lady Blake on the two gowns she had chosen as effusively as if she had bought all those listed earlier by Lady Beaumont. Meredith responded with a smile and did not concern herself with this *volte-face*. Obviously, the modiste would swallow her disappointment, maintaining her courtesy in the interests of good relations with such a valued customer as Lady Beaumont.

Arabella prudently put the rest of her planned morning aside since she rather suspected that visits to milliners and bootmakers would not find favor with her ferociously independent guest. Resolving to send a message to her brother at the earliest possible moment, she suggested to Meredith that they return home for luncheon and then perhaps Meredith would care to explore the neighborhood around Cavendish Square a little. She herself was in the habit of resting for an hour or so in the afternoon and hoped her guest would not mind being left to her own devices.

"Not at all," Meredith concurred easily. "I should like to walk outdoors of all things. It will not cause raised eyebrows?"

"Oh, no, for you will have a footman to escort you," Bella assured her.

That did not strike Meredith as at all necessary but, if it was considered to be so, she would accept it with a good grace.

Accordingly, she was safely out of the house when Lord Rutherford arrived to answer his sister's urgent summons.

"What's to do, Bella?" He greeted her in his usual forthright fashion. "From the tone of your message, I expected to find murder and mayhem."

"It is a great deal too bad of you, Damian, to put me in this abominable position," his sister told him roundly. She had received him in her boudoir where she reclined on a striped chaise longue, a copy of Mr. Southey's latest poem lying neglected but prominently displayed on the table beside her.

"Cut line, Bella," Rutherford advised equably, picking up the book and leafing through the pages.

Arabella told him the story in no uncertain terms. "I will not be put in the position of executing those tasks that you find distasteful, Rutherford, and so I tell you. It is not at all comfortable to be with Merrie when she is put out," she concluded, falling back against the cushions.

Rutherford could not help a rueful grin. "No, I do know what you mean. But do not rip up at me further, Bella. I swear that I had no intention of putting you in an abominable situation or of expecting you to deal with unpleasant tasks."

Bella, somewhat mollified by this assertion, demanded in robust tones to know what her brother intended doing about the pickle since his plan could clearly not go forward if Meredith was not to be persuaded into an ample and suitable wardrobe.

"To tell the truth, I had not envisaged this," he admitted. "I had thought that, having accepted the situation in principle, my obstinate little termagant would have no qualms with the details. Experience should have taught me otherwise."

"So, what will you do?" his twin persisted.

"Wait for her downstairs." Rutherford bent over the chaise longue, raising one elegant white hand to his lips. "Poor Bella, it was quite outrageous of me to expose you to a Merrie Trelawney tantrum."

Arabella smiled, completely appeased. "I would not describe it as such. But her eyes flashed in a most alarming fashion and her voice was quite different. I wish you will make all right so that I do not have to be always watching my step."

"I shall do so as soon as she returns," he promised, moving toward the door, adding casually, "I think it likely that you will be dining alone tonight, sister."

He left Bella in frowning contemplation of the implications of that statement. If her conclusions were correct, they should bring a blush to the marchioness's respectable cheek. They did not, however, Arabella being a pragmatic soul beneath the affectations demanded by society. She returned to Mr. Southey with a degree of reluctance. It was a tediously long poem, rejoicing in the title "The Curse of Kahama," but one must be able to talk of the latest poems should they happen to become the rage.

Lord Rutherford repaired to the library, meeting his

brother-in-law in the hall on the way. The two men had considerable respect for each other although they were little in each other's company.

"How d'ye do, George?" Damian shook the lean hand.

"Well enough, Damian," came the reply. "I'm glad you sent that relative of yours to Arabella, y'know. Just what she needs."

Rutherford pursed his lips, saying quietly, "a little more of her husband's company might not come amiss, Beaumont."

The marquis looked slightly taken aback at this blunt statement. "You know how things are, Rutherford."

His brother-in-law shrugged. "Just a piece of fraternal advice, George. Take it or leave it."

"When we've got these demmed Corn Laws passed, Damian, things will go easier." Beaumont gave a weary smile, clasping his brother-in-law's shoulder. "I am sensible of Bella's needs, but what's a man to do with only one body? I cannot be making love to my wife in her boudoir and arguing for the protection of agriculture in the Lords at one and the same time."

"True enough," Damian agreed. "Forgive me if I spoke out of turn."

Beaumont made haste to assure him that he had not done so, and the two parted, one with a thoughtful frown as if troubled by some uncomfortable reflections, the other satisfied that he had sown a necessary seed.

Meredith, having explored Piccadilly, which she knew from Patience to be the heart of the fashionable quarter, was in excellent spirits as she walked back to Cavendish Square, the footman a discreet ten paces behind her. She had discovered Hatchard's and had feasted her eyes on the bow window filled with all the newest publications. There was a sad dearth of new books in Cornwall, and the prospect of such riches on her doorstep was heady indeed. The annoying constraints of a tight budget were, as always, to be considered, but a small indulgence was surely permissible. In addition, there must be lending libraries in the vicinity. She would consult Bella on this score as soon as may be. This afternoon would also be a good opportunity to write letters to the boys. Her host had just this morning offered to frank her correspondence, and she had a myriad impressions to impart to her juniors although avoiding reference to Rutherford and his sister was going to prove a formidable task. That brought the other, most pleasurable thought. Damian would be joining them for dinner this evening. It had been agreed between brother and sister that Meredith would not venture upon the world until various necessary changes had been made in her appearance, and she had had time to settle down and learn her way about. Meredith, for her part, was not at all sorry for the delay. She was perfectly happy to submit to the artistry of Bella's hairdresser, perfectly happy to expand her wardrobe so long as she could do so without outrunning the carpenter, and, for entertainment, she found that the prospect of a family dinner in Rutherford's company was, for the moment, excitement enough.

Damian, who had left the library door ajar for this

purpose, heard her light tones in conversation with Grantly and went into the hall.

When she saw him, her cheeks flushed delicately with pleasure. "Why, Lord Rutherford, how delightful. We were not expecting you until this evening."

He raised her hand to his lips, feeling the slight tremor of her fingers. "I had some business to transact with Bella, then thought that I would wait until you returned from your walk. Did you enjoy it? Where did you go?" Chattering in this inconsequential fashion, he maneuvered her across the hall and into the library, closing the double doors firmly behind him.

Meredith gave him a sharp look as she pulled off her gloves and slipped out of her pelisse. "I had intended to run upstairs and leave my things," she said thoughtfully, tossing them on a chair and untying the ribbons of her hat. "It would appear, sir, that your business with me is somewhat urgent."

Damian, who had decided exactly how he was going to deal with this problem, fixed her with a grim eye. "Would you be good enough to explain to me why you saw fit to subject Arabella to such an awkward scene this morning?"

The color drained from her face. "I do not think you understand, sir. Your sister had some mistaken notions that I was obliged to correct. There was no scene, I can assure you. I do understand that poverty is considered a vulgar condition; nevertheless, it is *my* condition, and one for which I will not apologize. It was unfortunate that your sister did not fully understand my situation, but I would suggest, my lord, that it was your responsibility to have made her aware of

306

it."

Rutherford allowed the speech to continue without interruption, meeting the glaring, challenging sloe eyes with a level look. "Make no mistake, Meredith, Arabella is quite aware of your situation," he said with careful deliberation. "She was merely doing what *I* had asked her to do." He had decided that placation and cajoling would not achieve his object. They rarely did where Merrie Trelawney was concerned. One had to take her by storm, cut the ground from beneath her feet, set her spinning like a top, and then, when she was thoroughly off course, withdraw from the engagement and offer the peaceful solution.

"You dare to imagine that I would allow you to buy my wardrobe?" Meredith trembled with anger, an emotion exacerbated by her opponent's apparent calm.

"I wish you would sit down," he requested casually. "Since, if you do not, I may not."

Meredith set her teeth. "Pray be seated, sir. I prefer to stand."

"Thank you." Smiling, he took a seat on the sofa, crossed one leg over the other, and regarded her attentively. "I beg pardon, ma'am. You were saying?"

Meredith turned away from him and took two deep, steadying breaths. From the very first, he had had this ability to take control of their encounters by refusing to acknowledge her opposition. As a result, he usually won. This time, there was no question of his winning, but she must maintain control of herself and her anger, however outrageous the calculated provocation.

She turned back to face him, clasping her hands in front of her, lowering her eyes. "Lord Rutherford, I do not wish to appear ungrateful, and I am, indeed, most sensible of your many kindnesses, but I am afraid I cannot accept your charity in the matter of my wardrobe." She offered him that humble, self-deprecating little smile and saw with savage satisfaction that she had broken through.

"Damn you, Merrie Trelawney!" Springing to his feet he gripped her shoulders. "I have told you before that you will not smile at *me* in that fashion." Seeing the glint of triumph in her eyes, the contented lift of the corners of her mouth, Damian realized that he had fallen neatly into her trap. It were wise never to underestimate Meredith.

Releasing her instantly, he returned to the sofa. " 'Charity,' my dear, is not the correct word," he pointed out in a kindly tone. "I am merely fulfilling my obligations. Perhaps you do not fully understand the meaning of a carte blanche? Permit me to explain it to you."

Meredith, realizing what was coming, looked at him rather in the manner of a rabbit facing a rattlesnake. "I am entirely responsible for your welfare, dear girl," he continued. "And for all aspects of your living conditions." He paused, made a minute adjustment to his cravat. "And that, ma'am, includes the clothes on your back."

Merrie thought she would explode. Her palms felt damp and the blood pounded in her ears. They were not the symptoms of anger, she dimly recognized, but of incipient panic at the prospect of her imminent, impending defeat. Think, she told herself; for every trick, there was another. She looked around the room in search of inspiration and found it.

"I will agree, sir, that in a conventional arrangement, the obligations you describe would certainly fall to you. They would, after all, be payment for services rendered." Her smile this time was honeyed and Rutherford began to feel uneasy. When he said nothing, Merrie continued in the same sweet tones. "Since I am lodged under your sister's roof, my lord, it is really impossible for me to render those services. I must, therefore, consider our contract null and void. I shall be perfectly happy to return to Cornwall in the morning if you so wish."

To her consternation, she could read only relief on his countenance. Not an appropriate response to her *coup de grâce*, surely? But then that was something that had happened before, also. When she had thought she had said something that would leave him defenseless, he responded as if she had given him the one answer he craved.

"Make no mistake, ma'am, I intend that you shall have ample opportunity to fulfill your side of the bargain," said Rutherford softly, the gray eyes suddenly hooded in the way that set her heart racing for reasons other than panic or anger.

"How?" she managed, as her throat seemed to close.

Damian made a steeple of his fingers, pursed his lips reflectively, and kept her waiting.

"Do not be so insufferably smug!" Merrie yielded the dikes of control, wrenching his hands apart. "Tell me at once!"

He laughed, catching her wrists as she pummeled his chest. "No, do stop, Merrie!" Holding her arms at her sides, he stood up, towering over her as he looked down into her upturned face, shaking his head in a gesture of mild exasperation. "What an abominable girl you are. What am I to do with you?"

Merrie gasped at this blatant injustice. "It is you who have caused all this, and I will *not* make peace until this matter is resolved."

"Very well then." He gave her cheek a little pat. "It was a surprise I had intended to keep for a day or two until you were quite settled in, but, since you are so importunate—" She used her regained freedom to drive one fist into his midriff, meeting a rock-hard wall. Damian shook his head again. "I showed you yesterday how to hit me, Merrie. Eyes and nose are the only sensible targets. Now, put on your pelisse." Picking up the discarded garment from the chair, he held it for her as she pushed her arms into the sleeves.

"Where are we going?" It was a question designed to return some sense of reality to the trancelike state in which Merrie found herself, but it received a wholly unhelpful answer.

"Wait and see. Put on your bonnet." The chip hat went over the auburn knot, the ribbons tied beneath her chin. "Gloves."

"Thank you, I am able to put them on for myself." Meredith seized them when it appeared that he was about to manipulate her fingers into the holes as if she were a small child who had not yet learned to accomplish the task herself.

Rutherford pulled the bell rope and asked the footman to order his curricle brought around from the mews. He swung the caped driving coat around his shoulders, a handful of spare whip points thrust through one of the buttonholes, and drew on leather driving gloves. "Shall we go, ma'am?"

"I am amazed you are willing to be seen in public with one dressed so shabbily," Meredith threw out with lamentable lack of wisdom.

"Oh, we shall avoid places where I might be recognized," he returned airily.

The curricle stood at the door, drawn by a splendid team of grays. "They are magnificent," Merrie breathed, diverted from the need to find a suitably cutting response.

"I am thought to be something of a judge of horseflesh, Lady Blake," said Lord Rutherford, handing her up.

"And something of a whip, I presume," she replied dulcetly. "Tell me, sir, are you perhaps what they call a Nonpareil?"

He shot her a suspicious look. To judge from her innocent-seeming expression, that suspicion was justified. "Put up your sword, Merrie Trelawney. There's been enough quarreling between us for one afternoon. I have something infinitely more pleasurable in mind for the rest of the day. Stand away from their heads, Harry." He gave his horses the office to start as the tiger released the wheelers and leapt onto his perch.

Meredith decided to take the advice. She was in no doubt as to his meaning, in little doubt that the surprise was going to decimate what she had hoped was a *coup de grâce*. But, in all honesty, would she have wanted to be right in that instance? The answer was as plain as the nose on her face, as obvious as the now familiar fluttering of anticipation in her belly. She had asked for this from the first; somehow she must reconcile herself to the unpalatable aspects of an agreement that in its essentials was everything she desired.

Their direction took them rapidly away from the fashionable quarter. Meredith was granted ample opportunity to judge his lordship's skill with the team of high-couraged grays since their destination was clearly at some distance. They drove north, out of town, in the direction of Hampstead. Meredith was intrigued but, when she asked again where they were going, received the same amused answer as before. The grays easily took Highgate Hill, their stride lengthening as they came into the village. Rutherford turned them around the village green, past the Bull and Bear, and brought them to a halt in front of a pretty, thatched-roof cottage set in a garden of tall hollyhocks and gillyflowers.

Here he handed the reins to Harry and alighted, reaching up a hand to Merrie, who, her curiosity running out of bounds, sprang lightly into the street. "Take them to the inn, Harry. I'll send for you when I am ready to leave."

The tiger touched his forelock and led the team in the direction of the Bull and Bear.

"Who lives here? It is quite the prettiest house." Merrie went to the white wicket gate and pushed it open. Smiling, Damian followed as she skipped up

312

the narrow garden path to the green-painted door framed by a late-blooming Albertine climbing over a wooden trellis.

The door opened before she could knock. "I saw you from the front windows." A pink-and-white young woman bobbed a curtsy. "Welcome, my lord, my lady. Is there anything I can get you?"

"Not for the moment, thank you, Sally. My love, this is Sally, who will look after the house and will look after us when we visit," he said to the now clear-sighted Meredith. "Come into the parlor."

Merrie went through the door held by Sally, who said she would be in the kitchen should they need her, bobbed another curtsy, and disappeared. "So this is your surprise," Merrie murmured, looking around the cozy room where cheerful chintzes covered the furniture and hung at the small bow window. The scent of potpourri and beeswax filled the air.

Damian went to a little desk, opened a drawer, and took out a document. This he handed to Merrie with a quizzical little smile. It was the lease to the cottage made out in her name. Slowly she raised her eyes to meet his. "We have a love nest, it would seem," Merrie whispered as a warm glow spread from somewhere in the pit of her belly. She could never have imagined anything more perfect, more delicate than this romantic hideaway far from town, where they could be themselves, for the first time ever, away from all fears of observation, could create their own universe where there were no intruders, no distractions. At that moment, she loved him, if it were possible, more deeply than ever. It showed in her eyes as she came

313

into his arms.

"Let us go upstairs," he said on a husky note, lifting her with his usual ease. "You must inspect the rest of your property."

"If that is a double entendre, my lord, it is not very subtle," she chided, kissing his ear.

"It is the best I can do in the circumstances," he murmured, carrying her up a polished oak staircase to a small landing. "Unlatch the door, sweetheart, my hands are full."

Meredith reached for the latch, lifted it, and pushed open a door onto a country bedroom that in style and furnishing matched the parlor.

"I love you," Damian said, placing her on the patchwork coverlet of the posterbed.

"And I you," she replied.

Much later, when the early October dusk filled the small window, Damian gently disentangled himself from Merrie's warm, clinging limbs and slipped out of bed. He drew the curtains against the encroaching gloom, struck a flint, and bent to light the fire set ready in the hearth.

"May we stay here all night?"

"I thought you were still asleep." He stood up as the logs crackled, coming back to the bed where he drew down the covers, drinking in the nakedness, warm and glowing, firm yet soft, thus revealed. "We cannot this time, love." When she pulled a comical face of disappointment, he touched her lips. "I cannot leave Harry with my horses at the inn all night. Next time I will drive alone. If you remember, I had not intended our first visit to be unplanned."

A serious note had crept into his voice although his eyes remained soft and his fingers continued to trace the planes of her face.

"Dinner, at least?" Meredith inquired. She knew that he was now asking for her willing compliance in the matter that had brought them here, but she was not quite ready.

Damian nodded, accepting the delay, and drew the covers over her again. "Sally will have dinner prepared." He pulled on britches and shirt to pad barefoot down to the kitchen from whence emanated the most enticing aromas.

Sally was standing at the range, stirring a copper saucepan. She jumped at his lordship's soft-footed arrival. "Oh, m'lord, you startled me."

"I beg pardon, Sally," he apologized with a disarming smile. "We are exceeding sharp-set and something smells delicious."

The young woman beamed. "Will I lay the table in the parlor, m'lord? Or will you dine above stairs?"

Thinking of that glorious body beneath the covers on the wide bed, Rutherford said that they would eat above stairs for today and offered to carry the dishes. Sally making no demur, he bore a laden tray upstairs, entering the chamber to find Merrie sitting naked on the rug before the fire.

"Shameless creature," he chided, setting the tray on a gate-legged table which he then pulled before the fire. "Supposing it had been Sally who entered?"

"She would have knocked," Merrie said unarguably, getting up to examine the contents of the tray with a hungry sniff.

315

"That is not everything," he told her, running a lazy hand over her bottom as she leant over the table. "I will fetch the second course afterward. Sit down before you give me other ideas."

Chuckling, she complied, taking cutlery and napkins from the table, arranging them in two place settings while Damian ladled creamy artichoke soup into deep bowls.

He placed one bowl before Merrie, then very deliberately shook out the large linen napkin, tying it around her neck. "If you dribble soup, my dear, you might find yourself more than a little uncomfortable." A long finger ran between her breasts, circled her nipples, slid over her abdomen, and danced across her bare thighs in emphatic demonstration of his point.

The soup was followed by a duckling in a delicate orange sauce flavored with juniper berries, accompanied by fresh-picked green peas and roasted potatoes. A blackberry pie with heavy golden cream completed a simple but delectable dinner that seemed entirely in keeping with the charming simplicity of this perfect hideaway.

Meredith took a sip of the ruby claret in her glass and stretched with a sigh of repletion. She had abandoned the napkin some minutes previously and her breasts lifted, rose-tipped in the firelight. "Why may I not stay here?" she asked quietly. "I will await you in this love nest and you will come to me whenever you can, whenever you feel the need." A tender smile touched her lips, hovered in her eyes. "I would be most content, I promise. It is not so far from town that I may not visit to see the sights and, when you come to call upon me, then may we go out together also. It would be as I expected."

"But not as I intended," he replied, cracking a walnut between long fingers. "Must I remind you again of our agreement? Your unconditional acceptance of my conditions?" He leant across the table to lay the shelled nut on her plate, his eyes meeting hers in steady affirmation of his determination.

"No." Merrie shook her head. "I need no reminding. But why should it suit you better to have me lodged with your sister? To see me enter this society that is your home, not mine?" She popped the walnut between her lips and propped her elbows on the table, waiting for his answer.

Rutherford said nothing for a minute. So she still had not tumbled to his plan. The longer she remained in ignorance the better since he strongly suspected that, once she realized his fell intent, the fireworks he had seen so far would be damp squibs compared with her reaction then. He would not lie to her, though.

"Since you are not at all dull-witted, Meredith, I will leave you to work that out for yourself. You will do so sooner or later, I am convinced."

"I do not find that particularly reassuring, sir," she told him.

"Come here." Damian pushed back his chair, patting his knee in both invitation and demand.

The tip of her thumb disappeared between her teeth. "So you can cozen me into agreeing to anything?"

"Come." An imperative finger beckoned.

Meredith complied with a rueful little smile. The

317

battle was already lost anyway.

"I am going to give you a draft on my bank," Rutherford explained, once he had her safely captive. "If it is not sufficient to settle all your bills and for other necessities, then you will simply apply to me for more."

"That is so mortifying!" Meredith bit her lip angrily.

"I fail to see how. It is just what I would do for my wife," he replied evenly.

"But I am *not* your wife."

"No," he agreed drily. "You are not, are you?"

"Is this in some sort a punishment?" Meredith struggled to sit up, pushing against his chest. "Because I will not marry you?"

"Be still." He held her tighter. "You have a very strange notion of the concept of punishment, my love. I wish only to please you with the gift of an adventure that you would not otherwise have. My purse is a fat one and will in no wise be diminished by the gift. Will you not accept it willingly?"

"You are determined that I will accept it," she said thoughtfully. "Willing or no?"

His silence was confirmation enough and Meredith reluctantly accepted that she was *at point non plus*. She played with the buttons on his shirt for a few moments, then said. "Of course, my lord, you might regret your generosity. Supposing I should develop excessively expensive tastes? I have had to be so thrifty for so long that I may run wild. Secure in the knowledge that I may apply to you for further funds whenever necessary, I may set no restraints on my spending. Why, I might even discover a penchant for gaming. I am, after all, quite skilled at the cards."

"There is a risk in all enterprises," Rutherford said solemnly. "I had already decided that that one was quite acceptable."

Meredith's reaction to this provocation led them speedily back to the bed where Damian found some considerable effort was required to subdue the lean little body that twisted and wriggled, eluding his grasp like a greased pole. She was amazingly strong, as he had discovered before, and used her well-toned muscles to best advantage, levering herself skillfully against him to achieve her freedom.

Even as she wondered why they were wrestling, why she was fighting so hard to elude the captivity that would bring only joy, Meredith knew that the mock battle was the physical expression of their conflict. Damian had won the latter with trickery, using her own weapons against her; he would win this one eventually with his greater strength, but, before he did so, she would use all her wiles, exhaust her skills and strength in battle so that at the end she would be drained of all resentment, all lingering hostility, ready to be filled anew with pure, untarnished delight.

"I had not realized what a tigress I have taken into my bed," Damian gasped, breathless with effort as much as with the heat of desire engendered by the lithe body, by her stubborn defiance of the odds. "Permit me to tell you, madam, that you are not playing fair!" With a monumental heave, he managed to roll her onto her stomach. "I am so afraid of hurting you that I dare not rely simply on brawn."

"Well, what is this then?" she demanded, equally breathless, jerking her hips against his weight as he sat on her bottom and clipped her wrists in the small of her back.

"Brute strength, I admit." He chuckled. "But the most delicate parts of you are safely cushioned by the mattress." Merrie continue to jerk and heave, bringing up her heels to pummel his back until, finally exhausted, she lay still.

"Now," he whispered, leaning forward to nuzzle her neck. "Let us make an end of this business, my little adventuress, once and for all."

"Do you always understand?" Merrie whispered back, glowing through her exhaustion at the thought that he had known exactly what lay beneath the battle.

"Not always, but I will promise always to try."

Chapter Sixteen

"A very pretty behaved young woman," the Duchess of Keighley pronounced to her daughter. "I was most afraid that she would be *farouche*; it is so often the way with provincials."

"I do not think her exactly provincial," Arabella said thoughtfully. "To tell the truth, Mama, sometimes it is I who feel the simpleton, the naive one. George says she is one of the most sensible women he has ever met." She smiled, shrugged. "I should be jealous but am merely grateful. He has dined at home three times in the week since she came to us."

"And Rutherford?" the duchess inquired. "What interest does he have in the widow?"

"Oh, friendly, ma'am," Bella prevaricated, busying herself with the tea tray. "He felt some family obligation as Matthew's sole heir. Apparently Lady Blake could justifiably have expected something in the will herself."

Her mother nodded. She had heard the same from her son and judged that he had acted in a perfectly correct manner. She had, however, been most curious to make the acquaintance of this distant Cornish connection. Something had roused Rutherford from his gloom and despondency on that Cornish excursion, and her grace had now decided that, if it were the widow, she would have no need to fall into strong convulsions. The match was hardly brilliant, but the girl looked quite charming in an uncommon way and was possessed of a handsome fortune. In fact, if Damian had any intentions in that quarter, he would do well to make them known, the duchess thought pragmatically. Once the girl was properly launched, she would have no shortage of suitors. It behooved the Keighleys to take a most particular interest in Lady Blake's debut.

"I will talk to Sally Jersey about vouchers for Almack's," she said briskly. "I daresay she will call within the week. We will both let it be known that you have a guest, but you must give a party as soon as may be. George will have no objections, I trust?"

"None at all, ma'am," Bella assured with a serene smile. "I have already mentioned it to him. I have prepared a guest list." She handed her mother a paper, thinking it unnecessary to mention that the list had been compiled with Damian's more-than-active assistance.

"That will do very well," the duchess approved. "Brummell may well attend to oblige your brother, and I will ask Keighley to promise to bring York, if only for half an hour." She nodded in the manner her daughter recognized as denoting happy decision. "It would not surprise me at all if she were not to become all the rage if we play our cards right. Rutherford must be told that this dislike of his for dancing and parties must be overcome. He will be obliged to partner his cousin and most certainly to offer his escort when dear George must be in the House."

Lord Rutherford, favored with these instructions when next he called upon his mama, surprised that lady with his meek acquiescence. "I shall be most happy, ma'am, to do all in my power to assist Lady Blake. I see it in some way a duty since she is in London at my invitation."

The duchess regarded the son and heir over her lorgnette. "D'ye wish to fix your interest there, Rutherford?"

He stroked his chin reflectively before answering, "If she will have me, ma'am."

The Duchess of Keighley was betrayed into a somewhat unladylike exclamation. "Why, of course she will have you. What woman in her right mind would not? You are the most eligible catch on the market."

"I beg you will not say such a thing to Meredith, ma'am. It will not make my suit any the easier."

His mother stared. "Is she mad?"

"Proud, ma'am," he replied succinctly. "And very much out of the common way. I would not have it otherwise."

The duchess absorbed this in silence before saying bluntly. "Y're telling me not to take a hand in it, is that right?"

"Yes, Mama. Quite right."

The duchess recognized the note in her son's voice. Although never deficient in courtesy to his parent, or indeed to anyone, Rutherford could be alarmingly final when his mind was made up. "Hmph. Well, you know your own business best, I daresay. Arabella and George will bring her here for dinner tomorrow, and you may escort us to the play afterward."

Thus it was that Meredith found herself accepted into the Keighley family. The duke was perfectly pleasant although he appeared to take little notice of her, but, since this lack of attention seemed to extend universally, she could not feel slighted. His wife was kind, and Meredith was left in little doubt as to who was the power behind the family throne. It became clear that the duchess had decided to interest herself most energetically in Merrie's come-out, a fact that intrigued her ladyship. She understood Bella's part, but why the Duchess of Keighley should be more than ordinarily interested in a distant connection from the wilds of Cornwall was a definite puzzle.

Having bowed to necessity, Meredith typically wasted neither time nor energy in complaint. Throwing herself wholeheartedly into the enterprise after some initial hesitation, she rapidly lost her scruples about using Rutherford's purse. The bank draft he had given her seemed enormous until Madame Bernice sent in her bill for the ball dress of ivory crape with velvet ribbons spangled with gold. The gown had been bought for her first appearance at Almack's, and not even the undeniable vision reflected by her glass could reconcile Meredith to such a monstrous sum.

Damian, waiting in the hall to escort his sister and Meredith to the ball, caught his breath as she came down the stairs. That glorious auburn hair had been cut, not too much at his express desire but enough to accommodate the fashionably classic styles. Tonight, it clustered in a myriad loose curls confined by a ribbon with a bow over her left eye. A magnificent pearl necklace was clasped around a throat that rose long and creamy from a low-cut bodice that made the most of a bosom that Rutherford privately considered to be perfection. Had he once actually told his sister that he did not consider Merrie to be a beauty?

"You are quite ravishing, my love," he murmured in some awe, taking her hand as she stepped from the last stair. "That gown is quite magnificent."

"Yes, but Rutherford, the price!" she said, unable to contain her horror one more minute. "You would not credit the figure."

"I would," he answered, smiling. "But it is not a subject I wish to discuss now or at any time. Do we understand each other?"

"Yes, my lord. It shall be as you command, my lord," Merrie returned in dulcet accents, sweeping into a deep curtsy. "You must forgive the provincial values which betray me into such vulgar concerns."

He shook his head, refusing the mischievous invitation. Meredith looked a little disappointed, then laughed. "I must return the compliment, Rutherford. You are looking most elegant."

In fact, the word hardly did justice to the waisted black coat with long tails, the white waistcoat, the black silk knee britches and striped stockings, the single diamond pin in the folds of his cravat. His hair was brushed à la Brutus, and Merrie decided that she had never seen him looking more distinguished.

"I hope you realize what an honor this is, Merrie?" Bella said, adjusting the folds of a handsome silver mantilla. "Damian finds evenings such as we are about to pass the greatest form of insipidity. He would much rather be at White's or blowing a cloud at Cribb's parlor."

"You do me an injustice, Bella," her brother protested mildly. "Only a fool would pass up the opportunity to witness Merrie's first experience of this particular form of entertainment."

"You think I will not enjoy it?"

"I think you will find it lacking in excitement," he replied with a twinkle. "Let us go. It wants but half an hour to eleven and I would not care to be turned away for arriving one minute after the hour—not after the pains we have all taken to create a suitably devastating impression."

That evening, Meredith realized fully what it meant to be under the auspices of the Keighleys. The patronesses of Almack's all came forward when they arrived, greeting Damian with expressions of gratified surprise. Princess Esterhazy, who struck Merrie as a small round ball of vivacity, welcomed her kindly; Countess Lieven stared at her with an intensity that Merrie decided deserved no other name but rudeness. To Damian's amusement and Bella's slight alarm, she returned the stare. A chilly smile eventually touched the lips of the lady considered to be the best dressed and most knowledgeable in London.

"Do you waltz, Lady Blake?" she inquired.

Meredith, well taught by Bella, knew that a lady did not waltz at Almack's unless given permission to do so by one of the patronesses. "I do not find it objectionable, Countess," she responded. "It is not, however, a dance much practiced in Cornwall."

This reference to the provinces caused the countess a momentary flicker of pain, but she said with great condescension that she would later present Meredith to Lord Molyneux, reputed to be one of the most accomplished waltzers.

"And you are not, I suppose?" Meredith said to Damian as he partnered her in the boulanger.

"You will do better with Molyneux," he promised. "You should appear to best advantage on this first occasion."

Watching from the sidelines throughout the remainder of the evening, he was in no doubt that she did so. "Damian, I prophesy that your protegée will be all the rage." Mr. George Bryan Brummell, having spent twenty minutes in the company of the lady, came over to his friend where he stood, leaning negligently against the wall.

"You have just ensured that, George," replied Rutherford with a quirk of his lips. "Twenty minutes in your exclusive company will be more than sufficient to see her established."

"I like her," the beau said directly. "I do not think she cared a jot for my attentions."

"Probably not." Damian grinned. "But I am grateful, my friend, even if the lady is not."

"Lady Blake, permit me to introduce the Honorable Gerald Devereux." Lady Jersey beamed in her customary friendly fashion as she presented a lean, dark-haired young man, impeccably, if not spectacularly, attired in dove-gray silk. "He would like to solicit your hand for the cotillion."

"Mr. Devereux." Merrie smiled, giving him her hand. "I am honored." She had lost count of the number of partners presented to her this evening, names and features were beginning to blur in a rather pleasant haze. Gerald Devereux, however, had a most distinguished countenance. Cerulean-blue eyes pierced his surroundings from beneath sharply arched, black eyebrows, but most startling was the thick silver streak in the black locks brushed artlessly back from a broad white brow. It lent a most romantic air to an otherwise ascetic mien, and Meredith found herself both attracted and intrigued.

"The honor is all mine, your ladyship." He bowed low over the hand in his. "I hardly dared to hope for your partnership this evening, so well attended have you been."

"How gallant, sir," Merrie murmured as Sally Jersey, with a pleased little laugh, hurried off to spread elsewhere the cheerful nonstop chatter that had earned her the name of "Silence" amongst the ton.

"So, Lady Blake, are you suitably impressed by this bastion of proper social conduct, this bulwark of the ton?"

Merrie chuckled. "How could I not be, sir? My knees quake at the very thought of receiving a frown from one of the illustrious patronesses. And the refreshments—the epitome of elegance!"

Gerald Devereux laughed. He had not expected his sally to meet with quite such a mischievously forthright response. Since tea, orgeat, and lemonade accompanied by cakes and bread and butter could only be described as meager, he correctly surmised that his partner was indulging in a little sarcasm at the expense of one of society's gods—a most definitely daring venture for a newcomer who could be made or broken on this her first official appearance.

"Have I shocked you, Mr. Devereux?" Meredith inquired after executing a particularly complicated figure.

"Not at all, ma'am," he made haste to reassure her. "Surprised, perhaps, but most pleasantly so."

"I may be making my debut, sir," Meredith said, "but I am not a young chit in her first Season and cannot, I fear, behave in a suitably wide-eyed and impressionable fashion."

"Indeed not," Devereux agreed with a gravity belied by the admiring amusement in the blue eyes.

Meredith's dimples peeped. Such obvious admiration was very pleasant, she discovered. "I see we understand each other, sir."

"I most fervently hope we may further our understanding," her partner declared with an enthusiasm that Meredith found wholly satisfying.

"Merrie seems to be amusing herself," Bella observed to her brother as they went down the same set as Meredith and Devereux.

"Yes," Damian concurred drily. "Unless I much mistake the matter, she is flirting quite shamelessly with Devereux."

"Do you mind?" Arabella looked up at him a little anxiously but was instantly reassured by his smile.

"Not in the least, Bella. It is simply a talent I had not known she possessed. I daresay there are many others waiting to be discovered."

The subscription ball at Almack's was followed the next day by the small party given by Lady Beaumont for her guest. Meredith was hard-pressed to see how an occasion for which over two hundred invitations had been issued could be called small. From dawn till dinner time, the house was in an uproar, and Meredith, having narrowly avoided several disastrous collisions with intent servants laboring under burdens of silver, linen, and floral arrangements, followed Bella's example and retreated to her boudoir. It was mid afternoon when a footman brought the message that Lord Rutherford was below stairs, desirous of having speech with her ladyship.

Merrie found him in the crimson saloon, the only receiving room in the house, it would seem, to be untouched by the bustle. On the way, she paused to look through the open front door where men in leather aprons were erecting an awning to the street and others were unrolling a red carpet.

"I cannot help feeling this is an unconscionable amount of fuss for a country cousin," she remarked, closing the door of the saloon behind her.

"Have you not realized yet that Bella will seize any excuse to give a party?" Damian teased, holding open his arms.

"Thank you, sir. I am quite put in my place." She moved with dignified hauteur to the sofa, ignoring the welcoming arms. It was not a choice she was permitted though, and she managed only the faintest

330

squawk of protest as he spun her around and then collapsed, laughing, against his chest.

It was quite some minutes before Rutherford was able to reach the object of his visit. "I have a present for you," he said, drawing a flat, velvet box from his pocket. "No, do not say anything," he cautioned, seeing her about to make the protest he had been expecting. "Bella has told me how you will wear your hair tonight. You will accept this to please me."

Merrie opened the box. An opera comb of platinum, studded with seed pearls and tiny diamonds, lay on the satin lining. She looked at it for long minutes as that damnable Cornish pride warred with the loving desire to accept the gift of love. He would not oblige her to accept this as part of their contract, yet, if she refused it, Meredith knew he would be deeply wounded.

"It is beautiful," she said softly. "I will wear it with the utmost pleasure." Wear, but not accept, she thought. When it is time for this to be over, I will return the loan.

Damian did not hear the qualifying word, heard only the words of acceptance with a surge of relief at how easily it had been accomplished. He kissed her hungrily. "Tomorrow, my love, we will go to Highgate. I grow desperate at times, watching you flirt and cajole and play with those wicked eyes, and I cannot declare to the world that you are mine."

A cold finger touched between Merrie's shoulder blades. Sometimes, he still talked as if he did not understand that it was only a game they played, a game made even more precious by its temporal nature.

She was afforded little time to dwell on this unease when the evening began. Thirty people sat down to dinner at eight o'clock and Meredith found herself the guest of honor in spite of her inclination to retire into the background. She wore a dress of Pomona green crape over a white satin half-slip. Tiny puff sleeves of lace threaded with seed pearls complemented Rutherford's gift set behind the elaborate knot of hair on the crown of her head. Nan had brushed her side curls until they shone, burnished by the candlelight. For one delicious instant, Merrie contemplated the reactions of Lady Patience Barrat and her cronies if they could see the downtrodden widow at this moment. Then she thought of her brothers. Theo, at least, would approve wholeheartedly of his sister's transformation.

Meredith's hand had been solicited for almost every dance by a constant stream of callers to Cavendish Square in the days preceding the ball. She stood up for the first dance with the Marquis of Beaumont as was right and proper, but the waltz that followed was Rutherford's. "You are every inch as accomplished a dancer as Lord Molyneux," Meredith declared, a note of reproof in her voice. "Why do you dislike it so?"

"Curiously, I find that I do not," he returned, imperceptibly increasing the pressure of his hand on her back. "But then I have never before found a partner I could tolerate."

"But you cannot possibly now ignore the claims of all the fair damsels who are regarding me with such open envy." Merrie lifted her face to give him a smile brimming with mischief. "Having set a precedent, sir, you must continue. No one will believe you to be a reluctant or poor dancer any longer."

"Marry me," he said involuntarily, breaking his resolve not to bring up the subject until this way of life had become second nature to her.

"Do not spoil everything," she whispered. "I had thought we had agreed."

"To spoil things was not my intention," her partner said drily. "You are become quite flushed. Let us go onto the balcony for some air."

The balcony was a grandiose term for the narrow ledge built outside each one of the long windows of the ballroom. Low iron railings fenced in the tiny space where Meredith stepped, breathing deeply of the chilly night air. Damian partially closed the double windows behind them as he stood beside her, hidden from the ballroom by the heavy brocade curtains veiling the window.

"I do beg your pardon for bringing up a subject you find so repugnant," said Rutherford with ill-concealed sarcasm.

Meredith gripped the iron railing, heedless of the dirt transferred to her long white satin gloves. "How many times must I tell you that it will not do? I am not made to be a duchess, Damian. I am an adventuress, a smuggler, my birth is paltry, my fortune nonexistent. The only things I possess in any quantity are debts and brothers."

"In the past month," he said with quiet emphasis, "you have taken the town by storm. You are considered beautiful, accomplished, wellborn—"

"And rich!" She interrupted fiercely. "What does it

matter that I should be considered all of those things when you and I know that they are not true?"

"What society believes, my dear girl, is always the truth. Have you not realized that fact yet? Nothing else will ever be believed of you even if you hired a town crier to proclaim from the rooftops what you consider to be the truth."

The words sank in, bringing with them the final pieces of the puzzle. "I see," she said slowly. "That being the case then, I need not worry that you would commit social suicide by marrying an indigent, law-breaking widow since, as far as society is concerned, you would not be doing so." He did not respond and she turned in the confined space to face him. "You are as conniving and as full of duplicity as I am myself."

"True enough. But it is a perfectly respectable tactic to turn one's opponent's weapons against him."

"It is underhanded!" Merrie declared.

Damian laughed softly and tilted her chin. "You cannot blame me, love, for adopting whatever strategy seems necessary to achieve my object. You would do so yourself."

A gleam came into the sloe eyes. "*Will* do so, my lord. I give you fair warning."

"Just what is going through that pretty, but excessively devious, little head, now?" he demanded uneasily.

"Why, nothing." The slim white shoulders lifted in a careless shrug. "You issued a challenge, sir. I am merely telling you that I accept it. Perhaps we should return to the ballroom. We may be considered cousins, but rules of propriety still apply, do they not?"

That well-remembered crisp crackle was in her voice, and Damian's heart sank as his sense of unease increased. He held the rich curtains aside for her, ran his finger up the slender column of her neck as she passed him. Her skin, as always, rippled beneath his touch, and he felt that inevitable quiver run through the taut body. Angry with him she may be, the emotion did nothing to lessen her physical response to his caress.

He could derive only small comfort from this knowledge, however, as he watched her go off with a radiant smile on the arm of Gerald Devereux. She seemed to sparkle as lustrously as the great crystal chandelier whose hundreds of candles illuminated the ballroom, and Devereux quite obviously basked in that luminous warmth.

"I beg you will pardon my impertinence, ma'am, but I have the distinct impression that something has angered you." Gerald handed Merrie a glass of lemonade, taking up his place by her chair where she sat fanning herself vigorously after the exertions of the dance.

She looked at him in surprise not a little tinged with guilt. "I must have been lacking in manners, Mr. Devereux, to have given you such an impression."

"No—no, not at all," he protested. "I should never have mentioned it, but—forgive me—there is something about the way your eyes are sparkling that indicates an emotion other than pure enjoyment."

"You are remarkably perspicacious." She smiled wryly. "I have, perhaps, been a little out of temper, but I am quite restored to good humor now, I assure you."

He bowed, smiling. "I hope I can assume that I was not the author of your irritation."

"Indeed you were not!" Her eyes widened in horror. "Now, you have made me feel most dreadfully guilty."

"A thousand pardons, Lady Blake! That was never my intention." His voice dropped slightly. "I would only ensure your pleasure and happiness."

Meredith felt a small prickle of discomfort at the serious note, the intensity of the blue eyes bent upon her face. The light flirtatious veneer that she enjoyed with Gerald Devereux seemed suddenly to have been drawn aside, revealing something rather more purposeful. It was with a measure of relief that she greeted Viscount Allenby, coming at that moment to claim her hand for the quadrille.

For the remainder of the evening she danced every dance, seemingly indefatigable. Gerald Devereux partnered her several times but, to her relief, behaved with his usual amusing charm and light touch as if that moment of intensity had been a figment of her imagination. Meredith decided that it had been. Her imagination, after all, had a rich diet these days; it would be no wonder if it suffered from indigestion once in a while.

Damian found her smilingly polite, prepared to talk only the merest commonplace on the few occasions he could get close enough to her for speech. It was all very splendid that his plans should have succeeded so well, he reflected, finding his own hand relegated to a country dance where the need to concentrate on the figure made serious conversation impossible, but his success seemed somewhat Pyrrhic when his attempt to take her into supper met with a pretty apology as Meredith accepted the rival claim of the Marquis of Wolvey.

Much to Arabella's gratification, the band of the Scots Greys played at supper, Rutherford being good friends with their colonel, but she found her pleasure somewhat diminished when she saw her brother's moody expression. It was one she recognized all too well although it had been absent recently, but, when she asked him in a whisper what was amiss, he smiled, shrugged, denied that anything had occurred to disturb his serenity and reverted to his customary, charming sunny temper. In fact, Lord Rutherford was ruefully regretting the impulse that had led him to betray his intentions. Knowing better than to underestimate his mistress, he felt a considerable sense of foreboding when he sought his bed in the first faint flush of dawn.

"I do not think there has been such a sad crush this Season," Arabella announced complacently, rustling in a morning wrapper of rose-pink silk as she sat on her guest's bed the following morning. "I dare swear that by midnight one could hardly move."

"The floor was certainly crowded," Merrie agreed obligingly, smiling at Bella over her hot chocolate.

"My dear, only look at these billet-doux," Bella exclaimed, picking up a handful of the prettily penned

337

papers scattered over Merrie's satin coverlet. "Why, there must be one from every unattached male in the Upper Ten Thousand."

"Goose," Meredith said affectionately. "There is not one from your brother at any event."

"Well, it is not precisely his style," Arabella said, brushing away a stray curl. "My dear, you may snub me if you wish, but—have you and Damian perhaps quarreled? I could not help noticing that you were little in his company last night."

Meredith regarded her visitor thoughtfully. "I was as much in his as in anyone's. I would not care for it to be said that I was throwing myself at his head."

"No one would ever say such a thing." Bella sounded genuinely shocked at the idea. "It is perfectly proper for him to offer special attentions since you reside under his family's roof. Indeed, people would not be at all surprised."

"No?" Meredith inquired, eyebrows lifting. "Why would they not?"

"It is common knowledge that Rutherford must find a wife," Arabella said with blithe indiscretion. "Papa talks to him of little else, which is why Damian does not call upon him as often as he should. It would not be considered in the least extraordinary if you, as the family's protegée, caught his eye."

"Does your mother think this?"

"Oh, certainly." Bella smiled confidently. "She would be very well pleased with such an outcome, and it would not surprise me if it is not already thought about town to be almost settled."

"I see." Meredith sat back against her pillows,

responding to Bella's cheerful chatter automatically, her mind occupied with the infuriating knowledge of how thoroughly she had been duped. Damian had not for one minute accepted her proscription on marriage. Instead, he had set up a perfect arrangement whereby what he saw as her main objections to his proposal were made null and void. If society and the Keighleys considered such a match not only respectable but desirable, why should Merrie Trelawney have scruples? She had none about hoodwinking her Cornish neighbors as Rutherford knew only too well; the fraud she was now perpetuating on London society was simply on a more elaborate scale. There was no qualitative difference. She could almost hear his arguments, could almost be convinced by them. But nothing could overcome the dull certainty that a woman who drew the breath of life from flaunting the law and every rule and regulation of society would not make a suitable wife for the future Duke of Keighley. Rutherford enjoyed her unconventional ways, her recklessness excited him, and he found in the game they played the purpose and daring that had been lacking since he had left the army. But something that satisfied a momentary craving was no basis for the long years of a marriage that would have to be conventional. Suppose she could not adapt, could not become good and law-abiding or obedient to the rules and prohibitions of Damian's world? If she could not, she would bring him only misery, and Meredith was fairly convinced that she could not.

"Does the invitation to Belvoir please you, Merrie? If you do not like it, I daresay we can make an excuse, but it is most gratifying to receive it."

"I beg your pardon, Bella?" Meredith, realizing that she had heard nothing of the question, flushed guiltily.

"You have not been listening to me!" Bella rebuked her. "It is of all things what I most dislike. George does it to me and sometimes I could *kill* him!" She glared with unusual ferocity, and Merrie made haste to apologize, blaming her absent attention on pleasurable reminiscences of the previous evening.

Somewhat mollified, Arabella repeated that they had received an invitation from the Duchess of Rutland to join a house party at Belvoir Castle. Would Merrie enjoy it? Rutherford was also invited, she added. On receiving Merrie's agreement, Bella left her to get dressed, displaying no more than a discreet smile when her guest informed her that she would not be dining at home that evening.

Still thoughtful, Meredith got up herself, responding only absently to Nan's inquiries and comments. This distraction prompted Nan to demand acerbically what mischief she was planning and to receive Merrie's innocent disclaimers with a disbelieving grunt.

Meredith was indeed planning mischief. She had told Rutherford last night that she considered he had issued a challenge, one she had accepted. The statement then had been made simply out of anger at his duplicity; on reflection, the matter now assumed more serious proportions. She would pay him back in his own coin but, in so doing, would remind him forcibly of her true nature and convince him once and for all of the impossibility of anything more than glorious adventuring between them.

Rutherford, unsure of what he would find when he appeared that afternoon in Cavendish Square to spirit her away to the love nest in Highgate, was lulled into a sense of security by the bright, vivacious, definitely loving Meredith. Not once did she refer to their conversation on the balcony, and he made the grave error of allowing himself to assume that she had decided the issue was not worthy of battle.

"I would like you to teach me to drive," Meredith announced, watching appreciatively as he caught the thong of his whip with a slight turn of his wrist. "Then I should like to drive myself in a perch phaeton and pair."

"Very dashing," said Damian, amused. "I will engage to teach you, but, if you have no aptitude, then take my advice and forget the idea. Nothing looks more laughable than a cow-handed whip."

"Cow-handed," Merrie reflected, "is a most descriptive term."

He chuckled. "It is, but do not use it in polite circles; it is excessively vulgar."

Meredith, storing the term away for future reference, asked amiably, "Do you think that I will be cow-handed?"

"No." He shook his head. "I think it most unlikely. But as yet I have only seen you drive a gig and pony."

"I have good hands when riding. You said so yourself," Merrie pointed out. Soon after her arrival in Cavendish Square, Damian had presented her with a spirited chestnut gelding that had delighted her even as she refused the gift, insisting on accepting the horse

341

merely as a loan. He had conceded equably with the simple request that she exercise the loan regularly. As a result, Lady Blake's chestnut rapidly became a familiar sight in Hyde Park. Arabella, who did not herself care for riding, had quickly decided that riding habits became Meredith almost better than any other form of dress and had taken the matter in hand most energetically. Merrie now possessed more riding habits than she would once have thought it possible to wear in a single lifetime. Those considerations, however, belonged to another world, one that seemed to have receded into a dim and distant past.

"At Belvoir I will teach you," Damian now promised. "On one condition."

"What is that?"

"That you accept the fact that I know what I am talking about and do exactly as I bid," he replied with a grin. "I realize it will be a little difficult for you, believing as you do in your own supremacy—"

"I do not," Meredith protested, half laughing, but unsure whether he was only funning.

"And do you not?" Those expressive brows shot up. "I think, Merrie Trelawney, that there are few people you trust to manage things as well as you."

"Perhaps so." She played with her gloves restlessly. "I have reason to trust *you* though. You have demonstrated your ability to manage any number of things including me on more than one occasion."

Rutherford shot her a sharp look but her expression was as equable as her tone, and he decided to let the matter rest. "Do you look forward to visiting Belvoir, love?"

342

"I find the idea of Merrie Trelawney as guest of the Duke and Duchess of Rutland monstrous diverting," she replied, chuckling. "Can you imagine how Patience and Lady Collier would react?"

"Abominable girl!" he declared through his own mirth. "Have you no delicacy of feeling?"

"None whatsoever," she responded cheerfully. "I may acquire a veneer of London polish, Rutherford, but I am essentially abominable. You would do well to remember that."

"Is that a warning?" he asked, suddenly sober.

"Just a reminder, should you be in danger of forgetting."

Rutherford whistled softly through pursed lips. "Why do I feel so uneasy, Merrie Trelawney?"

"I cannot imagine," she replied with the smile that was as bland as milk pudding.

Chapter Seventeen

Meredith journeyed north to Belvoir in a state of cheerful anticipation. The prospect of spending a week under the same roof as Rutherford was heady indeed. They would be obliged to conduct themselves with due circumspection, of course, but the double game was one at which they were both skilled and one that they both enjoyed. The covert glance, discreet innuendo, the secret, intimate brush of a hand . . . Her heart danced. This week would provide an interlude before she set about her plan to convince Damian and the ton that the widow Blake was no eligible *partie* for the heir to the Duke of Keighley. A house party at Belvoir Castle was neither the place nor the occasion to put such a plan into action. While it would be most effective, it would be abominably uncomfortable for the Beaumonts in such close quarters.

Arabella, overjoyed that George had agreed to make one of the party, was bubbling with a pleasure that her husband could not help but find touching. It had been at his brother-in-law's energetic suggestion that the marquis now accompanied his wife but, in view of Arabella's heartwarming joy, Lord Beaumont was not about to award the credit where it was due.

It was late afternoon when the chaise turned in at the iron gates of the park, and they were all glad to see the gray stone building of Belvoir Castle looming majestically at the head of the driveway. Meredith gazed appreciatively around the great stone-flagged hall where an enormous fire blazed in the hearth, offering warmth and welcome to the arriving guests.

"Arabella, George, how delightful. And Lady Blake, you are most welcome." The Duchess of Rutland came forward from the fire where she had been standing with a party of men who, judging by their muddy boots and garments, had just returned from a day's shooting. "You must be exhausted after your journey. Come and warm your hands by the fire, then you shall go straight to your apartments and rest awhile before dinner." Chattering in this kindly fashion, she drew them over to the fire where introductions were performed.

"Why, Mr. Devereux, I did not know you were to be of this party." Meredith smiled pleasantly, greeting her acquaintance with well-concealed surprise. When Devereux had called in Cavendish Square only two days previously, he had made no mention of his intended visit to Belvoir although Meredith had been quite open about her own plans. Now, he gave her a somewhat enigmatic smile as his lips lightly brushed her fingertips.

"A little surprise, ma'am. A pleasant one, I trust."

"A delightful one," she responded politely, feeling again that slight prickle of unease. Gerald Devereux could not be intending to pursue a light-hearted flirtation into deeper woods, could he? No, of course not. Merrie dismissed the absurd thought as she followed the footman up the stairs to her bedchamber.

She did not feel remotely fatigued and, after some hesitation, decided that she would cause no offense to her hostess by taking a walk around the grounds. True, it was a damp, dank late October afternoon, but, after being boxed up in a chaise for the greater part of the day, her muscles ached for a stretching. A footman, recovering with well-trained speed from his surprise, opened the front door for her just as Lord Rutherford's curricle, drawn by a pair of blood chestnuts, drew up.

"Lady Blake." He sprang down, taking her hand. "If I were a coxcomb, I would dare to hope that you were come to meet me." His tone was jocular, offering a perfectly acceptable sally for the ears of footmen and grooms. The gray eyes, however, glowed and her fingers quivered in his palm in inevitable response.

"I was about to take a short stroll, my lord." Merrie smiled. "We are but newly arrived ourselves, and I have a need to shake out the fidgets from my legs."

"Like a restless colt," said Damian in an amused undertone before raising his voice. "We will meet at dinner, then." He bowed, released her hand, and disappeared into the house.

Merrie watched him go, a tiny smile playing over her lips as an outrageous idea glimmered, then burst gloriously in her mind. He would presumably be welcomed by the duke and duchess, a courtesy taking maybe ten minutes, then he would surely be shown to his apartments. Making a pretence of examining the shrubs bordering the gravel sweep occupied nearly ten minutes; then she returned to the house, reaching the hall just as Rutherford, escorted by a footman, attained the gallery at the head of the stairs. Casually and with the utmost discretion, Lady Blake followed, her demeanor indicating that she knew just where she was going as they turned down a corridor toward the west wing. If there were no ladies' apartments in this part of the castle, her presence might be remarked for all her apparent confidence, Merrie thought but was instantly reassured when a maid, bearing a dressing case, passed her, vanishing, after a discreet knock, behind a paneled door. Damian had not turned around, there was no reason why he should have, but Merrie fell back as her quarry reached the end of the corridor. Slipping into a deep window embrasure, she watched, making careful note of the door opened by the footman. It would not do to make a mistake! Merrie had to stifle a giggle at the thought before returning, with casually confident step, to her own chamber in the east wing.

Nan was awaiting her impatiently. "Just you come along now, Meredith. I had your water brought up an hour ago. Stone-cold it is by now, and serves you right, gallivanting about." The dark mutterings continued as Merrie was dressed in an evening gown of pale-lavender crape with long, full sleeves buttoned tightly at the wrist. Meredith gathered that Belvoir Castle was a nasty, drafty place, the staff so busy looking down their noses they were in danger of tripping over their feet. Nan did not care to share sleeping accommodation with anyone, not even Lady Beaumont's maid, but then she was always ready to

347

make sacrifices, as Meredith ought to know.

Merrie agreed that she did know, refraining from her usual fidgets as her hair was brushed, braided, and fastened in a coronet at the crown of her head, the side curls feathered about her ears. Nan fastened the tasseled cord at her waist, draped a silver embroidered scarf over her elbows, and nodded in satisfaction.

Merrie kissed her. "Do not wait up for me, Nan dear. I can undress myself, and you need have no fears for my safety here!" Her eyes twinkled wickedly and Nan smiled, albeit a little grimly. "Just you behave yourself," she admonished. "I know that look you've got, my girl, and it bodes no good."

"I cannot imagine what you mean." Laughing, Merrie whisked herself out of the chamber, remembering as she reached the head of the stairs to change her skip to a more decorous step.

The drawing room appeared to be full of a great many people, most of them strangers to her. There was no sign of Arabella or her husband, and it was with a measure of relief that Merrie greeted Mr. Brummell, who came over to her sofa, looking as unobtrusively elegant as ever.

"Do you hunt tomorrow, Lady Blake?" he inquired, taking a seat beside her.

"That rather depends," Merrie answered, "on whether I shall be quite outshone."

Mr. Brummell smiled appreciatively. "You are an apt pupil, Lady Blake. One should, indeed, never attempt anything in public if one is not quite sure of one's superiority." Raising his quizzing glass, he examined their fellow inhabitants of the drawing room and pronounced, "I do not think you need have any fears. There is no lady present to outshine you in the equestrian arena."

"Then I shall most definitely hunt," averred Meredith. "In fact, I enjoy the sport so much I should have been sadly disappointed to have been obliged to forgo it. I am doubly grateful to you, Mr. Brummell, for your reassurance."

"My pleasure, ma'am," he said gravely. "I am quite willing to be flattered although not accustomed to being so with such transparency."

Meredith chuckled and received a droll smile. She was, as her companion had noted before, quite indifferent to the consequence his attention bestowed upon her. She was totally unawed by Beau Brummell, found him merely amusing and a good conversationalist. She was not, however, unaware of the advantages his friendship bestowed on her socially and not at all averse to holding him at her side. It was all part of the game, after all—Beau Brummell entertaining and being entertained by such a one as Merrie Trelawney.

She felt Damian's approach before she saw him and, as Mr. Brummell's attention was claimed by a lady in a turquoise turban, patted the freed seat beside her.

"You are recovered from your journey, Lord Rutherford?"

"Thank you," he said with appropriate solemnity. "I trust you managed to rid yourself of the fidgets, Lady Blake."

"Yes, thank you," she responded primly. Then her dimples peeped. "Must we be so odiously formal for the entire week? I shall never be able to keep a straight face."

"I beg you will try," implored Rutherford. "I fear an entire week of this masquerade is going to prove a sore trial."

"Why did you come then?" Meredith fluttered her fan of frosted crape, showing him only a pair of utterly wicked eyes.

"Because I could not resist the opportunity to be under the same roof with you," he replied softly. "As well you know. If you will only behave with circumspection, we shall brush through quite tolerably. Just do not tempt me to laughter with any sly remarks."

"Bella did say that it would not be considered remarkable if you were to pay me more than ordinary attention," Merrie remarked in a casual manner. "The family connection, you understand?"

His sister was not always very wise, Rutherford reflected. "I do understand," he said drily. "It is that connection which will permit me to teach you to drive without undue remark. But unless you wish it said that you have set your cap at me, you would be advised to maintain a degree of formality."

"I was under the impression society considered a match between us to be quite settled," she said, closing her fan with a snap.

"Then society will be out of luck, will it not?"

It was a disappointing rejoinder. Meredith had hoped to see just a smidgeon of guilt. Instead, he appeared quite unperturbed. But then, when it came to verbal fencing, she had long ago become reconciled to the fact that Rutherford had the edge.

Damian, guessing accurately at her chagrin, looked sideways at the set profile. His lips twitched slightly. She looked so adorably put out but, in the interests of the greater good, he repressed his fond amusement, saying with a degree of sharpness, "I have not come all this way to quarrel with you, Meredith."

"That is not just," she accused in a fierce whisper. "The quarrels are of your making, not mine."

Damian sighed wearily. "I think that I must teach you to let sleeping dogs lie." He stood up and strolled away from her without so much as a nod of farewell.

Meredith watched indignantly as he joined an animated group by the fire while she sat neglected on her couch.

"Lady Blake, what has happened to displease you?" The Honorable Gerald Devereux appeared opportunely, looking at her with a flattering mixture of anxiety and sympathy.

"My face must be damnably revealing," Merrie said, then pressed her fingers to her lips in horror. "Oh, dear, Mr. Devereux, my wretched tongue! I do beg your pardon."

"It is not necessary, I assure you." The piercing blue eyes were alight with laughter. "It is not, as we once agreed, as if you had just emerged from the schoolroom."

"That is still no excuse, sir," she responded ruefully. "But it is kind in you to treat such a lapse as unimportant. Will you not be seated?"

Devereux accepted the invitation with alacrity. "How may I entertain you, my lady, so that you may forget whatever, or whomever, has caused your displeasure?"

Was there the slightest emphasis on "whomever"? Had Damian's abrupt departure been as revealing as her face? "Sir, it was but a passing thought," Merrie

351

replied swiftly. "And a singularly unimportant one at that. But I should be glad if you would identify those of our fellow guests with whom I am unacquainted. There seem to be a great many of them."

"Gladly," Devereux agreed. "Now, where shall I begin?"

Meredith found that her companion was as witty as he was knowledgeable and not at all averse to imparting wicked tidbits of gossip about their fellow guests. Damian, stealing a covert glance from across the room at her laughing face and sparkling eyes, recognized that his attempt at punishment had failed lamentably. Merrie appeared more than tolerably amused in his absence.

"Gerald is much taken with Arabella's protegée, Rutherford." The soft voice of his hostess broke into his musing.

"Indeed?" He looked as surprised as he felt, such an idea not having occurred to him, before composing his features into a suitably indifferent expression.

The duchess nodded. "He has begged most fervently to be allowed to take her into dinner." Her eyes rested on the two, side by side on the couch. "I wonder if she will succumb. While he is not precisely in financial straits, her fortune would certainly be of use to Devereux."

Damian experienced a surge of irritation at this matter-of-fact statement. He could not, however, deny it or even comment except in the lightest manner possible without causing undue remark. Clearly he must alert Merrie to the attention she was drawing by that harmless flirtation although, if it was harmless, why should he? Besides, he still intended to make his earlier point stick fast in her mind, and that plan prohibited speech with her until she exhibited some signs of repentance for her sharpness.

Devereux took Meredith in to dinner and she found herself seated at the opposite end of the table from Rutherford. It was not a deprivation for which she could hold him responsible, but the fact that he did not once look toward her during the long hours at table could only be construed as deliberate. She could not afford to appear distracted with her uncomfortably observant companion and so resolutely put thoughts of Damian, Lord Rutherford, to one side. After dinner, Damian joined his host and two other inveterate whist players in the card room, underscoring his intentional neglect, and Meredith began to feel distinctly forlorn in spite of the attentions of Devereux, entertainment offered by a rubber of cassino, and various performances on the pianoforte and the harp. Quite clearly, if Damian intended expressing his displeasure in this fashion for any length of time, the stay at Belvoir would not come up to expectations. However, Meredith had every intention of healing the breach in her own inimitable fashion.

Rutherford was in the hall with a group of men when the ladies appeared, on their way to bed. Merrie's eyes were downcast, her shoulders sagging just a little—body language that would be obvious and comprehensible to no one but himself, who was familiar with every one of the actress's tricks. He gave her her candle, clasping her wrist for a second as he bade her good-night.

"I am sorry," she whispered. "You will not still be

353

vexed tomorrow, will you?"

Rutherford's lip quivered. "Look at me." Obediently she raised her eyes. "As I conjectured," he said in a low voice. "You are quite unrepentant. I give you fair warning, Merrie, if you meant to quarrel with me this week, I shall simply absent myself."

"I do not mean to quarrel with you."

"That is all right, then." He gave a satisfied nod, eyes twinkling as he released her wrist. "Sweet dreams, Cousin Meredith."

The tip of her tongue touched her lips and her own eyes narrowed suggestively before she placed her hand on the banister, following Arabella upstairs.

Nan had clearly taken the advice and not waited up for her. Meredith undressed rapidly in the empty bedchamber, slipped into her nightgown and a dark hooded cloak, then sat by the fire to wait. It was well over an hour later before she was certain that the entire household had retired. There were no more soft voices in the corridor, sounds of doors opening and closing, muffled footsteps on the landing carpet. She cracked her door open. The corridor was deserted, lit dimly at either end by candles in wall sconces. Barefoot, drawing the hood of her cloak over her bright hair, Merrie stole into the corridor. Keeping against the wall, she crept toward the central gallery at the head of the stairs. The hall below was dark and shadowy, lit only by the dying embers of the great fire. Obviously, no one was still about if all the candles downstairs had been extinguished. On tiptoe, she darted across the gallery and into the passage leading to the west wing. She could always pretend she was sleepwalking—Lady Macbeth with a troubled conscience! Merrie pressed her fingers to her lips to keep back the bubble of laughter. It was quite hopeless. She could never learn to be respectable; it was so dull!

The castle was a warren of passages and wide corridors lined with doors. Fortunately, topography was a vital skill for a smuggler, one learned years ago, and she found her way to Damian's door without hesitation. No light showed in the crack beneath. Softly, she turned the porcelain knob and was in the room with the door closed on the outside world in the blink of an eye.

Rutherford, though, was even quicker. He still slept like a soldier, barely losing consciousness, ready to wake, instantly alert at the merest breath of disturbance. The silver-mounted pistol that he kept beneath his pillow was in his hand as the doorknob turned; his feet were on the floor as the dark figure whisked inside.

"What the devil?" he exclaimed softly, not sure whether he could believe the evidence of his eyes.

"Oh, you are awake. What a pity. I had planned a very special way of waking you." The mischievous chuckle convinced him that he was not in the grip of hallucination. "Is this not a famous adventure, love?"

Rutherford was, for once, speechless. Without taking his eyes off her, he pushed the pistol under his pillow again, lit the candle beside the bed, and swung himself back into a horizontal position. Merrie tossed back the hood of her cloak, shaking out her hair, her eyes shining. "Have you nothing to say, sir?" He shook his head, still watching as she threw off the cloak, untied the satin ribbon at the throat of the demure white nightgown, and drew the garment

355

slowly over her head. Damian exhaled on a long, slow breath as she stood still for a minute, offering her beauty to his gaze, a tiny smile curving her lips, head tilted quizzically. Then, with a sudden exultant little laugh, she sprang onto the bed beside him.

"Wicked creature!" Rutherford found his voice at last. But she just laughed and began with deft efficiency to remove his nightshirt.

"I am come to make love to you tonight," she informed him, pushing him flat as she moved her body over his. "You must lie still and let me pleasure you as you have so often done for me."

"Most willingly," he whispered, closing his eyes as she flicked his nipples with her eyelashes, her breath whispering over his skin. Her tongue, with swift little darts, grazed his skin, bringing every nerve ending to life. He was driven to the edge of torment by the delicacy of touches that appeared not to be corporeal, just a whisper of breath, a silky brush of hair or eyelash, the stroke of a tongue. All the while, her body, glowing in the candlelight, moved sinuously across and over him, available for his eyes and hands to roam wherever they wished. Merrie's own pleasure tonight was derived solely from Damian's so that, when she offered herself to his touch, it was for her lover's gratification, and the arousal she felt was purely secondary although nonetheless powerful for that. With lips and fingers, she brought him to the brink of ecstasy until, with an almost defeated groan, his hands locked in the auburn cascade on his belly and tugged her head up. "Enough," he said hoarsely. "We will share the end game."

Readily, Merrie swung herself astride his supine

form, sheathing him slowly within her welcoming body.

"Do not move," he demanded, holding her hips.

"I want to move," she murmured, her breathing rapid and shallow.

"No, I want you with me and, if you move, I shall be lost," he groaned.

"I *shall* be with you." She threw her head back, pressed her knees against his chest, resting her hands on her ankles, and very deliberately circled her body around the pulsing presence within. Damian moaned, his fingers biting convulsively into the firm flesh of her hips. As his body shuddered under the explosion, she drove hard against him, tightening her inner muscles until she was consumed in his fire.

It was a long time before either of them came back to a sense of the world around them. Merrie, lying collapsed on Damian's chest, their bodies still held at the point of fusion, wondered if she had died just a little. When she whispered this, he stroked her hair, telling her that they had touched the outermost limit of ecstasy and that was, indeed, a little death—a miraculous and rare experience. Lifting her off him with hands now gentle, he settled her into the crook of his arm and lay wide-eyed in the dimly lit room as Merrie's deep breathing told him she slept the sleep of satisfied exhaustion.

She was such a wondrous, irreverent, wild creature. How could he persuade her that he did not want her tamed, that marriage need not be a staid progress through a life confined and rigid? Rutherford knew well enough that Merrie would not change just as he knew that her own knowledge of this fact kept her so proud and obstinate in her refusal. But if she would not believe him when he told her that it was the wild and reckless Merrie Trelawney that he wanted as his duchess, it was hard to know what else he could do short of kidnapping her and marrying her by force over the anvil at Greta Green. It might well come to that, Damian reflected with a grim little smile, stroking the curve of her cheek. Her eyelashes fluttered, and she smiled in her sleep.

It was a pity to wake her, but he had no choice. His own eyes now drooped, and sleep sang a siren song on the horizon of consciousness. There was no way of guaranteeing that one of them would surface before the household arose. "Wake up, darling girl. You must go back to your own bed." He lifted her into a sitting position, but she flopped against his chest.

"Cannot," Merrie muttered. "Still asleep." Her breathing resumed its rhythm, and Damian swore under his breath. Quite obviously he was going to have to carry her back to bed, thus doubling the jeopardy. At least if she were discovered wandering the corridors alone, some story could be fabricated. He could not imagine what possible excuse he could produce for wandering through the castle with a night-gowned figure, dead to the world, in his arms. Apart from anything else, he did not know which was her room.

He managed to shake her into semiconsciousness, dressing the limp figure in nightgown and cloak, leaving her on the bed while he pulled on his shirt and britches. She was fast asleep again when he scooped her into his arms. "Merrie!" He made his voice sharp, setting her on her feet where she swayed dopily.

"If you cannot see your adventures through to the end, then you cannot be allowed to have them. You must wake up enough to direct me to your chamber."

Her eyes focused blearily but with a distinct flicker of awareness. "Beg pardon—east wing," she muttered.

"That's better." He picked her up again. "Now, stay awake to show me your door. You must not speak though, just point." A small nod indicated her comprehension. She forced her eyes wide open in such a determined effort to look alive that Damian was hard put not to laugh. "Some adventuress you are," he mocked, bending to kiss the freckled nose before softly opening the door.

The journey to the east wing seemed infinite, and he started at every creak of the boards beneath his feet. It was accomplished eventually, and with a sigh of relief he inserted the inert body beneath the coverlet on her own bed. The sloe eyes suddenly shot open, and a pair of wiry arms went around his neck, imprisoning him. Meredith laughed delightedly against his mouth. "Now, you can stay here and we may start all over again."

"You little devil!" Tearing her arms away, he forced them above her head, holding her hands, palm against palm on the bed as he glowered down into a face alight with mischief.

"You should have known I would not be so feeble," she chided. "Besides, it would not have been fair if only I had had the risk, would it?"

"One of these days, Merrie Trelawney, I am going to wring your neck and throw your body into the Serpentine," Rutherford threatened with a ferocity

359

not entirely feigned. "I have a very good mind not to teach you to drive."

"Oh, you would not be so unkind," she protested.

"No, I would not." He sighed, still leaning over her. "I can deny you nothing, and I am very much afraid that that is not good for either of us."

"Oh, pooh!" Merrie scoffed. "You talk as if I am a spoiled child to be overindulged. If I were not feeling so warm and loving, I could become very angry."

"Heaven forbid!" He kissed the corner of her mouth, still holding her palms. "I did not mean to imply anything of the kind. I do not believe you have ever been indulged, even to a reasonable extent. I would like to spoil you, but I know that you will not accept it, which is why it would not be good for either of us."

Merrie smiled in rueful understanding and apology. "You do spoil me quite shamelessly and, equally shamelessly, I enjoy it."

"If that is true, then am I content," Damian said simply. "Sleep now. If you meant to hunt, you must be up betimes."

"I will give you a lead," she promised.

"As always," he countered at the door.

In spite of her disturbed night, Meredith appeared at the breakfast table promptly the following morning. Her riding dress drew startled looks of envy from the three ladies who had also decided to take to the field and a smile of approval from Mr. Brummell, who drew out a chair for her beside his own. "You must promise me never to return to Cornwall," he said into her ear as she sat down. "Anyone who can so disconcert the Honorable Mrs. Astley and dear

360

daughter Helena is necessary to the comfort of all sensible people."

"They have not yet seen the hat," Merrie murmured, helping herself to a hot roll from a covered basket. "It has a tall crown, like a shako, with a peak and ostrich feathers."

"Perfect," Brummell declared. "What else would one wear with epaulettes?"

Gerald Devereux, arriving a few minutes later, greeted the table in general and Meredith in particular. "I hope you will not consider it an impertinence, Lady Blake, but that is a most dashing habit," he said, taking the vacant seat on her other side when she smiled her permission.

"Not at all impertinent, sir. Flattering, rather," Merrie replied automatically, concealing her disappointment under the warm smile. That seat had been intended for Damian, but then, if he were so dilatory about making an appearance, he had only himself to blame.

Rutherford, himself, however, did not make that connection when he entered the breakfast parlor to find Meredith in animated conversation with Devereux and Brummell and the nearest available seat to her across the table. The position did afford him an unrestricted view of her dress, though, and his eyebrows lifted slightly. His mistress was attired in a figure-hugging dark-blue habit. Epaulettes, frogged buttons, and braided sleeves emulated a hussar's uniform. That square little chin was lifted by a high, lace-trimmed collar, and a muslin cravat. Rutherford was not entirely sure that the habit met with his wholehearted approval. It certainly did not find favor with the highest sticklers such as the Honorable Mrs. Astley, whose disapproval was patent—as patent as Gerald Devereux's approval, Damian reflected with some annoyance as he helped himself to a dish of bacon and mushrooms on the sideboard.

"Good morning, Lord Rutherford." Merrie greeted him with a smile that was all sweet innocence except for the sensual suggestion lurking in the sloe eyes. Damian instantly forgot his irritation. If Devereux wanted to bask in a little of that radiance, his lordship could afford to be generous—just as long as that particular look was reserved for his eyes only.

Horses, hounds, red-coated huntsmen, grooms, and riders milled around the circular gravel sweep outside Belvoir Castle in the crisp chill of early morning.

"There is something immensely stirring about a meet," Merrie observed to Beau Brummell as they strolled down the castle steps, surveying the lively scene before them. "I enjoy the meet and the ride but not the kill," she confessed.

"How very poor-spirited of you, Lady Blake," Rutherford teased, drawing on his gloves. "May I assist you to mount?" Cupping his palms to receive her booted foot, he tossed her up effortlessly, asking softly as he handed her the reins, "Tell me, does Arabella approve that habit?"

"Why? Do you not?" She frowned down at him. "Mr. Brummell has been kind enough to offer only favorable comment."

"That settles the matter, then," he replied promptly. "It is not that I do not care for it, quite the contrary, but—uh—the audacity took me aback for the moment."

"You are a great deal too strict in your notions, Lord Rutherford," Merrie accused with a roguish gleam. "I would never have believed it—after last night."

"Minx!" he said softly. "I'll have my revenge for that later."

Mr. Brummell left the hunt at the fourth field, much to Merrie's amusement. "It is, of course, ridiculous to imagine him with splashed boots and muddy tops," she confided to Damian as he drew up alongside her at a check. "But I must confess, your friendship puzzles me."

"Because I am not of the Bow Window set?" He laughed.

"Yes. You always dress elegantly, but—"

"Nothing to compare with Brummell," he finished for her.

"No," she agreed. "Why, I have never even seen you in a pair of Hessians. You always wear riding boots and buckskins."

"Neither Brummell nor I are fool enough to believe that the clothes make the man," Rutherford told her, "for all that George would have the world believe it. Our friendship is based on genuine liking."

"I like him too." Merrie narrowed her eyes at a large hedge, carefully circumvented by those ahead of them in the field. "Shall we take the lead, sir, by jumping that barrier?" She was off without waiting for answer, and Damian set his raking bay to the jump minutes behind, offering up silent prayers that there be no ditch lurking on the other side. They landed safely, fortunately, and by early afternoon Meredith

363

agreed to his suggestion that they abandon the hunt and return to Belvoir for her first driving lesson.

This, Merrie discovered to her disgust, was not as amusing as she had expected. For a start, Damian had a quiet, stolid pair of horses from the Rutland stables put between the shafts of his curricle.

"Why are we not to drive your chestnuts?" she demanded naively.

"My dear girl, you do not imagine I would risk my horses' mouths on a rank novice," he replied, handing her into the curricle. "Besides, they have not been out today and will be very fresh. You could not possibly hold them."

Meredith's eyes flashed, but she swallowed the acerbic response as it rose to her lips and took the reins and whip. "We are going to the main gate," she was told. "Hold up your hands. If you drop them in your lap, even these staid creatures will break into a trot." She discovered, as they made their way down the wide driveway, that, quiet though they were, the pair between the shafts were an infinitely different breed from the dappled mare that pulled her gig at home. They were instantly responsive to the slightest tug of the bit, the merest flick of the whip, and Merrie found herself thankful that she did not have Rutherford's chestnuts in hand.

When they reached the iron gates at the entrance to the park, Rutherford told her to walk the horses through. Meredith did so, somewhat surprised at how narrow the gate seemed when one was responsible for negotiating it. She became very familiar with that gate over the next hour as she took the horses through it at a trot, a canter, and finally at full gallop. They approached the entrance head on, from the left, and from the right.

The gatekeeper's children clustered around, appearing to derive considerable amusement from this extraordinary, repetitive activity. When Merrie, taking the corner approach too sharply, shaved the side of the curricle against the stone gatepost, a gasp ran around the spectators.

"Why cannot they go in for their tea?" she muttered in chagrin. "I am sorry, Rutherford. Have I scraped the varnish?"

"Probably," he replied coolly. "But you'll not do it next time. Try the same angle again."

"But I do not want to damage your curricle further," she protested, more than a little shaken by the accident.

"Try it again, Meredith," he repeated. "Do I appear concerned?"

"No," she agreed with a rueful little chuckle. "But this is very tedious, and I do not think I have any aptitude."

"Do you wish to stop because it is tedious or because you think you cannot do it?" He looked at her, eyebrows raised.

"Well, it *is* tedious," she mumbled.

"And did you not agree to do exactly as I tell you?" Taking the reins from her, Rutherford backed the horses into the lane, positioning them for the corner approach. "As it happens, I think you show considerable aptitude. You just lack patience." He handed over the reins, and Meredith, unsure whether to be pleased with the compliment or incensed at the criticism, squared her shoulders and concentrated on the

365

task in hand. There were no further accidents, and by the time they returned to the house Merrie was convinced she would see those stone gateposts in her dreams.

"How did you enjoy your driving lesson, Lady Blake?" the Duke of Rutland inquired, coming over to her in the drawing room after dinner.

"I did not enjoy it in the least, your grace," Meredith replied with a smile. "But your gatekeeper's children had a most amusing afternoon, more entertaining than the circus, I am convinced. But you should know, sir, that I am now most proficient at driving through gates at any speed and from any angle. That is the sum total of my skill and is perhaps a little limiting, but I feel sure I shall find the opportunity to use the expertise at some other gate on some other occasion."

This lively speech brought a rumble of laughter from the duke and afforded those others around considerable amusement.

"Rutherford knows what he is about, ma'am." Sir Charles Stanton spoke up. "If one can drive through a gate at speed without mishap, one can handle most other situations."

"Thank you, Charles." Damian had been standing on the outskirts of the group, concealing his own amusement at Merrie's sardonic riposte, wondering when she would realize how well she fitted this scene and how much she would miss it if it were not there for her. Merrie Trelawney had carved herself a niche that had little now to do with the background he had invented. "I fear that my cousin found the lesson tiresomely repetitious."

"Mayhap the next one will be less so," Merrie suggested hopefully.

"Perhaps Lady Blake would agree to a race." A smooth female voice spoke. "You must know what an advantage such a teacher as Lord Rutherford must give you, ma'am. We ordinary mortals cannot hope to compete."

Meredith turned toward the speaker. The daughter of the Marquis of Blandford, Lady Margaret Pickering prided herself on her skill both with the ribbons and as a horsewoman. She had been outshone in the field this morning, both in dress and audacity by the widow, and now saw the possibility of a recoup.

"I would not presume to match myself against you, Lady Margaret," Meredith replied. "My instructor may well be a consummate practitioner, but that does not, unfortunately, guarantee his pupil's skill."

"Come now, Rutherford." Stanton's eyes lit up. "Surely you'll not let the challenge pass. I'll lay a pony you can turn Lady Blake into respectable competition for Lady Margaret within the week."

" 'Twill be an easy task, Rutherford, I declare," Devereux announced, laying his teacup on a rosewood sofa table. "Anyone with hands as light as Lady Blake's must prove an apt pupil. If you are unwilling, I'll be happy to take on the wager myself."

"That will not be necessary, Devereux," Rutherford said in cutting accents. The man was becoming the devil of a nuisance! He was continually at Merrie's side, and the object of his attentions showed little inclination to repulse him. Presumably, she did not realize how particular those attentions were becoming. Damian had noticed before that Merrie's lack of vanity tended to blind her to the effect she had upon those around her. It was an appealing quality but just a little dangerously naive on occasion.

Fortunately, in the general interest engendered by Stanton's idea, the sharpness of the exchange with Devereux went unnoticed by all save Meredith who, from her own standpoint, considered Devereux's suggestion outrageously presumptious. She was not entirely sure, either, that she cared to be the subject of an animated discussion that occurred without direct reference to herself. There was much talk of the impossibility of a complete beginner acquiring sufficient skill to match an experienced whip in a mere seven days, and many suggestions were offered as to the best methods of instruction.

Damian, guessing accurately at Merrie's indignant thoughts, looked across at her, his eyes narrowed speculatively. "What does the lady say?"

Meredith frowned. "Must I win the race?"

The question was debated at some length before it was eventually decided that she need only be a match for her opponent in order for Rutherford and Stanton to win this wager. The race itself would be a different gamble, on which they would take separate bets when they could judge her skill later in the week.

"I have seen the horses Lady Margaret drives," Meredith said thoughtfully. "I do not think I could engage to match her, let alone win against her, with the two I had today." Her eyes met Rutherford's, the challenge clear.

"If I win the first wager," he said, not troubling to hide his amusement, "you may race my chestnuts."

"A handsome offer, indeed, Rutherford," the duke

approved. "If Damian don't consider Lady Blake capable of holding his horses by the end of the week, he loses the wager. He'll not risk them, that's for sure."

It was agreed, but throughout that week Meredith frequently regretted her own agreement. Damian was unfailingly polite, always the soul of patience, but he was a ruthless perfectionist. His pupil was not simply going to be a good whip, she would be able to drive to an inch, not only with a pair but with a four-in-hand. For hours she practiced with the whip, learning how to catch the thong and send it up the stick with a turn of her wrist, how to loop a rein and let it run free again with deft elegance. She handled increasingly spirited horses from the Rutland stables, but never Damian's chestnuts, learning how to point her leaders so that she could round any corner with the utmost precision and take any entrance, however narrow without the slightest danger of scraped varnish.

"I do not think, when this week is over, that I shall ever wish to drive again," she declared bitterly, backing the team for the tenth time in half an hour into a narrow siding along the driveway. "Even in bed, you think of something you have forgotten to explain."

Damian chuckled but said only, "Ease your nearside wheeler a little more to the right."

"Why is this so damnably important to you?" Merrie demanded, absently dropping her hands. The team instantly broke into a canter. Merrie swore vigorously and unashamedly as she brought them under control again.

"If those had been my chestnuts, they would have bolted with you," Damian informed her with infuriating calm. "You must concentrate at all times."

Meredith bit her lip hard. "You did not answer my question."

"There are two reasons. First, if I decide to do something, I like to do it properly, and secondly— You had better give me the reins for a minute." He took them from her before continuing in a level voice. "Secondly, I have a great interest in your success—in anything that establishes you as a member of the ton."

It was as well he had taken the reins as Merrie once again felt the wash of frustration at this indication of his continued determination. "What must I do to prove to you that I can never belong in this world?" she asked, a note almost of desperation in her voice. "As play, as an adventure for a few short weeks, yes, I can enjoy it. But I could never learn to be a duchess, and I would suffocate under the weight of all the rules and prohibitions, and I would ruin you."

"I do not see how you can both ruin me and suffocate," Damian pointed out.

"You know what I mean. Do not be obtuse," she snapped.

"If you would pause to think clearly for a minute, my dear Merrie, you will see that you are in a fair way to becoming a duchess as it is. The interest of Gerald Devereux, for instance, would hardly be as pronounced if you were not so thoroughly established." He had been looking for an opportunity to drop what he hoped would be a word to the wise and now gave her a sidelong glance.

"What has Devereux to do with this?" Merrie demanded.

"Very little," her companion returned, "except that

he seems determined to fix his interest with you and is not very subtle in his manner of going about it."

"And you are accusing me of being indiscreet?"

"I am accusing you of nothing. Simply telling you that there is talk. Not malicious talk, but you might be well advised to—to be a little discouraging."

"Duchesses, of course, are never indiscreet," Merrie mused, blowing on the silver button at her cuff and rubbing it vigorously with her gloved hand. "They do not creep around corridors late at night on the way to their lover's bed." She held her wrist up to the sun, squinting at the button to check that there was no hint of tarnish.

"I fail to see why they should not," Damian objected. "Only, if you were the duchess in question, I should hope you would not be in need of a lover."

"Oh, you are being absurd," she said crossly. "I am a smuggler, or have you forgotten that small impediment?"

"You are not at the moment," Rutherford pointed out unarguably.

"Maybe not, but I will be."

Damian's lips tightened at this, but he kept silent.

"You cannot marry someone with such a past." Merrie tried again. "Only think of the scandal. If my activities were ever discovered, and it is not inconceivable that they might be—enough people in the village know my identity, and there is the cave and passage as evidence—I would hang."

"I am prepared to accept that risk."

"Well, I am not." They both fell silent at this impasse, then Meredith declared. "I do not wish to run this race any more. You may tell everyone that I

371

am a hopeless case and will never make a whip."

"And perjure my immortal soul!" Damian expostulated. "My good girl, you will leave Margaret Pickering at the starting line. When we return to London, you may lionize in a perch phaeton and pair."

"I do not wish to do so."

"Do not sulk, Meredith," Damian advised. "It is most unbecoming, and I am wholly impervious to such displays. Besides, you will simply be cutting off your own nose to spite your face."

Merrie accepted the truth of that, as he had known she would, with her usual self-knowledge, albeit reluctantly. On the Saturday, she drove Rutherford's chestnuts well up to their bits in front of an admiring audience. His lordship declined to sit beside her, maintaining that he was perfectly confident of her ability to control them, and only he was aware of his sweating palms. The following day, she won her race but handsomely conceded to Lady Margaret that the glory lay entirely with Rutherford's horses. If Lady Margaret had been driving them, she would have been assured of victory. Since no one was prepared to dispute this, the matter ended amicably without loss of face. Damian, in the privacy of the stables, examined his horses' mouths anxiously. If Meredith had damaged them, he would have borne the blow in silence; however, her hands had clearly been as light as he had hoped, and the gamble paid off.

Lady Blake and Lord Rutherford returned to London, each set on a course of action and a goal completely in opposition to the other. Rutherford was more than ever determined to bring his mistress to accept that, whatever she might say, she was firmly entrenched in society and became more so by the hour. Meredith was equally determined to demonstrate to Rutherford how uncomfortable it would be having a wife censured by society. It should not be difficult to be thought bad ton, and, in such an event, not even Damian could persist in his obstinacy. Maybe then, he would permit her to retire to Highgate, and they could enjoy their last few weeks together without further dissension. In fact, Meredith could not see why such an arrangement should not continue for as long as they both wished. She would have to return to Cornwall during school holidays, of course, but for the rest of the time . . . And in the summer, Rutherford could visit his Cornish estates and they could set up house in the cave again . . .

Some inner caution prevented her from outlining to Damian this splendid answer to all their problems. While he was still set on marriage, he would agree to nothing less. Once he realized how impossible it was, then would she offer the alternative. Of course, he would find a suitable wife at some point, sooner rather than later. But that was not a subject upon which Meredith cared to dwell.

Chapter Eighteen

"My dear sir, I am most honored, but do pray get up." Meredith stood in the drawing room of Cavendish Square several days after the return from Belvoir, struggling with laughter as she looked at the rather more than middle-aged gentleman on his knees before her.

Sir Tobias Morely staggered to his feet, somewhat red-faced with the exertion and extreme nature of his emotions. "Well, what d'ye say, dear lady?" he wheezed. "Shall we make a go of it?"

"A glass of claret, sir?" Meredith turned her back on her unexpected suitor, buying a little time as she poured wine. It was common knowledge that Sir Tobias Morely's affairs were in dire straits, and he had been hanging out for a rich wife for months. Her present predicament could be laid entirely at Damian's door. Why the devil had he put it about that she was a wealthy woman? A respectable competence would have served his purpose equally well. Since he had put her into the situation, he could extricate her,

Meredith resolved.

"Sir Tobias, you do me too much honor." Smiling and fluttering her eyelashes, she handed him the glass of claret. "But I fear that I am not in a position to answer for myself. Pray, sit down."

Sir Tobias, looking a little startled, eased a plump rear, straining against canary-yellow pantaloons, onto a chair. "Don't quite take your meaning, my lady."

"You should know sir, that Lord Rutherford is in some way responsible for me. I am not at all good at business." Her hands passed through the air in a gesture denoting total incompetence, if not complete idiocy. "My poor dear husband was well aware of my deficiencies in such matters—"

"My dear lady," Sir Tobias made haste to interrupt. "Not deficiencies, do not say such a thing. Ladies should not be troubling their heads about such matters. I should apply to Rutherford, I take it."

"Exactly so. He will know just how to answer you." Meredith smiled in a friendly way that sent Sir Tobias hotfoot to Brook Street in search of Lord Rutherford.

Damian was in his book room when his butler brought him Sir Tobias Morley's visiting card. "Thank you, Carlton. Tell Sir Tobias that I will join him in the library directly." Rutherford concealed his puzzlement at this extraordinary visitation. He and Morely moved in quite different circles and that gentleman was some ten years his senior. He was perfectly respectable, of course. Having pockets to let was hardly a social crime, it was far too common a condition. Curiosity considerably piqued, Rutherford went to join his visitor.

The house in Brook Street was definitely a bache-

375

lor's establishment, lacking the grandeur of the Keighley mansion in Grosvenor Square where Damian would eventually take up residence, but it lacked nothing to make it both elegant and comfortable. The staff were discreet and attentive, the apartments spacious, the furnishings of the finest, all of which Sir Tobias Morely noted with more than a degree of envy, consoling himself with the thought of the widow's fortune; eighty thousand pounds had been the figure generally agreed to be correct. It was a nice round sum, Sir Tobias considered, quite sufficient to support an elegant lifestyle, and once the notice was in the *Gazette*, his creditors would fall over themselves to accommodate him again. Matters were definitely improving, he decided, greeting the arrival of his host with a bow. Just this tiresome formality to be dispensed with.

"Sherry, Morely?" Rutherford offered. "Or madeira, if you prefer?"

"Sherry, if you please, dear boy," Morely said, reposing himself on a striped sofa, examining the gold tassels on his shining Hessians complacently. He certainly cut a more imposing figure sartorially than his host, clad in a plain cloth coat and buckskins. However, not even Sir Tobias could deceive himself when he contrasted his padded shoulders and corseted waist with his lordship's powerful physique that clearly needed no unnatural supports or additions.

"To what do I owe the pleasure, Morely?" Rutherford asked with a polite smile, taking a seat opposite his guest.

"A happy business." Sir Tobias beamed, sipping his sherry. "This is a fine wine, Rutherford." Damian inclined his head and waited patiently. "Fact is, Lady Blake has sent me to you." Sir Tobias sat back, still beaming, as if all had thus been explained.

Rutherford, however, was quite at sea. "Lady Blake? Forgive me, Morely, but why should she do such a thing?"

"For your consent, of course, dear fellow. A mere formality, I am sure, but she is such an innocent little thing—no head for business—y'know how the ladies are? Says you handle her affairs and will know just how to make things all right and tight."

Light was beginning to dawn. Rutherford found himself torn between amusement and annoyance—a not unfamiliar combination where Merrie Trelawney was concerned. He could not begin to imagine why the little wretch should involve him in a matter that she was more than capable of dealing with herself unless it were out of her usual mischief—which seemed more than likely. "Exactly what did Lady Blake say?" he asked cautiously.

"Just that she cannot manage her own affairs— such a sweet little thing, I wouldn't have her troubling her pretty head for the world . . ." Morely smiled, looking expectantly at Rutherford.

"No," Damian agreed blandly. "It would indeed be a pity if that pretty little head were to be troubled with such mundane affairs. In general, it is a great deal easier for all concerned when such pretty heads are left empty."

"Quite so," Morely concurred, his beam, if it were possible, widening to reveal yellowing teeth with a significant number of gaps. "Her late husband, she explained, understood her inability to grasp matters of business and appointed you as guardian of her affairs."

Damian began to wonder if a little judicious violence would be justified when next he faced his mistress. He could see her fluttering and simpering in front of this rotund idiot, apologizing for her stupidity when she had more brains in her little finger than this profligate fool had in his entire overweight body! What would she do if he refused to play her game? Of course, knowing Merrie's deviant thought processes, she probably thought he had caused the problem in the first place and therefore it was his responsibility to solve it. Rutherford decided that he would shoulder that responsibility on this occasion, but he would exact a subtle penalty for her mischief.

"There is one small problem, Morely," he said smoothly, refilling his visitor's glass with careful deliberation. "But it is hardly insuperable." He offered a reassuring smile at his guest's suddenly anxious countenance. "Not for a patient man." The smile broadened as Sir Tobias wriggled a little.

"Don't quite get your meaning, Rutherford."

"Oh, it is quite simple. Under the terms of Sir John Blake's will, his widow forfeits her inheritance should she remarry before her twenty-fifth birthday." He took a reflective sip of his sherry, regarding Morely over the rim of the glass. "Lady Blake's twenty-fourth birthday is in six months, as I recall. So you will need to be patient for a mere eighteen months. Unless, of course, you are willing to marry the lady as she stands? There is nothing to prevent you." Kindly, he averted his gaze as the discomfited suitor struggled to compose himself and find the most graceful words of retreat.

Meredith did not hear from her would-be bridegroom again, and it was not until the following evening that she saw Damian. He was a guest at a dinner party given by the Beaumonts so the opportunity for private conversation was inevitably limited, but it could have been found had he so wished. It became very clear to Meredith after the first five minutes that he did not. He greeted her with impeccable formality and that special smile but showed no inclination to move aside with her. She was obliged to participate in the general conversation and, when her urgent looks across the circle received only a puzzled smile, decided that either he was being deliberately obtuse or had some ulterior motive for ignoring her mute appeal. That motive became obvious when he took her into dinner and, in the general business of settling down at table, she was able to broach the matter on her mind.

"You have been tolerably amused, sir, since last we met?" she began, realigning the heavy silverware of her place.

"Yes, indeed, thank you," he responded. "And you also, I trust."

"Yes," she answered. "We have had a great many callers."

"Your popularity is without question," he said with a smile. "Did you attend the balloon ascension yesterday?"

The conversation was taking an unpromising turn, Meredith decided. Popularity and callers had been a much better avenue. "It was not particularly successful," she said dismissively. "You have, I am sure, received many callers yourself."

Damian had some difficulty maintaining his countenance. He had absolutely no intention of offering her any assistance, having decided that she would pay for her mischief by remaining in ignorance and suspense over the outcome of his meeting with her unwelcome suitor. "A few," he responded unhelpfully. "You seem remarkably interested, my lady, in the minute details of my social life."

"Not at all, sir," she replied loftily. "I was merely making polite conversation. Were any of your callers of particular interest?"

"None that comes to mind at this moment," he answered. "Tell me, have you yet visited the Elgin marbles? If you have not, I should be happy to escort you."

Meredith gave up. Pride prevented her from broaching the subject directly so she fretted and fumed for several days until honored by a second, even more passionate offer from the Honorable Francis Matthews. Since this young man suffered from the incompatible combination of expensive tastes and mediocre income, she had not far to look for the reason behind the honor done her. He, too, Meredith sent to Rutherford, this time receiving in return a message from his lordship. It read: Darling love, while I must always be more than happy to assist you in any way, I know from experience how adept you are at refusing offers of marriage. You need only tell future hopefuls that you are not free to marry under your late husband's will until you are twenty-five. It appears to be a sufficiently discouraging put-off.

Meredith tore the missive into shreds, which she was in the process of consigning to the wastepaper basket when Grantly opened the drawing room door to announce the Honorable Gerald Devereux. The smile she gave him was so clearly effortful that he crossed the room swiftly with an expression of concern. "What has happened to put you out?"

"Oh dear, Mr. Devereux." She smiled guiltily. "You always seem to come in when I am in the midst of one of my sad passions. You must have formed a dreadful impression of my temperament."

"How could you think such a thing?" he soothed, taking her hands in a grip that was a little too intense for propriety. Merrie, too angry with Damian to concern herself about such trivialities, left her hands where they were.

"You are very kind, sir, but let us talk of pleasanter matters."

"But will you not tell me what has distressed you?" He squeezed her hands. Merrie, suddenly remembering Damian's warning at Belvoir, withdrew them from captivity as discreetly as she could.

"It is a small enough matter," she said with a shrug, "just a little damaging to my pride. But that is no bad thing. One's vanity should be piqued on occasion for the good of the soul. Pray do be seated."

Devereux accepted the invitation, saying, "I do not mean to pry, Lady Blake, but sometimes it helps to share one's troubles with a sympathetic ear. I would be all sympathy, I assure you."

"Yes, I believe you would." She smiled with genuine warmth. Whatever the world and Damian might warn, Gerald Devereux had a nice touch when it came to soothing wounded spirits. "It is just that I find offers of marriage from fortune hunters most demeaning. Ridiculous of me, of course."

"Not at all ridiculous, dear lady," he expostulated with a most gratifying sincerity. "It must be unpleasant in the extreme. I have always thought ladies of substance are subjected to great insensitivity in that area."

"You do understand, then," she said.

"Indeed, yes. Will you not also sit down?" He moved invitingly on the sofa and Meredith, unwilling to appear unfriendly, sat beside him. "You have, I take it, received several of these unpleasant offers?"

"Yes," she agreed ruefully. "I am barely acquainted with my eager suitors and strongly suspect that it would not matter a jot if I had a crooked back and a walleye."

Devereux repossessed her hand. "Those suitors, dear Lady Blake, are definitely in the minority. There are those for whom your fortune is of no importance."

"If so, they have not shown themselves." Merrie fell neatly into the trap and could have kicked herself for her naivity. Removing her hand hastily, she rose to her feet and went to the mantelpiece to pull the bell rope. "You will take a glass of wine, Mr. Devereux?"

"Thank you." He stood up, a disconcertingly serious look on the ascetic countenance. "They are, perhaps, a little too discreet—unwilling to appear forward by declaring themselves too soon."

The arrival of the footman saved Merrie from the need to find an answer immediately, and, when he had left, she was able to offer some inconsequential remark about the extraordinarily clement autumn weather. Devereux appeared to take the hint and replied in kind. When he took his leave, however,

Meredith could not pretend to ignore the particular warmth in his voice or the pressure on her hand. She seemed to be in a pretty pickle, and, while Damian was certainly responsible for the unwelcome attentions of fortune hunters, she could hardly blame him for Devereux's interest. As far as she knew, he was perfectly well established for himself, and, while a rich wife was never to be sneezed at, it was not a matter of life and death for him. She must obviously do something to discourage him, but that was made difficult by the fact that she did not really wish to. He was pleasant company, and that ready sympathy and understanding of a predicament that Rutherford seemed to find merely amusing was most comforting.

She was in the mood for battle when Lord Rutherford appeared in the drawing room half an hour after Devereux's departure.

"I must thank you for your kind note, Lord Rutherford," she said stiffly, ignoring both his smile and outstretched hand.

Damian's eyebrows went up and his hand dropped to his side. "Dear me," he murmured. "I appear to have offended you. I wished only to be of assistance by explaining how you should deal with these unwelcome offers."

"That was not what you hoped!" she snapped.

"No," he agreed. "I hoped to teach you not to play tricks on me. Did I succeed?"

"I was not playing tricks," she protested somewhat unconvincingly. "Anyway, if I was, it was your own doing. To be courted by fortune hunters is of all things the most degrading, particularly when one has no fortune. Why did you have to put it about that I was

383

rich?"

He shrugged. "I felt you would prefer not to be thought of as a Keighley pensioner."

"I would have preferred not to be thought of at all," Meredith flashed.

"You refine too much upon it, my dear girl." Damian walked over to one of the long windows overlooking the square. "Come here and see something much more interesting."

How could he dismiss her distress so casually? She was *not* refining too much upon it. And if Lord Rutherford did not understand that, then Gerald Devereux did!

"Come over here, Merrie," Damian repeated, turning from the window, crooking an imperative finger. "I have a surprise for you."

"I have had my surfeit of surprises, thank you," she said crossly, standing her ground.

"You are sulking again," he chided gently. "Must I come and fetch you?"

"I am not sulking!" For some reason he had now made her feel like a silly little girl indulging in pointless obstinacy. It was most unfair when she was definitely the injured party.

Damian chuckled. "Your face, my love, is a picture, but I should tell you that I have no intention of quarreling with you further today. Now, will you please come here?" The soldier's crispness had entered his voice and Merrie sighed.

After a minute's hesitation, she crossed the room to look out of the window. A very sporty perch phaeton drawn by a pair of matched bays stood in charge of a groom at the front door. "Two of Cunningham's break-downs," she was informed with a degree of gleeful satisfaction. "I was able to get them before they came on the open market. You will be the envy of more than the ladies, my love."

"Those are for *me* to drive?" Merrie was momentarily diverted from her annoyance. It was, anyway, impossible to argue with Damian when he refused to enter the lists.

"Simply a loan," he assured her in a voice as dry as fallen leaves.

"Yes, of course," she replied matter-of-factly. "But I must change my dress."

"You may have twenty minutes." Satisfied that the danger had receded at least for the time being, Rutherford moved to a chair by the window.

Meredith returned within the quarter hour, drawing on a pair of York tan gloves. She had changed her muslins for a dark habit of severe cut. A velvet hat, turned up on one side, perched atop the auburn curls, kid half-boots encased small feet. Damian nodded in silent appreciation as he held the door for her.

"Tell me," Meredith said with one of her deceptively sweet smiles as she took her place on the driving seat, "do you accompany me on this occasion as instructor or companion?"

"I am honored, Lady Blake, that you should be so kind as to take me up," he responded promptly.

Merrie's lips twitched. "To the devil with the park. Let us go directly to Highgate. I do not like to be at odds with you, and it seems the only place these days where we do not quarrel."

"Once around the park first. I daresay it will be thronged at this hour, and I have a lively desire to see the effect you will have."

"You wish it known that you acquired Cunningham's break-downs," Merrie accused shrewdly and Damian chuckled.

"Several others had their eye on them, I admit."

"Men!" Merrie raised her eyes heavenward. "You are such little boys under that grand, powerful exterior. You are as bad as Rob with a winning marble."

"How are they? Have you heard?" He did not trouble to defend himself from such an accurate accusation.

"A letter from Hugo, just a scrawl from the other two," Meredith replied. "Theo hopes to make the First Eleven next cricket season, and Rob is hungry."

Damian gave a shout of laughter. "I remember the feeling only too well. I must send him supplies for his tuck box."

"Nan and I sent a fruitcake and shortbread," Merrie told him. "But I am sure that will not be enough to keep the wolf at bay. It has to be shared amongst twenty of them, I understand."

"Do not worry on that score," Damian assured her. "His consequence will increase to such an extent he will consider the sharing more than worth the sacrifice."

They had passed through the Stanhope Gate into Hyde Park by this time, and Meredith was obliged to pull up every few yards to greet acquaintances, who exclaimed in a suitably gratifying manner over her equippage, complaining mightily over the march Rutherford had stolen.

"Satisfied?" Meredith asked as they completed the circuit.

"More than satisfied. You are a capital whip, Merrie Trelawney. I have not experienced one moment's unease."

"Are you trying to provoke me, my lord?"

"In no wise," he protested. "It is the last thing I wish to do. To Highgate, and make all speed."

Chapter Nineteen

"My dear, are you feeling quite the thing?" The Duchess of Keighley looked at Meredith with some concern. The girl seemed unusually listless this afternoon and was certainly not looking her best, a fact which upset her grace since Meredith's presence at this tea party for the duchess's most favored cronies was designed in some way as a presentation. Remembering her son's instructions, she had, of course, not hinted at this ulterior motive, but Arabella was well aware of the facts and her mother had rather relied upon the marchioness to ensure Meredith's attendance in all her usual beauty.

"Of course, your grace," Meredith returned automatically, smiling with hoped-for enthusiasm. "It is most kind in you to invite me this afternoon."

"Not at all. You are quite one of the family, after all," her hostess said briskly.

Meredith stiffened, and her smile lost some of its spontaneity. The doors seemed to be closing on her from every side. She met only kindness, but that kindness was beginning to suffocate her as the assumptions underlying it became increasingly obvious.

Since her return from Belvoir there had been no opportunity to put into practice the plan that would hopefully extricate her from this tangle of Damian's making. And if the truth were told, her spirit shrank from creating the monumental stir that would be necessary if she were to achieve her object. It was a splendid plan on paper, but the reality that would involve her friends in embarrassment was much harder to stomach. Maybe she would try just once more to get Damian to see the light. Fundamentally, he was a perfectly reasonable individual—a little too accustomed to having his own way, but then that could be said of her too. Meredith was never less than honest about herself. And if he truly loved her as he said he did, then surely he would grant her the peace that would bring them both happiness.

"You are distracted, love," Arabella whispered under cover of the teapot. "Lady Brigham was talking to you for at least ten minutes and you hardly responded. Have you the headache?"

"No. I beg pardon, Bella." Merrie pulled herself together hastily, turning to an elderly dowager in a purple turban, offering an encouraging comment on Lord Byron's latest poem. One could never be sure, of course, whether *Marmion*'s notorious and eccentric author was an acceptable subject for conversation amongst such high sticklers, but his poems were generally considered respectable topics for discussion.

"Forgive me, love," Bella said, once they were in the barouche returning to Cavendish Square, "but is anything the matter? Mama was most concerned. She said you were sadly out of looks today." Bella smiled wryly. "For which I am held responsible, of course."

"That is hardly fair." Merrie sighed. "Your mama, Bella, is a formidable lady, but she has been most kind to me. I wish I did not feel that I was betraying her kindness—and yours and the marquis's, also."

"Fustian!" Bella declared vigorously. "Why should you think such a thing?"

"Because I will *not* marry your brother," Meredith said firmly, "and I know full well that that is what your mother hopes. And you, also?" She raised her eyebrows interrogatively.

Arabella played with the yellow silk ribbands of her lavender chip hat. "It is what we all hope because it is what Rutherford wishes, and I cannot imagine anyone I would liefer have for a sister."

"Tell me, Bella, what would your mother say if she knew the truth about me?" Meredith fixed her companion with a direct stare, under which Bella's eyes dropped.

"She must never find out," she replied candidly. "There is no reason why she should, is there? Only Damian and I know about the smuggling, and you have no relatives to reveal that the Blakes were not in some way related to Matthew Mallory."

"Only my brothers, who will never believe such a Banbury story," Merrie retorted.

"Rutherford said—" Bella began tentatively, and then her voice faded as Meredith's eyes crackled in that alarming fashion.

"Do go on, Bella," she prompted silkily.

Arabella sighed. "He said that your brothers were perfectly sensible and could safely be taken into your confidence on that score. He said that they would understand that your pride made such a fabrication

390

necessary."

"Oh, he did, did he?" Merrie muttered ominously. Damian obviously didn't know Rob as well as he thought.

"Oh, dear, Merrie, now I have made you cross, and Rutherford will be vexed with me for telling you what he had said." Bella sounded genuinely distressed, and Meredith made haste to reassure her that she was not at all annoyed. In fact, this further evidence of Rutherford's determination to manipulate Merrie into the position he wished merely wearied her. She would have it out with him when she made one last attempt to get him to see reason. Until then there was little point in fretting over one more pinprick.

Something that did give her reason for fretting occurred later that evening at a soirée given by the Countess of Maudsley. Merrie had gone to some considerable effort to shake off the languor that seemed to plague her these days everywhere except in the house at Highgate and was rewarded by Arabella's obvious relief at this return of the bright and cheerful companion and guest to whom she had become accustomed. At one point in the evening, Merrie observed brother and sister deep in conversation, and, if the looks cast in her direction were anything to judge by, it was not hard to guess the subject under discussion. Damian was looking unusually grave, and Meredith deduced that Arabella was telling him of their conversation that afternoon. Somehow, it seemed to add to her annoyance, to be treated as if she were an awkward child whose treatment by responsible adults needed to be concerted. Her chin went up and she greeted Gerald Devereux with a particularly ravishing smile.

In recent days, she had been carefully circumspect in her dealings with this gentleman, always ensuring that they met only in company and keeping the conversation light and frivolous. Tonight, however, she threw caution to the winds, responding to his flirtatious sallies in kind. The slight frown between Rutherford's expressive brows whenever he looked in her direction was distinctly satisfying. Not that he would be foolish enough to be jealous, of course, but it would do him no harm to feel a little uneasy for once. Unfortunately, the tactic backfired.

Meredith made the mistake of allowing Devereux to escort her into a quiet salon alongside the music room where the sounds of an imperfectly played harp twinged painfully.

"I fear I have no ear for fine music," she declared with the mischievous chuckle she would have given Rutherford. "It seems to set my teeth on edge. I must thank you for recognizing my predicament so promptly."

"It is one I share," he responded with a solemnity belied by the laughing eyes. "May I procure you a glass of champagne?"

"If you please." Meredith, left alone in the salon, smiled to herself. In the absence of Rutherford, Devereux was quite the most amusing companion and seemed refreshingly unshockable in addition to that pleasant sympathy he evinced. She greeted his return with smiling thanks for the champagne. "We should, perhaps, rejoin the party, Mr. Devereux, before our absence is remarked."

"In one minute." He laid an arresting hand on her

bare forearm and Merrie couldn't hide her jump. "I beg your pardon, I didn't mean to startle you," he said quietly, "but what I have to say cannot come as a surprise to you, Meredith."

Merrie cursed the self-indulgent idiocy that had landed her in this mess. "It would be better left unsaid, sir," she responded, seeing no gain in pretending to misunderstand him.

"I am in love with you," he declared simply. "Will you tell me that I may not hope?"

"Yes." It seemed kinder to settle for brutal honesty at the outset. "There is no possibility of anything other than friendship between us, Mr. Devereux."

"Will you tell me why?" He looked genuinely distressed and her heart ached for him. He had done nothing to deserve unkindness from her.

"I do not love you, my friend." Her hand lightly brushed his satin-clad arm. "I am sorry for it, but—"

"I have a rival?" He smiled quizzically.

Meredith thought rapidly. It would certainly provide a face-saving way out of this for both of them. "There is someone at home," she admitted, lowering her eyes.

"In Cornwall?"

She nodded. Cornwall was far enough away for safety. For the majority of the ton, it existed on another planet. "We should return to the drawing room, Mr. Devereux."

"Yes." With a bow, he took both her hands, raising them to his lips, his eyes smiling sadly. "You will not deprive me of your company as a result of my—my premature declaration?"

Meredith shook her head, unable to think of a

393

suitable response. She would have to work out a plan for dealing with this in the kindest and most definite way possible, but she could not do that here in Devereux's company.

He escorted her back to the drawing room, leaving her immediately. She watched as he made his farewells to his hostess and took his departure on the instant.

"That was not very wise, Merrie."

She swung round at Damian's low-voiced statement. "I beg your pardon, Lord Rutherford?"

"I think you heard me," he said. "And you know quite well to what I refer. To go apart in that particular manner with Devereux can only give rise to comment. What can you have been thinking of?"

"I do not need you to tell me how to behave," she said icily. "I am long past the age of requiring such counsel."

"You should be," he agreed with a sudden, wicked grin. "But, as I know from experience, you will behave exactly as you see fit and to the devil with the proprieties. Fetch your cloak. I think you have the headache, and I must instantly convey you home."

"What?" She stared at him, nonplussed by this extraordinary *volte-face.*

"*Home,*" he repeated with gentle emphasis, the gray eyes burning their message.

Home meant Highgate. "Dare we?" she whispered, looking around the crowded room. To escape this stuffy party for a night of illicit loving in their romantic hideaway was an utterly delicious thought, one that for the moment diverted her from her worries.

"Faint heart," he mocked.

"I will fetch my cloak, my lord."

Rutherford's town chaise deposited them in Cavendish Square, from where they strolled in cousinlike and respectable fashion into the side streets where Damian hailed a hackney. Upon hearing his destination, the jarvey beamed, closing the door on his passengers and climbing onto his box, muttering his satisfaction at the length of the journey and his fare. In the carriage's dark interior, Damian, in his own inimitable fashion, set about dispelling the tension in the supple frame in his arms. They had been bickering on and off ever since their return from Belvoir, and it seemed that only when they were alone like this could they be at peace. It was hardly a prescription for long-term marital bliss, he reflected before firmly putting aside all such gloomy thoughts as he reveled in the soft fragrance that promised only exquisite delight at journey's end.

Meredith, even as she lost herself in the familiar, yet eternal excitement of his embrace, knew that tonight she was going to transgress the unspoken rules of their hideaway. The debacle with Gerald Devereux had been the last straw. In the face of his honesty, she had had to live the lie she lived with Rutherford's parents and Bella's husband. The game held no savor anymore, and her false position was become intolerable. Tonight, in Highgate, she would make her last attempt to extricate herself from this mess with dignity for them both. If Damian persisted in his obstinacy, then she had but two options. Either she forced him to agree to her removal to Highgate, or she returned to Cornwall. The latter possibility filled her with such a bleak premonition of loss that she could hardly bear to contemplate it. That left her original plan. She would be obliged to scandalize society to such an extent that all respectable doors would be closed to her. It would be painful for Arabella at first, but she would receive ready sympathy for having nurtured a viper at her bosom, and, once her troublesome guest had vanished into outer darkness, all would be well again.

In the pretty bedroom under the thatched roof, Rutherford straightened from the hearth where he had lit the kindling always laid ready in anticipation of their arrival whenever it should be. Merrie had made no attempt to remove her cloak and stood by the window, one hand holding aside the curtain as she gazed out at the clear, star-filled night sky. There was something about the set of her shoulders, the determined tilt of her chin that filled him with a prescient foreboding.

"What is it?" he asked quietly, moving behind her and reaching over her shoulder for the clasp of her cloak.

"You know quite well," she said with dull simplicity. "I cannot continue in this way as I have told you over and over again. This time you must listen. I will *not* continue living this lie!"

"Then make it the truth," he replied, removing the cloak and tossing it over a chair. "The solution is, as always, in your hands."

"It is in *your* hands!" she said fiercely, twitching out of his hold. "All I ask is to be allowed to live here in Highgate. I must go home for the boys' holidays, of course, but can return here easily enough during term time. It would be perfect if only you would stop to consider alternatives to your own ideas for once."

"So that is your plan." Damian decided that he had had enough of being patient and reasonable with her. If Meredith wanted to sully the tranquillity of their haven with this conflict, then so be it. "I beg leave to inform you, ma'am, that it will not do at all. You seem to have forgotten that this entire arrangement was at your suggestion, and, for as long as you remain in London, Meredith, present conditions will persist."

"But I will *not* marry you!" she exclaimed.

"You will eventually, my stubborn little adventuress. You will marry me when you realize that I will accept no alternative." He did not add his conviction that the more uncomfortable she found the arrangement, the sooner she would capitulate. "You are being obstinate about this simply for the sake of it—"

"How dare you say that!" Merrie interrupted furiously. "You who categorically refuse even to consider another point of view. You have set your heart on one thing and cannot bear to be denied—"

"And you, Merrie Trelawney, having once made up your mind to something, are too damn proud to admit that you were wrong," he broke in, planting his hands firmly on his hips and fervently hoping that they would stay there. In this highly charged atmosphere, he could not vouch for the consequences if they did not.

Meredith was wrestling with her own problems of self-control and began pacing around the room, the embroidered flounce of the blue crape evening gown swishing around her celestial satin slippers. "If that is true of me, my lord, it is most certainly true of you," she said finally in a stifled voice. "I cannot imagine your ever admitting that you were in the wrong. You have spent too many years believing yourself to be infallible and having that belief strengthened by all those obedient souls under your command. How many years has it been since anyone dared to gainsay you?"

"You try me too far, Meredith," he said in a dangerously low voice. "My patience, believe it or not, is not inexhaustible."

"So now you must resort to threats," she taunted, scornfully and unwisely. "It is not unusual when the truth is too unpalatable to be faced."

"Why you—!" Speechless with fury, Damian advanced on her. Meredith backed away, whipping her hands behind her as he stalked her with grim purpose. She stopped when the bed at her back prevented a further retreat and looked at him with defiant bravery, determined that she would not apologize, would not back down from a statement that was only the truth.

"You are a termagant," Damian declared, "and you know how to go too far. Now, you are going to learn what happens when you do." Putting a flat palm against her shoulder, he pushed her. It seemed gentle enough, but Merrie landed flat on her back on the bed.

"What do you think you're doing?" she gasped, outraged, struggling to sit up.

"I am going to teach you a lesson that I had thought you had learned long ago." Catching her wrists in one large hand, he jerked them above her head. Merrie felt a stab of real fear as she realized for the first time how puny her own strength was beside

398

the soldier's whipcord body. When they had wrestled before in play, she had known he had held back, known that her victories had been given to her, but that intellectual knowledge was nothing compared with the reality of her helplessness now. His legs scissored hers into stillness, and his mouth came down in a kiss, punishing in its demand for response. She wriggled, squirming to get leverage with her hips, and he dropped the full weight of his body on hers without releasing her mouth. In the crimson-shot blackness behind her tightly closed eyes, the fear left her as the familiar scent of his skin filled her nostrils, the body pinioning hers assumed familiar contours, and her struggles ceased. However angry he was, Damian would never hurt her.

As she became still, Damian released her mouth, raising his head to look down at her. "You are going to ruin my gown," she murmured. "And it was monstrous expensive."

"You may count yourself fortunate I don't rip it from your back," he growled, still holding her with his weight. Meredith kept still and waited, but that inevitable excitement began stirring in her belly. It must have shown in her eyes because a small gleam of triumph appeared in the gray ones examining her. Very deliberately, he rolled away from her and stood up, still maintaining his grip on her wrists. Leaning over her supine body, he pushed up the skirts of her gown very slowly with his free hand. Meredith quivered, her tongue running over her swollen lips. The hand slid inside the waist of her pantalettes, flattened over her belly, the fingers reaching down. When she tugged at her imprisoned wrists, his grip tightened and the other hand moved in intimate exploration.

"Unfair, my lord," she accused weakly, trying to resist the inexorable honeyed flow created by those skillful, knowing fingers. Smiling, he shook his head in wordless denial, watching her face as he continued his devastating work. It was a losing battle she fought; her body was too well accustomed to taking its pleasure for her resistant mind to hold sway. And when she lay mindless with the glory of aftermath and her body opened, needing now to share that glory, he stripped them both of only those garments absolutely necessary before driving into her in fierce possession, all the while continuing to hold her wrists.

"When will you learn that I love you, Merrie Trelawney?" he demanded, pausing on the edge of her body as she hovered on the precipice of extinction.

"I do know it," she whispered, unable at this extremity of ecstasy to separate the strands that said that that was not the point at issue.

"Do you love me?" The gray eyes burned.

Her head moved in weak affirmative. "You know I do." But that isn't the point came the silent cry that was instantly lost in the maelstrom where protest and differences could never gain a foothold.

Chapter Twenty

It was an overcast November morning when Meredith, reluctantly but in the full knowledge that she had no choice, took the first step in her plan to compel Damian to agree to her solution. The idea of Lady Blake driving her phaeton unaccompanied through the city streets had deeply shocked the groom assigned to her on hearing that he was to remain behind in Cavendish Square, but it was not his place to question orders, and he had returned to the mews, there to express his horrified dismay.

The streets were busy, requiring all Meredith's concentration to negotiate a path between mail coaches and wagons, to avoid running down careless pedestrians darting through the traffic. The occupants of several barouches and landaulets cast frankly astonished looks at Lady Blake's very familiar equippage, looks that she returned with a small, but very definite bow. At the top of Piccadilly, she turned the horses onto St. James's Street.

Her courage almost foundered as she saw the length

of this, the one street where no respectable female dared be seen. Merrie lifted her chin determinedly, set the horses to a brisk trot, and began the journey. Since it was her object to be seen and recognized, she looked around her, acknowledging the stares of ogling bucks and town saunterers, examining the windows of the various clubs lining this male preserve, looking for the famous Bow Window of White's.

Lord Rutherford, having passed an energetic hour in Jackson's Saloon which he intended to follow with a little relaxation amongst congenial company in his club, was standing on the steps of White's, engaged in conversation with Colonel Armitage and Sir Charles Stanton, when Merrie's bombshell appeared at the head of the street. "Damme, Rutherford, if that ain't Lady Blake's set-up," Stanton exclaimed, raising his glass. "Know those horses anywhere."

Rutherford turned. His first reaction was shock, followed instantly by fury at himself as well as at Meredith. He should have known that that last scene in Highgate hadn't ended the matter. His abominable little adventuress was never one to give up easily, but she was *not* going to succeed in whatever devilish scheme lay behind this piece of mischief. "They must have got away with her," he said with swift improvisation.

"Looks like she has 'em well in hand," the colonel contradicted.

"No—no, Rutherford's right," Stanton said hastily. "Stands to reason. No groom with her. Must have dashed off before he had time to get up behind."

"Excuse me, gentlemen." Unhurriedly, Damian strolled into the path of the oncoming phaeton, where he stood idly slapping the palm of his hand with his gloves. Merrie felt a slight quiver of dismay as she saw the obstacle in her path. His face was quite impassive, but there was something about the way he was standing, apparently at ease but radiating determination that set off all her alarm bells. She was obliged to check her horses to avoid running him down although she did not bring them to a halt. Rutherford, with enviable agility, swung onto the high seat that hung precariously over the front axle.

"Hand me the reins, please," he requested pleasantly. Meredith was too startled to do anything but comply. He took the whip also and drove the bays down the street, swinging them round into Pall Mall.

"Am I to guess the reason for that? Or will you be so kind as to furnish me with an explanation?" he inquired, in the same pleasant tone.

"I was realizing a long-held ambition," she replied in similar accents. "You should know that I think it quite absurd to have a street exclusively for men. It is not as if there was a female equivalent."

"Indubitably unfair," he concurred. "But such inequities are frequently to be found in society."

"Then it seems to me that I have a duty to redress them," Meredith responded.

"Ah." Rutherford pursed his lips thoughtfully. "Well, I am grateful for the warning, Merrie Trelawney. It is to be hoped you will not regret it."

They turned into Cavendish Square and the carriage drew to a halt before the door. "I must ask you to alight unassisted," he said politely. "I cannot leave the horses."

"If you are taking them to the mews yourself, then I

will accompany you."

"I am taking them to *my* stables," he replied with gentle emphasis. "Buying them was a grave error of judgment. I had not realized that they would be too strong for you, but few people will be surprised to hear that you could not hold them."

Protest would simply be undignified, so Meredith alighted from the carriage without a further word. Rutherford waited to see her admitted to the house, then drove off, angry, although he would not give Meredith the satisfaction of seeing it, and not a little concerned. She had most definitely thrown down the glove, and he had equally definitely picked it up. The inevitable conflict would do nothing to advance his cause, but neither could he ignore it. He could not allow her to ruin herself as she so clearly intended doing. It would not suit his pride, quite apart from upsetting his plans. Perhaps he should yield the fight, allow her to retire to Highgate, accept what she would freely give, and no longer ask for what she believed so fervently she could not give. No, he would win this battle because he must, for both of them. Meredith was wrong about herself and about him. If he could not have that proud, obstinate Cornishwoman to wife, then he would have no one, and the years stretched emptily ahead.

Meredith, in the privacy of her boudoir, paced from window to door and back again, furious with herself for having been so easily outmaneuvered. Rutherford's presence in St. James's Street had been the most unfortunate occurrence. Now she would be an object of pity rather than censure, with not a few people deriving malicious satisfaction from her downfall. It would be said that Lord Rutherford had come opportunely to her rescue and, as incontrovertible proof, Lady Blake's perch phaeton would no longer be seen in Hyde Park. Perhaps she should give up the fight, return to Cornwall where she belonged, where the years stretched emptily ahead. Lifting a hand to her cheek to dash away a recalcitrant teardrop, Meredith decided that she would not be defeated, not just yet. Damian *must* acknowledge the truth eventually.

Over the next two days, it became clear that Meredith had correctly guessed society's reaction to her escapade. She was obliged to sit, a smile frozen on her lips, throughout an interminable flood of fellow sympathy from Lady Margaret Pickering. "So humiliating, Lady Blake, when one's horses bolt with one. It hasn't happened to me for quite some years, of course, and never so publicly, but I do assure you I know just how you feel."

"Well, it will not be happening again," the Duchess of Keighley pronounced. "Rutherford should have known better than to have procured such strong horses for you, my dear, but I understand he is intending to replace them with a pair more suitable for a lady to drive." The duchess spoke to Meredith in public, now, with all the familiarity she would have used to her daughter-in-law. Merrie bit back the childish retort that, if she couldn't have the bays back, she wanted no horses at all and maintained a steadfast silence.

"Lady Blake, I am sent to beg you will join the lottery table in the other salon." Gerald Devereux came to her rescue, his smile clearly expressing his sympathy for her mortification.

"With pleasure, Mr. Devereux," ~~she responded~~, rising with alacrity. Damian had made absolutely no attempt to intervene on her side, and, while justice told her he was entitled to be punitive, the recognition did little to lessen her resentment.

"How very unpleasant this must be for you," Devereux said quietly, escorting her from the room. "But it will be a nine days' wonder, I assure you. This time next week, no one will think of it."

"That would not be the case if I had done such a thing deliberately," Meredith said wryly.

"No, indeed not," he agreed. "It was certainly fortunate that Lord Rutherford was there to halt the runaways."

"Quite so," she agreed with a tight smile. "May we talk of something else, Mr. Devereux? I am heartily sick of the subject."

He turned the conversation deftly and kept her well amused throughout the game. Devereux appeared to have taken her rejection of his suit in good part and, since that evening, had behaved impeccably so that Meredith felt quite at ease in his company. Indeed, she saw no reason to keep at arm's length such an entertaining and cultivated companion, whose careful attentions never went beyond the line of what was pleasing and provided only gratification. If he was prepared to be satisfied with the friendship she was willing to offer, then there could be no possible danger.

Damian, hearing that rich chuckle, seeing the ravishing smile she bestowed on Devereux, began to wonder if she were deliberately ignoring the warning he had given her. There was nothing in the behavior of the two to give rise to malicious gossip, but Devereux's interest in the widow was very clear as his mother had just informed him in no uncertain terms. The duchess, of course, had simply urged her son to fix his own interest without delay, but Damian was hardly in a position to explain the truth to his fond and anxious parent. Deciding that the moment had come to bring an end to the present constraint, he waited until Merrie rose from the lottery table and went over to her.

"May I have a word, Cousin Meredith?" he asked politely, smiling at Devereux in clear dismissal.

"Mr. Devereux was about to procure me a glass of lemonade," Meredith said, not removing her hand from her escort's arm.

"Then we will wait here for him," Rutherford said smoothly. Devereux bowed, accepting gracefully the neat maneuver that ensured his departure.

"Well?" Meredith demanded ungraciously.

Rutherford's lips twitched. "Do not sulk," he advised in his usual fashion. "You have only yourself to blame for this unpleasantness. Let us cry peace, now. Do you care to drive with me in the park tomorrow? Your *own* horses," he added.

"Why should I?" She knitted her brow in puzzlement.

"To put an end to all this talk," he explained patiently. "The minute you are seen driving again, the story will lose its savor."

"I have promised to ride with Mr. Devereux in the morning," Meredith said. "Will the afternoon be convenient for you, sir?"

"Perfectly," he responded with the same formality.

"You will not, I trust, object if I join you on your ride?"

"Not at all. Why should I?" The sloe eyes were as candid as the voice, and Damian dismissed the suspicion that she was playing with him. Maybe Devereux had no ulterior motive in his attentions. Merrie was hardly a naive chit in her first Season, and, if she saw no harm in his companionship, then why should anyone else?

The following morning, Meredith and her two cavaliers proceeded in orderly fashion and at a sedate pace in the direction of Hyde Park. It was a pleasant day, crisp and sunny, and the park was thronged with pedestrians, riders, and carriages. Merrie's chestnut gelding lifted his head and sniffed the wind, the muscles rippling in the sinewy neck. "Is it a gallop you want?" Merrie leant forward, patting the long neck.

"Meredith, not in the park!" Rutherford said sharply.

"Oh, pshaw!" she scoffed. "You may tell everyone he ran away with me." With that she was off, leaning low over the saddle as the chestnut thundered down the tan.

Gerald Devereux, after an astonished second, gave a shout of laughter and set his own mount in pursuit. Rutherford, having no option if he was not to lose sight of her altogether, followed on the instant. It was a good ten minutes before Meredith eventually drew rein and turned her pink-cheeked, laughing face toward Rutherford. "I know it was outrageous, but it was quite irresistible," she said.

"By God, you can ride, ma'am," Devereux declared, making no attempt to hide his admiration. "It was as much as I could do to keep up with you."

"I have an excellent mount," Merrie laughed. "Besides, Trelawneys are taught to ride before they can walk. Where I come from, you should know, horseback is the only reliable form of transport."

"Damnation!" Rutherford muttered suddenly. "There is my mother."

"Where?" Meredith followed his gaze and gulped. The Duchess of Keighley was signaling to them imperatively from her smart barouche drawn up beside the track. "Oh, dear," she said apologetically. "She looks most dreadfully vexed."

"Well, I refuse to bear the blame alone," Damian announced. "Come." He turned his horse toward the carriage road. Meredith gave Devereux a small shrug, totally expressive of resignation, and followed. Devereux watched them go, a small frown knitting his brows. Since it was fairly clear that his presence was entirely superfluous, he continued on his way, leaving the errant pair to face an irate duchess.

The duchess spoke for nearly five minutes without pause. Her son was the chief recipient of the tongue-lashing since the only explanation his mother could come up with for their extraordinary behavior was that he had been negligent in warning Meredith of the rules pertaining in the park. Damian nobly bore his mama's strictures in meek silence, and Meredith murmured convincing apologies and promises that it would never happen again. The barouche moved off, and Damian, without a word, turned his horse toward the Stanhope Gate and home.

He looked so ludicrously chastened that Merrie's

shoulders began to shake. "I can see where your own eloquence comes from, my lord," she chuckled.

"You dare laugh, Merrie, and I'll make certain you don't sit that horse for a week!" he exclaimed. "I haven't been on the receiving end of my mother's tongue for ten years, and there was absolutely nothing I could do to defend myself without blaming you."

"Which would have been most unchivalrous," she murmured. "Whatever happened to Mr. Devereux?"

"I imagine he beat a hasty and well-timed retreat," her companion said dryly. "You are an abominable little wretch, Merrie Trelawney. Now, I am going to have to find you a mild-mannered lady's horse to ride in addition to a quiet pair to put between the shafts of your phaeton."

"You wouldn't," Merrie said, regarding him warily from beneath the brim of her velvet hat.

"And do you not deserve that I should?" he asked with complete justification.

"Probably," she agreed, offering him a hopefully winning smile. "But you will not, will you?"

"No, not this time. But the next time you decide to ride neck-or-nothing in the park, I should be grateful if you did not implicate me!"

Merrie's prank brought no social repercussions, but it had one result far worse than society's raised eyebrows. It brought a very grave Gerald Devereux to Cavendish Square the following afternoon.

Arabella was visiting a sick friend, and Meredith received her guest alone in the drawing room. "This is a pleasant surprise, Mr. Devereux," she greeted him cheerfully.

"You will pardon this intrusion," he began slowly,

not meeting her eye, "but there is something I must know. Perhaps I do not have the right to know it, but nevertheless I must ask."

Meredith's stomach began to flutter uncomfortably. "I am quite in the dark, sir," she said with an assumption of calm confidence. "Pray be seated." She sat herself on a low, delicate Sheraton chair without arms, a seat that obliged her to maintain an upright posture that was indicative of her alert watchfulness.

"You said to me that your affections were already engaged." Devereux did not accept the invitation but began instead to pace the long room. "I understood you to say that the fortunate man resided in Cornwall." Stopping beside the mantel, he looked directly at her.

Meredith thought rapidly. If Devereux was questioning the truth of that statement for a good reason, one she was as yet unaware of, and she persisted in the lie, then the tangle would merely become unknottable. "What is behind this, Mr. Devereux?" she asked quietly.

"Do you have an understanding with Lord Rutherford?"

Merrie inhaled sharply. "Why would you think such a thing?"

He sighed. "Yesterday, after that gallop—your manner of conversing with him—his with you—indicated a degree of intimacy . . ."

"We are in some way related," she interrupted sharply. "I reside under his family's roof."

"I do beg your pardon, but I formed the unmistakable impression that there was more to your friendship than that. Forgive me, ma'am, I should not be talking

411

in this manner, but, if what I suspect is the truth, I should like to know it so that I may no longer hope. If your suitor was indeed in Cornwall, then I would feel that perhaps I still had a chance, the advantage of presence, you understand."

Meredith felt the sticky tendrils of deception cling to her and enclose her. How could she answer him with any honesty? If she admitted that she and Rutherford had an understanding, it would be tantamount to admitting to a secret engagement. If she denied it, it would encourage Devereux in false hopes, always supposing she could deny it with conviction.

"I do not intend to marry Lord Rutherford," she said with great difficulty. That was, at least, the truth. "But that should not give you grounds for hope, my friend. I am not going to marry anyone."

"That is a very sweeping statement from one so young," Devereux observed, "but I will pry no further. Whatever reasons you may have for your secrecy, they are not for me to discover." Coming over to her chair, he took her hand and bowed low. "Yesterday, you said you were a Trelawney. You are not perchance sister to Hugo Trelawney?"

Meredith nodded her head, too startled to think clearly. "He is some years younger than you, sir. How do you know him?"

"We had some dealings at Harrow," Devereux said easily. "The dealings that sixth formers have with their juniors." Belatedly, Meredith thought, he released her hand. "I was unaware that Trelawneys were related to the Mallorys. That is the family connection, is it not?"

Meredith's tongue seemed stuck to the roof of her

412

mouth, and her body felt in the grip of a creeping paralysis. Why was he asking these questions? Don't be ridiculous, she scolded herself. In any other circumstances, the question would be considered perfectly innocuous. So Hugo, in that curious school tradition, had been obliged to act as Devereux's servant for one year, cleaning his boots and making his toast. It was hardly an uncommon relationship in these close-knit circles. Indeed, it would be strange if no one in London had come across the Trelawneys, father or sons, during their school days. "The connection is not with the Trelawneys," she said without a tremor. "It is with my late husband's family, the Blakes."

"Ah," he said noncommittally. "I don't think I know the family. My relatives in Truro have spoken of the Trelawneys on occasion. They are, after all, one of the oldest Cornish families." He smiled. "But I do not recall their mentioning the Blakes."

Of all the ill luck! To have drawn the attention of probably the only man in London, apart from Rutherford, to have Cornish connections! How long would it take him to discover the fabricated background? To discover the truth about Sir John Blake's poverty-stricken widow, living from hand to mouth? Meredith was not sure how she managed to see her appallingly knowledgeable visitor from the house. The only thing of which she was sure was that she must remove herself from Cavendish Square before Gerald Devereux delved any deeper.

Meredith planned her next step with great care, taking as her model Lady Caroline Lamb, the wife of Lord Melbourne and the accredited mistress of the

413

romantic Lord Byron. Lady Caroline defied convention with a gleeful deviltry that Meredith found most appealing. It was said that the lady inclined to madness on occasion, but Merrie was prepared to discount that as society malice. One thing was clear, Lady Caroline was no longer *persona grata*, and everyone felt very sorry for her husband. Lord Byron, on the other hand, since he was now all the fashion, could do no wrong. Yet another of society's inequities, Meredith decided as she prepared to join ranks with the lady, whose most recent scandalous behavior had involved attending an evening party attired in a transparent gown dampened in water so that it clung most immodestly to every inch of her body. There had been no underclothes beneath the gown to detract from the shocking effect, and Lady Caroline had certainly succeeded in becoming the talk of the town. One or two others, already considered disgracefully fast, had emulated the fashion but, since, like Lady Caroline, they were sufficiently bad ton to have already been denied vouchers for Almack's, the polite world was able to ignore their behavior. It would be a different matter altogether if the offender happened to be the protegée of the Keighleys.

Meredith laid her plans for the night of the Duchess of Dorset's ball with all the cunning she reserved for outwitting the king's revenue. It was essential that her dress not be revealed to anyone until they reached Dorset House. It was also essential that Nan be out of the way. Meredith was in no doubt that that formidable lady would lock her in her room and throw away the key before she would countenance such a costume.

On that night she allowed Nan to dress her in an

unimpeachable gown of spider gauze over satin. Before going down to dinner, Merrie, as usual, begged the elderly nurse not to wait up for her. Nan, who had a slight head cold and was looking forward to her bed and a hot posset, agreed without demur.

After dinner, Merrie went up to her chamber to fetch her cloak. The gauze and satin gown was changed for one of semitransparent jaconet muslin. Normally worn over a satin half-slip, the gown was considered a little daring but well within the bounds of respectability. Damp and unencumbered, it was all and more than Merrie had hoped. She could almost have been naked except that the gown was made up to the throat with a treble ruff of pointed lace, a decorous feature that seemed a subtle joke when compared with the whole effect. A midnight-blue velvet cloak hid the change of costume as she tripped down the stairs to where Arabella and George awaited her.

Her husband's escort so delighted Arabella that she would probably not have noticed if Meredith were in britches and boots and certainly did not remark the muslin peeping beneath the cloak where there should have been gauze and satin.

The pavement outside and the hall of Dorset House were thronged with guests, arriving and departing, flunkeys calling for carriages, helping guests from chairs and chaises. The line of guests on the stairs moving upward to be received by their hostess was two deep, much to Meredith's satisfaction. She did not wish to be noticed until, on reaching the head of the stairs, it would be too late for her companions to engineer a discreet retreat. Arabella, on her husband's arm, was ascending the bottom stair when Meredith, delayed by some judicious fumbling, handed her cloak to the maid who had accompanied them before blending into the crowd.

Rutherford, some ten steps higher, turned at the sound of his sister's voice. As he greeted the Beaumonts, his eye fell on Meredith's face behind, and he suffered a severe shock. Meredith bore an expression he remembered seeing on the face of young Rob outside the church in Landreth when the boy contemplated the havoc his little field mouse would create amongst the parishioners at their devotions. He could see nothing but her face and in the press was obliged to continue his ascent. Having greeted his hostess, he stepped to one side, waiting in some foreboding. Arabella and George exchanged pleasantries with the Duchess of Dorset, and Meredith mounted the last stair.

Arabella gave a little squeak and instantly suppressed it as her husband squeezed her arm urgently. The Duchess of Dorset had time to see only Lady Blake's face and the demure lace ruff at her throat before Lord Rutherford had taken her ladyship's right hand in a firm clasp, put his arm with slightly surprising familiarity around her waist, announced that he was come to claim his dance, and whisked her into the crowded ballroom.

The orchestra was playing a waltz, a fact of which Damian took instant advantage. He held the slight figure just a little too close for strict propriety but thus succeeded in shielding her front view from scandalized eyes. His gray silk arm and flattened palm covered as much of her back as legitimately possible as he led her expertly around the floor, choosing the most populous areas.

"This gown is sadly damp, my dear," he murmured solicitously. "I am very much afraid you will catch cold if you remain in it for very much longer."

"I am not in the least cold," she returned, gnashing her teeth in frustration.

"Stop scowling, sweetheart," he advised gently. "You may wish to draw attention to yourself, but you will not wish it said that I obliged you to listen to unpleasantness. I am afraid that is the only possible conclusion to draw from your expression."

They were moving inexorably to a door at the rear of the ballroom. Meredith struggled to find an expression that was at least neutral but was hampered by the absolute certainty that Damian, Lord Rutherford, was going to extricate her from this carefully engineered scrape without her reputation suffering the merest scratch. Fixing a gargoyle's smile upon her lips, she looked into his face, the sloe eyes glinting.

"I do not think that is much of an improvement," he said consideringly. "You look to be in some degree of pain. It is clearly incumbent upon me to escort you home with all due speed."

They found themselves in a small, deserted anteroom adjoining the ballroom. Damian, releasing his tight grip, took hold of her shoulders, stepping back to examine her minutely. He turned her around, subjecting her back view to the same unnerving scrutiny. "Tell me, my love, is this—uh—attire of yours intended as an invitation? I do hope so because I am minded to accept it."

"Whatever do you mean?" Meredith turned to look at him uneasily. There was a note in his voice that she did not care for in the least, and, while she had expected to be viewed with shock by a great many people, this inspection left her feeling small and hot and uncomfortable.

"Oh, come now, that must be obvious," he replied silkily. "You cannot expect any normal man to resist such blatant allure. You are hardly a naive little virgin, my dear ma'am—a fact you have gone to some pains to demonstrate this evening." Still holding her by one shoulder, he cupped her breast very deliberately with his free hand. With a gasp, she started back, but his fingers closed like spines over her shoulder, and the smooth caress continued. To Meredith's chagrin, she felt her nipples rise beneath the thin covering, lifting to the circling fingertip.

"Please, do not," she whispered, casting an anguished look in the direction of the door to the ballroom.

"Would it not suit your plans to be discovered in this so very compromising position?" he asked, sliding his hand round to her buttocks. "I would have thought it perfect. You would never be able to show your face in society again." His hand burned through the flimsy, clinging material. "And that, my wanton little adventuress, is your object, is it not?" Merrie yelped as a far-from-playful pinch punctuated his question. "Permit me to inform you, ma'am, that that is not an object I will support! Now, come along." Taking her wrist, he pulled her toward a door in the far wall, muttering, "I have no idea where this will lead us, but at least we are going away from the party."

An empty corridor appeared on the far side of the

door. "What about Bella and George?" Merrie asked, catching up her skirt to enable her to keep up with him. "They will wonder where I am."

"They will know perfectly well that I have you in charge," he replied curtly, leading her down another passage. A startled maidservant provided the information that they would reach a side door onto the street by taking the staircase at the end of the corridor.

It was not an entrance used by the owners of the house, to judge by the rather worn carpet and the faded flock paper. "I am going to fetch your cloak." Damian stood her against the wall. "If you move one inch before I get back, I'll have that dress off you and accept your far-from-subtle invitation right here!" So saying, he strode back the way they had come, leaving Meredith leaning against the wall, shivering in her damp dress in the drafty corridor, not at all prepared to put the threat to her test.

It took Rutherford ten minutes to find the maid with Meredith's cloak and to order his own chaise to make its way to the side door. By the time he returned to his errant mistress, his sense of humor had reasserted itself. "Shameless creature!" Wrapping the cloak securely around her, he could not hide the laughter in his eyes. "Just how did you contrive to slip past Nan? She would never have allowed you out like this."

"She went to bed with a cold," Merrie informed him, then sneezed herself.

"If you have made yourself ill with this prank, Merrie Trelawney, there really will be trouble!" Opening the door, he eased her out into the quiet side street. His chaise appeared round the corner and Meredith found herself bundled inside, enclosed in his arms, lapped by his body warmth. "When will you accept that I am more than a match for you in this business, my love?" His breath rustled against her hair. "Give up this plan please. It will not work and, if you hope to convince me that you are utterly abominable, you are wasting your time. I know it and have done so ever since I saw you sitting barefoot by the road in the middle of the night."

"I wish you would not make light of this." Merrie struggled vainly to sit upright. "There is something else that now makes it absolutely imperative that I leave Cavendish Square and society immediately." She had not been intending to tell him of Devereux's proposal and subsequent disclosures, having the suspicion that he would blame her for making herself vulnerable to the situation, but he still seemed to treat her fears and intentions as a tiresome joke, and it were high time he faced reality.

"Enlighten me, pray." There was a wearily patient note in his voice that infuriated Merrie.

"Gerald Devereux has Cornish connections. He was at school with Hugo and seems to know a fair amount about the Trelawneys," she told him succinctly. "How long do you think it will take him to discover the truth about my late husband and the reality of my situation? Cornish society is so inbred, no one there would believe in a suddenly discovered connection between Blakes and Mallorys. He will know the truth in a trice."

"Why would he want to find out what could only harm you?" Rutherford asked, allowing her to sit up.

Merrie did so, glad that at last she had his full attention. "I do not think he would want to harm me," she said slowly, "but—but I interest him. He suspects that there is something between you and me, and I could not deny it outright. If something interests one, it is surely only natural to exercise one's curiosity, is it not?"

"Has he proposed to you?"

"Yes," answered Merrie, wondering why she sounded self-conscious. "I thought he had accepted my refusal, but it seems—"

"That he was prepared to wait," Damian broke in. "I did warn you, Meredith, several times."

"I could not help his falling in love with me," she said in indignant defense.

"And I do not blame him for doing so," he replied with a dry little smile in the darkness of the carriage. "But you made no attempt to hold him at a distance. It is not surprising he should have thought there was still hope."

"Maybe I was a little at fault," she said with a sigh, "but inadvertently. However, admitting that does not alter the situation. If he makes inquiries, he will discover the truth. Perhaps he will say nothing, but supposing he does? Your mother would never forgive you for practicing such a deception. I am not ashamed of what I am and would gladly face her with that truth, but for her to discover this falsehood from some other source, for her to be exposed to society's pity in that way . . ." She shuddered. "I cannot bear to think of it, Damian. It makes me feel smirched and—and slimy!"

"Now you are being just a little melodramatic, my

love," said Damian quietly. "But I do take your point. You will leave this business in my hands."

"Let me remove to Highgate," she pleaded, knowing that it was the last time she would ever ask.

"No," he said with decisive finality. "Let me announce our engagement, then Devereux will have no reason to look into your background, and we may give my mother an edited version of the truth."

Meredith replied sadly, "I am not so mad as to believe that once the grand passion has died down, as it surely will, love, the chasm between us will not gape at our feet. I will *not* risk your happiness."

"You will destroy it, then," he told her flatly, as the chaise came to a halt. "By what right do you assume responsibility for my happiness? The consequences of my actions are mine to bear."

The footstep was lowered and he alighted nimbly, holding his hand for her. "I am going out of town for several days. I will also deal with Devereux. In my absence you will be pleased to behave yourself. If you get up to any more of your tricks, Meredith, I will make you very sorry. You would be wise to believe that." Merrie flushed in angry discomfiture but said nothing, knowing from experience that, when Colonel, Lord Rutherford, spoke in that particular tone, there was no possible dignified response.

He accompanied her into the house, explained to Grantly that Lady Blake had been taken unwell, kissed her hand with the recommendation that she repair instantly to bed, and left.

In her chamber, Merrie thankfully stripped off the chilly gown that she knew she could never bring herself to wear again, warmed herself before the fire, then dived into bed. Damian had accused her of taking responsibility for his happiness, but was he not also guilty of taking responsibility for hers? How could she be happy if marriage to him ensured that he was not?

She slept eventually, desolate in the certainty that her makeshift plans would never achieve her object. She must do what she should have done from the first, putting aside the childish methods that sprang from childish hopes.

Chapter Twenty-one

For the next two days, Meredith kept to her room, waiting for Damian's return so that she could inform him of her decision to return to Cornwall. It was not a decision he could argue with, not a matter on which he could impose his own will. While she remained in London, she gave tacit agreement to his arrangements, and he had taken ruthless advantage of that. The only way she could prove to him that she was serious was by leaving. Her heart shrank, however, from the inevitable confrontation even while she told herself that he had no right to object and must, in honor, accept her decision without demur. She was obliged to acknowledge the unpalatable truth that, if she could have quietened her conscience sufficiently, she would have yielded to cowardice and fled London in his absence.

During her self-imposed seclusion she was visited only by Arabella who, although she appeared much more subdued than usual, sad even, made no reference to Merrie's shameless conduct. With her brother's permission, she had told a little of their guest's extraordinary story to her husband, who deserved some explanation. The marquis had not been particularly mollified by the little she could tell him. He found it quite inexplicable that any woman should go to such lengths to avoid a brilliant marriage, particularly a woman who, he had thought, possessed more than average sense. He expressed the opinion that Rutherford would do well to forget the widow. Clearly she should never have been transplanted from the soil of Cornwall to the rarified London air, and the sooner she returned, the better.

Arabella did not, of course, impart any of this to Meredith, but neither was she as full of plans as usual. On the contrary, she encouraged her guest to keep to her room until she was quite certain she had thrown off her cold and was in no danger of the influenza.

Meredith drew her own conclusions. All her instincts told her to confront the subject with Arabella, but the thought of upsetting her hostess even further kept her in unhappy silence, pretending that nothing had happened, that she just had a simple cold and was a little fagged by the unceasing round of entertainment.

Nan, seeing little evidence of genuine illness, demanded an explanation for this pale-faced malingering. She received a judiciously censured version that nonetheless set her head nodding with comprehension. Something had to be done to break the deadlock, and Nan waited with patient trust for Lord Rutherford to make a move. Unfortunately, the one he did make had the opposite of the desired effect, sending Meredith into a passion that eclipsed all considerations of conscience and courtesy.

Rutherford had finally decided that matters were running out of hand. Their secret was now threatened, and, even if he dealt with this threat, there was always the possibility of others. It was time to bring an end to the deception. Since his own powers of persuasion seemed sadly inadequate, he would enlist support from an unexpected quarter. Before doing so, however, he paid a visit to Gerald Devereux. That gentleman received the bland statement that an understanding most definitely existed between Lord Rutherford and Lady Blake with a small nod and the offer of sherry. Rutherford accepted before going on to explain in the same bland tone that her ladyship, for family reasons to do with her brothers, wished to keep the engagement secret. She had felt she owed Mr. Devereux an explanation, but delicacy forbade her giving it to him herself. Rutherford was, therefore, her messenger. He was sure Mr. Devereux now understood the position perfectly. Mr. Devereux assured him that he did, and the gentlemen parted amicably: one satisfied that the explanation, while tenuous at the moment, would achieve unimpeachable credence the minute the notice of the marriage appeared in the *Gazette*; the other, remembering Lady Blake's declaration that she did not intend to marry Rutherford or anyone else, remained intrigued. But chivalry required that he accept Rutherford's statement at face value at least for the time being.

Within the week, the postman, in scarlet coat and cockaded hat, delivered three letters to Cavendish Square, addressed to Lady Blake.

Meredith, returning from a stroll in Hyde Park during the fashionable hour of five and six, recognised the handwriting on all three missives immediately and felt an instant sense of foreboding. All her correspondence was sent to a poste restante address and collected from there by a footman. Why then were her brothers writing directly to Cavendish Square when they had no idea she was here? But it seemed that they did know now, and, if they knew that, then how much more had been revealed and by whom?

Excusing herself to Bella, she took the letters and went upstairs. What she read left her shaking with rage. Rutherford had visited Hugo at Oxford, Rob and Theo at Harrow ostensibly to invite them all to spend Christmas at Rutherford Abbey, but the ulterior motive was clear. All three thought it capital that Meredith had met up with Rutherford in London and was now staying with his sister. Their opinions were expressed with their usual individuality. Hugo was restrained although he said Rutherford had entertained him to dinner in a most elegant fashion, and they had had a very sensible conversation about the Church and about running an estate the size of Pendennis. If Merrie wished to be at Rutherford Abbey for Christmas, then Hugo would be happy to join the party. Theo declared that Lord Rutherford was quite splendid, not at all toplofty, and all the fellows at school had been green with envy when he'd taken him and Rob out for exeat in a bang-up curricle with a team of grays. It was a pity they'd had to take Rob, but his lordship had insisted. If Merrie was intending to marry Lord Rutherford, Theo had no objections and was looking forward to Christmas at

Rutherford Abbey. They'd need evening clothes, though, since all the fellows said it would be very grand. Rob seemed to have difficulty finding sufficient superlatives. Not only had Lord Rutherford persuaded the Master to allow Rob to go on exeat, although first years were not allowed to leave the grounds, he had also brought enough tuck to feed the entire first form. They'd had luncheon in the town and a minute description of this repast followed. The letter ended with an impassioned plea that they spend Christmas at Rutherford Abbey because his lordship had promised him and Theo that they should join a proper shoot, and Rob was determined to bag the most grouse.

How dared Rutherford involve her brothers! It was one thing to employ underhand cunning when only she was affected. But to ingratiate himself with the boys, to show them what benefits there were in having such a magnificent figure for friend and relative! To imply that he and their sister were in a fair way to coming to an understanding! To dangle the riches and entertainments of a society Christmas before someone as susceptible as Theo! It was quite unpardonable.

Meredith left her boudoir, closing the door with a barely controlled slam, making her way to Arabella's apartments.

"Whatever is it?" Arabella looked at her friend's ashen face, blazing eyes and set lips.

"I beg your pardon for being so precipitate, Bella, but I shall be leaving for Cornwall in two days." Merrie struggled to calm the tremor in her voice.

"But why?" Bella faltered, aghast. "It is not because of that business the other evening, surely?

Because no one has said anything, or—"

"No, it is not that," Merrie interrupted. "At least, not directly. It was foolish of me, and I have been meaning to apologize to you for it. Your brother just makes reasonable action impossible at times."

"Oh, please, do not refine too much upon it," begged poor, bewildered Bella. "But I do not understand why you will not marry Damian when he wishes it so much."

"Your brother has been accustomed to having his own way for too long," Meredith said, quite unable to hide her own anger. "When he is thwarted, he becomes depressed and disagreeable. He did not wish to leave the army and suffered black moods that made everyone miserable until he decided he wished to marry me and so forgot about the army."

"I think you are being unfair!" Bella sprang to her brother's defense. "He was very unhappy after his furlough, but that was because he had always been a soldier and he did not know what else to do."

"So he decided to marry a totally unsuitable Cornishwoman," Merrie replied bluntly. "That gave him plenty to do and blinded him to the intransigent differences between us. I am not his equal in either rank or fortune, and it matters not that society believes otherwise. *I* know the truth. If things went wrong between us, I could not endure the humiliation of that truth, the knowledge that by marrying a duke's heir, all my material problems had been dissolved with one wave of the wand, and I was now responsible for making the fairy godfather unhappy because I did not fit in his world."

"But you do fit," Bella protested, "except when you

choose not to."

Meredith frowned. What that true? Did she sometimes *choose* not to? If that were so, then she could always choose the other path. She was still too enraged, however, to puzzle over that novel thought. "I am not the stuff of which duchesses are made, Bella," she said, her voice quite calm now. "Damian persists in ignoring this fact. He will not accept what I *can* offer him, and what he has just done makes it impossible for me to remain under your roof any longer. I must leave immediately, although"—smiling, she took the other woman's hand—"I shall miss you, my dear friend."

Arabella began to weep. "But what has he done?"

"You must ask him yourself," Meredith said. "I am not a tattletale. Please do not cry, Bella." The request went unheeded and Meredith stood by helplessly, unwilling to leave her so distraught but quite unable to do or say the one thing that would restore Bella's customary good cheer.

"You do not love him then?" Bella found her handkerchief and snuffled, pathetically red-eyed.

Meredith sighed, shaking her head sadly. "If that were true, my dear, I would marry him tomorrow. If I did not love him, I would not care if I made his life a misery."

Leaving Arabella then, she returned to her own boudoir where she informed a grim-faced Nan of their impending departure.

"And just what bee have you got in your bonnet this time?" Nan demanded. "Seems to me you don't know when you're well off, my girl."

"I do not wish to discuss it," Meredith said coldly.

430

"You will pack only those things I brought with me, please." She marched into her bedchamber, emerging pale, red-eyed, but firm of purpose an hour later. They would have to travel by stage coach at least as far as Honiton since she could not begin to afford the cost of a post chaise for the entire journey. In the morning, she would go to the George in the Strand and reserve their places on the waybill. It would be an horrendously uncomfortable journey, but there was little point in complaining.

Damian, blithely unaware of these events, passed a pleasant evening with friends, intending to call in Cavendish Square on the morrow, having decided that he had left Meredith to her own devices for long enough. On returning to his house after dinner, however, he found a hastily penned, distraught scrawl from his sister: Bella did not understand anything, but Merrie was going home to Cornwall and, if he intended to prevent her, he had best make haste.

It was too late to seek an explanation that night so Rutherford was obliged to bide his time until the morning, which found him, at an unconscionably early hour, in Cavendish Square.

Grantly, upon informing his lordship that the ladies were not yet up, found himself holding my lord's hat and gloves while their owner mounted the stairs to the upper region two at a time. Damian walked without ceremony into Meredith's boudoir where he found her, in a simple morning wrapper, packing her dressing case. A dour-faced Nan was folding gowns preparatory to laying them in the trunk standing open beneath the window.

"What the devil is this nonsense?" Rutherford

demanded.

"I am going home," Meredith informed him. "I was about to write you a letter."

"I am honored," said he, sarcastically. "However, it will not do. Will you please get dressed? We shall go to Highgate where we may discuss this nonsensical business properly."

"There is nothing nonsensical about it. If you have anything to say, you may say it here. I have a great deal to do this morning."

"Meredith, must I request you again to get dressed?" There was a distinct note of menace in the usually level tones, but Merrie was beyond caution. A panicky feeling in the pit of her stomach told her that she could not afford to be alone with him, and the fear merely increased her legitimate anger.

"I am going nowhere, my lord. I will, of course, do you the courtesy of listening to whatever you may wish to say." She began to roll up a pair of long evening gloves with hands that shook slightly.

Nan sniffed derisively and Rutherford said, "Very well, if you wish to take the hard road, that is your choice. Since you will not dress yourself, I must do it for you."

Before she could guess at his intention, he had swept her off her feet and carried her to the chaise longue where he sat down, imprisoning her legs between his own, holding her wrists in one large hand behind her back while he began unbuttoning the wrapper with his free hand.

"Stop this!" 'Meredith spoke with fierce desperation, jerking at her captive wrists. "You cannot compel me in this manner."

432

"Can I not?" he replied grimly. "Nan, bring me a driving dress."

"Nan, don't you dare!" Meredith exclaimed.

"I've waited nigh on twenty-four years to see you broke to bridle, Meredith," Nan announced, shaking out the folds of a dark-green driving habit. "If you'd be a little less worried about the happiness of others, then maybe you'd find your own. It's as plain as the nose on your face where it lies." So saying, she tossed the dress over Merrie's head.

Meredith, realizing with a sick horror that, between them, these two would have her dressed regardless of struggles and protest, knew that she could not bear the humiliation and capitulated the minute her head emerged from the folds of material. "Let me go. I will come with you if you insist."

She was instantly set on her feet by a greatly relieved Damian. Shaking off Nan's assisting hands, she said, "I can manage myself."

"Yes, I am sure you think you can," Nan muttered, returning to her packing.

"I will wait for you downstairs." Damian beat a hasty retreat, hoping by this withdrawal to lessen the effects of that regrettable show of force.

Meredith, when she joined him in a very few minutes, offered little reassurance that he need not regret it. The sloe eyes were coldly blank, her face set, her voice a monotone. She sat beside him in the curricle, hands folded in her lap, staring at the road ahead.

When they reached the house in Highgate, she walked into the parlor, turning to face him as he closed the door quietly. "Well, sir, what is it you wish

433

to say to me?"

"What the devil is the matter?" he exclaimed in frustration. "Why are you behaving in this manner?"

"How can you ask such a question? After the way you have just treated me—that brutal, humilating—"

"Merrie, I beg your pardon. It was insufferable, but what else was I to do?"

"Accede to my wishes, of course," she clipped. "But then, that is something you cannot bring yourself to do if they run counter to your own."

Damian took a deep breath and went to the sherry decanter on the marquetry sideboard. "Do you care for a glass?"

"No, thank you," she answered stiffly. "It is a little early for me."

"Will you please tell me what precipitated this—this crisis?" he asked, taking a deep draft of the tawny wine. "The only fault which I am aware of having committed is in preventing you from making yourself the talk of the town."

"You do not consider going behind my back to my brothers a fault then?" she inquired, one mobile eyebrow lifted. "You consider it perfectly acceptable to issue invitations to *my* wards without consulting me? You do not consider it in the least despicable to enlist the unwitting support of total innocents in your own interests—interests that run against mine and, therefore, against theirs?"

Rutherford's startled expression told her very clearly that he had not considered the matter in this light. He had, in fact, seen it as a perfectly legitimate move. Only now did he realize his mistake. It was a mistake based on the firm belief that Meredith's true interests did not run counter to his, quite the opposite. Unless she could be brought to believe this also, then his action was indeed despicably underhanded.

Meredith, seeing him for once at a loss for a reply, pressed her advantage. "I will no longer be compelled to run between your shafts, Rutherford. It is quite clear that you will use any method to obtain your way, including force. I can no longer continue with this masquerade, continue to deceive your mother and my host. Since you cannot see your way to accepting what I have to give, then I am returning by stage to Cornwall tomorrow." The slight figure radiated resolution and a pride that could not be gainsaid. Dimly, Rutherford began to see that his tactics had been wrong from the start. In trying to overcome that damnable, proud independence, he had simply reinforced it. By trying to make her a part of his world, he had merely emphasized the chasm that lay between them. Certainly, he had demonstrated that *she* could bridge that chasm, but he had not shown that so could he also. Unless he did so, Meredith would remain convinced that the gap was not to be traversed.

"You will not return by stage," he informed her crisply, putting his now empty glass back on the tray. "You will return home exactly as you came. At Okehampton, you may engage your own conveyance."

If Meredith felt any satisfaction at this evidence of an instantaneous, effortless victory, it did not show on her face. "Thank you, but that will not be necessary."

"It *is* necessary," he said forcefully. "Do you think that I do not have *my* pride? You came here under my protection, you have lived here under that protection, and you will leave here under it. You cannot refuse to end this without a veneer of grace at least."

"No," Meredith said quietly. "I cannot and would not under any circumstances. I accept your offer, sir. May we now go back to Cavendish Square?"

Damian thought of the bedchamber upstairs under the thatched roof, the wide bed with its patchwork quilt. In that room there had been laughter, love, friendship between them, the glorious heights of ecstasy. Only once had there been anger, quickly dissipated by the passion that was, after all, only the reverse side of the coin. Would it work this time? Would the act of love dissipate the desolation of that anger? The bodily fusion cement the division of spirit? Looking at Meredith, so pale and set and unhappy in her resolution, he did not think so, and, if it did not work, the failure would tarnish the gold of a memory that they must both keep bright. It was not a risk he could afford to take.

"By all means, ma'am." Rutherford bowed her out of the room, out of the house and left her at the gate while he went to the inn to fetch the curricle.

Meredith looked back at the cottage, its garden now neat and dark with the onset of winter. She had imagined this moment after that first glorious summer night in the cave—the moment when they would both accept the parting of the ways. She had told herself then that she would give thanks for what she had had, would make the memories last a lifetime. Putting that resolution into practice was a deal harder than it had seemed then in the roseate dawn when this reality existed in a vague, indefinite future. But if she were to continue to live her life, to support her brothers and ensure their future, there was no time to mope over what had been and might have been.

It was a face quiet with determination and acceptance that she showed Lord Rutherford when he appeared with the curricle. It was the same face he saw the following morning as he handed her into the chaise in Cavendish Square. It fell to Nan to cradle Merrie's head against an ample bosom as the sobs racked the slight frame and the tears of loss fell.

Chapter Twenty-two

"Jacques will not come tonight,' Meredith said with finality, turning to her companion as they huddled in the lee of the cliff. "He'll not risk the reef in that sea."

"Aye, reckon not," Bart agreed. "This'll be the third put-off this month. We're all a-wearied of turning out in foul weather, cowering out of the wind like sheep on Bodmin moor, and all for nought. Why do we not forget the runs until these storms are over? Jacques'll not be sorry, I'll be bound. It's what we've always done in years past."

"I know." Merrie blew on her freezing hands before tucking them into her armpits. "But in past years, we were not out of business from September to December. We could afford to leave January and February fallow."

Bart peered at her in the darkness. "There's more to it than that, I reckon."

Meredith stamped her numb feet on the sand. "The

438

revenue don't think we'd dare operate during the winter. They're off guard, Bart, even more so after the months of inactivity. It's too good an opportunity to miss."

The burly fisherman grunted. "That's not the whole story, and you'll not bamboozle me into believing it is." When he received no reply from his companion, Bart shrugged, whistling tunelessly through his teeth. "Shall we call it a night, then?" he asked eventually. "Try for next Wednesday?"

"Not much else we can do." Meredith sighed. "Jacques's out there somewhere. It's so damnably infuriating!" Turning, she addressed the rest of the shivering group, keeping her voice low. "Another wasted night, I'm afraid, lads. Let's be off to our beds and try for this day next week."

There were a few muttered grumbles as the group dispersed, and Meredith, as she made her own lonely way back to the cave beneath Pendennis, wondered if she were being selfish by refusing to call off the operation until the spring. The reasons she had given Bart for continuing were all good, but there was another one—a personal reason. Only when she was engaged in smuggling did she seem to come alive these days. Only then did her flight from London and Rutherford continue to make sense. When she was Merrie Trelawney, smuggler, she *knew* she could never be Lady Rutherford, let alone the Duchess of Keighley.

The boys had come home for the Christmas holidays, disgruntled and full of questions. She had answered them as honestly as she could, but their disappointment only increased her own wretchedness. It had not been a particulary happy holiday, for which Meredith, without reservation, blamed Damian. If he had not dangled the infinitely exciting prospect of Christmas at Rutherford Abbey before them, they would have been perfectly satisfied with their customary celebration. In an effort to make up for their disappointment, Meredith had been much more lavish with presents and entertainment than a tight budget could stand. As a result, she felt cross with herself for a piece of self-indulgence designed simply to allay a guilt that was not hers to bear. All in all, life these days was as gray as the sea and the sky, as barren as the bare trees, and as dull as ditchwater.

The outer cave was dark and empty as usual, and she nerved herself for the crawl through the narrow tunnel to the inner cavern where the lantern would be burning its welcome. Somehow, in winter, everything seemed so much more menacing. In summer, nothing was ever this dark and cheerless. Edging her way through the tunnel, she kept her eyes peeled for the first glimmer of light ahead. It did not come, however, and she found herself at the mouth of the cavern, staring into inky, disorienting darkness. Her palms began to sweat, her heart to thud. The damn lantern must have gone out although she was sure she had remembered to fill it with oil. The problem now lay in negotiating the vast cavern, finding the other passage that would take her up to the house. The dark, dank chill seemed to infiltrate the marrow of her bones, and she fancied she could hear the rapid beat of her heart in the eerie silence. Keeping one hand on the rough wall of the cavern, Merrie began to edge her way along, feeling for the gap that would indicate the tunnel's opening.

When a hand closed over her mouth and an arm circled her waist from behind, lifting her off her feet, Meredith reacted with blind, automatic self-defense. Her teeth bit deeply into the palm, her feet flailed, kicking backward against her captor's shins, her elbows drove hard into the ribs at her back.

The grip didn't slacken, but a familiar voice exclaimed in the darkness, "Damn you, Meredith! Stop it!" She went limp suddenly and then, feeling the ground beneath her feet again, sank slowly down on her rear, keeping the wall at her back. A flint scraped on a tinderbox, and the soft yellow of the oil lamp glowed.

Meredith, still speechless, stared over her drawn-up knees at Damian, who was examining his bitten palm with a rueful grimace. "I forgot what a tigress you were," he said. "My ribs and shins will be black and blue."

"I hope you don't expect me to apologize." Merrie found her voice at last. "That was a *dastardly* thing to do."

"I hoped to bring a little adventure and excitement into your otherwise dull existence," he replied with a grin. "Take off that cap, will you? You look just like a pixie, sitting like that."

Meredith obliged, her gaze roaming around the cavern in some amazement. In the three hours since she had been here, the place was transformed back to their playhouse of last summer. As she watched,

Rutherford again struck a flint, setting a light to a fire of neatly laid driftwood set in a circle of flat stones.

"I am hoping there is sufficient ventilation to avoid suffocating us," he remarked prosaically. "Will you take a glass of champagne, my lady?"

"Please." Meredith found herself in that familiar, dreamlike state so often engenderd by her companion when, as now, he took complete control over the situation.

"Come over by the fire then. You can lean against me rather than the wall if you are still in need of support." Sitting down on a bright cushion, Damian patted one beside him. Meredith complied, stretching her hands to the comforting blaze, leaning against his knees at her back. She took the glass of champagne, sipping appreciatively. It was a fine wine.

"Hungry?" asked Damian, unfastening the pins in her hair, shaking free the rich burnished mass. "I have Cornish pasties. A little crude with the champagne, but quite appropriate for a healthy, outdoor appetite."

"Actually, I find that I am," Meredith said in some surprise. "I cannot imagine why. We have had little enough exercise this night, just standing shivering on the beach, watching for a phantom boat."

"The weather?" he questioned, opening a wicker hamper and passing her a warm, cloth-wrapped pasty.

"Mmm." Merrie mumbled through a satisfying mouthful. "Surf's too high and the riptide's running like the devil."

What on earth were they doing, sitting in this cave,

talking so easily, so naturally? As if London had never happened, as if they were back in the carefree days of last summer when Rutherford had stopped mentioning marriage and they had loved gloriously and illicitly.

"Why are you here?" The question was so bald it could have been interpreted as hostile except that her body was warm and pliant against his knees, and her head rested trustingly beneath his stroking fingers.

"I missed you," he said frankly. "I thought I would come and pay you a short visit."

"How short?"

"Two weeks. I have to be back in London by the end of January for a wedding."

"Oh." She didn't ask whose wedding. It was hardly her business although she would probably know the celebrants. "Two weeks is a long time."

"Yes," he agreed, reaching a hand round, slipping inside her shirt to cup one round breast. "Take off your clothes."

Meredith quivered. "Will you not take them off yourself, my lord?"

"No," he said. "Not this time. This time I want to watch you become naked for me." Slowly she began to unbutton her shirt until he softly insisted. "Stand up. I cannot see you properly."

Standing in the glow of the fire, feeling its warmth lap her skin, Meredith bared herself before the unmoving gray eyes that burned their desirous message into her very self. Afterward, with hands and mouth, he seared her body, branding her as his own for this one night, in this magic kingdom where all things

For the next few days, Meredith walked on air. Rutherford had informed her that they would not meet socially on this visit because he did not think he could again stand by while she played the socially inept nincompoop. This suited Merrie very well, and the only sufferers were Patience Barrat and her like, who found their illustrious neighbor had become sadly reclusive. The lovers rode and walked together, well off the beaten track and away from curious eyes, and enjoyed each other with gay abandon in the cave. Not a word of dissension came between them. It was as if, knowing this was borrowed time, they were determined to drain it to the last drop of joy.

"Love, we must dismantle our home." It was the following Tuesday when Meredith gestured expressively around the cozy, firelit, lamplit scene.

"You are going to work again, then?" Damian, refilling their glasses with a rich, ruby burgundy and nibbling on a hunk of cheese, asked his question carelessly.

"Tomorrow night," she told him. "Jacques will try again to make landfall if conditions are fair. Bart thinks there will be little problem for once. The fish are biting apparently." She scrunched into a crisp, green apple. "I do not know quite why that should promise good weather, but Bart is rarely mistaken. We will store the goods here as usual and leave the ponies in the cave overnight. It reduces the risk of drawing undue attention, you understand, if we make our way

444

home on foot. The following morning, no one will remark a man and his pony on the road."

"Quite," he concurred. "Very sensible."

Meredith looked at him sharply. "Are you mocking me, Damian?"

"What an idea!" he protested. "To make mock of such a daring, experienced, skillful little adventuress—" Laughing, he held up his hands to shield himself from the attack, rolling with her onto the cushions.

There was no laughter the following evening when Meredith joined her fellow smugglers on the beach. The ponies were dark shapes, huddled against the cliff, the wind cut an ice-tipped swath from the sea across the cove, the surf gleamed white as the breakers rose, curled, and crashed onto the sand. But there was nothing about this sea, wild though it appeared, that Jacques and his men could not handle. The fishermen had been out beyond the headland earlier in the evening and pronounced the rip navigable. The beacon at Devil's Point had flashed its intermittent, unmistakable message, and the coastguard, it was to be hoped and assumed, were tucked up in their beds.

Merrie cast an eye over the group. There was an air of suppressed excitement, the sense that this night would make up for all the wasted ones. Someone chuckled softly, a pipe glowed redly as the smoker drew on the stem, feet stamped, and breath rose. Suddenly, Merrie froze. Something was wrong, badly wrong. What was it? She looked again at the dark, cloaked figures. All as familiar shapes to her as her own brothers. There was Luke, Tod, Jess. Matt, Dan,

Bart, of course, and—and—that figure by the ponies on the outskirts of the circle, a part of the group, yet not a part. As familiar as the rest, yet not belonging. Her mouth opened to give the alarm as her hand closed over the shaft of the knife in her belt. Then her mouth shut on a shuddering breath. She walked across the sand toward him.

"Are you run quite mad?"

Rutherford smiled in the darkness. "Only as mad as you, my love. A smuggler can surely wed a smuggler?"

"Who's this?" Bart's voice hissed urgently behind her where he stood, cutlass in hand.

"A fellow traveler, Bart," Merrie said quietly. "You need have no fear. He is here to help, not hinder."

The fisherman peered at the cloaked figure, shook his head in disbelief. "It's that fancy lord what's inherited old Mallory's place!"

"True enough," Damian replied, "but I hope to prove worthy of this enterprise."

"Worthy?" Merrie gasped.

"Yes, you stubborn little adventuress! Worthy of the Trelawneys, as you have proved yourself worthy of the Keighleys."

"Here she comes!" A voice spoke sharply and Merrie swung round. The French boat had rounded the headland, riding high on the surf under minimum sail.

"I do not understand what you have said," she spoke swiftly to Damian, "but we cannot take the time now. If you will join with me in this, I shall be right glad of your partnership."

"You have it, now and for always." For a moment, their hands touched, and then Merrie was off and running down the beach, Rutherford behind her.

"Dear God!" At the shoreline, she stopped with the others, staring in horror at the second boat rounding the headland. "Coastguard!" As if in confirmation, a musket bellowed, fire sparking in the night sky. Jacques's boat was still out of range and on the open sea could probably remain so. In the confines of the bay, with the riptide and his pursuers behind, only the shore ahead, he was as trapped as any rat in a burning barn.

"We gotta get out of here," Luke whispered hoarsely, "before they land." He turned to the cliff path, then found a slight figure barring his way, a knife in her hand.

"Understand this, Luke! No one is going anywhere!" Merrie said savagely. "Jacques is ahead by five minutes. It's a start. We use the trail and take them with us to the cave." Her eyes ran around the group, daring any one of them to object.

Damian, his hand on his own sword, found, even in the midst of crisis, something amusing as well as admirable about that indomitable little figure daring this group of hulking men to leave their comrades in the lurch.

Luke dropped his eyes before the ferocious stare. "Get ready," Bart ordered. "We'll pull 'em in. That way, we'll gain a few more minutes."

Another musket shot rang out as Jacques swung his boat into the wind, letting the sails flap as the craft sped on the crest of a wave to the beach.

"You must not stay here," Merrie hissed urgently, finding Damian beside her in the surf. "Not now—now that there is danger of discovery."

"When this night is over, Merrie Trelawney, I shall take immense pleasure in ensuring that you regret that remark," he gritted. "How dare you tell me to desert when you hold others to their post at knife point!"

"I beg your pardon," she said, acknowledging her mistake instantly, shooting him a mischievous grin that entranced him even as it amazed.

Then the boat was upon them, and for a moment all was chaos as its crew leapt into the surf, cursing up hill and down dale. "Leave the boat, Jacques." Merrie's voice rose urgently as the Frenchmen struggled to beach the laden vessel. "There is nothing to be done now except save our necks."

"Leave the contraband. *Sacré bleu*! You are out of your mind, Meredith!" Jacques tugged at the painter. "You know how much that cargo is worth."

"And I know how much I value my life," she snapped. "A deal more than brandy and tobacco, *mon ami*. Besides, it will distract the revenue for a few precious minutes. *Allons-y*."

With a vicious oath, the French smuggler released his boat and cargo as if consigning precious offspring to the flames before leaping through the shallows onto the beach where the others were already making for the narrow trail snaking up to the cliff road.

Meredith glanced over her shoulder as she reached the base of the cliff. The cutter was about to land, but its skipper, not as canny as Jacques, had turned too late into the wind, and it was listing heavily in the crosscurrent. She drew her pistol from her belt, squinting along the barrel as she held it at arm's length.

"Damn you, Meredith!" Damian knocked her arm to one side. "I refuse to marry a murderess. Get up that trail!"

"I wasn't aiming to kill, just to make the landing more difficult," she protested. He put a hand beneath her backside, shoved her upward, and turned to put what he had to admit was a sound plan into action. His pistol cracked, the bullet spurting sand. The men in the boat paused. He reloaded with the speed garnered from years of battlefield experience and kept firing until a quick glance behind him showed that the others were almost at the top. Meredith, from halfway up, was firing doggedly in support, but someone in the cutter had come to his senses and fired back as the boat bucked on the unruly surf, and the revenue men were torn between the lure of the contraband waiting to be seized and chasing the smugglers. A musket ball whined over Damian's head, burying itself in the cliff a few inches from the cowering Meredith.

"Move!" he yelled. "Now!"

"I'll cover you," she called back.

"You'll do as you're damn well told! Climb! And keep your head down!"

Meredith, recognizing the colonel's incisive accents in her lover's voice, found herself scrambling upward as if all the devils in hell were on her heels as, indeed, they were. More than one musket was firing now, but she dared not turn to look behind, could only go on, keeping her head low, wincing as musket balls hit the dust around her. How had they not hit Damian, so much more in range? Unable to bear the suspense any longer, she risked slowing her pace to look over her shoulder.

"If we're going to continue in this crazy business, I am going to have to give you some instruction in guerrilla warfare." The cool, amazingly controlled voice accompanied that hand on her behind again, propelling her upward. He did not seem to be remotely out of breath and had caught her up as soundlessly as it had been swiftly.

"You would know, of course," she gasped, "after all those years in the Peninsula."

"Just so. Now save your breath and keep up your speed."

The shooting from below had become sporadic. Meredith realized the reason as she hauled herself over the cliff and onto the road. Only a few coastguard remained on the beach, the rest were streaming up the broad path that would bring them onto the road a quarter mile behind their quarry. That quarter mile was the only advantage the smugglers had.

"We have to hold them off," Meredith said breathlessly as Damian joined her on the path. "Give the others time to hide until the pursuit dies down. There are dozens of places for those who know them, and Bart knows them all. Eventually, they will make their way to the cavern, but we cannot risk relying on being able to outrun the revenue."

Damian looked up and down the road, eyes narrowed speculatively. "You will obey orders implicitly?"

"Yes, Colonel," she agreed instantly, shooting him the same impish grin she had given him on the beach. Damian shook his head in amazement. The greater the danger, it seemed, the greater her stimulation. Nothing seemed to frighten her at all events.

"Very well. Give me your pistol and ammunition. Now, run and keep running for five minutes. Then set fire to the scrub beside the road."

Swallowing the temptation to ask what Damian intended to do himself, Merrie ran obediently. The sound of rapid firing broke out behind her. Rutherford, using both pistols, was creating as much havoc as he could, sprawled on the cliff top, firing down onto the path where the coastguard, suddenly as exposed as tall trees on a moor, milled around, firing blindly in the direction of the sniper. Damian knew he could not keep them confused for long, and he needed to keep some ammunition in case of further emergency. When he judged that Merrie had had a little over five minutes, he backed away, still firing, then turned and ran.

Merrie had had difficulty initially in getting the damp scrub to catch and in the end set fire to her jacket, which burned easily, and then set the light to the recalcitrant brush. When Damian appeared, covering the ground easily with long strides, she followed the curt order to fan the flames as he dragged sticks and fallen branches into the road, throwing a burning brand into their midst. The wind tugged merrily at the sparks, and the damp fuel created a thick, oily blanket of smoke that billowed down the road. The fire in the scrub beside the road was burning well so the coastguard would meet a barrier ahead and to the left when they rounded the corner. On their right, the cliff dropped sheer to the sea.

"It will not hold them for long," Damian said. "Run now as you've never run before."

"In half a mile we can go over the cliff," she gasped. "They will run right past us."

Recalling the manner in which they had all disappeared on that first memorable night that had turned his life inside out and upside down, Rutherford agreed to the plan. There was no sign of their fellow smugglers, who had clearly taken advantage of the delayed pursuit. Shouted oaths and expletives rent the air as their pursuers reached the fire. They would find a way around it soon enough, and Meredith, for all her wiry strength, was flagging, fighting for breath, her lungs bursting, her legs screaming for relief. Rutherford, with the dispassion of a commanding officer, closed his mind to her plight; if he showed any concern, she would probably collapse, and he could not possibly carry her while maintaining the necessary speed. She must manage alone, knowing that he expected it of her.

When Merrie fell suddenly to her knees at the edge of the cliff, his heart sank as he made to haul her upright. Unable to speak, she shook her head weakly, pointing to the cliff edge.

"Here?" He peered over, seeing only the black space of a sheer drop.

Meredith nodded. "Just drop," she gasped, "exactly where I do." She had no breath to expand the statement, but Damian realized grimly that, if he missed the exact spot, he would plummet down to the rocks beneath. Then she had disappeared, just like on that other occasion, and he approached the edge gingerly, lying on his belly, inching backward until his legs hung free. To his inexpressible relief, he felt something grasp, then guide his feet. "Drop now!" the urgent whisper came from what seemed a great distance below. "Straight as you can." For a dizzying instant he held onto nothing, then his feet touched solid ground. "Don't step back," she hissed, and he hugged the cliff face convulsively.

"One of your ancestors must have been a goat," Damian muttered. "Guerrilla warfare as a necessary component of marriage is one thing, emulating mountain goats quite another. Don't you ever expect me to do this again!"

"I won't," Merrie promised with a feeble chuckle. Then she fell silent at the sound of pounding feet and raised voices from above.

As she had predicted, the coastguard ran straight past them. When the noise of pursuit had faded, she whispered to Damian that she was going to climb behind him to his other side so that she could lead the way along the ledge. They would come up on the road a quarter of a mile back, thus putting even more ground between themselves and the revenue. They could reach Pendennis across the fields, going behind their pursuers.

"Be careful," he enjoined, trying to shrink into the cliff as he felt her hands on his waist, the brush of her body against his back, and then she was beside him again, but this time on his left.

Crabwise, they traversed the narrow ledge until it petered out, and they hauled themselves up onto the road. "I do not suppose we could go back to the beach and recover some of the contraband," Merrie said wistfully.

"For God's sake, have you never had enough!" Rutherford grasped the nape of her neck between pincerlike fingers, pushing her across the road into the field. "You have not considered that the boat is bound to be guarded. Or does that minor detail not concern you?"

"Jacques is going to be enraged," she said. "He will have to get another boat since the coastguard will impound that one. So, not only will he have lost his cargo, but he will have the expense of replacing his vessel. I will have to share the cost," she added gloomily.

"Well, permit me to inform you, my love, that that is one burden I shall not remove from your shoulders. All financial transactions with the Frenchman are yours to bear!"

"I would not dream of asking you to do any such thing," she said indignantly, trying to turn her head against the pressure of his fingers. "You talk, sir, as if matters are in a fair way to being settled between us."

"So they are," replied Damian in uncompromising accents. "A few details remain to be discussed, that is all."

"More than a few," Merrie muttered, squelching through a deep ditch.

Damian grinned to himself, unperturbed by this minor recalcitrance. They had reached the copse on

Pendennis land by this time, and Merrie made straight for the side door of the house. "We will go to the cave from inside," she whispered, unlatching the door, which opened soundlessly on well-oiled hinges.

Damian followed her through the sleeping house, into the pantry where she lifted the slab, revealing the secret passage. In the lamplit cavern, they found the relieved French crew and the disconsolate Jacques. Bart was the only Cornishman in attendance, informing Meredith that the others had chosen to go their separate ways, but as far as he knew all were safe.

"Thank God!" Meredith sighed with relief. "That was too narrow an escape."

"I am glad to hear it," Rutherford declared, sitting on a rock and stretching his legs. "Perhaps, in future, we can avoid further such narrow ones."

"Who's this?" Jacques demanded, scrutinizing the long, lean Englishman whose aristocratic bearing seemed not a whit disguised by the filth on his hands, the tears in his clothes, the black smoke streaks on his face.

"Lord Rutherford," Meredith introduced absently. "It seems that we are to be married. Jacques, you must calculate your losses for this night's work, and I will contrive to meet half of them. Is that fair?"

"Married?" said Jacques, obviously intrigued by this idea. "When?"

"In three weeks' time," Damian informed him with a serene smile.

"What?" Meredith squeaked. "Do not be absurd."

"They are already calling the bans in St. George's, Hanover Square," Damian said calmly, "and the notice appeared in the *Gazette* last week. Madame Bernice is making your wedding gown, and you cannot possibly postpone Bella's preparations for the reception, it would be too unkind."

"This wedding you said you must attend . . ." She stared in disbelief.

"My own," he corroborated. "I think, gentlemen, if you will excuse me, Merrie and I have matters of some moment to discuss."

"I will fetch blankets and wine," Merrie said in a dazed voice. "You will not be too uncomfortable, and in the morning we will decide what to do next."

Jacques chuckled richly. "I would never have believed it possible, *mon amie*, but I think you have found a man your equal in determination. Bring us wine, by all means. Blankets we can do without. As to my losses—" he shrugged—"I will bear them myself. A wedding present, *comprenez*?"

Meredith smiled, returning the bear hug, before turning to Bart. "Will you go home now, Bart? Or do you keep our friends company until morning?"

"I'll stay," the fisherman pronounced. "No sense running further risks." He looked at Rutherford and then nodded, as if satisfied. "You'll do, I reckon, m'lord."

Damian felt absurdly pleased, as if somehow his suit had been approved by two people who had the right to judge. Meredith, still somewhat bemused, allowed herself to be directed back to the pantry. Food and wine were passed down to Bart, the slab was firmly replaced, and Damian and Meredith crept upstairs on stockinged feet to her bedchamber.

"Lawks-a-mercy!" Nan, shocked out of her usual composure, jumped upright at the sight of them. "Whatever have you been a-doing now? You look as if you've been stoking Lucifer's furnace."

"So we have, in a manner of speaking," said Meredith. "Can you fetch us hot water, Nan, dear?"

"Aye, that I can. It's a bath you'll both be needing before you get between the sheets." She bustled from the room and Meredith began to laugh helplessly.

"As far as Nan is considered, you're just another one of her nurslings. She is not at all surprised to see you."

Damian did not respond, indeed appeared as if he had not heard her. "If I agree to be a Trelawney during the summer months, will you agree to be Lady Rutherford from October to May?" he asked, his expression grave.

"Is this a proposal, sir? I was under the impression I had no choice in this matter of marriage." She smiled tentatively.

"Not in the fact," he said quietly. "But in the manner of its conduct. You accept the fact now, do you not?"

"Yes." Meredith nodded, her expression equaling his in gravity. "I accept that a smuggler may wed a smuggler. I accept that you risked your life as well as your family's honor to prove to me that my fears were groundless. I accept that I am able to take my place in your world if I choose to do so. The only barriers would be of my own construction."

"You once said that marriage would confer upon me the honor of giving, while allowing you only to accept. What say you now, Merrie Trelawney?"

"That I will give to you as I know you will give to me." She smiled a distinctly misty smile. "Do I know my catechism, sir?"

"It has taken you a while to learn it," he replied. "But then it has taken me as long to learn mine." His arms opened, and Merrie stepped into the loving circle of his embrace.

"There'll be time enough for that later," Nan said, thumping two jugs of hot water inside the door. "Get out of those filthy clothes now, the pair of you. Meredith, fetch the bath in front of the fire."

"I'll fetch it. Where is it?" Damian's shoulders shook as, following Meredith's directions, he pulled the porcelain hip bath from a cupboard, drawing it in front of the fire. Nan poured steaming water from the jugs, then took them away to refill.

"There's only room for one of us at a time," Merrie choked. "Perhaps I should go in first since Nan will be back any minute. She would not be at all perturbed to encounter you in the bath, but perhaps you might."

"Doubtless I would," he agreed equably, beginning to unbutton her shirt. "I have to tell you, Merrie, in spite of my partiality, that you resemble a particularly repulsive little boy at the moment."

"And I must tell you, Lord Rutherford, in spite of *my* partiality, that you look excessively villainous. Not someone I would care to meet alone in a dark alley," she countered, not taking her eyes from his as he stripped off her clothes.

"Then we are in a fair way to suiting one another very well," he responded. "Get in the bath."

Merrie did so, resting her head against the rim with a sigh of deep contentment as those knowing hands began to stroke her body beneath the water. "I still do not know how I will manage to be a duchess," she murmured, arching her back luxuriously.

"As well as I may manage to be a smuggler," Damian said. "Although, on the whole, I would feel happier if we could satisfy your adventurous spirit with some activity that is not outside the law."

"That, if I may be so bold, is the most sensible thing I've heard said in a long while." The blunt comment came from Nan, who brought two more steaming jugs over to the bath. "You'll not be needing me any further tonight, I imagine."

"No. Thank you, Nan." Merrie tried to look sweetly innocent in denial of the soaping hands busily at work beneath the water.

"Good-night, Nan," said Damian firmly. "You may safely leave matters in my hands."

"What a thing to say!" Merrie expostulated through her mirth as the door finally closed on the departing Nan. Then she became serious again although the sloe eyes smiled still. "Will we always laugh together, love? It is so much a part of being with you."

"Always," he affirmed, kissing her eyes. "As we will always love together."

"And quarrel?" Her wet arms slipped around his neck.

"Oh, yes." He chuckled. "Life with you, my little adventuress, will be no bed of roses."

"Well, of all things!" Merrie protested indignantly,

with a sudden jerk of her arms. Caught off balance, Damian tumbled atop her into the bath.

"Abominable girl!" he declared against her mouth. "You are, love of my life, the most maddening, infuriating creature."

"And you, love of my life, are autocratic, tyrannical, and cunning," Merrie retorted with considerable satisfaction. "Perhaps you should take off your clothes if we are to continue in this fashion . . ."